WITHDRAWN

WITHDRAWN

SONG

&

DANCE

SONG & DANCE

An Encyclopedia of Musicals

by

Sheryl Aumack

Sea-Maid Press
Newport Beach, California

Library of Congress Catalog Card Number: 89-92707

Copyright ©1990 by Sheryl Aumack

All Rights Reserved

First Printing June 1990

ISBN 0-9625180-1-8

Additional copies may be obtained by contacting:

Sea-Maid Press
P.O. Box 1322
Newport Beach, CA 92659
(714) 548-9065

Printed in the United States of America

For Otto, Elaine and Tréy

. . . with love

Acknowledgements

I would like to thank the following people for their help in the making of this book: the staff of the public library system of Newport Beach, California; the staff of the Margaret Herrick Library of the Academy of Motion Picture Arts and Sciences; the people at ASCAP; Jennifer Hendrickson of the Walt Disney Studios Archives; my mother, Elaine Aumack, for all her help just when I needed it most; and to Dr. Aaron Rosenzweig who, probably without his knowing it, first planted the idea for this book in my mind when I was a student of his at college.

Whenever possible I have listed a soundtrack for the various films listed in this book. Although many of these recordings have since been deleted from a company's inventories they can often be found in used record stores. One that has been of great help to me in my own collection is the following:

Disc-Connection
10970 West Pico Boulevard
West Los Angeles, California 90064
(213) 208-7211

The owner, Bernie Nifoussi, is very knowledgeable in his field and has a wide range of recordings in his establishment. Also, many of the older film recordings which have been deleted in album (LP) form are now being released in compact disc form with excellent sound quality. They can be found in most popular record stores.

Once again, to all those who have helped me compile the data for this book,

Thanks!

Sheryl Aumack
Newport Beach, California

A

AARON SLICK FROM PUNKIN CRICK
Paramount, 1952

Producer: William Perlberg and George Seaton
Director: Claude Binyon
Screenplay: Claude Binyon; based on the play by Walter Benjamin Hare
Choreography: Charles O'Curran
Music and Lyrics: Ray Evans and Jay Livingston
Running time: 95 minutes, color

CAST:

Alan Young (*Aaron Slick*); Dinah Shore (*Josie Berry*); Robert Merrill (*Bill Merridew*); Adele Jergens (*Gladys*); Minerva Urecal (*Mrs. Peabody*); Martha Stewart (*Soubrette*); Fritz Feld (*Headwaiter*) and Veda Ann Borg (*Hotel Con-Artist*).

SONGS:

Chores, Chores, Chores; My Beloved; Saturday Night in Punkin Crick; Why Should I Believe in Love?; Still Water; It's Pert 'Nigh, But Not Plum; Life is a Beautiful Thing; Marshmallow Moon; I'd Like to Baby You; The Tenth Part of a Buck.

SYNOPSIS:

When singer and con-man Bill Merridew tries to swindle innocent widow Josie Berry out of her farm, shy farmer Aaron Slick decides to take action.

SOUNDTRACK: Motion Picture Tracks - 4

* * * * * * * * *

ABOUT FACE
Warner Bros., 1952

Producer: William Jacobs
Director: Roy Del Ruth
Screenplay: Peter Milne; based on the play by John Monks, Jr. and Fred F.
    Finklehoffe
Choreography: LeRoy Prinz
Music and Lyrics: Peter De Rose and Charles Tobias
Running time: 93 minutes, color

CAST:

Gordon MacRae (*Tony Williams*); Eddie Bracken (*"Boff" Roberts*); Dick Wesson (*Dave Crouse*); Virginia Gibson (*Betty Long*); Phyllis Kirk (*Alice Wheatley Roberts*); Aileen Stanley, Jr. (*Lorna Carter*); Joel Grey (*Cadet Bender*); Larry Keating (*Colonel Long*); Cliff Ferre (*Lt. Jones*); John Baer (*Hal Carlton*) and Mabel Albertson (*Mrs. Carter*).

SONGS:

Reveille; S.M.I. March; Tar Heels; If Someone Had Told Me; Wooden Indian; Spring Has Sprung; They Haven't Lost a Father Yet; I'm Nobody; I'm Gonna Take My Baby Out Tonight; There's No Other Girl For Me.

SYNOPSIS:

Musical remake of *Brother Rat* about a trio of cadets at Southern Military Institute and the problems of one, Boff Roberts, who is secretly married and whose wife is expecting a baby.

SOUNDTRACK: No soundtrack available

* * * * * * * * * *

THE AFFAIRS OF DOBIE GILLIS
Metro-Goldwyn-Mayer, 1953

Producer: Arthur M. Loew, Jr.
Director: Don Weis
Screenplay: Max Shulman
Choreography: Alex Romero
Music and Lyrics: see below with song titles
Running time: 74 minutes, B/W

CAST:

Debbie Reynolds (*Pansy Hammer*); Bobby Van (*Dobie Gillis*); Hans Conried (*Professor Amos Pomfritt*); Lurene Tuttle (*Mrs. Hammer*); Bob Fosse (*Charlie Trask*); Barbara Ruick (*Lorna Ellingboe*); Hanley Stafford (*Mr. Hammer*); Charles Lane (*Professor Obispo*) and Kathleen Freeman (*Happy Stella*).

SONGS:

All I Do Is Dream Of You - *Nacio Herb Brown and Arthur Freed*

2

You Can't Do Wrong Doin' Right - *Al Rinker and Floyd Huddleston*
I'm Through With Love - *Matt Malneck, Fud Livingston and Gus Kahn*
Those Endearing Young Charms - *Philip Boulter*

SYNOPSIS:

Bumbling college student Dobie Gillis basically finds classes a waste of time when he'd rather be spending it with his girlfriend Pansy just having a good time.

SOUNDTRACK: No soundtrack available

* * * * * * * * *

ALEXANDER'S RAGTIME BAND
20th Century Fox, 1938

Producer: Darryl F. Zanuck
Director: Henry King
Screenplay: Kathryn Scola, Lamar Trotti and Richard Sherman
Choreography: Seymour Felix
Music and Lyrics: Irving Berlin
Running time: 105 minutes, B/W

CAST:

Tyrone Power (*Roger Grant/"Alexander"*); Alice Faye (*Stella Kirby*); Don Ameche (*Charlie Dwyer*); Ethel Merman (*Jerry Allen*); Jack Haley (*Davey Lane*); Jean Hersholt (*Professor Heinrich*); Helen Westley (*Aunt Sophie*); John Carradine (*Taxi Driver*); Paul Hurst (*Bill*); Ruth Terry (*Ruby*); Douglas Fowley (*Snapper*) and Joe King (*Charles Dillingham*).

SONGS:

Alexander's Ragtime Band; Ragtime Violin; The International Rag; Everybody's Doin' It; Now It Can Be Told; This is the Life; Oh, How I Hate To Get Up in the Morning!; We're On Our Way to France; Say It With Music; A Pretty Girl is Like a Melody; I'm Marching Along With Time; Blue Skies; Everybody Step; What'll I Do?; All Alone; Heat Wave.

SYNOPSIS:

In turn-of-the-century San Francisco Roger Grant finds himself leading a double life: as a respected violin player under the tutelage of Professor Heinrich and as "Alexander", who with his friends play in a Barbary Coast night club.

3

* * * * * * * * *

ALICE IN WONDERLAND
RKO, 1951

Producer: Walt Disney
Director: Clyde Geronimi, Hamilton Luske and Wilfred Jackson
Screenplay: Winston Hibler, Ted Sears, Bill Peet, Erdman Penner, Joe Rinaldi, Milt Banta, Bill Cottrell, Dick Kelsey, Joe Grant, Dick Huemer, Del Connell, Tom Oreb and John Walbridge; based on the stories by Lewis Carroll
Music and Lyrics: Bob Hilliard and Sammy Fain
Running time: 75 minutes, color

VOCAL TALENTS:

Kathryn Beaumont (*Alice*); Ed Wynn (*The Mad Hatter*); Richard Haydn (*The Caterpillar*); Sterling Holloway (*The Cheshire Cat*); Jerry Colonna (*The March Hare*); Verna Felton (*The Queen of Hearts*); J. Pat O'Malley (*The Walrus/The Carpenter/Tweedledum & Tweedledee*); Bill Thompson (*The White Rabbit/The Dodo*); James MacDonald (*The Dormouse*); Heather Angel (*Alice's sister*); Larry Grey (*Bill*); Joseph Kearns (*The Doorknob*); Doris Lloyd (*The Rose*) and Dink Trout (*The King of Hearts*).

SONGS:

Alice in Wonderland; In a World of My Own; I'm Late; The Caucus Race; The Walrus and the Carpenter; Old Father William*; We'll Smoke the Blighter Out*; All in a Golden Afternoon; A-E-I-O-U*; 'Twas Brillig**; A Very Merry Un-Birthday***; Very Good Advice; Painting the Roses Red.

   **music and lyrics by Oliver Wallace and Ted Sears*
  ***music and lyrics by Don Raye and Gene DePaul*
****music and lyrics by Mack David, Al Hoffman and Jerry Livingston*

SYNOPSIS:

Animated Disney tale based on Lewis Carroll's *Alice in Wonderland* and *Through the Looking Glass* has a little girl named Alice who encounters several strange creatures as she searches for a mysterious white rabbit.

SOUNDTRACK: No soundtrack available

* * * * * * * * *

ALICE'S ADVENTURES IN WONDERLAND
American National Enterprises, 1972

Producer: Derek Horne
Director: William Sterling
Screenplay: William Sterling; based on the stories by Lewis Carroll
Choreography: Terry Gilbert
Music and Lyrics: John Barry and Don Black
Running time: 96 minutes, color

CAST:

Michael Crawford (*The White Rabbit*); Davy Kaye (*The Mouse*); Robert Helpmann (*The Mad Hatter*); Peter Sellers (*The March Hare*); Dudley Moore (*The Dormouse*); Ralph Richardson (*The Caterpillar*); Peter Bull (*The Duchess*); Flora Robson (*The Queen of Hearts*); Michael Hordern (*The Mock Turtle*); Spike Milligan (*The Gryphon*); Michael Jayston (*Dodgson*) and Fiona Fullerton (*Alice*).

SONGS:

Curiouser and Curiouser; You've Gotta Know When to Stop; The Last Word is Mine; Dum and Dee Dance/Nursery Rhyme*; The Pun Song; I've Never Been This Far Before; Off With Their Heads; The Moral Song; Will You Walk a Little Faster?*; They Told Me That You Had Been To Her*; The Me I Never Knew.

*music and lyrics by John Barry and Lewis Carroll

SYNOPSIS:

The classic children's story by Lewis Carroll about a young girl named Alice who, while in pursuit of a mysterious white rabbit, falls down a rabbit hole and into Wonderland where a series of incredible adventures await her.

SOUNDTRACK: Warner Bros. BS-2671

* * * * * * * * *

ALL HANDS ON DECK
20th Century Fox, 1961

Producer: Oscar Brodny
Director: Norman Taurog

Screenplay: Jay Sommers; based on a novel by Donald R. Morris
Choreography: Hal Belfer
Music and Lyrics: Ray Evans and Jay Livingston
Running time: 98 minutes, color

CAST:

Pat Boone (*Lt. Victor Donald*); Barbara Eden (*Sally Hobson*); Buddy Hackett (*Seaman "Shrieking Eagle" Garfield*); Dennis O'Keefe (*Captain Ryan O'Gara*); Warren Berlinger (*Ensign Rush*); Gale Gordon (*Commander Bintle*); David Brandon (*Lt. Kutley*); Joe E. Ross (*Bos'n*); Jody McCrea (*Lt. J.G. Schuyler*) and Ann B. Davis (*Nobby*).

SONGS:

All Hands On Deck; I've Got It Made; Somewhere There's Home; There's No One Like You.

SYNOPSIS:

Lt. Vic Donald is assigned the job of "babysitting" seaman Garfield, an Indian from a wealthy Chicasaw tribe in Oklahoma, but he finds his pursuit of reporter Sally Hobson a much more attractive job.

SOUNDTRACK: No soundtrack available

* * * * * * * * *

ANCHORS AWEIGH
Metro-Goldwyn-Mayer, 1945

Producer: Joe Pasternak
Director: George Sidney
Screenplay: Isobel Lennart; based on a story by Natalie Marcin
Choreography: Gene Kelly
Music and Lyrics: see below with song titles
Running time: 140 minutes, color

CAST:

Frank Sinatra (*Clarence Doolittle*); Kathryn Grayson (*Susan Abbott*); Gene Kelly (*Joseph Brady*); José Iturbi (*Himself*); Dean Stockwell (*Donald Martin*); Billy Gilbert (*Café Manager*); Henry O'Neill (*Admiral Hammond*); Leon Ames (*Commander*); Pamela Britton (*"Brooklyn"*) and Sharon McManus (*Little Beggar Girl*).

SONGS:

We Hate to Leave - *Jule Styne and Sammy Cahn*
Lullaby - *Johannes Brahms*
I Begged Her - *Jule Styne and Sammy Cahn*
If You Knew Susie, Like I Know Susie - *B.G. DeSylva and Joseph Meyer*
Jealousy - *Jacob Gade*
What Makes the Sunset? - *Jule Styne and Sammy Cahn*
(All of a Sudden) My Heart Sings - *Henri Herpin and Harold Rome*
The Donkey Serenade (instrumental) - *Rudolf Friml, Robert Wright and George Forrest*
The Worry Song - *Ralph Freed and Sammy Fain*
The Charm Of You - *Jule Styne and Sammy Cahn*
I Fall in Love Too Easily - *Jule Styne and Sammy Cahn*
Mexican Hat Dance (instrumental) - *arranged by F.A. Partichela*
Anchors Aweigh - *Charles A. Zimmerman, Alfred Hart Miles and Royal Lovell*

SYNOPSIS:

When Joe Brady and Clarence Doolittle, sailor on leave in Los Angeles, find a young runaway boy named Donald they return him to his "Aunt Susan" who turns out to be a lovely young woman.

SOUNDTRACK: Curtain Calls 100/17

* * * * * * * * *

AN AMERICAN IN PARIS
Metro-Goldwyn-Mayer, 1951

Producer: Arthur Freed
Director: Vincente Minelli
Screenplay: Alan Jay Lerner, based·on his story
Choreography: Gene Kelly
Music and Lyrics: George Gershwin and Ira Gershwin
Running time: 113 minutes, color

CAST:

Gene Kelly (*Jerry Mulligan*); Leslie Caron (*Lise Bouvier*); Oscar Levant (*Adam Cook*); Georges Guetary (*Henri Baurel*); Nina Foch (*Milo Roberts*); Martha Bamaltre (*Martine Mattieu*); Eugene Borden (*Georges Mattieu*) and Anna Q. Nilsson (*Kay Jansen*).

SONGS:

By Strauss; I Got Rhythm; Tra-La-La; Our Love is Here to Stay; I'll Build a Stairway to Paradise*; 'S Wonderful; An American in Paris (instrumental).

*music and lyrics by George Gershwin, B.G. DeSylva and E. Ray Goetz

SYNOPSIS:

Jerry Mulligan, a WWII ex-G.I., decides to stay on in Paris after his discharge to paint. He soon finds himself in love with shopgirl Lise but indebted to wealthy patroness Milo.

SOUNDTRACK: MGM Select 2353-068 (with *Les Girls*)

* * * * * * * * * *

ANNIE
Columbia, 1982

Producer: Ray Stark
Director: John Huston
Screenplay: Carol Sobieski; based on the stage musical book by Thomas Meehan
Choreography: Arlene Phillips
Music and Lyrics: Charles Strouse and Martin Charnin
Running time: 128 minutes, color

CAST:

Albert Finney (*Oliver "Daddy" Warbucks*); Carol Burnett (*Miss Hannigan*); Bernadette Peters (*Lily St. Regis*); Ann Reinking (*Grace Farrell*); Tim Curry (*Rooster*); Geoffrey Holder (*Punjab*); Edward Herrmann (*Franklin D. Roosevelt*); Roger Minami (*The Asp*); Toni Ann Gisondi (*Molly*); Lois de Banzie (*Eleanor Roosevelt*); Peter Marshall (*Bert Healy*) and Aileen Quinn (*Annie*).

SONGS:

Maybe; It's the Hard-Knock Life; Dumb Dog; Sandy; I Think I'm Gonna Like It Here; Little Girls; We Got Annie; Let's Go to the Movies; Sign; You're Never Fully Dressed Without a Smile; Tomorrow; Easy Street; I Don't Need Anything But You.

SYNOPSIS:

Based on the adventures of comic strip heroine "Little Orphan Annie" as she tried

8

to locate her real parents with the help of "Daddy" Warbucks.

SOUNDTRACK: Columbia JS-38000

* * * * * * * * * *

ANNIE GET YOUR GUN
Metro-Goldwyn-Mayer, 1950

Producer: Arthur Freed
Director: George Sidney
Screenplay: Sidney Sheldon; based on the stage musical book by Herbert Fields and
         Dorothy Fields
Choreography: Robert Alton
Music and Lyrics: Irving Berlin
Running time: 107 minutes, color

CAST:

Betty Hutton (*Annie Oakley*); Howard Keel (*Frank Butler*); Louis Calhern (*Buffalo Bill*); Keenan Wynn (*Charlie Davenport*); J. Carrol Naish (*Sitting Bull*); Edward Arnold (*Pawnee Bill*); Benay Venuta (*Dolly Tate*) and Clinton Sundberg (*Foster Wilson*).

SONGS:

Doin' What Comes Natur'lly; The Girl That I Marry; You Can't Get a Man With a Gun; They Say It's Wonderful; My Defenses Are Down; I Got the Sun in the Morning; Anything You Can Do; There's No Business Like Show Business.

SYNOPSIS:

Farm girl Annie Oakley grows up to become a professional sharpshooter and eventually joins Buffalo Bill's Wild West Show where her rivalry with Frank Butler soons turns to love.

SOUNDTRACK: MGM 2-SES-42ST (with *Show Boat*/1951)

* * * * * * * * * *

ANYTHING GOES
Paramount, 1956

Producer: Robert Emmett Dolan
Director: Robert Lewis
Screenplay: Sidney Sheldon; based on the play by P.G. Wodehouse and Guy Bolton,
       revised by Howard Lindsay and Russel Crouse
Choreography: Nick Castle
Music and Lyrics: Cole Porter
Running time: 106 minutes, color

CAST:

Bing Crosby (*Bill Benson*); Donald O'Connor (*Ted Adams*); Mitzi Gaynor (*Patsy Blair*); Jeanmarie (*Gaby Duval*); Phil Harris (*Steve Blair*); Kurt Kasznar (*Victor Lawrence*); Richard Erdman (*Ed Brent*); Walter Sande (*Alex Todd*); Archer MacDonald (*Otto*) and Argentina Brunetti (*Suzanne*).

SONGS:

You've Gotta Give the People Hokum*; Anything Goes; I Get a Kick Out Of You; You're the Top; It's De-Lovely; All Through the Night; You Can Bounce Right Back*; A Second-Hand Turban and a Crystal Ball*; Blow, Gabriel, Blow.

music and lyrics by James Van Heusen and Sammy Cahn

SYNOPSIS:

The stars of a new Broadway show, Bill Benson and Ted Adams, go to Europe looking for a leading lady--and both sign the girl they've fallen for!

SOUNDTRACK: Decca DL-8318

* * * * * * * * *

APRIL IN PARIS
Warner Bros., 1953

Producer: William Jacobs
Director: David Butler
Screenplay: Jack Rose and Melville Shavelson
Choreography: LeRoy Prinz
Music and Lyrics: Vernon Duke and Sammy Cahn
Running time: 101 minutes, color

CAST:

Doris Day (*Dynamite Jackson*); Ray Bolger (*S. Winthrop Putnam*); Claude Dauphin (*Philippe Fouquet*); Eve Miller (*Marcia*); George Givot (*François*); Paul Harvey (*Secretary Sherman*); Herbert Farjeon (*Joshua Stevens*); Wilson Millar (*Sinclair Wilson*); Raymond Largay (*Joseph Weimar*) and John Alvin (*Tracy*).

SONGS:

April in Paris*; It Must Be Good; Life is Such a Pleasure; Give Me Your Lips; That's What Makes Paris Paree; I'm Gonna Ring the Bell Tonight; The Diff'rence; I Know the Place; Who Needs It?; I Ask You.

*music and lyrics by Vernon Duke and E.Y. Harburg

SYNOPSIS:

The U.S. State Department sends chorus girl Dynamite Jackson to Paris for an arts festival by mistake but she is unaware of it and falls in love aboard ship for fellow passenger (and real diplomat) Winthrop Putnam.

SOUNDTRACK: Titania 500 (with *Young at Heart*)

* * * * * * * * * *

APRIL LOVE
20th Century Fox, 1957

Producer: David Weisbart
Director: Henry Levin
Screenplay: Winston Miller; based on a novel by George Agnew Chamberlain
Choreography: Bill Foster
Music and Lyrics: Sammy Fain and Paul Francis Webster
Running time: 99 minutes, color

CAST:

Pat Boone (*Nick Conover*); Shirley Jones (*Liz Templeton*); Dolores Michaels (*Fran*); Arthur O'Connell (*Jed*); Matt Crowley (*Dan Templeton*); Jeanette Nolan (*Henrietta*) and Brad Jackson (*Al Turner*).

SONGS:

April Love; The Bentonville Fair; Clover in the Meadow; Give Me a Gentle Girl;

Do It Yourself.

SYNOPSIS:

City boy Nick Conover moves to Kentucky to escape his problems with the police. Once there he falls in love with Liz Templeton and decides to become a sulky driver.

SOUNDTRACK: Dot 9000

* * * * * * * * *

THE ARISTOCATS
Buena Vista, 1970

Producer: Wolfgang Reitherman and Winston Hibler
Director: Wolfgang Reitherman
Screenplay: Larry Clemmons, Vance Gerry, Frank Thomas, Julius Svendsen, Ken Anderson, Eric Cleworth and Ralph Wright; based on a story by Tom McGowan and Tom Rowe
Music and Lyrics: see below with song titles
Running time: 78 minutes, color

VOCAL TALENTS:

Eva Gabor (*Duchess*); Phil Harris (*O'Malley*); Hermione Baddeley (*Mme. Bonfamille*); Dean Clark (*Berlioz*); Liz English (*Marie*); Gary Dubin (*Toulouse*); Nancy Kulp (*Frou-Frou*); Pat Buttram (*Napoleon*); George Lindsay (*Lafayette*); Roddy Maude-Roxby (*Edgar*); Sterling Holloway (*Roquefort*); Monica Evans (*Abigail*); Carole Shelley (*Amelia*); Charles Lane (*Georges Hautecourt*) and "Scatman" Crothers (*Scat Catt*).

SONGS:

My Paree (Theme from *The Aristocats*)* - *George Bruns*
She Never Felt Alone - *Richard M. Sherman and Robert B. Sherman*
Scales and Arpeggios - *Richard M. Sherman and Robert B. Sherman*
Nice Melody - *George Bruns*
Pretty Melody - *George Bruns*
Thomas J. O'Malley Cat - *Terry Gilkyson*
The Goose Steps High (Goose Walk) - *George Bruns*
Blues - *George Bruns*
Ev'rybody Wants to Be a Cat - *Floyd Huddleston and Al Rinker*
Cats Love Theme (Meow) - *George Bruns*
The Aristocats - *Richard M. Sherman and Robert B. Sherman*

*vocal by Maurice Chevalier

SYNOPSIS:

Animated tale about a cat named Mewsette and her three kittens--Berlioz, Toulouse and Marie--who are kidnapped from Mme. Bonfamille's home by the evil butler Edgar. They manage to escape and are befriended by an affable alley cat named O'Malley who help them on their way.

SOUNDTRACK: Disneyland ST-3995

* * * * * * * * *

ARTISTS AND MODELS
Paramount, 1955

Producer: Hal B. Wallis
Director: Frank Tashlin
Screenplay: Frank Tashlin, Hal Kanter and Herbert Baker; based on a play by
        Michael Davidson and Norman Lessing
Choreography: Charles O'Curran
Music and Lyrics: Harry Warren and Jack Brooks
Running time: 108 minutes, color

CAST:

Dean Martin (*Rick Todd*); Jerry Lewis (*Eugene Fullstack*); Dorothy Malone (*Abigail Parker*); Shirley MacLaine (*Bessie Sparrowbush*); Eddie Mayehoff (*Mr. Murdock*); Eva Gabor (*Sonia*); Anita Ekberg (*Anita*); George Winslow (*Richard Stilton*); Jack Elam (*Ivan*) and Herbert Rudley (*Chief Samuels*).

SONGS:

When You Pretend; You Look So Familiar; My Lucky Song; Inamorata.

SYNOPSIS:

Unemployed artist Rick Todd finds the dreams of his roommate Eugene Fullstack are the perfect material for a new series of comic book adventures.

SOUNDTRACK: No soundtrack available

* * * * * * * * *

13

ATHENA
Metro-Goldwyn-Mayer, 1954

Producer: Joe Pasternak
Director: Richard Thorpe
Screenplay: William Ludwig and Leonard Spigelgass
Choreography: Valerie Bettis
Music and Lyrics: Hugh Martin and Ralph Blane
Running time: 95 minutes, color

CAST:

Jane Powell (*Athena Mulvain*); Edmund Purdom (*Adam Calhorn Shaw*); Debbie Reynolds (*Minerva Mulvain*); Vic Damone (*Johnny Nyles*); Louis Calhern (*Grandpa Mulvain*); Linda Christian (*Beth Hallson*); Ray Collins (*Mr. Tremaine*); Carl Benton Reid (*Mr. Griswalde*); Evelyn Varden (*Grandma Salome Mulvain*); Virginia Gibson (*Niobe*); Nancy Kilgas (*Aphrodite*); Dolores Starr (*Calliope*); Jane Fischer (*Medea*); Cecile Rogers (*Ceres*); Howard Wendel (*Mr. Grenville*); Henry Nakamura (*Roy*); Kathleen Freeman (*Miss Seely*); Steve Reeves (*Ed Perkins*) and Richard Sabre (*Bill Nichols*).

SONGS:

The Girl Next Door; Vocalize; Imagine; Love Can Change the Stars; I Never Felt Better; Chacun le sait (*La Fille du Régiment*)*; Venezia.

music and lyrics by Gaetano Donizetti

SYNOPSIS:

After stuffy Boston lawyer Adam Shaw falls in love with Athena Mulvain he finds that his life is turned upside-down by her family's rather eccentric lifestyle.

SOUNDTRACK: Motion Picture Tracks - 2

B

BABES IN ARMS
Metro-Goldwyn-Mayer, 1939

Producer: Arthur Freed
Director: Busby Berkeley
Screenplay: Jack McGowan and Kay Van Riper; based on the stage musical book
        by Richard Rodgers and Lorenz Hart
Choreography: Busby Berkeley
Music and Lyrics: see below with song titles
Running time: 97 minutes, B/W

CAST:

Mickey Rooney (*Mickey Moran*); Judy Garland (*Patsy Barton*); Charles Winninger (*Joe Moran*); Guy Kibbee (*Judge Black*); June Preisser (*Rosalie "Baby" Essex*); Grace Hayes (*Florrie Moran*); Betty Jaynes (*Molly Moran*); Douglas McPhail (*Don Brice*); Rand Brooks (*Jeff Steele*); Leni Lynn (*Dody Martini*); John Sheffield (*Bobs*); Margaret Hamilton (*Margaret Steele*); Ann Shoemaker (*Mrs. Lillian Barton*) and Henry Hull (*Mr. Madox*).

SONGS:

Good Morning - *Nacio Herb Brown and Arthur Freed; arranged by Roger Edens*
Opera vs. Jazz - *arranged by Roger Edens*
Babes in Arms - *Richard Rodgers and Lorenz Hart*
Where or When? - *Richard Rodgers and Lorenz Hart*
I Cried For You - *Nacio Herb Brown and Arthur Freed*
My Daddy Was a Minstrel Man - *Roger Edens*
Ida, Sweet as Apple Cider - *Eddie Munson and Eddie Leonard*
On Moonlight Bay - *Edward Madden and Percy Wenrich*
I'm Just Wild About Harry - *Eubie Blake and Noble Sissle*
God's Country - *Harold Arlen and E.Y. Harburg*

SYNOPSIS:

Mickey Moran, Patsy Barton and their friends, children of a group of vaudeville actors, decide to put on a show to raise money to help the adults through a rough time--as well as prove their folks are fit parents.

SOUNDTRACK: Curtain Calls 100/6-7 (with *Babes on Broadway*)

* * * * * * * * *

BABES IN TOYLAND
Buena Vista, 1961

Producer: Walt Disney
Director: Jack Donohue
Screenplay: Joe Rinaldi, Ward Kimball and Lowell S. Hawley; based on the stage
        musical book by Victor Herbert and Glen McDonough
Choreography: Tom Mahoney
Music and Lyrics: Victor Herbert
Running time: 105 minutes, color

CAST:

Ray Bolger (*Barnaby*); Tommy Sands (*Tom Piper*); Ed Wynn (*The Toymaker*);
Annette Funicello (*Mary Contrary*); Henry Calvin (*Gonzorgo*); Gene Sheldon
(*Roderigo*); Tommy Kirk (*Grumio*); Mary McCarty (*Mother Goose*); Kevin Corcoran
(*Boy Blue*); Brian Corcoran (*Willie Winkie*): Marilee & Melanie Arnold (*The Twins*)
and Ann Jilliann (*Bo Peep*).

SONGS:

Down in the Village Square; Lemonade; We Won't Be Happy 'Till We Get It; Just
a Whisper Away; Slowly He Sank Into the Sea*; Castle in Spain; My Sheep Are
Gone For Good; I Can't Do the Sum; Floretta; The Forest of No Return*; Go to
Sleep; Toyland; The Workshop Song*; Just a Toy; March of the Wooden Soldiers
(instrumental); Tom and Mary.

music and lyrics by George Bruns and Mel Leven

SYNOPSIS:

In Mother Goose Land the big event is the impending marriage of Mary Contrary
and Tom Piper but the evil Barnaby plots to kill Tom so that he can marry Mary
himself--for her inheritance!

SOUNDTRACK: Disneyland 1219

* * * * * * * * *

BABES ON BROADWAY
Metro-Goldwyn-Mayer, 1942

Producer: Arthur Freed
Director: Busby Berkeley

Screenplay: Fred Finklehoffe and Elaine Ryan; based on a story by Fred Finklehoffe
Choreography: Busby Berkeley
Music and Lyrics: see below with song titles
Running time: 121 minutes, B/W

CAST:

Mickey Rooney (*Tommy Williams*); Judy Garland (*Penny Morris*); Fay Bainter (*Jonesy*); Virginia Weidler (*Barbara Jo Conway*); Ray McDonald (*Ray Lambert*); Richard Quine (*Morton "Hammy" Hammond*); Donald Meek (*Mr. Stone*); James Gleason (*Thornton Reed*); Emma Dunn (*Mrs. Williams*); Frederick Burton (*Mr. Theodore Morris*); Cliff Clark (*Inspector Moriarity*); William F. Post, Jr. (*Announcer*); Luis Alberni (*Nick*) and Alexander Woolcott (*Himself*).

SONGS:

Anything Can Happen in New York - *Burton Lane and E.Y. Harburg*
How About You? - *Burton Lane and Ralph Freed*
Hoe Down - *Roger Edens and Ralph Freed*
Chin Up! Cheerio! Carry On! - *Ralph Freed*
Mary is a Grand Old Name - *George M. Cohan*
She is Ma Daisy - *Harry Lauder and J.D. Harper*
I've Got Rings On My Fingers - *Maurice Scott, R.P. Weston and F.J. Barnes*
Yankee Doodle Dandy - *George M. Cohan*
Bombshell From Brazil - *Roger Edens*
Mama Yo Quiero - *Jararaca Paiva and Vincente Paiva*
Blackout Over Broadway - *Burton Lane and Ralph Freed*
By the Light of the Silvery Moon - *Gus Edwards and Edward Madden*
Franklin D. Roosevelt Jones - *Harold J. Rome*
Waitin' For the Robert E. Lee - *L. Wolfe Gilbert and Lewis F. Muir*

SYNOPSIS:

Tommy Williams, Ray Lambert and Morton Hammond--"The Three Ball of Fire"--try and raise enough money with a block party to rent a theatre for a benefit to help send the children from a settlement house on a country vacation.

SOUNDTRACK: Curtain Calls 100/6-7 (with *Babes in Arms*)

* * * * * * * * *

THE BANDWAGON
Metro-Goldwyn-Mayer, 1953

Producer: Arthur Freed
Director: Vincente Minelli
Screenplay: Betty Comden and Adolph Green
Choreography: Michael Kidd
Music and Lyrics: Arthur Schwartz and Howard Dietz
Running time: 112 minutes, color

CAST:

Fred Astaire (*Tony Hunter*); Cyd Charisse* (*Gabrielle "Gaby" Gerard*); Oscar Levant (*Lester Marton*); Nanette Fabray (*Lily Marton*); Jack Buchanan (*Jeffrey Cordova*); James Mitchell (*Paul Byrd*); Robert Gist (*Hal Benton*); Thurston Hall (*Colonel Tripp*); LeRoy Daniels (*Bootblack*) and Ava Gardner (*Herself*).

vocals dubbed by India Adams

SONGS:

By Myself; A Shine On Your Shoes; That's Entertainment; Dancing in the Dark (instrumental); You and the Night and the Music; I Love Louisa; New Sun in the Sky; I Guess I'll Have to Change My Plans; Louisiana Hayride; Triplets; The Girl Hunt Ballet (instrumental).

SYNOPSIS:

Tony Hunter is a faded movie idol who agrees to appear in a Broadway show written by old friends Lester and Lily Marton but is soon in conflict with his leading lady Gaby and slightly maniacal director Jeff.

SOUNDTRACK: MGM 2-SES-44ST (with *Kiss Me, Kate!*)

* * * * * * * * * *

THE BARKLEYS OF BROADWAY
Metro-Goldwyn-Mayer, 1949

Producer: Arthur Freed
Director: Charles Walters
Screenplay: Betty Comden and Adolph Green
Choreography: Robert Alton
Music and Lyrics: Harry Warren and Ira Gershwin
Running time: 109 minutes, color

CAST:

Fred Astaire (*Josh Barkley*); Ginger Rogers (*Dinah Barkley*); Oscar Levant (*Ezra Millar*); Billie Burke (*Mrs. Livingston Belney*); Gale Robbins (*Shirlene May*); Jacques François (*Jacques Pierre Barredout*); George Zucco (*The Judge*); Clinton Sundberg (*Bert Felsher*); Inez Cooper (*Pamela Driscoll*); Gloria Amboy (*Carol Brewster*) and Wilson Wood (*Larry*).

SONGS:

Swing Trot; Sabre Dance* (instrumental); You'd Be Hard to Replace; Bouncin' the Blues (instrumental); My One and Only Highland Fling; Weekend in the Country; Shoes With Wings On; Piano Concerto No. 1 in B Flat Minor** (instrumental); They Can't Take That Away From Me***; Manhattan Downbeat.

music by Aram Khachaturian
**music by Peter Ilitsch Tchaikovsky*
***music and lyrics by George Gershwin and Ira Gershwin*

SYNOPSIS:

Josh and Dinah Barkley's husband-and-wife act--and marriage--is threatened when Dinah decides to quit to try her luck at drama.

SOUNDTRACK: MGM 2-SES-51ST (with *Silk Stockings* and *Les Girls*)

* * * * * * * * * *

BARNUM
British Broadcasting Corporation, 1986

Producer: Harold Fielding
Director: Peter Coe and Terry Hughes
Book: Mark Bramble
Choreography: Joe Layton and Buddy Schwab
Music and Lyrics: Cy Coleman and Michael Stewart
Running time: 113 minutes, color

CAST:

Michael Crawford (*Phineas Taylor Barnum*); Eileen Battye (*Charity "Chairy" Barnum*); Michael Heath (*The Ringmaster/Julius Goldschmidt/James A. Bailey*); Christina Collier (*Jenny Lind*); Sharon Benson (*Joice Heth/Blues Singer*) and Paul Miller (*tom thumb*).

There's a Sucker Born Ev'ry Minute; Thank God I'm Old; The Colors of My Life; One Brick at a Time; Museum Song; I Like Your Style; Bigger Isn't Better; Love Makes Such Fools Of Us All; Out There; Come Follow the Band; Black and White; The Prince of Humbug; Join the Circus.

SYNOPSIS:

Master showman P.T. Barnum's life is chronicled from his "humble beginnings" in the exhibition and museum business through to his partnership with James A. Bailey to form Barnum and Bailey's circus.

SOUNDTRACK: Air CDL-1348

* * * * * * * * *

BEAUTY AND THE BEAST
Cannon Films, 1987

Producer: Menahem Golan and Yoram Globus
Director: Eugene Marner
Screenplay: Carole Lucia Satrina; based on the fairy tale by Madame de Villeneuve
Choreography: Christine Oren
Music and Lyrics: Lori McKelvey
Running time: 96 minutes, color

CAST:

Rebecca De Mornay (*Beauty*); John Savage (*Beast/The Prince*); Yossi Graber* (*Father*); Joseph Bee** (*Oliver*); Ruth Harlap (*Isabelle*); Carmela Marner (*Bettina*); Jack Messinger (*Frederick*) and Michael Schneider (*Mr. Kuppel*).

 vocals dubbed by George Little
**vocals dubbed by Nick Curtis*

SONGS:

What Would You Do Without Me?; This Life For Me; See With Your Heart; Wish For the Moon.

SYNOPSIS:

When he unintentionally steals a rose from a mysterious castle, a merchant finds he must sacrifice his youngest daughter, Beauty, to the owner of the castle--the Beast.

SOUNDTRACK: Kid Stuff CMT-6622 (cassette only)

* * * * * * * * *

BECAUSE YOU'RE MINE
Metro-Goldwyn-Mayer, 1952

Producer: Joe Pasternak
Director: Alexander Hall
Screenplay: Karl Tunberg and Leonard Spigelgass; based on a story by Ruth Brooks
          Flippen and Sy Gomberg
Music and Lyrics: see below with song titles
Running time: 103 minutes, color

CAST:

Mario Lanza (*Renaldo Rossano*); Doretta Morrow (*Bridget Batterson*); James
Whitmore (*Sgt. Batterson*); Dean Miller (*Ben Jones*); Paula Corday (*Francesca
Landers*); Jeff Donnell (*Patty Ware*); Spring Byington (*Mrs. Montville*); Curtis
Cooksey (*General Montville*); Don Porter (*Capt. Burton Loring*); Eduard Franz
(*Albert Parkson Foster*); Bobby Van (*Artie Pilcer*); Celia Lovsky (*Mrs. Rossano*) and
Ralph Reed (*Horsey*).

SONGS:

The Song Angels Sing - *Johannes Brahms, Irving Aaronson and Paul Francis Webster*
You Do Something To Me - *Cole Porter*
Lee-Ah-Loo - *John Lehmann and Raymond Sinatra*
The Lord's Prayer - *Alfred Hay Malotte*
Because You're Mine - *Nicholas Brodsky and Sammy Cahn*
Be My Love - *Nicholas Brodsky and Sammy Cahn*
Granada - *Agustin Lara*

SYNOPSIS:

After opera star Renaldo Rosanno is drafted into the Army he finds that, with the
help of his music-loving sergeant, he can still continue to make recordings in New
York City with his partner Francesca. But complications develop when he falls for
Sgt. Batterson's sister Bridget.

SOUNDTRACK: No soundtrack available

* * * * * * * * *

BEDKNOBS AND BROOMSTICKS
Buena Vista, 1970

Producer: Bill Walsh
Director: Robert Stevenson
Screenplay: Bill Walsh and Don DaGradi; based on the book by Mary Norton
Choreography: Donald McKayle
Music and Lyrics: Richard M. Sherman and Robert B. Sherman
Running time: 117 minutes, color

CAST:

Angela Lansbury (*Eglantine Price*); David Tomlinson (*Professor Emelius Brown*); Roddy McDowall (*Mr. Jelk*); Sam Jaffe (*The Bookman*); John Ericson (*Colonel Heller*); Reginald Owen (*General Teagler*); Bruce Forsyth (*Swinburne*); Ian Weighill (*Charles Rawlins*); Cindy O'Callaghan (*Carrie Rawlins*) and Roy Snart (*Paul Rawlins*).

SONGS:

The Old Home Guard; The Age of Not Believing; With a Flair; A Step in the Right Direction; Eglantine; Don't Let Me Down; Portobello Road; The Beautiful Briny; Substitutiary Locomotion.

SYNOPSIS:

Eglantine Price, an apprentice with, tries to utilize her talents to help in some way with the war effort in WWII Britain.

SOUNDTRACK: Buena Vista 5003

* * * * * * * * *

THE BELLE OF NEW YORK
Metro-Goldwyn-Mayer, 1952

Producer: Arthur Freed
Director: Charles Walters
Screenplay: Robert O'Brien and Irving Elinson, adapted by Chester Erskine; based
             on a play by Hugh Morton
Choreography: Robert Alton
Music and Lyrics: Harry Warren and Johnny Mercer
Running time: 82 minutes, color

CAST:

Fred Astaire (*Charlie Hill*); Vera-Ellen* (*Angela Collins*); Marjorie Main (*Mrs. Phineas Hill*); Keenan Wynn (*Max Ferris*); Alice Pearce (*Elsie Wilkins*); Clinton Sundberg (*Gilfred Spivak*); Gale Robbins (*Dixie McCoy*) and Henry Slate (*Officer Clancy*).

vocals dubbed by Anita Ellis

SONGS:

When I'm Out With the Belle of New York; Who Wants to Kiss the Bridegroom?; Let a Little Love Come In*; Seeing's Believing; Baby Doll; Oops!; Thank You Mr. Currier, Thank You Mr. Ives; Naughty But Nice; I Wanna Be a Dancin' Man.

music and lyrics by Roger Edens

SYNOPSIS:

Playboy Charlie Hill is dependent on his puritanical aunt, Mrs. Phineas Hill, for his livelihood and soon finds himself falling in love with her pretty assistant Angela Collins.

SOUNDTRACK: Stat DS-15004

* * * * * * * * *

BELLE OF THE YUKON
RKO, 1945

Producer: William A. Seiter
Director: William A. Seiter
Screenplay: James Edward Grant; based on a story by Houston Branch
Choreography: Don Loper
Music and Lyrics: Johnny Burke and James Van Heusen
Running time: 84 minutes, color

CAST:

Randolph Scott (*"Honest" John Calhoun*); Gypsy Rose Lee (*Belle Devalle*); Dinah Shore (*Lettie Candless*); Bob Burns (*Sam Slade*); Charles Winninger (*Pop Candless*); William Marshall (*Steve*); Guinn Williams (*Marshal Mervyn Maitland*); Florence Bates (*Viola*) and Robert Armstrong (*George*).

SONGS:

Belle of the Yukon; Sleighride in July; Every Girl is Different; Like Someone in Love; I Can't Tell Why I Love You But I Do.

SYNOPSIS:

John Calhoun is trying to start a new life in Alaska running a dance hall but George, a local crook, has other ideas about its operation.

SOUNDTRACK: No soundtrack available

* * * * * * * * *

BELLS ARE RINGING
Metro-Goldwyn-Mayer, 1960

Producer: Arthur Freed
Director: Vincente Minelli
Screenplay: Betty Comden and Adolph Green, based on their stage musical book
Choreography: Charles O'Curran
Music and Lyrics: Jule Styne, Betty Comden and Adolph Green
Running time: 127 minutes, color

CAST:

Judy Holliday (*Ella Peterson*); Dean Martin (*Jeffrey Moss*); Fred Clark (*Larry Hastings*); Eddie Foy, Jr. (*J. Otto Prantz*); Jean Stapleton (*Sue*); Ruth Storey (*Gwynne*); Dort Clark (*Inspector Barnes*); Frank Gorshin (*Blake Barton*); Ralph Roberts (*Francis*); Bernie West (*Dr. Joe Kitchell*) and Hal Linden (*Night Club Singer*).

SONGS:

Bells Are Ringing; It's a Perfect Relationship; Do It Yourself; It's a Simple Little System; It's Better Than a Dream; I Met a Girl; Mu Cha Cha; Just in Time; Drop That Name; The Party's Over; The Midas Touch; I'm Goin' Back.

SYNOPSIS:

Ella Peterson, a switchboard operator for an answering service, finds that she has become involved in the lives of her subscribers and fallen in love with playwright Jeffrey Moss.

24

SOUNDTRACK: Capitol SW-1435

* * * * * * * * * *

BERT RIGBY, YOU'RE A FOOL
Warner Bros., 1989

Producer: George Shapiro
Director: Carl Reiner
Screenplay: Carl Reiner
Choreography: Larry Hyman
Music and Lyrics: see below with song titles
Running time: 94 minutes, color

CAST:

Robert Lindsay (*Bert Rigby*); Robbie Coltrane (*Sid Trample*); Cathryn Bradshaw (*Laurel Pennington*); Jackie Gayle (*I.I. Perlestein*); Bruno Kirby (*Kyle DeForest*); Corbin Bernsen (*Jim Shirley*); Anne Bancroft (*Meredith Perlestein*); Carmen du Sautoy (*Tess Trample*); Liz Smith (*Mrs. Rigby*); Lila Kaye (*Mrs. Pennington*) and Fanny Carby (*Aunt Aggie*).

SONGS:

The Continental - *Con Conrad and Herb Magidson*
That's How I Turned Out to Be Mister Elvis P. - *Earl Brown*
Isn't It Romantic? - *Richard Rodgers and Lorenz Hart*
Singin' in the Rain - *Nacio Herb Brown and Arthur Freed*
Fit as a Fiddle - *Al Goodhart, Arthur Freed and Al Hoffman*
You Are My Lucky Star - *Nacio Herb Brown and Arthur Freed*
Good Morning - *Nacio Herb Brown and Arthur Freed*
You Were Meant For Me - *Nacio Herb Brown and Arthur Freed*
Moses Supposes - *Betty Comden, Adolph Green and Roger Edens*
Make 'Em Laugh - *Nacio Herb Brown and Arthur Freed*
Broadway Rhythm - *Nacio Herb Brown and Arthur Freed*
Broadway Melody - *Nacio Herb Brown and Arthur Freed*
My Little Ukelele - *Jack Cottrell*
I'll See You Again - *Noël Coward*
All Of You - *Cole Porter*
Dream a Little Dream - *Wilbur Schwandt, Fabian Andre and Gus Kahn*
Whitegold Beer Commercial - *Earl Brown*
Puttin' on the Ritz - *Irving Berlin*
They've Opened the Ritz Tonight - *Earl Brown*

SYNOPSIS:

Out-of-work British coal miner Bert Rigby is a big fan of old movies, especially musicals, and joins a touring amateur company to earn enough money to buy the run-down theatre in his home town and turn it into a first-class establishment.

SOUNDTRACK: No soundtrack available

* * * * * * * * *

BEST FOOT FORWARD
Metro-Goldwyn-Mayer, 1943

Producer: Arthur Freed
Director: Edward Buzzell
Screenplay: Irving Brecher and Fred F. Finklehoff; based on the stage musical book
           by John Cecil Holm
Choreography: Charles Walters
Music and Lyrics: Hugh Martin and Ralph Blane
Running time: 95 minutes, color

CAST:

Lucille Ball (*Herself*); William Gaxton (*Jack O'Riley*); Tommy Dix (*Elwood C. "Bud" Hooper*); Virginia Weidler (*Helen Schlessenger*); Nancy Walker (*Nancy*); Gloria De Haven (*Minerva*); June Allyson (*Ethel*); Kenny Bowers (*Dutch*); Jack Jordan (*Hunk*); Chill Wills (*Chester Short*); Sara Haden (*Miss Talbert*); Bobby Stebbins (*Greenie*); Henry O'Neill (*Major Reeber*); Donald MacBride (*Captain Bradd*) and Harry James (*Himself*).

SONGS:

Wish I May; Three Men on a Date; Two O'Clock Jump (instrumental)*; Ev'ry Time; The Flight of the Bumblebee (instrumental)**; The Three B's; My First Prom; Alive and Kicking; You're Lucky; Buckle Down, Winsocki.

  *music by Count Basie, Harry James and Benny Goodman
**music by Nikolai Rimski-Korsakov

SYNOPSIS:

When Winsocki Military Institute cadet Bud Hooper invites movie star Lucille Ball to his senior prom she accepts to further her career. But when she arrives she finds that he wants her to impersonate his real girlfriend, Helen.

SOUNDTRACK: Caliban 6039

* * * * * * * * *

THE BEST LITTLE WHOREHOUSE IN TEXAS
Universal, 1982

Producer: Thomas Miller, Edward Milkis and Robert Boyett
Director: Colin Higgins
Screenplay: Larry L. King, Peter Masterson and Colin Higgins; based on the stage
            musical book by Larry L. King and Peter Masterson
Choreography: Tony Stevens
Music and Lyrics: Carol Hall
Running time: 111 minutes, color

CAST:

Burt Reynolds (*Sheriff Ed Earl Dodd*); Dolly Parton (*Miss Mona Stangley*); Dom
DeLuise (*Melvin P. Thorpe*); Charles Durning (*Governor*); Jim Nabors (*Deputy Fred*);
Robert Mandan (*Senator Charles Wingwood*); Lois Nettleton (*Dulcie Mae*); Theresa
Merritt (*Jewel*) and Noah Beery (*Edsel*).

SONGS:

Twenty Fans; A Lil' Ole Bitty Pissant Country Place; Sneakin' Around*; Watchdog
Report/Texas Has a Whorehouse In It; The Aggie Song; The Sidestep; Hard Candy
Christmas; I Will Always Love You*.

music and lyrics by Dolly Parton

SYNOPSIS:

The title of the film refers to the infamous "Chicken Ranch" in Texas where the
activities of Miss Mona and her girls becomes the obsession of television consumer
advocate Melvin P. Thorpe and his determination to close them down.

SOUNDTRACK: MCA 1499

* * * * * * * * *

THE BEST THINGS IN LIFE ARE FREE
20th Century Fox, 1956

Producer: Henry Ephron
Director: Michael Curtiz
Screenplay: William Bowers and Phoebe Ephron; based on a story by John O'Hara
Choreography: Rod Alexander
Music and Lyrics: B.G. DeSylva, Lew Brown and Ray Henderson
Running time: 104 minutes, color

CAST:

Gordon MacRae (*Buddy DeSylva*); Dan Dailey (*Ray Henderson*); Ernest Borgnine
(*Lew Brown*); Sheree North (*Kitty*); Tommy Noonan (*Carl*); Murvyn Vye (*Manny*);
Phyllis Avery (*Maggie Henderson*); Larry Keating (*Sheehan*); Tony Galento (*Fingers*);
Norman Brooks (*Al Jolson*); Jacques d'Amboise (*Dancer*); Roxanne Arlen (*Perky
Nichols*); Byron Palmer (*Hollywood Star*); Linda Brace (*Jeannie Henderson*); Patty
Lou Hudson (*Susie Henderson*); Eugene Borden (*Louis*); Julie Van Zandt (*Miss Van
Seckland*).

SONGS:

Lucky Day; The Black Bottom; The Birth of the Blues; This is the Missus; Without
Love; Lucky in Love; Good News; The Best Things in Life Are Free; Don't Hold
Everything; Button Up Your Overcoat; Strike Me Pink (instrumental); Sunny Side
Up; If I Had a Talking Picture Of You; It All Depends On You; Sonny Boy; One
More Time; You Try Somebody Else; Here Am I Broken-Hearted; Just a Memory;
Together.

SYNOPSIS:

The biography of songwriters B.G. DeSylva, Lew Brown and Ray Henderson
chronicles their relationship over the years as they write some of their biggest hits.

SOUNDTRACK: No soundtrack available

* * * * * * * * *

BILLIE
United Artists, 1965

Producer: Don Weis
Director: Don Weis
Screenplay: Ronald Alexander, based on his play *Time Out For Ginger*
Choreography: David Winters
Music and Lyrics: Bernice Ross, Lor Crane and Jack Gold
Running time: 87 minutes, color

CAST:

Patty Duke (*Billie Carol*); Jim Backus (*Howard Carol*); Warren Berlinger (*Mike Benson*); Jane Greer (*Agnes Carol*); Susan Seaforth (*Jean Carol Matthews*); Charles Lane (*Coach Jones*); Dick Sargent (*Matt Bullitt*); Billy DeWolfe (*Mayor Davis*); Ted Bessell (*Bob Matthews*) and Richard Deacon (*Principal Wilson*).

SONGS:

Billie*; The Beat (instrumental); Lonely Little In-Between; Funny Little Butterflies; A Girl is a Girl is a Girl.

music and lyrics by Dominic Frontiere and Diane Lampert

SYNOPSIS:

The star of the boys' track team is a fifteen-year-old girl named Billie Carol which creates numerous headaches for her father Howard as he attempts to run for town mayor.

SOUNDTRACK: United Artists UAL-5131

* * * * * * * * * *

BILLY ROSE'S DIAMOND HORSESHOE
20th Century Fox, 1945

Producer: William Perlberg
Director: George Seaton
Screenplay: George Seaton; based on a play by John Kenyon Nicholson
Choreography: Hermes Pan
Music and Lyrics: Harry Warren and Mack Gordon
Running time: 104 minutes, color

CAST:

Betty Grable (*Bonnie Collins*); Dick Haymes (*Joe Davis, Jr.*); Phil Silvers (*Blinky Walker*); William Gaxton (*Joe Davis, Sr.*); Beatrice Kay (*Claire Williams*); Margaret Dumont (*Mrs. Standish*); George Melford (*Pop*); Hal K. Dawson (*Sam Carter*); Roy Benson (*Harper*) and Carmen Cavallaro (*Himself*).

SONGS:

Welcome to the Diamond Horseshoe; In Acapulco; I Wish I Knew; The More I See

You; Carrie Marry Harry*; Play Me An Old-Fashioned Melody; A Nickel's Worth of Jive.

music and lyrics by Albert Von Tilzer and Junie McCree

SYNOPSIS:

The headliner at Billy Rose's Diamond Horseshoe club, Joe Davis, Sr., tries to break up the romance of his medical student son Joey and singer Bonnie Collins when Joey decides to quit school to follow his girlfriend onto the stage.

SOUNDTRACK: Caliban 6028

* * * * * * * * * *

BILLY ROSE'S JUMBO
Metro-Goldwyn-Mayer, 1962

Producer: Joe Pasternak and Martin Melcher
Director: Charles Walters
Screenplay: Sidney Sheldon; based on the stage musical book by Ben Hecht and
         Charles MacArthur
Choreography: Busby Berkeley
Music and Lyrics: Richard Rodgers and Lorenz Hart
Running time: 125 minutes, color

CAST:

Doris Day (*Kitty Wonder*); Jimmy Durante (*Anthony "Pop" Wonder*); Stephen Boyd* (*Sam Rawlins*); Martha Raye (*Lulu*); Dean Jagger (*John Noble*); Joseph Waring (*Harry*); Lynn Wood (*Tina*); Charles Watts (*Ellis*); James Chandler (*Parsons*) and Robert Burton (*Madison*).

vocals dubbed by James Joyce

SONGS:

Over and Over Again; Circus On Parade; Why Can't I?; This Can't Be Love; The Most Beautiful Girl in the World; My Romance; Little Girl Blue; Sawdust, Spangles and Dreams*.

music and lyrics by Richard Rodgers, Lorenz Hart and Roger Edens

Pop Wonder's circus operates on a shoestring and the big Noble circus literally steals Pop's show and his prize attraction--Jumbo the elephant--with the help of Sam Rawlins, John Noble's son.

SOUNDTRACK: Columbia OS-2260

* * * * * * * * *

BITTER SWEET
Metro-Goldwyn-Mayer, 1940

Producer: Victor Saville
Director: W.S. Van Dyke II
Screenplay: Lesser Samuels; based on the stage musical book by Noël Coward
Choreography: Ernst Matray
Music and Lyrics: Noël Coward and Gus Kahn
Running time: 94 minutes, color

CAST:

Jeanette MacDonald (*Sarah Millick/Sari Linden*); Nelson Eddy (*Carl Linden*); George Sanders (*Baron von Tranisch*); Ian Hunter (*Lord Shayne*); Felix Bressart (*Max*); Edward Ashley (*Harry Daventry*); Lynne Carver (*Dolly*); Diana Lewis (*Jane*); Curt Bois (*Ernst*); Fay Holden (*Mrs. Millick*); Sig Rumann (*Herr Schlick*); Janet Beecher (*Lady Daventry*); Charles Judels (*Herr Wyler*); Veda Ann Borg (*Manon*); Herman Bing (*Market Keeper*) and Greta Meyer (*Mama Luden*).

SONGS:

I'll See You Again; If You Could Only Come With Me; What is Love?; Tokay; Love in Any Language Means Oui, Oui; Sweet Little Café; Kiss Me; Ladies of the Town; Zigeuner; Evermore and a Day.

SYNOPSIS:

When Sarah Millick elopes with her singing teacher Carl Linden to his home in Vienna they find that trying to get Carl's operetta *Zigeuner* published difficult and the unwanted attentions of military officer Baron von Tranisch only add to their difficulties.

SOUNDTRACK: Bright Tight Discs BIS-1377

31

BLUE HAWAII
Paramount, 1961

Producer: Hal B. Wallis
Director: Norman Taurog
Screenplay: Hal Kanter; based on a story by Allan Weiss
Choreography: Charles O'Curran
Music and Lyrics: see below with song titles
Running time: 101 minutes, color

CAST:

Elvis Presley (*Chad Gates*); Joan Blackman (*Maile Duval*); Angela Lansbury (*Sara Lee Gates*); Nancy Walters (*Abigail Prentice*); Roland Winters (*Fred Gates*); John Archer (*Jack Kelman*) and Howard McNear (*Mr. Chapman*).

SONGS:

Blue Hawaii - *Leo Robin and Ralph Rainger*
Almost Always True - *Fred Wise and Ben Weisman*
Aloha Oe - *Queen Liliuokalani; arranged by Elvis Presley*
No More - *Don Robertson and Hal Blair*
Can't Help Falling in Love With You - *Hugo Peretti, Luigi Creatore and George David Weiss*
Rock-a-Hula Baby - *Fred Wise, Ben Weisman and Dolores Fuller*
Moonlight Swim - *Dee Fuller and Ben Weisman*
Ku-u-i-po (Hawaiian Sweetheart) - *Hugo Peretti, Luigi Creatore and George David Weiss*
Ito Eats - *Sid Tepper and Roy C. Bennett*
Slicin' Sand - *Sid Tepper and Roy C. Bennett*
Hawaiian Sunset - *Sid Tepper and Roy C. Bennett*
Beach Boy Blues - *Sid Tepper and Roy C. Bennett*
Island of Love - *Sid Tepper and Roy C. Bennett*
Hawaiian Wedding Song - *Charles E. King, Al Hoffman and Dick Manning*

SYNOPSIS:

Recently out of the Army, Chad Gates returns home to Hawaii where his parents hope he will go into his father's business, but he opts to work as a tour guide for his girlfriend Maile's company.

SOUNDTRACK: RCA LSP-2426

* * * * * * * * *

BLUE SKIES
Paramount, 1946

Producer: Sol C. Siegel
Director: Stuart Heisler
Screenplay: Arthur Sheekman, adapted by Allan Scott; based on an idea by Irving
        Berlin
Choreography: Hermes Pan
Music and Lyrics: Irving Berlin
Running time: 104 minutes, color

CAST:

Bing Crosby (*Johnny Adams*); Fred Astaire (*Jed Potter*); Joan Caulfield (*Mary O'Dare*); Billy DeWolfe (*Tony*); Olga San Juan (*Nita Nova*); Mikhail Rasumny (*François*); Frank Faylen (*Mack*); Victoria Horne (*Martha*) and Karolyn Grimes (*Mary Elizabeth Adams*).

SONGS:

A Pretty Girl is Like a Melody; I Got My Captain Working For Me Now; You'd Be Surprised; All By Myself; Puttin' On the Ritz; A Couple of Song and Dance Men; You Keep Coming Back Like a Song; Blue Skies; Everybody Step; How Deep is the Ocean?; Running Around in Circles; Heat Wave; Any Bonds Today?; This is the Army, Mr. Jones; White Christmas.

SYNOPSIS:

When dancer Jed Potter and night club owner/singer Johnny Adams fall in love with the same girl, Mary O'Dare, their personal and professional relationships span twenty years.

SOUNDTRACK: Sountrak 104

* * * * * * * * *

BORN TO DANCE
Metro-Goldwyn-Mayer, 1936

Producer: Jack Cummings
Director: Roy Del Ruth

33

Screenplay: Jack McGowan and Sid Silvers; based on a story by Jack McGowan and
             B.G. DeSylva
Choreography: Dave Gould
Music and Lyrics: Cole Porter
Running time: 108 minutes, B/W

CAST:

Eleanor Powell (*Nora Paige*); James Stewart (*Ted Barker*); Virginia Bruce (*Lucy James*); Una Merkel (*Jenny Saks*); Sid Silvers (*"Gunny" Saks*); Frances Langford (*"Peppy" Turner*); Raymond Walburn (*Captain Dingby*); Alan Dinehart (*James McKay*); Buddy Ebsen (*"Mush" Tracy*); Juanita Quigley (*Sally Saks*) and Reginald Gardiner (*Policeman in Park*).

SONGS:

Rolling Home; Rap-Tap on Wood; Hey, Babe, Hey; Love Me, Love My Pekinese; Easy to Love; I've Got You Under My Skin; Swingin' the Jinx Away.

SYNOPSIS:

Nora Paige is an aspiring dancer but soon finds her chance for a career in jeopardy when she and the show's star, Lucy James, fall for the same guy.

SOUNDTRACK: Classic International Filmusicals 3001

* * * * * * * * * *

THE BOY FRIEND
Metro-Goldwyn-Mayer, 1971

Producer: Ken Russell
Director: Ken Russell
Screenplay: Ken Russell; based on the stage musical book by Sandy Wilson
Choreography: Christopher Gable, Gillian Gregory and Terry Gilbert
Music and Lyrics: Sandy Wilson
Running time: 135 minutes, color

CAST:

Twiggy (*Polly*); Christopher Gable (*Tony*); Max Adrian (*Max*); Bryan Pringle (*Percy*); Murray Melvin (*Alphonse*); Moyra Fraser (*Mme. Dubonnet*); Georgina Hale (*Fay*); Sally Bryant (*Nancy*); Antonia Ellis (*Maisie*); Caryl Little (*Dulcie*); Graham Armitage (*Michael*); Tommy Tune (*Tommy*) and Glenda Jackson (*Rita Monroe*).

SONGS:

Perfect Young Ladies; The Boy Friends; Won't You Charleston With Me?; Fancy Forgetting; I Could Be Happy With You; You Are My Lucky Star*; Sur Le Plage; A Room in Bloomsbury; It's Nicer in Nice; The You-Don't-Want-to-Play-With-Me Blues; Safety in Numbers; All I Do is Dream Of You*; It's Never Too Late to Fall in Love; Poor Little Pierette; The Riviera.

*music and lyrics by Nacio Herb Brown and Arthur Freed

SYNOPSIS:

A spoof of British musical comedy has the star-struck assistant stage manager, Polly, suddenly thrust into the spotlight when the star, Rita Monroe, breaks her foot.

SOUNDTRACK: MGM 1SE-32

* * * * * * * * * *

BRIGADOON
Metro-Goldwyn-Mayer, 1954

Producer: Arthur Freed
Director: Vincente Minelli
Screenplay: Alan Jay Lerner, based on his stage musical book
Choreography: Gene Kelly
Music and Lyrics: Frederick Loewe and Alan Jay Lerner
Running time: 108 minutes, color

CAST:

Gene Kelly (*Tommy Albright*); Van Johnson (*Jeff Douglas*); Cyd Charisse* (*Fiona Campbell*); Elaine Stewart (*Jane Ashton*); Barry Jones (*Mr. Lundie*); Hugh Laing (*Harry Beaton*); Albert Sharpe (*Andrew Campbell*); Virginia Bosler (*Jean Campbell*); Tudor Owen (*Archie Beaton*) and Jimmy Thompson** (*Charlie Chisholm Dalrymple*).

 *vocals dubbed by Carole Richards
**vocals dubbed by John Gustafson

SONGS:

Once in the Highlands; Brigadoon; Down on MacConnachy Square; Waitin' For My Dearie; I'll Go Home With Bonnie Jean; The Heather on the Hill; Almost Like Being in Love; The Wedding Dance (instrumental); The Chase.

SYNOPSIS:

Two vacationing hunters from New York, Tommy Albright and Jeff Douglas, stumble across a village in the Scottish Highlands while lost only to discover that it only appears once every hundred years.

SOUNDTRACK: MGM 2-SES-50ST (with *Lovely to Look At*)

* * * * * * * * * *

BROADWAY MELODY OF 1936
Metro-Goldwyn-Mayer, 1935

Producer: John W. Considine, Jr.
Director: Roy Del Ruth
Screenplay: Jack McGowan and Sid Silvers; based on a story by Moss Hart
Choreography: Dave Gould and Albertina Rasch
Music and Lyrics: Nacio Herb Brown and Arthur Freed
Running time: 103 minutes, B/W

CAST:

Jack Benny (*Bert Keeler*); Robert Taylor (*Bob Gordon*); Una Merkel (*Kitty Corbett*); Eleanor Powell (*Irene Foster/Mlle. Arlette*); June Knight (*Lillian Brent*); Buddy Ebsen (*Ted Burke*); Vilma Ebsen (*Sally Burke*); Nick Long, Jr. (*Basil*); Robert Wildhack (*"The Snorer"*); Sid Silvers (*Snoop*); Paul Harvey (*Managing Editor*) and Frances Langford (*Herself*).

SONGS:

Broadway Melody; You Are My Lucky Star; I've Gotta Feelin' You're Foolin'; Sing Before Breakfast; On a Sunday Afternoon; Broadway Rhythm.

SYNOPSIS:

After radio announcer Bert Keeler's editor tells him that he has to find a "hot" story he decides to invent a French musical star, Mlle. La Belle Arlette, to entice producer Bob Gordon into an exclusive story.

SOUNDTRACK: No soundtrack available

* * * * * * * * * *

BROADWAY MELODY OF 1938
Metro-Goldwyn-Mayer, 1937

Producer: Jack Cummings
Director: Roy Del Ruth
Screenplay: Jack McGowan; based on a story by Jack McGowan and Sid Silvers
Choreography: Dave Gould
Music and Lyrics: Nacio Herb Brown and Arthur Freed
Running time: 115 minutes, B/W

CAST:

Robert Taylor (*Steve Raleigh*); Eleanor Powell (*Sally Lee*); George Murphy (*Sonny Ledford*); Binnie Barnes (*Caroline Whipple*); Buddy Ebsen (*Peter Trot*); Sophie Tucker (*Alice Clayton*); Judy Garland (*Betty Clayton*); Charles Igor Gorin (*Nicki Papaloopas*); Raymond Walburn (*Herman Whipple*); Robert Benchley (*Duffy*); Willie Howard (*Waiter*); Charley Grapewin (*James K. Blakeley*); Robert Wildhack (*"The Sneezer"*); Billy Gilbert (*George Papaloopas*); Barnett Parker (*Jerry Jason*) and Helen Troy (*Emma Snipe*).

SONGS:

Follow in My Footsteps; Everybody Sing; I'm Feeling Like a Million; Sun Showers; Dear Mr. Gable (You Made Me Love You); Yours and Mine; Your Broadway and My Broadway; Broadway Rhythm.

SYNOPSIS:

Steve Raleigh needs financial backing for his new show and when the horse that the show's star, Sally Lee, raised wins at Saratoga he thinks he has found it.

SOUNDTRACK: No soundtrack available

* * * * * * * * *

BROADWAY MELODY OF 1940
Metro-Goldwyn-Mayer, 1940

Producer: Jack Cummings
Director: Norman Taurog
Screenplay: Leon Gordon and George Oppenheimer; based on a story by Jack
            McGowan and Dore Schary
Choreography: Bobby Connolly

Music and Lyrics: Cole Porter
Running time: 102 minutes, B/W

CAST:

Fred Astaire (*Johnny Brett*); Eleanor Powell (*Clare Bennett*); George Murphy (*King Shaw*); Frank Morgan (*Bob Casey*); Ian Hunter (*Bert C. Matthews*); Florence Rice (*Amy Blake*); Lynne Carver (*Emmy Lou Lee*) and Ann Morriss (*Pearl*).

SONGS:

Please Don't Monkey With Broadway; Rocked in the Cradle of the Deep; Between You and Me; I've Got My Eyes On You; I Concentrate On You; Begin the Beguine.

SYNOPSIS:

Dance partners Johnny Brett and King Shaw both fall for Clare Bennett but, when their chance for a part in a big new show comes along, King's irresponsibility threatens to ruin everything.

SOUNDTRACK: Classic International Filmusicals 3002

* * * * * * * * *

BROADWAY RHYTHM
Metro-Goldwyn-Mayer, 1944

Producer: Jack Cummings
Director: Roy Del Ruth
Screenplay: Dorothy Kingsley and Harry Clork; based on the stage musical *Very Warm For May* by Jerome Kern and Oscar Hammerstein II
Choreography: Charles Walters, Jack Donohue, Robert Alton and Don Loper
Music and Lyrics: see below with song titles
Running time: 114 minutes, color

CAST:

George Murphy (*Jonnie Demming*); Ginny Simms (*Helen Hoyt*); Charles Winninger (*Sam Demming*); Gloria De Haven (*Patsy Demming*); Nancy Walker (*Trixie Simpson*); Ben Blue (*Felix Gross*); Lena Horne (*Fernway de le Fer*); Eddie "Rochester" Anderson (*Eddie*); Kenny Bowers (*Ray Kent*); Hazel Scott (*Herself*) and Tommy Dorsey (*Himself*).

38

SONGS:

Irresistible You - *Don Raye and Gene DePaul*
What Do You Think I Am? - *Hugh Martin and Ralph Blane*
Amor - *Gabriel Ruiz and Ricardo Lopez Mendez*
Brazilian Boogie - *Hugh Martin and Ralph Blane*
Solid Potato Salad - *Don Raye and Gene DePaul*
That Lucky Fellow - *Jerome Kern*
In Other Words, Seventeen - *Jerome Kern*
All in Fun - *Jerome Kern*
All the Things You Are - *Jerome Kern*
Somebody Loves Me - *George Gershwin and Ira Gershwin*
Pretty Baby - *Tony Jackson, Gus Kahn and Egbert Van Alstyne*
Milkman, Keep Those Bottles Quiet! - *Don Raye and Gene DePaul*
Oh, You Beautiful Doll! - *Fred Fisher and Alfred Bryan*
Who's Who - *Don Raye and Gene DePaul*

SYNOPSIS:

Producer Jonnie Demming wants Hollywood star Helen Hoyt for his new show but she opts instead for one with Jonnie's father Sam and his sister Patsy.

SOUNDTRACK: No soundtrack available

* * * * * * * * * *

THE BUDDY HOLLY STORY
Columbia, 1978

Producer: Fred Bauer
Director: Steve Rash
Screenplay: Robert Gittler; based on a story by Steve Rash and Fred Bauer
Choreography: Maggie Rush
Music and Lyrics: see below with song titles
Running time: 113 minutes, color

CAST:

Gary Busey (*Buddy Holly*); Don Stroud (*Jesse*); Charles Martin Smith (*Ray Bob*); Bill Jordan (*Riley Randolph*); Maria Richwine (*Maria Elena Holly*); Conrad Janis (*Ross Turner*); Albert Popwell (*Eddie Foster*); Amy Johnston (*Jenny Lou*); Jim Beach (*Mr. Wilson*); John F. Goff (*T.J.*); Fred Travalena (*Madman Mancuso*) and Dick O'Neil (*Sol Zuckerman*).

39

SONGS:

That'll Be the Day - *Norman Petty, Buddy Holly and Joe Allison*
Oh Boy! - *Sunny West, Bill Tilghman and Norman Petty*
Peggy Sue - *Jerry Allison, Norman Petty and Buddy Holly*
Maybe Baby - *Norman Petty and Charles Hardin*
Not Fade Away - *Charles Hardin and Norman Petty*
Everyday - *Norman Petty and Charles Hardin*
I'm Gonna Love You Too - *Joe Mauldin, Niki Sullivan and Norman Petty*
It's So Easy - *Buddy Holly and Norman Petty*
Listen to Me - *Charles Hardin and Norman Petty*
Rave On - *Sunny West, Bill Tilghman and Norman Petty*
Rock Around with Ollie Vee - *S. Curtis*
True Love Ways - *Norman Petty and Buddy Holly*
Well All Right - *Norman Petty, Buddy Holly, Jerry Allison and Joe Maudlin*
Whole Lotta Shakin' Goin' On - *Sunny David and David Williams*

SYNOPSIS:

The biography of 1950's rock and roll singer Buddy Holly whose life, and career, were tragically cut short by his death in a plane crash in 1959 (along with the Big Bopper and Richie Valens.)

SOUNDTRACK: Epic/American International SE-35412

* * * * * * * * *

BYE BYE BIRDIE
Columbia, 1963

Producer: Fred Kohlmar
Director: George Sidney
Screenplay: Irving Brecher; based on the stage musical book by Michael Stewart
Choreography: Onna White
Music and Lyrics: Charles Strouse and Lee Adams
Running time: 112 minutes, color

CAST:

Dick Van Dyke (*Albert Petersen*); Ann-Margret (*Kim McAfee*); Janet Leigh (*Rosie DeLeon*); Paul Lynde (*Harry McAfee*); Bobby Rydell (*Hugo Peabody*); Jesse Pearson (*Conrad Birdie*); Maureen Stapleton (*Mama Peterson*); Mary LaRoche (*Mrs. McAfee*) and Ed Sullivan (*Himself*).

40

<u>SONGS</u>:

Bye Bye Birdie; How Lovely to Be a Woman; The Telephone Hour; Put On a Happy Face; Honestly Sincere; Hymn For a Sunday Evening; One Last Kiss; One Boy; Kids; A Lot of Livin' to Do; Rosie.

<u>SYNOPSIS</u>:

When rock star Conrad Birdie is drafted into the Army, his manager arranges for a farewell performance on the Ed Sullivan show with a kiss going to one lucky All-American teenage girl.

SOUNDTRACK: RCA LSO-1081

* * * * * * * * *

BY THE LIGHT OF THE SILVERY MOON
Warner Bros., 1953

Producer: William Jacobs
Director: David Butler
Screenplay: Robert O'Brien and Irving Elinson; based on the *Penrod* stories by
              Booth Tarkington
Choreography: Donald Saddler
Music and Lyrics: see below with song titles
Running time: 103 minutes, color

<u>CAST</u>:

Doris Day (*Marjorie Winfield*); Gordon MacRae (*William Sherman*); Leon Ames (*George Winfield*); Rosemary De Camp (*Mrs. Winfield*); Billy Gray (*Wesley Winfield*); Mary Wickes (*Stella*); Russell Arms (*Chester Finley*); Maria Palmer (*Miss La Rue*); Howard Wendell (*Mr. Harris*); Geraldine Wall (*Mrs. Harris*); Walter Flannery (*Pee Wee*); John Maxwell (*Ike Hickey*); Minerva Urecal (*Mrs. Simmon*) and Carl Forman (*Dangerous Dora*).

<u>SONGS</u>:

If You Were the Only Girl in the World - *Nat D. Ayer and Clifford Grey*
Your Eyes Have Told Me So - *Gus Kahn, Walter Blaufuss and Egbert Van Alstyne*
Ain't We Got Fun? - *Richard Whiting and Gus Kahn*
Be My Little Baby Bumblebee - *Henry I. Marshall and Stanley Murphy*
Just One Girl - *Lyn Udall and Karl Kennett*
I'll Forget You - *Ernest R. Ball and Annalu Burns*

King Chanticleer - *A. Seymour Brown and Nat D. Ayer*
My Home Town is a One Horse Town, But It's Big Enough For Me - *Abner Silver and Alex Gerber*
By the Light of the Silvery Moon - *Gus Edwards and Edward Madden*

<u>SYNOPSIS</u>:

Bill Sherman comes home from WWI and his girlfriend Marjorie Winfield expects him to marry her right away and can't understand why he insists on waiting awhile in order to save some money. Sequel to *On Moonlight Bay*.

SOUNDTRACK: No soundtrack available

C

CABARET
Allied Artists, 1972

Producer: Cy Feuer
Director: Bob Fosse
Screenplay: Jay Allen; based on the stage musical book by Joe Masteroff
Choreography: Bob Fosse
Music and Lyrics: John Kander and Fred Ebb
Running time: 119 minutes, color

CAST:

Liza Minelli (*Sally Bowles*); Michael York (*Brian Roberts*); Helmut Griem (*Maximillian Von Heune*); Joel Grey (*Master of Ceremonies*); Fritz Wepper (*Fritz Wendel*); Marisa Berenson (*Natalia Landauer*); Elisabeth Neumann-Viertel (*Fraülein Schneider*); Sigrid Von Richthofen (*Fraülein Mayr*); Helen Vita (*Fraülein Kost*); Gerd Vespermann (*Bobby*); Ralf Woller (*Herr Ludwig*); Georg Hartmann (*Willi*) and Ricky Renee (*Elke*).

SONGS:

Wilkommen; Mein Herr; Maybe This Time; The Money Song; Two Ladies; Tomorrow Belongs To Me; If You Could See Her (The Gorilla Song); Cabaret.

SYNOPSIS:

Berlin, 1931: Free-spirited Sally Bowles is an American who performs at the sleazy Kit Kat Klub and dreams of becoming a film star--a dream she can't abandon even when she falls in love with British philosophy student Brian Roberts.

SOUNDTRACK: ABC Records 752

* * * * * * * * *

CABIN IN THE SKY
Metro-Goldwyn-Mayer, 1943

Producer: Arthur Freed
Director: Vincente Minelli
Screenplay: Joseph Schrank; based on the stage musical book by Lynn Root
Choreography: Busby Berkeley

Music and Lyrics: see below with song titles
Running time: 99 minutes, B/W

CAST:

Ethel Waters (*Petunia Jackson*); Eddie "Rochester" Anderson (*Little Joe Jackson*); Lena Horne (*Georgia Brown*); Louis Armstrong (*The Trumpeter*); Rex Ingram (*Lucius/Lucifer Jr.*); Kenneth Spencer (*Rev. Green/The General*); John W. Sublett (*Domino Johnson*); Oscar Polk (*The Deacon/Sgt. Fleetfoot*); Mantan Moreland (*First Idea Man*); Willie Best (*Second Idea Man*); Fletcher Rivers (*Third Idea Man*); Leon James (*Fourth Idea Man*); Bill Bailey (*Bill*); Ford L. Washington (*Messenger Boy*); Butterfly McQueen (*Lily*); Ruby Dandridge (*Mrs. Kelso*); Nicodemus (*Dude*); Ernest Whitman (*Jim Henry*) and Duke Ellington (*Himself*).

SONGS:

Li'l Black Sheep - *Harold Arlen and E.Y. Harburg*
Happiness is Just a Thing Called Joe - *Harold Arlen and E.Y. Harburg*
Cabin in the Sky - *Vernon Duke and John LaTouche*
Taking a Chance on Love - *Vernon Duke, John LaTouche and Ted Fetter*
Life's Full O' Consequence - *Harold Arlen and E.Y. Harburg*
S-H-I-N-E - *Ford Dabney, Cecil Mack & Lew Brown*
Going Up (instrumental) - *Duke Ellington*
Honey in the Honeycomb - *Vernon Duke and John LaTouche*

SYNOPSIS:

Little Joe Jackson is mortally wounded in a barroom brawl but is given a second chance to mend his ways by God after his wife Petunia prays strongly to save his soul.

SOUNDTRACK: Hollywood Soundstage 5003

* * * * * * * * *

CALAMITY JANE
Warner Bros., 1953

Producer: William Jacobs
Director: David Butler
Screenplay: James O'Hanlon
Choreography: Jack Donohue
Music and lyrics: Sammy Fain and Paul Francis Webster
Running time: 101 minutes, color

CAST:

Doris Day (*Calamity Jane*); Howard Keel (*Will Bill Hickock*); Allyn McLerie (*Katie Brown*); Philip Carey (*Lt. Daniel Gilmartin*); Dick Wesson (*Francis Fryer*); Paul Harvey (*Henry "Milly" Miller*); Gale Robbins (*Adelaid Adams*) and Chubby Johnson (*Rattlesnake*).

SONGS:

The Deadwood Stage; I've Got a Hive Full of Honey; I Could Do Without You; It's Harry I'm Planning to Marry; I Just Blew in From the Windy City; Better Keep It Under Your Hat; A Woman's Touch; Higher Than a Hawk; The Black Hills of Dakota; Secret Love.

SYNOPSIS:

Calamity Jane, the tomboy of the Black Hills, soon decides to change her ways when she falls in love with Wild Bill Hickock.

SOUNDTRACK: No soundtrack available

* * * * * * * * *

CALL ME MADAM
20th Century Fox, 1953

Producer: Sol C. Siegel
Director: Walter Lang
Screenplay: Arthur Sheekman; based on the stage musical book by Howard Lindsay and Russel Crouse
Choreography: Robert Alton
Music and Lyrics: Irving Berlin
Running time: 117 minutes, color

CAST:

Ethel Merman (*Mrs. Sally Adams*); Donald O'Connor (*Kenneth*); Vera-Ellen* (*Princess Maria*); George Sanders (*Cosmo Constantine*); Billy De Wolfe (*Pemberton Maxwell*); Helmut Dantine (*Prince Hugo*); Walter Slezak (*Tantinnin*); Steven Geray (*Sebastian*); Ludwig Stossel (*Grand Duke*); Lilia Skala (*Grand Duchess*); Charles Dingwell (*Senator Brockway*); Emory Parnell (*Senator Gallagher*) and Percy Helton (*Senator Wilkins*).

*vocals dubbed by Carole Richards

The Hostess With the Mostes' on the Ball; You're Just in Love; Best Thing For Me Would Be You; It's a Lovely Day Today; The International Rag; Something to Dance About; Can You Use Any Money Today?; Marrying For Love.

SYNOPSIS:

Sally Adams is appointed the ambassador to Lichtenburg and is soon involved with Cosmo Constantine as well as helping out her assistant Kenneth in his romance with the Princess Maria.

SOUNDTRACK: Stet DS-25001 (with *Guys and Dolls* and *I'll Cry Tomorrow*)

* * * * * * * * *

CALL ME MISTER
20th Century Fox, 1951

Producer: Fred Kohlmar
Director: Lloyd Bacon
Screenplay: Albert E. Lewin and Burt Styler; based on the musical revue by Harold J. Rome and Arnold M. Auerbach
Choreography: Busby Berkeley
Music and Lyrics: see below with song titles
Running time: 96 minutes, color

CAST:

Betty Grable (*Kay Hudson*); Dan Dailey (*Shep Dooley*); Danny Thomas (*Stanley*); Dale Robertson (*Capt. Johnny Comstock*); Benay Venuta (*Billie Barton*); Richard Boone (*Mess Sergeant*); Jeffrey Hunter (*"The Kid"*); Frank Fontaine (*Sergeant*); Harry Von Zell (*General Steele*); Dave Willock (*Jones*); Robert Ellis (*Ackerman*) and Jerry Paris (*Brown*).

SONGS:

Japanese Girl Like American Boy - *Mack Gordon and Sammy Fain*
I'm Gonna Love That Guy (Like He's Never Been Loved Before) - *Frances Ash*
Lament to the Pots and Pans - *Jerry Seeler and Earl K. Brent*
Going Home Train - *Harold J. Rome*
I Just Can't Do Enough For You, Baby - *Mack Gordon and Sammy Fain*
Call Me Mister - *Harold J. Rome*

Military Life - *Harold J. Rome and Jerry Seeler*
Love is Back in Business - *Mack Gordon and Sammy Fain*

SYNOPSIS:

Trying to win his estranged wife Kay back at the end of WWII, Sgt. Shep Dooley goes AWOL from his unit in Japan to join a revue that she is organizing.

SOUNDTRACK: Titania 510

* * * * * * * * *

CAMELOT
Warner Bros., 1967

Producer: Jack L. Warner
Director: Joshua Logan
Screenplay: Alan Jay Lerner, based on his stage musical book
Choreography: Buddy Schwab
Music and Lyrics: Frederick Loewe and Alan Jay Lerner
Running time: 177 minutes, color

CAST:

Richard Harris (*King Arthur*); Vanessa Redgrave (*Guenevere*); Franco Nero (*Lancelot*); David Hemmings (*Mordred*); Lionel Jeffries (*King Pellinore*); Laurence Naismith (*Merlin*); Gary Marshall (*Sir Lionel*); Anthony Rogers (*Sir Dinadan*); Peter Bromilow (*Sir Sagramore*) and Estelle Winwood (*Lady Clarinda*).

SONGS:

I Wonder What the King is Doing Tonight?; The Simple Joys of Maidenhood; Camelot; C'est Moi; The Lusty Month of May; How to Handle a Woman; Take Me to the Fair; If Ever I Would Leave You; What Do the Simple Folk Do?; Follow Me; I Loved You Once in Silence; Guenevere.

SYNOPSIS:

The tale of the mythical kingdom of Camelot, origin of the Knights of King Arthur's Round Table and the tragic love triangle that brought about it's ruin.

SOUNDTRACK: Warner Bros. BS-1712

* * * * * * * * *

CAN-CAN

20th Century Fox, 1960

Producer: Jack Cummings
Director: Walter Lang
Screenplay: Dorothy Kingsley and Charles Lederer; based on the stage musical book
        by Abe Burrows
Choreography: Hermes Pan
Music and Lyrics: Cole Porter
Running time: 131 minutes, color

CAST:

Frank Sinatra (*François Durnais*); Shirley MacLaine (*Simone Pistache*); Maurice Chevalier (*Paul Barriere*); Louis Jourdan (*Philippe Forrestier*); Juliet Prowse (*Claudine*); Marcel Dalio (*André*); Nestor Paiva (*Bailiff*) and Leon Belasco (*Arturo*).

SONGS:

Montmart'; Maidens Typical of France; C'est Magnifique; Live and Let Live; You Do Something to Me; Let's Do It; It's All Right With Me; Come Along With Me; Just One of Those Things; Can-Can (instrumental); I Love Paris.

SYNOPSIS:

Paris, 1896: The scandalous can-can dance is illegal but Montmartre café owner/dancer Simone Pistache keeps on performing it assured that her lawyer boyfriend François can keep her out of jail. However, complications arise when an investigating judge falls in love with her.

SOUNDTRACK: Capitol SM-1301

* * * * * * * * * *

CARMEN JONES

20th Century Fox, 1954

Producer: Otto Preminger
Director: Otto Preminger
Screenplay: Harry Kleiner; based on the stage musical book by Oscar Hammerstein
        II
Choreography: Herbert Ross

Music and Lyrics: Georges Bizet and Oscar Hammerstein II
Running time: 105 minutes, color

CAST:

Dorothy Dandridge* (*Carmen*); Harry Belafonte** (*Joe*); Olga James (*Cindy Lou*); Pearl Bailey (*Frankie*); Diahann Carroll*** (*Myrt*); Roy Glenn (*Rum*); Nick Stewart○ (*Dink*); Joe Adams○○ (*Husky*); Brock Peters (*Sgt. Brown*); Sandy Lewis (*T-Bone*) and Mauri Lynn (*Sally*).

   vocals dubbed by Marilyn Horne
  **vocals dubbed by LeVern Hutcherson*
 ***vocals dubbed by Bernice Peterson*
   ○*vocals dubbed by Joe Crawford*
  ○○*vocals dubbed by Marvin Hayes*

SONGS:

Stand Up and Fight; Beat Out That Rhythm on a Drum; Dere's a Café on De Corner; Lift 'Em Up and Put 'Em Down; Dat's Love (I Got For You, But You're Taboo); You Talk Just Like My Maw; Dis Flower; De Cards Don't Lie; My Joe; Dat's Our Man; Whizzin' Away Along De Track.

SYNOPSIS:

An Americanized version of Bizet's *Carmen* has Carmen a saloon singer who falls for soldier Joe but when her flirting with a boxer becomes serious, tragedy results.

SOUNDTRACK: RCA LM-1881

* * * * * * * * *

CARNIVAL IN COSTA RICA
20th Century Fox, 1947

Producer: William A. Bacher
Director: Gregory Ratoff
Screenplay: John Larkin, Samuel Hoffenstein and Elizabeth Reinhardt
Choreography: Leonide Massine
Music and Lyrics: Ernesto Lecuona and Harry Ruby
Running time: 96 minutes, color

CAST:

Dick Haymes (*Jeff Stephens*); Vera-Ellen (*Luisa Molina*); Cesar Romero (*Pepe Castro*); Celeste Holm (*Celeste*); Anne Revere (*Elsa Molina*); J. Carrol Naish (*Ricardo "Rico" Molina*); Pedro de Cordoba (*Mr. Castro*); Barbara Whiting (*Maria Molina*); Nestor Paiva (*Father Rafael*); Fritz Feld (*Desk Clerk*); Tommy Ivo (*Juanito Molina*) and Mimi Aguglia (*Mrs. Castro*).

SONGS:

I'll Know It's Love; Gui-Pi-Pia*; Maracas; Mi Vida; Costa Rica*; Rhumba Bomba; Another Night Like This.

music and lyrics by Albert Stillman, Sunny Skylar and Harry Ruby

SYNOPSIS:

In San José, Costa Rica, the parents of Luisa Molina and Pepe Castro arrange a marriage for them unaware that they had each found other mates.

SOUNDTRACK: No soundtrack available

* * * * * * * * * *

CAROUSEL
20th Century Fox, 1956

Producer: Henry Ephron
Director: Henry King
Screenplay: Phoebe Ephron and Henry Ephron; based on the stage musical book by
             Oscar Hammerstein II
Choreography: Rod Alexander and Agnes DeMille
Music and Lyrics: Richard Rodgers and Oscar Hammerstein II
Running time: 128 minutes, color

CAST:

Gordon MacRae (*Billy Bigelow*); Shirley Jones (*Julie Jordan*); Cameron Mitchell (*Jigger Craigin*); Barbara Ruick (*Carrie Pipperidge*); Claramae Turner (*Nettie Fowler*); Richard Rounseville (*Enoch Snow*); Gene Lockhart (*The Starkeeper*); Susan Luckey (*Louise Bigelow*); Audrey Christie (*Mrs. Mullin*) and Jacques d'Amboise (*Louise's Dancing Partner*).

SONGS:

You're a Queer One, Julie Jordan!; When I Marry Mister Snow; If I Loved You; June is Bustin' Out All Over; When the Children Are Asleep; Blow High, Blow Low; Soliloquy; A Real Nice Clambake; Stonecutters Cut It On Stone; What's the Use of Wond'rin'?; The Carousel Waltz (instrumental); You'll Never Walk Alone.

SYNOPSIS:

When shiftless carousel barker Billy Bigelow falls in love with innocent Julie Jordan he tries to mend his ways but with tragic results.

SOUNDTRACK: Capitol SW-694

* * * * * * * * *

CENTENNIAL SUMMER
20th Century Fox, 1946

Producer: Otto Preminger
Director: Otto Preminger
Screenplay: Michael Kanin; based on the novel by Albert E. Idell
Choreography: Dorothy Fox
Music and Lyrics: Jerome Kern, Leo Robin, Oscar Hammerstein II & E.Y. Harburg
Running time: 104 minutes, color

CAST:

Jeanne Crain* (*Julia Rogers*); Cornel Wilde (*Philippe Lascalles*); Linda Darnell (*Edith Rogers*); William Eythe (*Dr. Benjamin Franklin Phelps*); Walter Brennan (*Jesse Rogers*); Constance Bennett (*Zenia Lascalles*); Dorothy Gish (*Harriet Rogers*); Barbara Whiting (*Susanna Rogers*); Larry Stevens (*Richard Lewis, Esq.*); Kathleen Howard (*Deborah*); Buddy Swan (*Dudley Rogers*); Charles Dingle (*Snodgrass*); Eddie Dunn (*Mr. Phelps*) and Lois Austin (*Mrs. Phelps*).

vocals dubbed by Louanne Hogan

SONGS:

Cinderella Sue; Up With the Lark; Centennial; In Love in Vain; All Through the Day; The Right Romance.

51

The centennial celebration of 1876 in Philadelphia is the event which the Rogers family is preparing to attend when Philippe Lascalles arrives from Paris to help with the French exhibit and falls for daughter Julia.

SOUNDTRACK: Classic International Filmusicals 3009 (with *State Fair*/1945)

* * * * * * * * * *

CHARLOTTE'S WEB
Paramount, 1973

Producer: Joseph Barbera and William Hanna
Director: Charles A. Nichols and Iwao Takamoto
Screenplay: Earl Hamner, Jr.; based on the novel by E.B. White
Music and Lyrics: Richard M. Sherman and Robert B. Sherman
Running time: 85 minutes, color

VOCAL TALENTS:

Debbie Reynolds (*Charlotte*); Henry Gibson (*Wilbur*); Paul Lynde (*Templeton*); Agnes Moorehead (*The Goose*); Dave Madden (*Old Sheep*); Pam Ferdin (*Fern*) and Rex Allen (*Narrator*).

SONGS:

There Must Be Something More; I Can Talk; Chin Up; Mother Earth and Father Time; We've Got Lots in Common; A Veritable Smorgasbord; Deep in the Dark; Zuckerman's Famous Pig.

SYNOPSIS:

Animated tale of a little girl named Fern and her pet pig Wilbur, who is destined for the slaughterhouse--but is saved by the ingenuity of his new friend, Charlotte the spider.

SOUNDTRACK: Paramount 1008

* * * * * * * * * *

CHITTY CHITTY BANG BANG
United Artists, 1968

Producer: Albert R. Broccoli
Director: Ken Hughes
Screenplay: Roald Dahl and Ken Hughes; based on the novel by Ian Fleming
Choreography: Marc Breaux and Dee Dee Wood
Music and Lyrics: Richard M. Sherman and Robert B. Sherman
Running time: 142 minutes, color

CAST:

Dick Van Dyke (*Caractacus Potts*); Sally Ann Howes (*Truly Scrumptious*); Lionel Jeffries (*Grandpa*); Gert Frobe (*Baron Bomburst*); Anna Quayle (*Baroness Bomburst*); Benny Hill (*The Toymaker*); Robert Helpmann (*The Childcatcher*); James Robertson Justice (*Lord Scrumptious*); Adrian Hall (*Jeremy*) and Heather Ripley (*Jemima*).

SONGS:

You Two; Toot Sweets; Hushabye Mountain; Me Ol' Bam-boo; Chitty Chitty Bang Bang; Truly Scrumptious; Lovely Lonely Man; Posh!; The Roses of Success; Doll on a Music Box.

SYNOPSIS:

When the two children of a poor eccentric inventor named Caractacus Potts convince their father to buy a broken-down racing car he transforms it into a magical vehicle that can float and fly!

SOUNDTRACK: United Artists 5188

* * * * * * * * *

THE CHOCOLATE SOLDIER
Metro-Goldwyn-Mayer, 1941

Producer: Victor Saville
Director: Roy Del Ruth
Screenplay: Leonard Lee and Keith Winter; based on the play *The Guardsman* by
         Ferenc Molnar
Choreography: Ernst Matray
Music and Lyrics: see below with song titles
Running time: 102 minutes, B/W

CAST:

Nelson Eddy (*Karl Lang*); Risë Stevens (*Maria Lanyi*); Nigel Bruce (*Bernard Fischer*); Florence Bates (*Madame Helene*); Dorothy Gilmore (*Magda*); Nydia Westman (*Liesl*); Max Barwyn (*Anton*) and Charles Judels (*Klementov*).

SONGS:

My Hero - *Oscar Straus and Stanislaus Stange*
Thank the Lord the War is Over - *Oscar Straus and Stanislaus Stange*
Mon coeur sòuvre à ta voix (*Samson et Dalila*) - *Camille Saint-Saëns*
Sympathy - *Oscar Straus and Stanislaus Stange*
Seek the Spy - *Oscar Straus and Stanislaus Stange*
Song of the Flea - *Modest Petrovich Moussorgsky*
Evening Star (*Tannhäuser*) - *Richard Wagner*
While My Lady Sleeps - *Bronislau Kaper and Gus Kahn*
Ti-Ra-La-La - *Oscar Straus, Stanislaus Stange and Gus Kahn*
The Chocolate Soldier - *Oscar Straus and Stanislaus Stange*
Forgive - *Oscar Straus and Stanislaus Stange*

SYNOPSIS:

In Vienna, Karl Lang and his wife Maria Lanyi are performing in *The Chocolate Soldier* when Karl's jealousy of Maria's flirtations reaches such a point that he decides to impersonate a dynamic Russian to woo Maria--unaware that she knows all along who he really is.

SOUNDTRACK: No soundtrack available

* * * * * * * * *

A CHORUS LINE
Columbia, 1985

Producer: Cy Feuer and Ernest Martin
Director: Richard Attenborough
Screenplay: Arnold Schulman; based on the stage musical book by James Kirkwood
            and Nicholas Dante
Choreography: Jeffrey Hornaday
Music and Lyrics: Marvin Hamlisch and Edward Kleban
Running time: 113 minutes, color

CAST:

Michael Douglas (*Zach*); Terrence Mann (*Larry*); Alyson Reed (*Cassie*); Cameron English (*Paul*); Vicki Frederick (*Sheila*); Audrey Landers (*Val*); Gregg Burge (*Richie*); Nicole Fosse (*Kristine*); Yamil Borges (*Morales*); Charles McGowan (*Mike*); Matt West (*Bobby*); Michael Blevins (*Mark*); Michelle Johnston (*Bebe*); Janet Jones (*Judy*); Pam Klinger (*Maggie*); Jan Gan Boyd (*Connie*); Blane Savage (*Don*); Justin Ross (*Greg*); Tony Fields (*Al*) and Sharon Brown (*Pam*).

SONGS:

I Hope I Get It; Who Am I Anyway?; I Can Do That: At the Ballet; Surprise, Surprise; Nothing; Dance: Ten, Looks: Three; Let Me Dance For You; What I Did For Love; One.

SYNOPSIS:

Adapted from the stage musical about a group of young hopeful dancers trying out for the chorus of a new Broadway show under the critical eye of caustic choreographer Zach.

SOUNDTRACK: Casablanca 826306-1

* * * * * * * * *

CINDERELLA
RKO, 1950

Producer: Walt Disney
Director: Wilfred Jackson, Hamilton Luske and Clyde Geronimi
Screenplay: Ken Anderson, Ted Sears, Homer Brightman, Joe Rinaldi, William Peet, Harry Reeves, Winston Hibler and Erdman Penner; based on the story by Charles Perrault
Music and Lyrics: Mack David, Jerry Livingston and Al Hoffman
Running time: 76 minutes, color

VOCAL TALENTS:

Ilene Woods (*Cinderella*); William Phipps (*Prince Charming*); Verna Felton (*Fairy Godmother*); Eleanor Audley (*Stepmother*); James MacDonald (*Jaq/Gus*); Rhoda Williams (*Stepsister*); Lucille Bliss (*Stepsister*) and Luis Van Rooten (*King/Grand Duke*).

SONGS:

A Dream is a Wish Your Heart Makes; Sing, Sweet Nightingale; The Work Song (Cinderelly); Bibbidi Bobbidi Boo; So This is Love.

SYNOPSIS:

Animated fairy tale classic has Cinderella being helped out not only by her Fairy Godmother but by an adorable pair of mice named Jaq and Gus.

SOUNDTRACK: Disneyland 1207

* * * * * * * * *

CLAMBAKE
United Artists, 1967

Producer: Jules Levy, Arthur Gardner and Arnold Laven
Director: Arthur H. Nadel
Screenplay: Arthur Browne, Jr.
Choreography: Alex Romero
Music and Lyrics: see below with song titles
Running time: 100 minutes, color

CAST:

Elvis Presley (*Scott Heyward*); Shelley Fabares (*Dianne Carter*); Bill Bixby (*James Jamison III*); Will Hutchins (*Tom Wilson*); Gary Merrill (*Sam Burton*); James Gregory (*Duster Heyward*); Suzie Kaye (*Sally*); Jack Good (*Mr. Hathaway*) and Hal Peary (*Hal the Doorman*).

SONGS:

Who Needs Money? - *Randy Starr*
A House That Has Everything - *Sid Tepper and Roy C. Bennett*
Confidence - *Sid Tepper and Roy C. Bennett*
Clambake - *Sid Wayne and Ben Weisman*
You Don't Know Me - *Eddy Arnold and Cindy Walker*
Hey, Hey, Hey - *Joy Byers*
The Girl I Never Loved - *Randy Starr*

SYNOPSIS:

Millionaire Duster Heyward's son Scott just wants to be recognized for himself so he swaps identities with water-ski instructor Tom Wilson to work at a Florida resort hotel.

SOUNDTRACK: RCA APL1-2565

* * * * * * * * *

COAL MINER'S DAUGHTER
Universal, 1980

Producer: Bernard Schwartz
Director: Michael Apted
Screenplay: Tom Rickman; based on the book by Loretta Lynn and George Vecsey
Music and Lyrics: see below with song titles
Running time: 124 minutes, color

CAST:

Sissy Spacek (*Loretta Lynn*); Tommy Lee Jones (*Doolittle "Mooney" Lynn*); Beverly D'Angelo (*Patsy Cline*); Levon Helm (*Ted Webb*); Phyllis Boyens (*Clara Webb*); Bob Hannah (*Charlie Dick*); Robert Elkins (*Bobby Day*) and Ernest Tubb (*Himself*).

SONGS:

Blue Moon of Kentucky - *Bill Monroe*
The Great Titanic - *traditional*
There He Goes - *Eddie Miller, Durwood Haddock and W.S. Stevenson*
I'm a Honky Tonk Girl - *Loretta Lynn*
Amazing Grace - *traditional*
Walking After Midnight - *Don Hecht and Alan Block*
Crazy - *Willie Nelson*
I Fall to Pieces - *Hank Cochran and Harlan Howard*
Sweet Dreams - *Don Gibson*
Back in Baby's Arms - *Bob Montgomery*
You Ain't Woman Enough to Take My Man - *Loretta Lynn*
You're Lookin' at Country - *Loretta Lynn*
One's on the Way - *Shel Silverstein*
Coal Miner's Daughter - *Loretta Lynn*

SYNOPSIS:

Biography of country music star Loretta Lynn from her childhood in Butcher Hollow, Kentucky, marriage at thirteen to Doolittle Lynn and her rise in the industry that is plagued by self-doubt and illness.

SOUNDTRACK: MCA 1699

* * * * * * * * * *

COLLEEN
Warner Bros., 1936

Producer: The Vitaphone Corporation
Director: Alfred E. Green
Screenplay: Peter Milne, F. Hugh Herbert and Sid Herzig; based on a story by
         Robert Lord
Choreography: Bobby Connolly and Paul Draper
Music and Lyrics: Harry Warren and Al Dubin
Running time: 89 minutes, B/W

CAST:

Dick Powell (*Donald Ames III*); Ruby Keeler (*Colleen Reilly*); Jack Oakie (*Joe Cork*); Joan Blondell (*Minnie Hawkins*); Hugh Herbert (*Cedric Ames*); Louise Fazenda (*Alicia Ames*); Paul Draper (*Paul Gordon*); Luis Alberni (*Carlo*); Marie Wilson (*Mabel Reynolds*) and J.M. Kerrigan (*Pop Reilly*).

SONGS:

I Don't Have to Dream Again; A Boulevardier From the Bronx; An Evening With You; You've Gotta Know How to Dance.

SYNOPSIS:

After dilettante millionaire Cedric Ames buys Carlo's dress shop for his "ward" Minnie Hawkins his nephew Donald finds himself falling for the shop's manager, Colleen Reilly.

SOUNDTRACK: Caliban 6007 (with *Variety Girl*)

* * * * * * * * * *

CONEY ISLAND
20th Century Fox, 1943

Producer: William Perlberg
Director: Walter Lang
Screenplay: George Seaton
Choreography: Hermes Pan

58

Music and Lyrics: see below with song titles
Running time: 96 minutes, color

CAST:

Betty Grable (*Kate Farley*); George Montgomery (*Eddie Johnson*); Cesar Romero
(*Joe Rocco*); Charles Winninger (*Finnegan*); Phil Silvers (*Frankie*); Matt Briggs
(*William Hammerstein*); Paul Hurst (*Louie*); Frank Orth (*Bartender*); Phyllis Kennedy
(*Dolly*); Andrew Tombes (*Carter*) and Hal K. Dawson (*Cashier*).

SONGS:

Put Your Arms Around Me, Honey - *Albert Von Tilzer and Junie McCree*
Who Threw the Overalls in Mrs. Murphy's Chowder? - *George L. Geifer*
In My Harem - *Irving Berlin*
When Irish Eyes Are Smiling - *Ernest R. Ball, Chauncey Olcott and George Graff*
Cuddle Up a Little Closer, Lovey Mine - *Karl Hoschna and Otto Harbach*
Winter - *Albert Gumble and Alfred Bryan*
Pretty Baby - *Tony Jackson, Egbert Van Alstyne and Gus Kahn*
Get the Money - *Leo Robin and Ralph Rainger*
Miss Lulu From Louisville - *Leo Robin and Ralph Rainger*
Take It From There - *Leo Robin and Ralph Rainger*
Beautiful Coney Island - *Leo Robin and Ralph Rainger*
There's Danger in a Dance - *Leo Robin and Ralph Rainger*

SYNOPSIS:

Kate Farley is the star performer at a Coney Island, New York music hall and long-
standing rivals Eddie Johnson and Joe Rocco are both in love with her.

SOUNDTRACK: Caliban 6001 (with *Moon Over Miami*)

* * * * * * * * *

A CONNECTICUT YANKEE IN KING ARTHUR'S COURT
Paramount, 1949

Producer: Robert Fellows
Director: Tay Garnett
Screenplay: Edmund Beloin; based on the novel by Mark Twain
Music and Lyrics: James Van Heusen and Johnny Burke
Running time: 108 minutes, color

Bing Crosby (*Hank Martin*); Rhonda Fleming (*Alisande La Carteloise/Sandy*); Sir Cedric Hardwicke (*King Arthur/Lord Pendragon*); William Bendix (*Sir Sagramore*); Murvyn Vye (*Merlin*); Virginia Field (*Morgan Le Fay*); Joseph Vitale (*Sir Logris*); Henry Wilcoxen (*Sir Lancelot*); Richard Webb (*Sir Galahad*); Alan Napier (*High Executioner*); Julia Faye (*Lady Penelope*); Mary Field (*Peasant Woman*) and Ann Carter (*Peasant Girl*).

SONGS:

If You Stub Your Toe on the Moon; When is Sometime?; Once and For Always; Busy Doing Nothing.

SYNOPSIS:

Blacksmith Hank Martin gets knocked unconscious in a storm in his hometown of Bridgeport, Connecticut and wakes up in Camelot and has to help King Arthur thwart the evil doings of Merlin and his followers.

SOUNDTRACK: No soundtrack available

* * * * * * * * *

THE COURT JESTER
Paramount, 1956

Producer: Norman Panama and Melvin Frank
Director: Norman Panama and Melvin Frank
Screenplay: Norman Panama and Melvin Frank
Choreography: James Starbuck
Music and Lyrics: Sammy Cahn and Sylvia Fine
Running time: 101 minutes, color

CAST:

Danny Kaye (*Hubert Hawkins*); Glynis Johns (*Maid Jean*); Basil Rathbone (*Sir Ravenhurst*); Angela Lansbury (*Princess Gwendolyn*); Cecil Parker (*King Roderick*); Mildred Natwick (*Griselda*); Robert Middleton (*Sir Griswold*); Edward Ashley (*The Black Fox*); Herbert Rudley (*Captain of the Guard*) and John Carradine (*Giacomo*).

SONGS:

Life Could Not Better Be; Outfox the Fox; I'll Take You Dreaming; My Heart

Knows a Lovely Song; The Maladjusted Jester*.

*music and lyrics by Sylvia Fine

SYNOPSIS:

Hubert Hawkins is an unemployed circus actor in medievel times who desparately wants to be a hero. He gets his chance when he impersonates first an assassin, then a forest bandit in order to save the life of the baby king.

SOUNDTRACK: Decca 8212

* * * * * * * * *

COVER GIRL
Columbia, 1944

Producer: Arthur Schwartz
Director: Charles Vidor
Screenplay: Virginia Van Upp, adaptation by Marion Parsonnet and Paul Gangelin;
          based on a story by Erwin Gelsey
Choreography: Gene Kelly, Stanley Donen and Seymour Felix
Music and Lyrics: Jerome Kern and Ira Gershwin
Running time: 107 minutes, color

CAST:

Rita Hayworth* (*Rusty Parker/Maribelle Hicks*); Gene Kelly (*Danny McGuire*); Lee Bowman (*Noel Wheaton*); Phil Silvers (*Genius*); Jinx Falkenburg (*Jinx*); Leslie Brooks (*Maurine Martin*); Eve Arden (*Cornelia "Stonewall" Jackson*) and Otto Kruger (*Jess Barker*).

*vocals dubbed by Nan Wynn

SONGS:

Long Ago and Far Away; Cover Girl; Sure Thing; The Show Must Go On; Who's Complaining?; Put Me to the Test; Make Way For Tomorrow*.

*music and lyrics by Jerome Kern, Ira Gershwin and E.Y. Harburg

SYNOPSIS:

Rusty Parker works at Danny McGuire's night club in Brooklyn where Jess Barker sees her and offers her a chance to be on the cover of his magazine. She is soon offered a part in a big Broadway show and it leads to a fight with Danny.

SOUNDTRACK: Curtain Calls 100/24 (with *You Were Never Lovelier*)

* * * * * * * * *

CURLY TOP
20th Century Fox, 1935

Producer: Winfield Sheehan
Director: Irving Cummings
Screenplay: Patterson McNutt and Arthur Beckhard
Choreography: Jack Donohue
Music and Lyrics: Ray Henderson, Ted Koehler, Irving Caesar and Edward Heyman
Running time: 75 minutes, B/W (has been colorized)

CAST:

Shirley Temple (*Elizabeth "Curly" Blair*); John Boles (*Edward Morgan*); Rochelle Hudson (*Mary Blair*); Jane Darwell (*Mrs. Denham*); Rafaela Ottiano (*Mrs. Higgins*); Esther Dale (*Aunt Genevieve Graham*); Etienne Girardot (*Mr. Wyckoff*); Maurice Murphy (*Jimmie Rogers*) and Arthur Treacher (*Reynolds*).

SONGS:

Animal Crackers in My Soup; It's All New To Me; The Simple Things in Life; When I Grow Up; Curly Top.

SYNOPSIS:

Lawyer Edward Morgan would like to adopt orphan Curly Blair but when her sister Mary says she promised their parents they'd never be parted he decides that he must become an anonymous benefactor--"Mr. Hiram Jones".

SOUNDTRACK: No soundtrack available

D

DADDY LONG LEGS
20th Century Fox, 1955

Producer: Samuel G. Engel
Director: Jean Negulesco
Screenplay: Phoebe Ephron and Henry Ephron; based on the play by Jean Webster
Choreography: Fred Astaire, David Robel and Roland Petit
Music and Lyrics: Johnny Mercer
Running time: 126 minutes, color

CAST:

Fred Astaire (*Jervis Pendleton*); Leslie Caron (*Julie André*); Terry Moore (*Linda*); Thelma Ritter (*Miss Pritchard*); Fred Clark (*Griggs*); Charlotte Austin (*Sally*); Larry Keating (*Alexander Williamson*); Kathryn Givney (*Gertrude*); Kelly Brown (*Jimmy McBride*) and Ann Codee (*Mme. Sevanne*).

SONGS:

That'll Get It When It's Almost Gone; C-A-T Spells Cat; Welcome Egghead; Sluefoot; Dream; Something's Gotta Give.

SYNOPSIS:

Wealthy bachelor Jervis Pendleton decides to finance French orphan Julie André's college education but due to his desire for anonymity she addresses her reports and letters to him as "Dear Daddy Long Legs".

SOUNDTRACK: Caliban 6000 (with *The Story of Vernon and Irene Castle*)

* * * * * * * * * *

DAMES
Warner Bros., 1934

Producer: Darryl F. Zanuck
Director: Ray Enright
Screenplay: Delmer Daves; based on a story by Robert Lord and Delmer Daves
Choreography: Busby Berkeley
Music and Lyrics: Harry Warren and Al Dubin
Running time: 90 minutes, B/W

CAST:

Joan Blondell (*Mabel Anderson*); Dick Powell (*Jimmy Higgens*); Ruby Keeler (*Barbara Hemingway*); ZaSu Pitts (*Mathilda Hemingway*); Guy Kibbee (*Horace P. Hemingway*); Hugh Herbert (*Ezra Ounce*); Arthur Vinton (*Bulger*); Phil Regan (*Johnny Harris*) and Sammy Fain (*Buttercup Baumer*).

SONGS:

When You Were a Smile On Your Mother's Lips and a Twinkle in Your Daddy's Eye*; I Only Have Eyes For You; Try To See It My Way**; The Girl at the Ironing Board; Dames.

  *music and lyrics by Irving Kahal and Sammy Fain
 **music and lyrics by Mort Dixon and Allie Wrubel

SYNOPSIS:

In order to receive his $10,000,000 inheritance Horace Hemingway must prove to his eccentric brother-in-law Ezra that he is a moral person--not an easy task with actress Mabel Anderson blackmailing him for $20,000 to back a new show for Jimmy Higgens, the "black sheep" of the family.

SOUNDTRACK: Caliban 6014 (with *St. Louis Blues*)

* * * * * * * * *

DAMN YANKEES
Warner Bros., 1958

Producer: George Abbott and Stanley Donen
Director: George Abbott and Stanley Donen
Screenplay: George Abbott, based on his stage musical book
Choreography: Bob Fosse
Music and Lyrics: Richard Adler and Jerry Ross
Running time: 110 minutes, color

CAST:

Tab Hunter (*Joe Hardy*); Ray Walston (*Mr. Applegate*); Gwen Verdon (*Lola*); Russ Brown (*Van Buren*); Shannon Bolin (*Meg Boyd*); Nathaniel Frey (*Smokey*); Jimmie Komack (*Rocky*); Rae Allen (*Gloria*); Robert Shafer (*Joe Boyd*) and Jean Stapleton (*Sister*).

64

SONGS:

Six Months Out of Every Year; Goodbye, Old Girl; Heart; Shoeless Joe From Hannibal Mo; A Little Brains, a Little Talent; Whatever Lola Wants; Who's Got the Pain?; The Game; There's Something About an Empty Chair; Those Were the Good Old Days; Two Lost Souls.

SYNOPSIS:

In order to help out his beloved Washington Senators baseball team, middle-aged Joe Boyd agrees to sell his soul to the Devil in exchange for the body of a young man, Joe Hardy, with an amazing talent for the game.

SOUNDTRACK: RCA LOC-1047

* * * * * * * * * *

A DAMSEL IN DISTRESS
RKO, 1937

Producer: Pandro S. Berman
Director: George Stevens
Screenplay: P.G. Wodehouse, Ernest Pagano and S.K. Lauren; based on a story by
                P.G. Wodehouse
Choreography: Hermes Pan
Music and Lyrics: George Gershwin and Ira Gershwin
Running time: 100 minutes, B/W

CAST:

Fred Astaire (*Jerry Halliday*); George Burns (*George*); Gracie Allen (*Gracie*); Joan Fontaine (*Lady Alyce Marshmorton*); Reginald Gardiner* (*Keggs*); Ray Noble (*Reggie*); Montagu Love (*Lord John Marshmorton*); Constance Collier (*Lady Caroline Marshmorton*) and Harry Watson (*Albert*).

vocals dubbed by Mario Berini

SONGS:

I Can't Be Bothered Now; The Jolly Tar and Milkmaid; Put Me to the Test (instrumental); Stiff Upper Lip; Things Are Looking Up; A Foggy Day in London Town; Nice Work If You Can Get It.

SYNOPSIS:

After her aunt has her grounded for her behavior, Lady Alyce Marshmorton slips away to London where she meets stage star Jerry Halliday and everyone assumes that the accidental meeting is really a secret rendezvous.

SOUNDTRACK: Curtain Calls 100/19 (with *The Sky's the Limit*)

* * * * * * * * *

DANCING IN THE DARK
20th Century Fox, 1949

Producer: George Jessel
Director: Irving Reis
Screenplay: Mary C. McCall, Jr. and Jay Dratler, adaptation by Marion Turk; based on the stage musical book *The Bandwagon* by George S. Kaufman
Choreography: Seymour Felix
Music and Lyrics: Howard Dietz and Arthur Schwartz
Running time: 92 minutes, color

CAST:

William Powell (*Emery Slade*); Mark Stevens (*Bill Davis*); Betsy Drake (*Julie Clarke*); Adolphe Menjou (*Melvin Grossman*); Randy Stuart (*Rosalie Brooks*); Lloyd Corrigan (*Barker*); Hope Emerson (*Mrs. Schlaghammer*); Walter Catlett (*Joe Brooks*); Don Beddoe (*Barney Basset*) and Jean Hersholt (*Himself*).

SONGS:

Something to Remember You By; New Sun in the Sky; Dancing in the Dark; I Love Louisa.

SYNOPSIS:

Washed-up movie star Emery Slade is promised a job by the head of 20th Century Fox studios if he can persuade Broadway star Rosalie Brooks to sign a movie contract--but he double-crosses his boss and signs unknown Julie Clarke instead.

SOUNDTRACK: No soundtrack available

* * * * * * * * *

66

DANGEROUS WHEN WET
Metro-Goldwyn-Mayer, 1953

Producer: George Wells
Director: Charles Walters
Screenplay: Dorothy Kingsley
Choreography: Charles Walters and Billy Daniel
Music and Lyrics: Arthur Schwartz and Johnny Mercer
Running time: 96 minutes, color

CAST:

Esther Williams (*Katy Higgins*); Fernando Lamas (*André Lanet*); Jack Carson (*Windy Webbe*); Charlotte Greenwood (*Ma Higgins*); Denise Darcel (*Gigi Mignon*); William Demarest (*Pa Higgins*); Donna Corcoran (*"Junior" Higgins*); Barbara Whiting (*Suzi Higgins*); Bunny Waters (*Greta*); Henri Letondal (*Joubert*); Paul Bryar (*Pierre*); Richard Alexander (*Egyptian swimmer*); Tudor Owen (*Old Salt*); Jack Raine (*Stuart Frye*) and Ann Codee (*Mrs. Lanet*).

SONGS:

I Got Out of Bed on the Right Side; I Like Men; Fifi; In My Wildest Dreams; Ain't Nature Grand?

SYNOPSIS:

"Liquapep" promoter Windy Webbe convinces his boss to sponser the Higgins family of Arkansas in a contest to swim the English Channel but is upset when eldest daughter Katy falls for French champagne heir André Lanet.

SOUNDTRACK: No soundtrack available

* * * * * * * * * *

DARLING LILI
Paramount, 1970

Producer: Blake Edwards
Director: Blake Edwards
Screenplay: Blake Edwards and William Peter Blatty
Choreography: Hermes Pan
Music and Lyrics: Henry Mancini and Johnny Mercer
Running time: 136 minutes, color

CAST:

Julie Andrews (*Lili Smith*); Rock Hudson (*Major William Larrabee*); Jeremy Kemp (*Colonel Kurt von Ruger*); Lance Percival (*Twombley-Crouch*); Jacques Marin (*Captain Duvalle*); André Maranne (*Lt. Liggett*); Michael Whitney (*Lt. George Youngblood Carson*); Gloria Paul (*Crêpe Suzette*); Doreen Keogh (*Emma*); Bernard Kay (*Bedford*); Carl Duering (*General Kessler*); Ingo Mogendorf (*The Red Baron*) and Vernon Dobtcheff (*Kraus*).

SONGS:

Whistling Away the Dark; It's a Long Way to Tipperary*; The Girl in No Man's Land; Smile Away Each Raining Day; I'll Give You Three Guesses; La Marseillaise**; Your Good Will Ambassador.

  *music and lyrics by Harry H. Williams and Jack Judge
  **music and lyrics by Roget de Lisle

SYNOPSIS:

WWI German spy Lili Smith finds her newest mission compromised when she finds herself falling in love with her "assignment"--Major William Larrabee.

SOUNDTRACK: RCA LSPX-1000

* * * * * * * * *

A DATE WITH JUDY
Metro-Goldwyn-Mayer, 1948

Producer: Joe Pasternak
Director: Richard Thorpe
Screenplay: Dorothy Cooper and Dorothy Kingsley; based on characters created by
          Aleen Leslie
Choreography: Stanley Donen
Music and Lyrics: see below with song titles
Running time: 113 minutes, color

CAST:

Wallace Beery (*Melvin Colner Foster*); Jane Powell (*Judy Foster*); Elizabeth Taylor (*Carol Pringle*); Carmen Miranda (*Rosita Conchellas*); Xavier Cugat (*Himself*); Robert Stack (*Stephen I. Andrews*); Selena Royle (*Mrs. Dora Foster*); Scotty Beckett (*Ogden "Oogie" Pringle*); Leon Ames (*Lucien T. Pringle*); George Cleveland

(*Gramps*); Lloyd Corrigan (*Sam "Pop" Scully*); Clinton Sundberg (*Jameson*); Jerry Hunter (*Randolph*) and Jean McLaren (*Mitzi Hoffman*).

SONGS:

It's a Most Unusual Day - *Harold Adamson and Jimmy McHugh*
Through the Years - *Vincent Youmans and Edward Heyman*
Love is Where You Find It - *Nacio Herb Brown and Earl Brent*
I'm Strictly On the Corny Side - *Stella Unger and Alec Templeton*
Judaline - *Don Raye and Gene DePaul*
Home, Sweet, Home - *Sir Henry Rowley Bishop and John Howard Payne*
Cuanto la Gusta - *Ray Gilbert and Gabriel Ruiz*

SYNOPSIS:

Melvin Foster decides to secretly hire Rosita Conchellas to teach him how to rhumba for his wife for their anniversary party, but his daughter Judy mistakenly assumes he is having an affair with her.

SOUNDTRACK: No soundtrack available

* * * * * * * * *

THE DAUGHTER OF ROSIE O'GRADY
Warner Bros., 1950

Producer: William Jacobs
Director: David Butler
Screenplay: Jack Rose, Melville Shavelson and Peter Milne; based on a story by
             Jack Rose and Melville Shavelson
Choreography: LeRoy Prinz
Music and Lyrics: see below with song titles
Running time: 104 minutes, color

CAST:

June Haver (*Patricia O'Grady*); Gordon MacRae (*Tony Pastor*); James Barton (*Dennis O'Grady*); Debbie Reynolds (*Maureen O'Grady*); S.Z. Sakall (*Miklos Teretzky*); Gene Nelson (*Doug Martin*); Sean McClory (*James Moore*); Marsha Jones (*Katie O'Grady*); Jane Darwell (*Mrs. Murphy*) and Irene Seidner (*Mama Teretzky*).

SONGS:

The Daughter of Rosie O'Grady - *Walter Donaldson and Monty C. Bricem*

Rose of Tralee - *Charles Glover and C. Mordaunt Spencer*
A Farm On Old Broadway - *Jack Scholl and M.K. Jerome*
My Own True Love and I - *Jack Scholl and M.K. Jerome*
What Am I Going to Tell Them at the Yacht Club? - *Jack Scholl and M.K. Jerome*
Winter Serenade - *Jack Scholl and M.K. Jerome*
As We Are Today - *Ernest Lecuona and Charles Tobias*
The Picture That's Turned (Toward) the Wall - *Charles Graham*

SYNOPSIS:

Patricia O'Grady takes a job in Tony Pastor's new show much to the chagrin of her father Dennis who doesn't want her on the stage like her late mother.

SOUNDTRACK: No soundtrack available

* * * * * * * * *

DELIGHTFULLY DANGEROUS
United Artists, 1945

Producer: Charles R. Rogers
Director: Arthur Lubin
Screenplay: Walter DeLeon and Arthur Phillips; based on a story by Irving Phillips, Edward Verdier and Frank Tashlin
Choreography: Ernst Matray
Music and Lyrics: Morton Gould and Edward Heyman
Running time: 93 minutes, B/W

CAST:

Jane Powell (*Sherry Williams*); Ralph Bellamy (*Arthur Hale*); Constance Moore (*Josephine Williams*); Morton Gould (*Himself*); Arthur Treacher (*Jeffers*); Louise Beavers (*Hannah*); Ruth Tobey (*Molly Bradley*) and André Charlot (*Professor Bremond*).

SONGS:

In a Shower of Stars; Once Upon a Song; I'm Only Teasin'; Through Your Eyes . . . To Your Heart; Mr. Strauss Goes to Town*.

**music and lyrics by Johann Strauss and Edward Heyman*

70

After discovering that her sister Jo is really a burlesque stripper instead of a musical comedy star teenager Sherry Williams decides to find a way to get them both into Arthur Hale's new show.

SOUNDTRACK: Curtain Calls 100/4

* * * * * * * * * *

THE DESERT SONG
Warner Bros., 1944

Producer: Robert Buckner
Director: Robert Florey
Screenplay: Robert Buckner; based on the stage musical book by Otto Harbach, Oscar Hammerstein II and Frank Mandel
Choreography: LeRoy Prinz
Music and Lyrics: Sigmund Romberg, Otto Harbach, Oscar Hammerstein II and Frank Mandel
Running time: 96 minutes, color

CAST:

Dennis Morgan (*Paul Hudson/"El Khobar"*); Irene Manning (*Margot*); Bruce Cabot (*Fontaine*); Lynne Overman (*Johnny Walsh*); Gene Lockhart (*Fanfan*); Faye Emerson (*Hajy*); Victor Francen (*Caid Yousseff*); Curt Bois (*François*); Jack LaRue (*Lt. Bertin*); Marcel Dalio (*Tarbouch*); Nestor Paiva (*Benoit*); Fritz Leiber (*Ben Sidi*) and Gerald Mohr (*Hassan*).

SONGS:

The Riff Song; Gay Parisienne*; One Alone; The Desert Song; The French Military March; Long Live the Night.

music and lyrics by Jack Scholl and Serge Walter

SYNOPSIS:

Paul Hudson goes to Morocco after the Spanish Civil War and soon becomes the infamous "El Khobar"--helping the Arab nomads fight against an evil sheik.

SOUNDTRACK: No soundtrack available

71

* * * * * * * * *

THE DESERT SONG
Warner Bros., 1953

Producer: Rudi Fehr
Director: Bruce Humberstone
Screenplay: Roland Kibbee; based on the stage musical book by Otto Harbach,
      Oscar Hammerstein II and Frank Mandel
Choreography: LeRoy Prinz
Music and Lyrics: Sigmund Romberg, Otto Harbach, Oscar Hammerstein II and
      Frank Mandel
Running time: 110 minutes, color

CAST:

Kathryn Grayson (*Margot Birabeau*); Gordon MacRae (*Paul Bonnard/"El Khobar"*);
Steve Cochran (*Captain Claude Fontaine*); Raymond Massey (*Sheik Yousseff*); Dick
Wesson (*Benjamin Kidd*); Allyn McLerie (*Azuri*); Ray Collins (*General Birabeau*);
Paul Picerni (*Hassan*); Frank DeKova (*Mindar*); William Conrad (*Lachmed*); Trevor
Bardette (*Neri*) and Mark Dana (*Lt. Duvalle*).

SONGS:

The Riff Song; Romance; Gay Parisienne*; One Flower Grows Alone in Your
Garden; One Alone; The Desert Song; Long Live the Night.

music and lyrics by Jack Scholl and Serge Walter

SYNOPSIS:

Shy anthropology professor Paul Bonnard masquerades as the Arab renegade "El
Khobar" in order to help the desert nomads of North Africa in their fight against the
evil Sheik Yousseff.

SOUNDTRACK: Titania 505 (with *My Wild Irish Rose*)

* * * * * * * * *

DIMPLES
20th Century Fox, 1936

Producer: Darryl F. Zanuck
Director: William A. Seiter

Screenplay: Arthur Sheekman and Nat Perrin
Choreography: Bill Robinson
Music and lyrics: Jimmy McHugh and Ted Koehler
Running time: 78 minutes, B/W

CAST:

Shirley Temple (*Sylvia Dolores "Dimples" Appleby*); Frank Morgan (*Professor Eustace Appleby*); Helen Westley (*Mrs. Caroline Drew*); Robert Kent (*Allen Drew*); Astrid Allwyn (*Cleo Marsh*); Delma Byron (*Betty Loring*); Berton Churchill (*Colonel Loring*); Paul Stanton (*Mr. St. Clair*); Stepin Fetchit (*Cicero*); Julius Tannen (*Hawkins*); John Carradine (*Richards*); Billy McClain (*Rufus*); Jack Clifford (*"Uncle Tom"*); Betty Jean Hainey (*"Topsy"*) and Arthur Aylsworth (*Pawnbroker*).

SONGS:

Hey, What Did the Bluejay Say?; He Was a Dandy; Picture Me Without You; Get on Board; Swing Low, Sweet Chariot*; Dixie-Anna.

traditional Black American spiritual

SYNOPSIS:

In 1850 New York City Prof. Appleby is a pickpocket who uses his little granddaughter Dimples to distract the crowds. But when wealthy widow Caroline Drew offers Appleby $5,000 to let the little girl come live with her he wonders if she wouldn't be better off with her.

SOUNDTRACK: No soundtrack available

* * * * * * * * *

DIXIE
Paramount, 1943

Producer: B.G. DeSylva
Director: A. Edward Sutherland
Screenplay: Karl Tunberg and Darrell Ware, adaptation by Claude Binyon; based on
　　　　　a story by William Rankin
Choreography: Seymour Felix
Music and Lyrics: Johnny Burke and James Van Heusen
Running time: 89 minutes, color

CAST:

Bing Crosby (*Daniel Decatur Emmett*); Dorothy Lamour (*Millie Cook*); Marjorie Reynolds (*Jean Mason Emmett*); Billy DeWolfe (*Mr. Bones*); Lynne Overman (*Mr. Whitlock*); Raymond Walburn (*Mr. Cook*); Eddie Foy, Jr. (*Mr. Pelham*); Grant Mitchell (*Mr. Mason*) and Clara Blandick (*Mrs. Mason*).

SONGS:

Sunday, Monday and Always; She's From Missouri; Miss Jemima Walks By; If You Please; Kinda Peculiar Brown; A Horse That Knows His Way Back Home; Dixie*.

music and lyrics by Daniel Decatur Emmett

SYNOPSIS:

Fictional biography of composer Daniel Decatur Emmett who leaves his Kentucky home, travels to New Orleans and eventually comes to write "Dixie" but then has difficulty getting anyone to sing it.

SOUNDTRACK: Decca 4257

* * * * * * * * *

DOCTOR DOLITTLE
20th Century Fox, 1967

Producer: Arthur P. Jacobs
Director: Richard Fleischer
Screenplay: Leslie Bricusse; based on the books by Hugh Lofting
Choreography: Herbert Ross
Music and Lyrics: Leslie Bricusse
Running time: 145 minutes, color

CAST:

Rex Harrison (*Dr. John Dolittle*); Samantha Eggar (*Emma Fairfax*); Anthony Newley (*Matthew Mugg*); Richard Attenborough (*Albert Blossom*); William Dix (*Tommy Stubbins*); Peter Bull (*General Bellowes*); Portia Nelson (*Sarah Dolittle*); Norma Varden (*Lady Petherington*); Muriel Landers (*Mrs. Blossom*) and Geoffrey Holder (*Willie Shakespeare III*).

SONGS:

My Friend, the Doctor; The Vegetarian; Talk to the Animals; At the Crossroads; I've Never Seen Anything Like It; Beautiful Things; When I Look in Your Eyes; Like Animals; After Today; Fabulous Places; Where Are the Words?; I Think I Like You; Doctor Dolittle; Something in Your Smile.

SYNOPSIS:

In the English village of Puddleby-on-the-Marsh Dr. John Dolittle finds he would rather care for the local animals than the villagers. When his activities ultimately land him in jail his friends break him out and set out on an expedition to the South Seas.

SOUNDTRACK: 20th Century Fox DTCS-5101

* * * * * * * * *

DOLL FACE
20th Century Fox, 1946

Producer: Bryan Foy
Director: Lewis Seiter
Screenplay: Leonard Praskins, adaptation by Harold Buchman; based on a play by
             Louise Hovick
Choreography: Kenny Williams
Music and Lyrics: Harold Adamson and Jimmy McHugh
Running time: 81 minutes, B/W

CAST:

Vivian Blaine (*Doll Face*); Dennis O'Keefe (*Mike Hannegan*); Perry Como (*Nicky Ricci*); Carmen Miranda (*Chita*); Martha Stewart (*Frankie Porter*); Michael Dunne (*Gerard*) and Reed Hadley (*Flo Hartman*).

SONGS:

Somebody's Walkin' in My Dreams; Red Hot and Beautiful; Here Comes Heaven Again; Dig You Later; Chico-Chico (From Puerto Rico).

SYNOPSIS:

Burlesque stripper "Doll Face" gets the once-over from her boyfriend Mike after he decides that a little refinement is needed in order for her to make it in the legitimate theatre.

SOUNDTRACK: No soundtrack available

* * * * * * * * * *

THE DOLLY SISTERS
20th Century Fox, 1945

Producer: George Jessel
Director: Irving Cummings
Screenplay: John Larkin and Marian Spitzer
Choreography: Seymour Felix
Music and Lyrics: see below with song titles
Running time: 114 minutes, color

CAST:

Betty Grable (*Jenny Dolly*); John Payne (*Harry Fox*); June Haver (*Rosie Dolly*); S.Z. Sakall (*Uncle Latsie*); Reginald Gardiner (*Tony, Duke of Breck*); Frank Latimore (*Irving Netcher*); Sig Rumann (*Tsimmis*); Gene Sheldon (*Professor Winnup*); Trudy Marshall (*Leonore*); Collette Lyons (*Flo Daly*) and Robert Middlemass (*Oscar Hammerstein*).

SONGS:

The Vamp - *Byron Gay*
I Can't Begin to Tell You - *Mack Gordon and James V. Monaco*
Give Me the Moonlight - *Lew Brown and Albert Von Tilzer*
We Have Been Around - *Mack Gordon and Charles Henderson*
Carolina in the Morning - *Gus Kahn and Walter Donaldson*
Powder, Lipstick and Rouge - *Mack Gordon and Harry Revel*
I'm Always Chasing Rainbows - *Frederick Chopin, Joseph McCarthy and Harry Carroll*
Darktown Strutters' Ball - *Shelton Brooks*
Arrah Go On I'm Gonna Go Back to Oregon - *Joe Young, Sam M. Lewis and Bert Grant*
Smiles - *J. Will Callahan and Lee M. Roberts*
The Sidewalks of New York - *James Blake and Charles B. Lawlor*

SYNOPSIS:

The life and times of entertainers the Dolly sisters, Jenny and Rosie, from their

76

arrival in America in 1904 from Hungary through the 1920's.

SOUNDTRACK: Classic International Filmusicals 3010

* * * * * * * * * *

DOUBLE TROUBLE
Metro-Goldwyn-Mayer, 1967

Producer: Judd Bernard and Irwin Winkler
Director: Norman Taurog
Screenplay: Jo Heims; based on a story by Marc Brandel
Choreography: Alex Romero
Music and Lyrics: see below with song titles
Running time: 90 minutes, color

CAST:

Elvis Presley (*Guy Lambert*); Annette Day (*Gillian Conway*); John Williams (*Gerald Waverly*); Yvonne Romain (*Claire Dunham*); Michael Murphy (*Morley*); Chips Rafferty (*Arthur Babcock*); Leon Askin (*Inspector de Groote*); Norman Rossington (*Archie Brown*); Monty Landis (*Georgie*) and the Wiere Brothers (*Belgian Detectives*).

SONGS:

Double Trouble - *Doc Pomus and Mort Shuman*
Baby, If You Give Me All Your Love - *Joy Byers*
Could I Fall in Love? - *Randy Starr*
Long-Legged Girl (With the Short Dress On) - *J. Leslie McFarland and Winfield Scott*
City By Night - *Bill Giant, Bernie Baum and Florence Kaye*
Old MacDonald - *arranged by Randy Starr*
I Love Only One Girl - *Sid Tepper and Roy C. Bennett*
There is So Much World to See - *Sid Wayne and Ben Weisman*

SYNOPSIS:

When teenage British heiress Gillian Conway develops a crush on singer Guy Lambert she follows him to Belgium--unaware that someone is trying to kill her.

SOUNDTRACK: RCA APL1-2564

* * * * * * * * * *

DOWN AMONG THE SHELTERING PALMS
20th Century Fox, 1953

Producer: Fred Kohlmar
Director: Edmund Goulding
Screenplay: Claude Binyon, Albert Lewin and Burt Styler; based on a story by
             Edward Hope
Choreography: Seymour Felix
Music and Lyrics: Harold Arlen and Ralph Blane
Running time: 86 minutes, color

CAST:

William Lundigan (*Capt. Bill Willoby*); Jane Greer (*Diana Forrester*); Mitzi Gaynor (*Rozoulia*); David Wayne (*Lt. Carl O. Schmidt*); Gloria De Haven (*Angela Toland*); Gene Lockhart (*Rev. Edgett*); Jack Paar (*Lt. Mike Sloan*); Alvin Greenman (*Corporal Kolta*); Billy Gilbert (*King Jilouili*); Henry Kulky (*First Sergeant*); Lyle Talbot (*Major Curwin*); Ray Montgomery (*Lt. Everly*) and George Nader (*Lt. Homer Briggs*).

SONGS:

Friendly Island; The Opposite Sex; I'm a Ruler of a South Sea Island; Who Will It Be When the Time Comes?; What Make De Difference?

SYNOPSIS:

Capt. Bill Willoby is assigned the occupation of a post-WWII South Seas island but finds the "no fraternization" policy he is to enforce difficult to follow--especially as he is in love with pretty Diana Forrester.

SOUNDTRACK: No soundtrack available

* * * * * * * * *

DOWN ARGENTINE WAY
20th Century Fox, 1940

Producer: Darryl F. Zanuck
Director: Irving Cummings
Screenplay: Darrell Ware and Karl Tunberg; based on a story by Rian James and
             Ralph Spence
Choreography: Nick Castle and Geneva Sawyer

Music and Lyrics: Mack Gordon and Harry Warren
Running time: 89 minutes, color

CAST:

Don Ameche (*Ricardo Quintana*); Betty Grable (*Glenda Crawford*); Carmen Miranda
(*Herself*); Charlotte Greenwood (*Binnie Crawford*); J. Carrol Naish (*Casiano*); Henry
Stephenson (*Don Diego Quintana*); Katharine Aldridge (*Helen Carson*); Leonid
Kinskey (*Tito Acuna*); Chris-Pin Martin (*Esteban*); Robert Conway (*Jimmy Blake*);
Gregory Gaye (*Sebastian*); Bobby Stone (*Panchito*); Charles Judels (*Ambassador*);
Edward Fielding (*Willis Crawford*); The Nicholas Brothers (*Dancers at Nightclub*) and
Edward Conrad (*Anastasio*).

SONGS:

South American Way; Down Argentina Way; Mama eu Quero; Sing to Your Señorita;
Two Dreams Met.

SYNOPSIS:

Argentine horse-breeder Don Diego Quintana holds a long-standing grudge against
the Crawford family and the fact that his son Ricardo is in love with Glenda
Crawford is something he cannot accept.

SOUNDTRACK: Caliban 6003 (with *Tin Pan Alley*)

* * * * * * * * * *

DO YOU LOVE ME?
20th Century Fox, 1946

Producer: George Jessel
Director: Gregory Ratoff
Screenplay: Robert Ellis, Helen Logan and Dorothy Bennett; based on a story by
              Bert Granet
Choreography: Seymour Felix
Music and Lyrics: see below with song titles
Running time: 91 minutes, color

CAST:

Maureen O'Hara (*Katherine Hilliard, Jr.*); Dick Haymes (*Jimmy Hale*); Harry James
(*Barry Clayton*); Reginald Gardiner (*Herbert Benham*); Richard Gaines (*Ralph
Wainwright*); Stanley Prager (*Dilly*); B.S. Pully (*Taxi Driver*); Chick Chandler (*Earl

Williams); Alma Kruger (*Mrs. Joshua Frederick Crackleton*); Almira Sessions (*Miss Wayburn*); Douglas Wood (*Dr. Dunfee*); Harlan Briggs (*Mr. Higbee*); Julia Dean (*Mrs. Allen*) and Harry Hays Morgan (*Professor Allen*).

SONGS:

As If I Didn't Have Enough On My Mind - *Charles Henderson, Lionel Newman and Harry James*
The More I See You - *Harry Warren and Mack Gordon*
I Didn't Mean a Word I Said - *Harold Adamson and Jimmy McHugh*
Moonlight Propaganda - *Herb Magidson and Matt Malneck*
Do You Love Me? - *Harry Ruby*

SYNOPSIS:

Staid music professor Katherine Hilliard goes to New York to make arrangements for a concert and suddenly finds herself involved with both bandleader Barry Clayton and singer Jimmy Hale.

SOUNDTRACK: Caliban 6011 (with *One Hour With You*)

* * * * * * * * * *

DU BARRY WAS A LADY
Metro-Goldwyn-Mayer, 1943

Producer: Arthur Freed
Director: Roy Del Ruth
Screenplay: Irving Brecher, Nancy Hamilton and Wilkie Mahoney; based on the stage musical book by Herbert Fields and B.G. DeSylva
Choreography: Charles Walters
Music and Lyrics: see below with song titles
Running time: 96 minutes, color

CAST:

Red Skelton (*Louis Blore/King Louis XV*); Lucille Ball* (*May Daly/Mme. DuBarry*); Gene Kelly (*Alec Howe/The Black Arrow*); Virginia O'Brien (*Ginny*); "Rags" Ragland (*Charlie/Dauphin*); Zero Mostel (*Rami the Swami/Taliostro*); Douglass Dumbrille (*Willie/Duc de Rigor*); Donald Meek (*Mr. Jones/Duc de Choiseul*); George Givot (*Cheezy/de Roquefort*); Louise Beavers (*Niagara*); Dick Haymes (*Palace Singer*) and Tommy Dorsey (*Himself/Duc de Dorsey*).

**vocals dubbed by Martha Mears*

80

SONGS:

DuBarry Was a Lady - *Burton Lane and Ralph Freed*
Do I Love You, Do I? - *Cole Porter*
No Matter How You Slice It, It's Still Salome - *Roger Edens*
I Love an Esquire Girl - *Ralph Freed, Lew Brown and Roger Edens*
Ladies of the Bath - *Roger Edens*
Katie Went to Haiti - *Cole Porter*
Madame, I Love Your Crêpe Suzettes - *Burton Lane, Lew Brown and Ralph Freed*
On to Combat - *Daniele Amfitheatrof*
Friendship - *Cole Porter*

SYNOPSIS:

Night club checkroon attendant Louis Blore wins the Irish Sweepstakes and convinces singer May Daly to marry him--even if only for his money. But to make sure that his rival Alec doesn't try to stop things, he slips him a "mickey" but inadvertently drinks it himself and dreams that he is King Louis XV and May is Mme. DuBarry!

SOUNDTRACK: Titania 509 (with *Can't Help Singing*)

* * * * * * * * *

THE DUCHESS OF IDAHO
Metro-Goldwyn-Mayer, 1950

Producer: Joe Pasternak
Director: Robert Z. Leonard
Screenplay: Dorothy Cooper and Jerry Davis
Choreography: Jack Donohue
Music and Lyrics: Al Rinker and Floyd Huddleston
Running time: 98 minutes, color

CAST:

Esther Williams (*Christine Riverton Duncan*); Van Johnson (*Dick Layn*); John Lund (*Douglas J. Morrisen, Jr.*); Paula Raymond (*Ellen Hallet*); Clinton Sundberg (*Matson*); Connie Haines (*Peggy Elliott*); Mel Tormé (*Cyril*); Amanda Blake (*Linda Kinston*); Tommy Farrell (*Chuck*); Sig Arno (*Monsieur LeBlanche*); Dick Simmons (*Alec J. Collins*); Lena Horne (*Herself*); Eleanor Powell (*Herself*) and Red Skelton (*Himself*).

SONGS:

Baby, Come Out of the Clouds*; Let's Choo-Choo to Idaho; Of All Things; You Can't Do Wrong Doin' Right.

*music and lyrics by Lee Pearl and Henry Nemo

SYNOPSIS:

To help her friend Ellen win her boss, Doug Morrisen, Chris Duncan arranges to make him realize how much he really cares for her but Chris' new beau Dick Layn doesn't approve of her methods.

SOUNDTRACK: Titania 508 (with *You Can't Have Everything*)

* * * * * * * * * *

DUMBO
RKO, 1941

Producer: Walt Disney
Director: Ben Sharpsteen
Screenplay: Joe Grant and Dick Huemer; based on a story by Helen Aberson and Harold Pearl
Music and Lyrics: Oliver Wallace, Frank Churchill and Ned Washington
Running time: 63 minutes, color

VOCAL TALENTS:

Edward Brophy (*Timothy J. Mouse*); Verna Felton (*Mrs. Jumbo*); Herman Bing (*The Ringmaster*); Sterling Holloway (*The Stork*) and Cliff Edwards (*Jim Crow*).

SONGS:

Look Out For Mr. Stork; Casey Junior; Baby Mine; Pink Elephants on Parade; When I See an Elephant Fly.

SYNOPSIS:

Animated Disney tale about a circus elephant who is diminutive in every way except one--his ears--and with the aid of his friend Timothy J. Mouse and his "magic feather" he learns to fly thus becoming the hit of the circus.

SOUNDTRACK: Disneyland 1204

E

EASTER PARADE
Metro-Goldwyn-Mayer, 1948

Producer: Arthur Freed
Director: Charles Walters
Screenplay: Sidney Sheldon, Frances Goodrich and Albert Hackett; based on a story
        by Frances Goodrich and Albert Hackett
Choreography: Robert Alton
Music and Lyrics: Irving Berlin
Running time: 104 minutes, color

CAST:

Judy Garland (*Hannah Brown*); Fred Astaire (*Don Hewes*); Peter Lawford (*Jonathan Harrow III*); Ann Miller (*Nadine Hale*); Jules Munshin (*François*); Clinton Sundberg (*Mike*) and Jeni LeGon (*Essie*).

SONGS:

Happy Easter; Drum Crazy; It Only Happens When I Dance With You; I Want to Go Back to Michigan; A Fella With an Umbrella; I Love a Piano; Snooky Ookums; Ragtime Violin; When That Midnight Choo Choo Leaves For Alabam'; Shaking the Blues Away; Steppin' Out With My Baby; A Couple of Swells; The Girl on the Magazine Cover; Better Luck Next Time; Easter Parade.

SYNOPSIS:

When dancer Don Hewes' partner Nadine Hale deserts him for a chance at a big show he vows that he can turn an awkward chorus girl named Hannah Brown (who can't tell her left leg from her right without help from her garter!) into a star.

SOUNDTRACK: MGM 2-SES-40ST (with *Singin' in the Rain*)

* * * * * * * * * *

EASY COME, EASY GO
Paramount, 1967

Producer: Hal B. Wallis
Director: John Rich
Screenplay: Allan Weiss and Anthony Lawrence
Choreography: David Winters

Music and Lyrics: see below with song titles
Running time: 95 minutes, color

CAST:

Elvis Presley (*Ted Jackson*); Dodie Marshall (*Jo Symington*); Pat Priest (*Dina Bishop*); Pat Harrington (*Judd Whitman*); Frank McHugh (*Captain Jack*); Skip Ward (*Gil Carey*); Elsa Lanchester (*Madame Neherina*); Sandy Kenyon (*Lt. Schwartz*); Elaine Beckett (*Vicki*) and Shari Nims (*Mary*).

SONGS:

Easy Come, Easy Go - *Sid Wayne and Ben Weisman*
The Love Machine - *Gerald Nelson, Chuck Taylor and Fred Burch*
Yoga is as Yoga Does - *Gerald Nelson and Fred Burch*
You Gotta Stop - *Bill Giant, Bernie Baum and Florence Kaye*
Sing, You Children - *Gerald Nelson and Fred Burch*
I'll Take Love - *Dee Fuller and Mark Barkan*

SYNOPSIS:

Former Navy frogman Ted Jackson agrees to help Jo Symington look for the sunken treasure that her grandfather left her a map to.

SOUNDTRACK: RCA EPA-4387

* * * * * * * * *

EASY TO LOVE
Metro-Goldwyn-Mayer, 1953

Producer: Joe Pasternak
Director: Charles Walters
Screenplay: Laslo Vadnay and William Roberts; based on a story by Laslo Vadnay
Choreography: Busby Berkeley
Music and Lyrics: see below with song titles
Running time: 96 minutes, color

CAST:

Esther Williams (*Julie Hallerton*); Van Johnson (*Ray Lloyd*); Tony Martin (*Barry Gordon*); John Bromfield (*Hank*); Edna Skinner (*Nancy Parmel*); King Donovan (*Ben*); Paul Bryar (*Mr. Barnes*); Carroll Baker (*Clarice*); Eddie Oliver (*Band Leader*) and Benny Rubin (*Oscar Levendon*).

SONGS:

Didja' Ever - *Vic Mizzy and Mann Curtis*
Look Out! I'm Romantic - *Vic Mizzy and Mann Curtis*
Coquette - *Carmen Lombardo, Johnny Green and Gus Kahn*
Easy to Love - *Cole Porter*
That's What a Rainy Day is For - *Vic Mizzy and Mann Curtis*

SYNOPSIS:

The star of a Cypress Gardens, Florida aquacade, Julie Hallerton, is in love with her boss, Ray Lloyd, amd decides to make him jealous by flirting with crooner Barry Gordon.

SOUNDTRACK: No soundtrack available

* * * * * * * * *

EASY TO WED
Metro-Goldwyn-Mayer, 1946

Producer: Jack Cummings
Director: Edward Buzzell
Screenplay: Dorothy Kingsley; based on the screenplay *Libeled Lady* by Maurice
           Watkins, Howard Emmett Rogers and George Oppenheimer
Choreography: Jack Donohue
Music and Lyrics: see below with song titles
Running time: 110 minutes, color

CAST:

Van Johnson (*Bill Chandler*); Esther Williams (*Connie Allenbury*); Lucille Ball (*Gladys Benton*); Keenan Wynn (*Warren Haggerty*); Cecil Kellaway (*J.B. Allenbury*); Carlos Ramirez (*Himself*); Ben Blue (*Spike Dolan*); Ethel Smith (*Herself*); June Lockhart (*Babs Norvell*); Grant Mitchell (*Homer Henshaw*); Josephine Whittell (*Mrs. Burns Norvell*) and Paul Harvey (*Farwood*).

SONGS:

Easy to Wed - *Johnny Green and Ted Duncan*
Goosey-Lucy - *Johnny Green and Robert Franklin*
Come Closer to Me - *Osvaldo Farres*
Continental Polka - *Johnny Green and Ralph Blane*

(Tell You What I'm Gonna Do) Gonna Fall in Love With You - *Johnny Green and Ralph Blane*
It Shouldn't Happen to a Duck - *Johnny Green and Robert Franklin*
Can't I Do Anything But Swim? - *Harriet Lee*

SYNOPSIS:

Socialite Connie Allenbury sues newspaperman Warren Haggerty for libel after he criticizes her wild lifestyle in print. To get her to drop the suit, Haggerty hires former employee Bill Chandler to woo her and get her to change her mind.

SOUNDTRACK: No soundtrack available

* * * * * * * * *

THE EMPEROR'S NEW CLOTHES
Cannon Films, 1987

Producer: Menahem Golan and Yoram Globus
Director: David Irving
Screenplay: Anna Mathias, Len Talan and David Irving; based on the fairy tale by
            Hans Christian Andersen
Choreography: Yaacov Kalusky
Music and Lyrics: Stephen Lawrence and Michael Korie
Running time: 85 minutes, color

CAST:

Sid Caesar (*The Emperor*); Robert Morse (*Henry Spencer*); Clive Revill (*The Prime Minister*); Jason Carter* (*Nicholas Spencer*); Lysette Anthony** (*Princess Gilda*); Julian Joy-Chagrin (*The Duke*); Israel Gurion (*Wenceslas*); Susan Berlin (*Lady Christine*); Danny Segev (*Prince Nino*) and Eli Gorenstein (*Sergeant*).

 vocals dubbed by Danny Street
**vocals dubbed by Joan Baxter*

SONGS:

Clothes Make the Man; Adventure; Weave-o; Is This a Love Song?; Red or Blue?

SYNOPSIS:

Based on the fairy tale is the story of swindler Henry Spencer and his nephew Nicholas who pass themselves off as tailors to a vain emperor and promise to supply

86

him with a wondrous new cloth that is invisible to anyone who is stupid.

SOUNDTRACK: No soundtrack available

* * * * * * * * *

EVERYTHING I HAVE IS YOURS
Metro-Goldwyn-Mayer, 1952

Producer: George Wells
Director: Robert Z. Leonard
Screenplay: George Wells and Ruth Brooks Flippen
Choreography: Gower Champion and Nick Castle
Music and Lyrics: see below with song titles
Running time: 92 minutes, color

CAST:

Marge Champion (*Pamela Hubbard*); Gower Champion (*Chuck Hubbard*); Dennis O'Keefe (*Alec Tackabury*); Eduard Franz (*Phil Meisner*); Monica Lewis (*Sybil Meriden*); Dean Miller (*Monty Dunstan*) and John Gallaudet (*Ed Holly*).

SONGS:

Like Monday Follows Sunday - *Johnny Green, Clifford Grey, Rex Newman and Douglas Furber*
Casablanca (instrumental) - *Richard Priborsky*
My Heart Skips a Beat - *Walter Donaldson, Robert Wright and George Forrest*
Seventeen Thousand Telephone Poles - *Saul Chaplin*
Serenade For a New Baby (instrumental) - *Johnny Green*
Everything I Have is Yours - *Burton Lane and Harold Adamson*
Derry Down Dilly - *Johnny Green and Johnny Mercer*
General Hiram Johnson Jefferson Brown - *Walter Donaldson and Gus Kahn*

SYNOPSIS:

Husband-and-wife dance team Chuck and Pamela Hubbard find that their first big Broadway show is in trouble when Pamela discovers that she's pregnant.

SOUNDTRACK: MGM 2-SES-52ST (with *Summer Stock* and *I Love Melvin*)

* * * * * * * * *

EXCUSE MY DUST
Metro-Goldwyn-Mayer, 1951

Producer: Jack Cummings
Director: Roy Rowland
Screenplay: George Wells
Choreography: Hermes Pan
Music and Lyrics: Arthur Schwartz and Dorothy Fields
Running time: 82 minutes, color

CAST:

Red Skelton (*Joe Belden*); Sally Forrest* (*Liz Bullitt*); Macdonald Carey (*Cyrus Random, Jr.*); William Demarest (*Harvey Bullitt*); Monica Lewis (*Daisy Lou Schulzer*); Raymond Walburn (*Mayor Fred Haskell*); Jane Darwell (*Mrs. Belden*); Lillian Bronson (*Mrs. Matilda Bullitt*); Paul Harvey (*Cyrus Random, Sr.*); Marjorie Wood (*Mrs. Cyrus Random, Sr.*); Guy Anderson (*Ben Parrot*) and Will Wright (*Race Judge*).

vocals dubbed by Gloria Grey

SONGS:

I'd Like to Take You Out Dreaming; Lorelei Brown; Going Steady; Spring Has Sprung; Get a Horse; That's For the Children.

SYNOPSIS:

It's 1895 in Willow Falls, Indiana and inventor Joe Belden is determined to make his "Gas-a-mobile" a success despite the fact that his girlfriend Liz's father owns the local livery stable.

SOUNDTRACK: No soundtrack available

88

F

THE FARMER TAKES A WIFE
20th Century Fox, 1953

Producer: Frank P. Rosenberg
Director: Henry Levin
Screenplay: Walter Bullock, Sally Benson and Joseph Fields; based on the novel
        Rome Haul by Walter D. Edmonds
Choreography: Jack Cole
Music and Lyrics: Harold Arlen and Dorothy Fields
Running time: 81 minutes, color

CAST:

Betty Grable (*Molly Larkins*); Dale Robertson (*Daniel Harrow*); Thelma Ritter (*Lucy Cashdollar*); John Carroll (*Jotham Klore*); Eddie Foy, Jr. (*Fortune Friendly*); Charlotte Austin (*Pearl Dowd*); Kathleen Crowley (*Susanna*); Merry Anders (*Hannah*); Donna Lee Hickey (*Eva Gooch*); Donald Kerr (*Jacob*); Mel Pogue (*Abner Green*); Howard Negley (*Governor Hamilton Fish*) and Gwen Verdon (*Abigail*).

SONGS:

Today I Love Everybody; We're Doing It For the Natives in Jamaica; Schenectady; Somethin' Real Special; On the Erie Canal; With the Sun Warm Upon Me; We're in Business.

SYNOPSIS:

Rome, New York, 1850: Molly Larkins is a boat cook on the Erie Canal for Jotham Klore and Dan Harrow is the farmer who takes a job as a driver on the boat and soon falls for Molly.

SOUNDTRACK: No soundtrack available

* * * * * * * * *

FIDDLER ON THE ROOF
United Artists, 1971

Producer: Norman Jewison
Director: Norman Jewison
Screenplay: Joseph Stein, based on his stage musical book
Choreography: Jerome Robbins and Tom Abbott

Music and Lyrics: Jerry Bock and Sheldon Harnick
Running time: 150 minutes, color

CAST:

Topol (*Tevye*); Norma Crane (*Golde*); Leonard Frey (*Motel*); Molly Picon (*Yente*); Paul Mann (*Lazar Wolf*); Rosalind Harris (*Tzeitel*); Michele Marsh (*Hodel*); Neva Small (*Chava*); Michael Glaser (*Perchik*); Raymond Lovelock (*Fyedka*); Elaine Edwards (*Shprintze*); Candy Bonstein (*Bielke*); Louis Zorich (*Constable*); Zvee Scooler (*Rabbi*); Ruth Madoc (*Fruma Sarah*) and Patience Collier (*Grandma Tzeitel*).

SONGS:

Tradition; Matchmaker; If I Were a Rich Man; Sabbath Prayer; To Life; Miracle of Miracles; Tevye's Dream; Sunrise, Sunset; The Bottle Dance (instrumental); Do You Love Me?; Far From the Home I Love; Chava's Ballet (Little Bird); Anatevka.

SYNOPSIS:

Tevye, a poor Jewish milkman in turn-of-the-century Russia, wonders why God has given him five daughters to marry off with no hopes of dowries to provide them with--but nevertheless manages to look on the bright side of things.

SOUNDTRACK: United Artists 10900

* * * * * * * * * *

FINIAN'S RAINBOW
Warner Bros., 1968

Producer: Joseph Landon
Director: Francis Ford Coppola
Screenplay: E.Y. Harburg and Fred Saidy, based on their stage musical book
Choreography: Hermes Pan
Music and Lyrics: Burton Lane and E.Y. Harburg
Running time: 145 minutes, color

CAST:

Fred Astaire (*Finian McLonergan*); Tommy Steele (*Og*); Petula Clark (*Sharon McLonergan*); Don Francks (*Woody Mahoney*); Keenan Wynn (*Senator Billboard Rawkins*); Al Freeman, Jr. (*Howard*); Barbara Hancock (*Susan the Silent*); Louil Silas (*Henry*) and Dolph Sweet (*Sheriff*).

SONGS:

This Time of the Year; How Are Things in Glocca Morra?; Look to the Rainbow; Old Devil Moon; Something Sort of Grandish; If This Isn't Love; That Great Come-and-Get-It Day; When the Idle Poor Become the Idle Rich; Rain Dance Ballet (instrumental); The Begat; When I'm Not Near the Girl I Love.

SYNOPSIS:

Finian McLonergan steals a crock of gold from the leprechauns back in Ireland and comes to America with his daughter to make his fortune--by burying the crock near Fort Knox!

SOUNDTRACK: Warner Bros. 2550

* * * * * * * * *

THE FIREFLY
Metro-Goldwyn-Mayer, 1937

Producer: Hunt Stromberg
Director: Robert Z. Leonard
Screenplay: Albert Hackett and Frances Goodrich, adapted by Ogden Nash; based
      on the stage musical book by Otto A. Harbach
Choreography: Albertina Rasch
Music and Lyrics: Rudolf Friml and Otto A. Harbach
Running time: 131 minutes, B/W

CAST:

Jeanette MacDonald (*Nina Maria Azara*); Allan Jones (*Don Diego/Captain François André*); Warren William (*Colonel DeRougement*); Billy Gilbert (*Innkeeper*); Henry Daniell (*General Savary*); Douglass Dumbrille (*Marquis de Melito*); Leonard Penn (*Captain Etienne DuBois*); Tom Rutherford (*King Ferdinand*); Belle Mitchell (*Lola*) and George Zucco (*Secret Service Chief*).

SONGS:

Love is Like a Firefly; When the Wine is Full of Fire; A Woman's Kiss; The Donkey Serenade*; Giannina Mia; He Who Loves and Runs Away; Sympathy; When a Maid Comes Knocking at Your Heart.

**music and lyrics by Rudolf Friml, Robert Wright and George Forrest*

SYNOPSIS:

Café singer Nina Maria is really a spy for Spain, extracting information from French soldiers to find out what the Emperor Napoleon is planning next.

SOUNDTRACK: Caliban 6027

* * * * * * * * *

THE FIVE PENNIES
Paramount, 1959

Producer: Jack Rose
Director: Melville Shavelson
Screenplay: Melville Shavelson and Jack Rose; based on a story by Robert Smith
Choreography: Earl Barton
Music and Lyrics: see below with song title
Running time: 117 minutes, color

CAST:

Danny Kaye (*Ernest Loring "Red" Nichols*); Barbara Bel Geddes* (*Bobbie Meredith*); Louis Armstrong (*Himself*); Bob Crosby (*Wil Paradise*); Harry Guardino (*Tony Valani*); Susan Gordon (*Dorothy Nichols, age 6*); Tuesday Weld (*Dorothy 12-14*); Valene Allen (*Tommye Eden*); Ray Anthony (*Jimmy Dorsey*); Shelly Manne (*Dave Tough*); Bobby Troup (*Artie Schutt*) and Ray Daley (*Glenn Miller*).

vocals dubbed by Eileen Wilson

SONGS:

Bill Bailey, Won't You Please Come Home? - *Hughie Cannon*
Follow the Leader - *Sylvia Fine*
Lullaby in Ragtime - *Sylvia Fine*
Good Night-Sleep Tight - *Sylvia Fine*
The Music Goes 'Round and 'Round - *Edward Farley, Michael Riley and Red Hodgson*
The Five Pennies - *Sylvia Fine*
When the Saints Go Marching In - *James M. Black and Katharine E. Purvis, new lyrics and adaptation by Sylvia Fine*
Jingle Bells - *J.S. Pierpont*

The biography of jazz cornet player Red Nichols, from his initiation into the "big time" in a Harlem, New York night club with Louis Armstrong through his premature retirement due to his daughter's battle with polio and his comeback in the early 1940's.

SOUNDTRACK: Dot 29500

* * * * * * * * * *

THE FLEET'S IN
Paramount, 1942

Producer: B.G. DeSylva
Director: Victor Schertzinger
Screenplay: Walter DeLeon, Sid Silvers and Ralph Spence; based on a story by
         Monte Brice and J. Walter Ruben
Choreography: Jack Donohue
Music and Lyrics: Johnny Mercer and Victor Schertzinger
Running time: 93 minutes, B/W

CAST:

Dorothy Lamour (*"The Countess"*); William Holden (*Casey Kirby*); Eddie Bracken (*Barney Waters*); Betty Hutton (*Bessie Dale*); Leif Erickson (*Jake*); Betty Jane Rhodes (*Diana Golden*); Barbara Britton (*Eileen Wright*); Cass Daley (*Cissie*); Gil Lamb (*Spike*); Jack Norton (*Kellogg*) and Jimmy Dorsey (*Himself*).

SONGS:

The Fleet's In; Tangerine*; I Remember You; If You Build a Better Mousetrap; Arthur Murray Taught Me Dancing; It's Somebody Else's Moon; Tomorrow You Belong to Uncle Sam.

music and lyrics by Frank Loesser and Victor Schertzinger

SYNOPSIS:

Casey Kirby is a girl-shy sailor whose friends make a bet that he can get a kiss from an icy entertainer known as "The Countess".

SOUNDTRACK: Hollywood Soundstage 405

* * * * * * * * * *

FLOWER DRUM SONG
Universal, 1961

Producer: Ross Hunter
Director: Henry Koster
Screenplay: Joseph Fields; based on the stage musical book by Joseph Fields and
                      Oscar Hammerstein II
Choreography: Hermes Pan
Music and Lyrics: Richard Rodgers and Oscar Hammerstein II
Running time: 133 minutes, color

CAST:

Nancy Kwan* (*Linda Low*); James Shigeta (*Wang Ta*); Miyoshi Umeki (*Mei Li*); Jack
Soo (*Sammy Fong*); Juanita Hall (*Mme. Liang*); Benson Fong (*Wang Chi-Yang*); Kam
Tong** (*Dr. Li*); Patrick Adiarte (*Wang San*); Reiko Sato*** (*Helen Chao*); Victor
Sen Yung (*Frankie Wing*) and Soo Yung (*Mme. Fong*).

   **vocals dubbed by B.J. Baker*
  ***vocals dubbed by Jack Dodson*
****vocals dubbed by Marilyn Horne*

SONGS:

A Hundred Million Miracles (The Flower Drum Song); Fan Tan Fanny; The Other
Generation; I Enjoy Being a Girl; I Am Going to Like It Here; Gliding Through My
Memoree; Love, Look Away; You Are Beautiful; Sunday; Don't Marry Me.

SYNOPSIS:

A young Chinese girl, Mei Li, arrives from Hong Kong illegally for an arranged
marriage with nightclub manager Sammy Fong--who is already engaged to the club's
singer Linda Low.

SOUNDTRACK: Decca 79098

* * * * * * * * * *

FLYING DOWN TO RIO
RKO, 1933

Producer: Lou Brock
Director: Thornton Freeland
Screenplay: Cyril Hume, H.W. Haneman and Erwin Gelsey; based on a play by
          Anne Caldwell
Choreography: Dave Gould
Music and Lyrics: Vincent Youmans, Edward Eliscu and Gus Kahn
Running time: 89 minutes, B/W

CAST:

Dolores del Rio (*Belinha de Rezende*); Gene Raymond (*Roger Bond*); Raul Roulien (*Julio Rubeiro*); Ginger Rogers (*Honey Hale*); Fred Astaire (*Fred Ayres*); Blanche Friderci (*Doña Elena de Rezende*) and Walter Walker (*Carlos de Rezende*).

SONGS:

Music Makes Me; The Carioca; Orchids in the Moonlight; Flying Down to Rio.

SYNOPSIS:

Playboy bandleader Roger Bond takes his orchestra down to Rio de Janeiro when he falls for Brazilian beauty Belinha de Rezende.

SOUNDTRACK: Classic International Filmusicals 3004 (with *Carefree*)

* * * * * * * * * *

FOLLOW THAT DREAM
United Artists, 1962

Producer: David Weisbart
Director: Gordon Douglas
Screenplay: Charles Lederer; based on the novel *Pioneer, Go Home!* by Richard
          Powell
Music and Lyrics: see below with song titles
Running time: 110 minutes, color

CAST:

Elvis Presley (*Toby Kwimper*); Arthur O'Connell (*Pop Kwimper*); Anne Helm (*Holly Jones*); Joanna Moore (*Alicia Claypoole*); Alan Hewitt (*H. Arthur King*); Simon Oakland (*Nick*); Jack Kruschen (*Carmine*); Howard McNear (*George*); Herbert Rudley (*Mr. Endicott*) and Roland Winters (*Judge*).

SONGS:

What a Wonderful Life - *Sid Wayne and Jerry Livingston*
I'm Not the Marrying Kind - *Sherman Edwards and Mack David*
Sound Advice - *Bill Giant and Anna Shaw*
Follow That Dream - *Bernie Weisman and Fred Wise*
Angel - *Sid Tepper and Roy C. Bennett*

SYNOPSIS:

When the Kwimper family decide to homestead a stretch a state land in Florida they run into a wall of bureaucracy.

SOUNDTRACK: RCA EPA-4368

* * * * * * * * *

FOLLOW THE FLEET
RKO, 1936

Producer: Pandro S. Berman
Director: Mark Sandrich
Screenplay: Dwight Taylor and Allan Scott; based on the play *Shore Leave* by
            Hubert Osborne
Choreography: Hermes Pan
Music and Lyrics: Irving Berlin
Running time: 110 minutes, B/W

CAST:

Fred Astaire (*Seaman "Bake" Baker*); Ginger Rogers (*Sherry Martin*); Randolph Scott (*CPO "Bilge" Smith*); Harriet Hilliard (*Connie Martin*); Astrid Allwyn (*Iris Manning*); Ray Mayer (*Dopey*); Harry Beresford (*Captain Hickey*); Addison Randall (*Lt. Williams*); Russell Hicks (*Jim Nolan*); Brooks Benedict (*Sullivan*) and Lucille Ball (*Kitty Collins*).

SONGS:

We Saw the Sea; Let Yourself Go; Get Thee Behind Me, Satan; I'd Rather Lead a Band; Here Am I, But Where Are You?; I'm Putting All My Eggs in One Basket; Let's Face the Music and Dance.

SYNOPSIS:

While sailors "Bake" Baker and Bilge Smith are on shore leave in San Francisco, Bake tries to team up again with his former dance partner Sherry Martin, while her sister Connie makes a play for Bilge.

SOUNDTRACK: Sountrak 118

* * * * * * * * *

FOOTLIGHT PARADE
Warner Bros., 1933

Producer: Darryl F. Zanuck
Director: Lloyd Bacon
Screenplay: Manuel Seff and James Seymour
Choreography: Busby Berkeley
Music and Lyrics: Sammy Fain and Irving Kahal
Running time: 102 minutes, B/W

CAST:

James Cagney (*Chester Kent*); Joan Blondell (*Nan Prescott*); Ruby Keeler (*Bea Thorn*); Dick Powell (*Scotty Blair*); Frank McHugh (*Francis*); Guy Kibbee (*Silas Gould*); Ruth Donnelly (*Harriet Bowers Gould*); Hugh Herbert (*Charlie Bowers*); Claire Dodd (*Vivian Rich*); Gordon Wescott (*Harry Thompson*); Arthur Hohl (*Al Frazer*) and Renee Whitney (*Cynthia Kent*).

SONGS:

Ah, the Moon is Here; Sitting On a Backyard Fence; Honeymoon Hotel*; Shanghai Lil*; By a Waterfall.

*music and lyrics by Harry Warren and Al Dubin

SYNOPSIS:

Chester Kent is a producer of "prologues"--production numbers that precede the new talking pictures--for Sid Gould and Al Frazer but soon finds that his best ideas are being stolen by a rival.

SOUNDTRACK: No soundtrack available

* * * * * * * * *

FOOTLIGHT SERENADE
20th Century Fox, 1942

Producer: William LeBaron
Director: Gregory Ratoff
Screenplay: Robert Ellis, Helen Logan and Lynn Starling; based on a story by Fidel LaBarba and Kenneth Earl
Choreography: Hermes Pan
Music and Lyrics: Leo Robin and Ralph Rainger
Running time: 81 minutes, B/W

CAST:

John Payne (*Bill Smith*); Betty Grable (*Pat Lambert*); Victor Mature (*Tommy Lundy*); Jane Wyman (*Flo LaVerne*); James Gleason (*Bruce McKay*); Phil Silvers (*Slap*); Cobina Wright, Jr. (*Estelle Evans*); Frank Orth (*Doorman*); Irving Bacon (*Mike*); George Dobbs (*Frank*) and Charles Tannen (*Charlie*).

SONGS:

Are You Kidding?; I'm Still Crazy For You; I Hear the Birdies Sing; I'll Be Marching to a Love Song.

SYNOPSIS:

Boxing star Tommy Lundy is given a part in a new Broadway show and promptly makes a play for the understudy, Pat Lambert--who is secretly married to Bill Smith, Lundy's sparring partner in the show.

SOUNDTRACK: Caliban 6002 (with *Rose of Washington Square*)

* * * * * * * * *

FOR ME AND MY GAL
Metro-Goldwyn-Mayer, 1942

Producer: Arthur Freed
Director: Busby Berkeley
Screenplay: Richard Sherman, Fred Finklehoffe and Sid Silvers; based on a story by Howard Emmett Rogers
Choreography: Bobby Connolly
Music and Lyrics: see below with song titles
Running time: 104 minutes, B/W

98

CAST:

Judy Garland (*Jo Hayden*); George Murphy (*Jimmy K. Metcalfe*); Gene Kelly (*Harry Palmer*); Marta Eggerth (*Eve Minard*); Ben Blue (*Sid Simms*); Horace McNally (*Bert Waring*); Richard Quine (*Danny Hayden*); Lucille Norman (*Lily*) and Keenan Wynn (*Eddie Melton*).

SONGS:

Oh, You Beautiful Doll! - *Fred Fisher and Alfred Bryan*
Don't Leave Me Daddy - *Joe Vergas*
By the Beautiful Sea - *Harold Atteridge and Harry Carroll*
For Me and My Gal - *Edgar Leslie, F. Ray Goetz and George W. Meyer*
When You Wore a Tulip - *Jack Mahoney and Percy Wenrich*
Do I Love You? - *F. Ray Goetz and Henri Christine*
After You've Gone - *Henry Creamer and Turner Layton*
Tell Me - *Max Kortlander and J. Will Callahan*
Till We Meet Again - *Raymond B. Egan and Richard A. Whiting*
We Don't Want the Bacon - *Howard Carr, Harry Russell and Jimmie Havens*
Ballin' the Jack - *James Henry Burris and Chris Smith*
What Are You Gonna Do For Uncle Sammy? - *Gus Kahn and Egbert Van Alstyne*
How You Gonna Keep 'Em Down on the Farm? - *Sam M. Lewis, Joe Young and Walter Donaldson*
Where Do We Go From Here? - *Howard Johnson and Percy Wenrich*
It's a Long Way to Tipperary - *Henry H. Williams and Jack Judge*
Goodbye Broadway, Hello France - *Francis Riesner, Benny Davis and Billy Baskette*
Smiles - *J. Will Callahan and Lee M. Roberts*
Oh Frenchy - *Sam Ehrlich and Con Conrad*
Pack Up Your Troubles - *George Asaf and Felix Powell*
When Johnny Comes Marching Home - *Louis Lambert, arranged by Roger Edens*

SYNOPSIS:

In the heyday of vaudeville, performers Jo Hayden and Harry Palmer find their lives in turmoil with the advent of WWI.

SOUNDTRACK: Sountrak 107

* * * * * * * * *

FOR THE FIRST TIME
Metro-Goldwyn-Mayer, 1959

99

Producer: Alexander Grueter
Director: Rudolph Maté
Screenplay: Andrew Solt, based on his story
Music and Lyrics: see below with song titles
Running time: 95 minutes, color

CAST:

Mario Lanza (*Tony Costa*); Zsa Zsa Gabor (*Countess Gloria de Vadnuz*); Johanna von Kozian (*Christa Bruckner*); Kurt Kasznar (*Ladislas Tabory*); Hans Sonker (*Albert Bruckner*); Peter Capell (*Leopold Huebner*); Renzo Cesana (*Angelo*) and Sandro Giglio (*Alessandro*).

SONGS:

La donna è mobile (*Rigoletto*) - *Giuseppe Verdi*
Come Prima (For the First Time) - *Taccani-di Paola Panzerzi*
Capri Capri - *George Stoll*
O Solo Mio - *Eduardo di Capua*
Vesti la giubba (*Pagliacci*) - *Ruggiero Leoncavallo*
Avé Maria - *Franz Schubert*
Bavarian Drinking Song - *Karl Bette*
Pineapple Picker - *George Stoll*
Grand March (*Aida*) - *Giuseppe Verdi*

SYNOPSIS:

While vacationing in Capri tempermental opera singer Tony Costa falls in love with Christa Bruckner, a beautiful deaf girl. He then decides to set up a series of concerts throughout Europe to raise money for an operation that will restore her hearing.

SOUNDTRACK: RCA LSC-2338

* * * * * * * * * *

42nd STREET
Warner Bros., 1933

Producer: Darryl F. Zanuck
Director: Lloyd Bacon
Screenplay: James Seymour and Rian James; based on the novel by Bradford Ropes
Choreography: Busby Berkeley

Music and Lyrics: Harry Warren and Al Dubin
Running time: 98 minutes, B/W

CAST:

Warner Baxter (*Julian Marsh*); Bebe Daniels (*Dorothy Brock*); George Brent (*Pat Denning*); Ruby Keeler (*Peggy Sawyer*); Guy Kibbee (*Abner Dillon*); Una Merkel (*Lorraine Fleming*); Ginger Rogers (*Ann Lowell*); Ned Sparks (*Thomas Barny*); Dick Powell (*Billy Lawler*); Allen Jenkins (*Mac Elory*); Edward J. Nugent (*Terry Neil*); Robert McWade (*Al Jones*) and George E. Stone (*Andy Lee*).

SONGS:

It Must Be June; You're Getting to Be a Habit With Me; Shuffle Off to Buffalo; Young and Healthy; 42nd Street.

SYNOPSIS:

Director Julian Marsh is on the verge of another nervous breakdown trying to ready a new show for Broadway and his troubles only get worse when the star, Dorothy Brock, breaks her leg.

SOUNDTRACK: No soundtrack available

* * * * * * * * *

FRANKIE AND JOHNNY
United Artists, 1966

Producer: Edward Small
Director: Frederick de Cordova
Screenplay: Alex Gottlieb; based on a story by Nat Perrin
Choreography: Earl Barton
Music and Lyrics: see below with song titles
Running time: 88 minutes, color

CAST:

Elvis Presley (*Johnny*); Donna Douglas (*Frankie*); Harry Morgan (*Cully*); Nancy Kovack (*Nellie Bly*); Anthony Eisley (*Clint Braden*); Sue Ane Langdon (*Mitzi*); Robert Strauss (*Blackie*); Audrey Christie (*Peg*) and Joyce Jameson (*Abigail*).

SONGS:

Come Along - *David Hess*
Petunia - *Sid Tepper and Roy C. Bennett*
Chesay - *Ben Weisman, Sid Wayne and Fred Karger*
What Every Woman Lives For - *Doc Pomus and Mort Shuman*
Frankie and Johnny - *new lyrics and arranged by Fred Karger, Alex Gottlieb and Ben Weisman*
Lookout Broadway - *Fred Wise and Randy Starr*
Angel in My Arms - *Sid Tepper and Roy C. Bennett*
Down By the Riverside - *arranged by Fred Wise and Randy Starr*
When the Saints Go Marching In - *James M. Black and Katharine E. Purvis; arranged by Fred Wise and Randy Starr*
Shout It Out - *Bill Giant, Bernie Baum and Florence Kaye*
Hard Luck - *Ben Weisman and Sid Wayne*
Please Don't Stop Loving Me - *Joy Byers*
Everybody Come Aboard - *Bill Giant, Bernie Baum and Florence Kaye*

SYNOPSIS:

The popular ballad comes to life as a musical set aboard a Mississippi River showboat with Frankie and Johnny as the romantic duo of the stage who find that Johnny's compulsive gambling leads them into danger.

SOUNDTRACK: RCA LSP-3553

* * * * * * * * *

THE FRENCH LINE
RKO, 1954

Producer: Edmund Grainger
Director: Lloyd Bacon
Screenplay: Mary Loos and Richard Sale; based on a story by Matty Kemp and Isabel Dawn
Choreography: Billy Daniel
Music and Lyrics: Josef Myrow, Ralph Blane and Robert Wells
Running time: 102 minutes, color

CAST:

Jane Russell (*Mary Carson*); Gilbert Roland (*Pierre Ducane*); Arthur Hunnicutt (*Waco Mosby*); Mary McCarty (*Annie Farrell*); Joyce MacKenzie (*Myrtle Brown*); Paula Corday (*Celeste*); Scott Elliott (*Bill Harris*); Craig Stevens (*Phil Barton*); Laura

102

Elliott (*Katherine Hodges*); Michael St. Angel (*George Hodges*) and Steven Geray (*François*).

SONGS:

Well, I'll Be Switched!; With a Kiss; Comment Allez-Vous?; Wait Till You See Paris; What is This That I Feel?; Poor André; Any Gal From Texas; By Madame Firelli; Lookin' For Trouble.

SYNOPSIS:

Texas millionaire Mary Carson believes people are only attracted to her money so she decides to take a sea cruise and hires Myrtle Brown to impersonate her so that she can see if a man can love her for herself.

SOUNDTRACK: No soundtrack available

* * * * * * * * *

THE FROG PRINCE
Cannon Films, 1986

Producer: Menahem Golan and Yoram Globus
Director: Jackson Hunsicker
Screenplay: Jackson Hunsicker; based on the fairy tale by the Brothers Grimm
Choreography: Christine Oren
Music and Lyrics: Kenn Long
Running time: 75 minutes, color

CAST:

Aileen Quinn (*Princess Zora*); Clive Revill (*The King*); Helen Hunt (*Henrietta*); John Paragon* (*The Frog Prince*); Seagull Cohen (*Dulcey*); Jeff Gurner (*Emissary*) and Shimuel Atzmon (*Baron Von Whobble*).

vocals dubbed by Nick Curtis

SONGS:

Lucky Day; A Promise is a Promise; Too Tall Frog; Music Box Waltz (instrumental); Friendship; Have You Forgotten Me?

SYNOPSIS:

Princess Zora is a very lonely little girl with only her special ball for entertainment. But When she loses it in a pond a magical frog agrees to retrieve it in return for her friendship.

SOUNDTRACK: No soundtrack available

* * * * * * * * *

FUN IN ACAPULCO
Paramount, 1963

Producer: Hal B. Wallis
Director: Richard Thorpe
Screenplay: Allan Weiss
Choreography: Charles O'Curran
Music and Lyrics: see below with song titles
Running time: 97 minutes, color

CAST:

Elvis Presley (*Mike Windgren*); Ursula Andress (*Margarita Dauphin*); Elsa Cardenas (*Dolores Gomez*); Paul Lukas (*Maximillian Dauphin*); Larry Domasin (*Raul Almeido*); Alejandro Rey (*Moreno*); Robert Carricart (*José*); Teri Hope (*Janie Harkins*) and Charles Evans (*Mr. Harkins*).

SONGS:

Fun in Acapulco - *Sid Wayne and Ben Weisman*
Viva el Amor - *Sid Tepper and Roy C. Bennett*
I Think I'm Gonna Like It Here - *Hal Blair and Don Robertson*
Mexico - *Sid Tepper and Roy C. Bennett*
El Toro - *Bill Giant, Bernie Baum and Florence Kaye*
Margarita - *Don Robertson*
The Bullfighter Was a Lady - *Sid Tepper and Roy C. Bennett*
(There's) No Room to Rhumba (in a Sports Car) - *Fred Wise and Dick Manning*
Bossa Nova Baby - *Jerry Leiber and Mike Stoller*
You Can't Say No in Acapulco - *Dee Fuller, Lee Morris and Sid Feller*
Guadalajara - *Pepe Guizar*

SYNOPSIS:

Mike Windgren gets a job as a lifeguard at the Acapulco Hilton hotel in an attempt to overcome his fear of heights--developed when his partner in a circus aerial act, his brother, was killed in a fall he feels was his fault.

SOUNDTRACK: RCA LSP-2756

* * * * * * * * *

FUNNY FACE
Paramount, 1957

Producer: Roger Edens
Director: Stanley Donen
Screenplay: Leonard Gershe
Choreography: Eugene Loring and Fred Astaire
Music and Lyrics: George Gershwin and Ira Gershwin
Running time: 103 minutes, color

CAST:

Fred Astaire (*Dick Avery*); Audrey Hepburn (*Jo Stockton*); Kay Thompson (*Maggie Prescott*); Michel Auclair (*Professor Emile Flostre*); Robert Flemyng (*Paul Duval*); Ruta Lee (*Lettie*); Dovima (*Marian*); Virginia Gibson (*Babs*) and Alex Gerry (*Dovitch*).

SONGS:

Think Pink*; How Long Has This Been Going On?; Funny Face; Bonjour, Paris!*; Let's Kiss and Make Up; He Loves and She Loves; On How To Be Lovely*; Clap Yo' Hands; 'S Wonderful.

music and lyrics by Roger Edens and Leonard Gershe

SYNOPSIS:

Fashion photographer Dick Avery spots a young girl, Jo Stockton, in a Greenwich Village book shop and persuades her to become a model--with a trip to Paris as an incentive.

SOUNDTRACK: Verve 15001

* * * * * * * * *

105

FUNNY GIRL
Columbia, 1968

Producer: Ray Stark
Director: William Wyler
Screenplay: Isobel Lennart, based on her stage musical book
Choreography: Herbert Ross
Music and Lyrics: Jule Styne and Bob Merrill
Running time: 155 minutes, color

CAST:

Barbra Streisand (*Fanny Brice*); Omar Sharif (*Nick Arnstein*); Kay Medford (*Rose Brice*); Anne Francis (*Georgia James*); Walter Pidgeon (*Florenz Ziegfeld*); Lee Allen (*Eddie Ryan*); Mae Questel (*Mrs. Strakosh*); Gerald Mohr (*Tom Branca*); Frank Faylen (*Mr. Keeney*) and Mittie Lawrence (*Emma*).

SONGS:

If a Girl Isn't Pretty; I'm the Greatest Star; Roller Skate Rag; I'd Rather Be Blue*; Second Hand Rose**; His Love Makes Me Beautiful; People; You Are Woman, I Am Man; Don't Rain On My Parade; Sadie, Sadie; The Swan; Funny Girl; My Man***.

  *music and lyrics by Fred Fisher and Billy Rose
 **music and lyrics by Grant Clark and James Hanley
***music and lyrics by Maurice Yvoin and Channing Pollock

SYNOPSIS:

The life of entertainer Fanny Brice from her start on the Lower East Side of New York through her rise to the Ziegfeld shows as well as her turbulent relationship with gambler Nick Arnstein.

SOUNDTRACK: Columbia JS-3220

* * * * * * * * *

FUNNY LADY
Columbia, 1975

Producer: Ray Stark
Director: Herbert Ross

Screenplay: Arnold Schulman and Jay Presson Allen; based on a story by Arnold
             Schulman
Choreography: Herbert Ross
Music and Lyrics: see below with song titles
Running time: 136 minutes, color

CAST:

Barbra Streisand (*Fanny Brice*); James Caan (*Billy Rose*); Omar Sharif (*Nick
Arnstein*); Roddy McDowall (*Bobby Moore*); Ben Vereen (*Bert Robbins*); Carole
Wells (*Norma Butler*); Larry Gates (*Bernard Baruch*); Heidi O'Rourke (*Eleanor
Holm*); Matt Emery (*Buck Bolton*); Corey Fisher (*Conductor*); Cliff Norton (*Stage
Manager*); Gene Troobnick (*Ned*); Garrett Lewis (*Production Singer*); Royce Wallace
(*Adele*) and Samantha Huffaker (*Fran Arnstein*).

SONGS:

Blind Date - *John Kander and Fred Ebb*
More Than You Know - *Vincent Youmans, Edward Eliscu and Billy Rose*
I Like Him/I Like Her - *John Kander and Fred Ebb*
It's Only a Paper Moon - *Harold Arlen, E.Y. Harburg and Billy Rose*
Beautiful Face, Have a Heart - *Fred Fisher, James V. Monaco and Billy Rose*
I Found a Million Dollar Baby in a Five and Ten Cent Store - *Harry Warren, Mort
                                                  Dixon and Billy Rose*
If You Want the Rainbow, You Must Have the Rain - *Oscar Levant, Mort Dixon
                                                  and Billy Rose*
I Caught a Code in My Dose - *Arthur Fields, Fred Hall and Billy Rose*
Clap Hands, Here Comes Charley - *Joseph Meyer, Ballard MacDonald and Billy
                                                  Rose*
Great Day - *Vincent Youmans, Edward Eliscu and Billy Rose*
How Lucky Can You Get? - *John Kander and Fred Ebb*
Isn't This Better? - *John Kander and Fred Ebb*
If I Love Again - *Jack Murray and Ben Oakland*
Let's Hear It For Me - *John Kander and Fred Ebb*
Me and My Shadow - *Al Jolson, Dave Dreyer and Billy Rose*

SYNOPSIS:

Sequel to *Funny Girl* picks up the life of entertainer Fanny Brice in the 1930's
during the Depression and her marriage to songwriter/producer Billy Rose.

SOUNDTRACK: Arista 9004

* * * * * * * * *

A FUNNY THING HAPPENED ON THE WAY TO THE FORUM
United Artists, 1966

Producer: Melvin Frank
Director: Richard Lester
Screenplay: Melvin Frank and Michael Pertwee; based on the stage musical book
          by Burt Shevelove and Larry Gelbart
Choreography: George Martin and Ethel Martin
Music and Lyrics: Stephen Sondheim
Running time: 99 minutes, color

CAST:

Zero Mostel (*Pseudolus*); Phil Silvers (*Marcus Lycus*); Buster Keaton (*Erronius*);
Michael Crawford (*Hero*); Jack Gilford (*Hysterium*); Michael Hordern (*Senex*);
Annette Andre (*Philia*); Patricia Jessel (*Domina*); Inga Neilsen (*Gymnasia*) and Leon
Greene (*Miles Gloriosus*).

SONGS:

Comedy Tonight; Lovely; Everybody Ought to Have a Maid; My Bride; The Dirge;
Riot at the Funeral (instrumental); The Chase (instrumental).

SYNOPSIS:

Based on the Broadway show is the story that revolves around the various efforts of
Pseudolus, a slave in Ancient Rome, to obtain his freedom.

SOUNDTRACK: United Artists 5144

G

G.I. BLUES
Paramount, 1960

Producer: Hal B. Wallis
Director: Norman Taurog
Screenplay: Edmund Beloin and Henry Garson
Choreography: Charles O'Curran
Music and Lyrics: see below with song titles
Running time: 100 minutes, color

CAST:

Elvis Presley (*Tulsa McClain*); Juliet Prowse (*Lili*); Robert Ivers (*Cookie*); James Douglas (*Rick*); Letitia Roman (*Tina*); Sigrid Maier (*Marla*); Arch Johnson (*Sgt. McGraw*); Edward Stroll (*Dynamite*); Jeremy Slate (*Turk*) and Ludwig Stossel (*Puppet Show Owner*).

SONGS:

G.I. Blues - *Sid Tepper and Roy C. Bennett*
Doin' the Best I Can - *Doc Pomus and Mort Shuman*
Frankfort Special - *Sid Wayne and Sherman Edwards*
Shoppin' Around - *Sid Tepper, Roy C. Bennett and Aaron Schroeder*
Tonight is So Right For Love - *Sid Wayne and Silver Joe Lilly*
Wooden Heart - *Fred Wise, Ben Weisman, Kathleen G. Twomey and Berhard
                Kaempfert*
Pocketful of Rainbows - *Fred Wise and Ben Weisman*
Big Boots - *Sid Wayne and Sherman Edwards*
Didja' Ever - *Sid Wayne and Sherman Edwards*

SYNOPSIS:

In Frankfort, West Germany, Tulsa McClain reluctantly accepts a bet from some Army buddies that he can spend the night alone with an aloof dancer named Lili.

SOUNDTRACK: RCA LSP-2256

* * * * * * * * *

THE GANG'S ALL HERE
20th Century Fox, 1943

Producer: William LeBaron
Director: Busby Berkeley
Screenplay: Walter Bullock; based on a story by Nancy Wintner, George Root, Jr.
and Tom Bridges
Choreography: Busby Berkeley
Music and Lyrics: Harry Warren and Leo Robin
Running time: 103 minutes, color

CAST:

Alice Faye (*Eadie Allen*); Carmen Miranda (*Dorita*); Eugene Pallette (*H.A. Mason*); Charlotte Greenwood (*Mrs. Blossom Potter*); Edward Everett Horton (*Peyton Potter*); James Ellison (*Andy Mason, Jr.*); Sheila Ryan (*Vivian Potter*); Dave Willock (*Sgt. Pat Casey*); Phil Baker (*Himself*); Benny Goodman (*Himself*) and Tony DeMarco (*Himself*).

SONGS:

Brazil*; You Discover You're in New York; Minnie's in the Money; The Lady in the Tutti-Frutti Hat; A Journey to a Star; No Love, No Nothin'; Paducah; The Polka-Dot Polka.

music and lyrics by Ary Barroso and S.K. Russell

SYNOPSIS:

Showgirl Eadie Allen finds that her boyfriend, Sgt. Andy Casey, is really Sgt. Andy Mason, Jr. when she goes to perform at a war bond benefit at the home of Vivian Potter--Andy's fianceé!

SOUNDTRACK: Classic International Filmusicals 3003

* * * * * * * * * *

THE GAY DIVORCÉE
RKO, 1934

Producer: Pandro S. Berman
Director: Mark Sandrich
Screenplay: George Marion, Jr., Dorothy Yost and Edward Kaufman; based on the
stage musical book by Dwight Taylor
Choreography: Dave Gould
Music and Lyrics: see below with song titles
Running time: 107 minutes, B/W

CAST:

Fred Astaire (*Guy Holden*); Ginger Rogers (*Mimi Glossop*); Alice Brady (*Hortense Ditherwell*); Edward Everett Horton (*Egbert Fitzgerald*); Erik Rhodes (*Rudolfo Tonetti*); Eric Blore (*Waiter*); William Austin (*Cyril Glossop*) and Betty Grable (*Hotel Guest*).

SONGS:

Don't Let It Bother You - *Harry Revel and Mack Gordon*
A Needle in a Haystack - *Con Conrad and Herb Magidson*
Let's K-nock K-nees - *Harry Revel and Mack Gordon*
Night and Day - *Cole Porter*
The Continental - *Con Conrad and Herb Magidson*

SYNOPSIS:

American dancer Guy Holden falls in love with Mimi Glossop and inadvertently helps his lawyer friend Egbert win her a divorce.

SOUNDTRACK: Sountrak (with *Top Hat*)

* * * * * * * * * *

GAY PURR-EE
Warner Bros., 1962

Producer: Henry G. Saperstein
Director: Abe Levitow
Screenplay: Dorothy Jones, Chuck Jones and Ralph Wright
Music and Lyrics: Harold Arlen and E.Y. Harburg
Running time: 85 minutes, color

VOCAL TALENTS:

Judy Garland (*Mewsette*); Robert Goulet (*Jaune Tom*); Red Buttons (*Robespierre*); Hermione Gingold (*Mme. Rubens-Chatte*) and Paul Frees (*Meowrice*).

SONGS:

Take My Hand, Paree; Roses Red-Violets Blue; The Money Cat; The Horse Won't Talk; Bubbles; Little Drops of Rain; Paris is a Lonely Town; Mewsette.

SYNOPSIS:

Animated tale about a young naïve cat named Mewsette who, after spurning her boyfriend Jaune Tom, goes to Paris but falls in with a "slavery" ring.

SOUNDTRACK: Warner Bros. 1479

* * * * * * * * * *

GENTLEMEN MARRY BRUNETTES
United Artists, 1955

Producer: Richard Sale and Robert Westerfield
Director: Richard Sale
Screenplay: Richard Sale and Mary Loos; based on a story by Anita Loos
Choreography: Jack Cole
Music and Lyrics: see below with song titles
Running time: 99 minutes, color

CAST:

Jane Russell (*Bonnie/Mimi Jones*); Jeanne Crain* (*Connie/Mitzi Jones*); Alan Young (*Charlie Biddle/Mrs. Biddle/Mr. Biddle, Sr.*); Scott Brady** (*David Action*); Rudy Vallee (*Himself*); Guy Middleton (*Earl of Wickenware*); Eric Pohlmann (*Monsignor Ballard*); Ferdy Mayne (*Monsignor Dufond*); Leonard Sachs (*Monsignor Duffy*) and Guido Lorraine (*Monsignor Marcel*).

 **vocals dubbed by Anita Ellis*
***vocals dubbed by Robert Farnon*

SONGS:

Gentlemen Marry Brunettes* - *Herbert Spencer, Earle Hagen and Richard Sale*
You're Driving Me Crazy - *Walter Donaldson*
Have You Met Miss Jones? - *Richard Rodgers and Lorenz Hart*
Miss Annabelle Lee - *Sidney Clare and Lew Pollack*
Daddy, I Want a Diamond Ring - *Bob Troup*
My Funny Valentine - *Richard Rodgers and Lorenz Hart*
I Wanna Be Loved By You - *Harry Ruby and Bert Kalmar*
Ain't Misbehavin' - *Thomas "Fats" Waller and Andy Razaf*
I've Got Five Dollars - *Richard Rodgers and Lorenz Hart*

**vocal by Johnny Desmond*

SYNOPSIS:

SYNOPSIS:

Mimi and Mitzi Jones are sisters and entertainers who decide to move to Europe because they are tired of being bothered by stage-door admirers. Their mother and aunt were the rage there a generation ago and they hope to emulate their success but love soon gets in the way.

SOUNDTRACK: Coral 57013

* * * * * * * * *

GENTLEMEN PREFER BLONDES
20th Century Fox, 1953

Producer: Sol C. Siegel
Director: Howard Hawks
Screenplay: Charles Lederer; based on the stage musical book by Joseph Fields and
        Anita Loos
Choreography: Jack Cole
Music and Lyrics: Jule Styne and Leo Robin
Running time: 92 minutes, color

CAST:

Jane Russell* (*Dorothy Shaw*); Marilyn Monroe (*Lorelei Lee*); Charles Coburn (*Sir Francis Beekman*); Elliott Reid (*Malone*); Tommy Noonan (*Gus Esmond, Jr.*); George Winslow (*Henry Spofford III*); Marcel Dalio (*Magistrate*); Taylor Holmes (*Gus Esmond, Sr.*); Norma Varden (*Lady Beekman*); Howard Wendel (*Watson*); Steven Geray (*Hotel Manager*) and Leo Mostovoy (*Phillipe*).

**vocals dubbed by Eileen Wilson*

SONGS:

Two Little Girls From Little Rock; Bye, Bye, Baby; Anyone Here For Love?*; When Love Goes Wrong*; Diamond's Are a Girl's Best Friend.

**music and lyrics by Hoagy Carmichael and Harold Adamson*

SYNOPSIS:

When entertainers Dorothy Shaw and Lorelei Lee leave for Paris aboard the *Ile de France* the cynical father of Lorelei's fiancé, Gus Esmond, Jr., hires private detective

113

Malone to spy on her to get some incriminating evidence of her suspected gold-digging.

SOUNDTRACK: No soundtrack available

* * * * * * * * *

GIGI
Metro-Goldwyn-Mayer, 1958

Producer: Arthur Freed
Director: Vincente Minelli
Screenplay: Alan Jay Lerner; based on the novel by Colette
Choreography: Charles Walters
Music and Lyrics: Frederick Loewe and Alan Jay Lerner
Running time: 116 minutes, color

CAST:

Leslie Caron* (*Gigi*); Maurice Chevalier (*Honoré Lachaille*); Louis Jourdan (*Gaston Lachaille*); Hermione Gingold (*Mme. Alvarez*); Eva Gabor (*Liane d'Exelmans*); Isabel Jeans (*Aunt Alicia*); Jacques Bergerac (*Sandomir*) and John Abbott (*Mañuel*).

**vocals dubbed by Betty Wand*

SONGS:

Thank Heaven For Little Girls; It's a Bore; The Parisians; She is Not Thinking Of Me (Waltz at Maxim's); The Night They Invented Champagne; I Remember It Well; Gigi (Gaston's Soliloquy); I'm Glad I'm Not Young Anymore; Say a Prayer For Me Tonight.

SYNOPSIS:

Gigi is a teenage schoolgirl in 1900 Paris who is being groomed to be a courtesan--without her knowledge!

SOUNDTRACK: MGM SE-3641

* * * * * * * * *

GIRL CRAZY
Metro-Goldwyn-Mayer, 1943

Producer: Arthur Freed
Director: Norman Taurog
Screenplay: Fred F. Finklehoffe; based on the stage musical book by Guy Bolton
and John McGowan
Choreography: Charles Walters and Busby Berkeley
Music and Lyrics: George Gershwin and Ira Gershwin
Running time: 99 minutes, B/W

CAST:

Mickey Rooney (*Danny Churchill, Jr.*); Judy Garland (*Ginger Gray*); Gil Stratton (*Bud Livermore*); Robert E. Strickland (*Henry Lathrop*); "Rags" Ragland (*Rags*); June Allyson (*Band Singer*); Nancy Walker (*Polly Williams*); Guy Kibbee (*Dean Phineas Armour*); Frances Rafferty (*Marjorie Tait*); Henry O'Neill (*Mr. Daniel Churchill, Sr.*); Howard Freeman (*Governor Tait*) and Tommy Dorsey (*Himself*).

SONGS:

Treat Me Rough; Bidin' My Time; Could You Use Me?; Embraceable You; Fascinating Rhythm (instrumental); But Not For Me; I Got Rhythm.

SYNOPSIS:

Danny Churchill, Jr. is sent out West to Cody College by his father to keep him away from girls, but Danny soon discovers Ginger, the Dean's granddaughter, and together they plan a rodeo to help bolster enrollment.

SOUNDTRACK: Curtain Calls 100/9-10 (with *Strike Up the Band*)

* * * * * * * * * *

GIRL HAPPY
Metro-Goldwyn-Mayer, 1965

Producer: Joe Pasternak
Director: Boris Sagal
Screenplay: Harvey Bullock and R.S. Allen
Choreography: David Winters
Music and Lyrics: see below with song titles
Running time: 96 minutes, color

CAST:

Elvis Presley (*Rusty Wells*); Shelley Fabares (*Valerie Frank*); Gary Crosby (*Andy*);

Joby Baker (*Wilbur*); Nita Talbot (*Sunny Daze*); Mary Ann Mobley (*Deena*); Fabrizio Mioni (*Romano*); Jimmy Hawkins (*Doc*); Harold J. Stone (*Big Frank*) and Jackie Cooper (*Sgt. Benson*).

SONGS:

Girl Happy - *Doc Pomus and Norman Mead*
Spring Fever - *Bill Giant, Bernie Baum and Florence Kaye*
Fort Lauderdale Chamber of Commerce - *Sid Tepper and Roy C. Bennett*
Startin' Tonight - *Lenore Rosenblatt and Victor Millrose*
Wolf Call - *Bill Giant, Bernie Baum and Florence Kaye*
Do Not Disturb - *Bill Giant, Bernie Baum and Florence Kaye*
Cross My Heart and Hope to Die - *Ben Weisman and Sid Wayne*
The Meanest Girl in Town - *Joy Byers*
Do the Clam - *Ben Weisman, Sid Wayne and Dolores Fuller*
Puppet on a String - *Sid Tepper and Roy C. Bennett*
I've Got to Find My Baby - *Joy Byers*

SYNOPSIS:

Rusty Wells and his combo work in Big Frank's Chicago nightclub but are hired to "escort" his daughter Valerie (without her knowledge) during spring break in Fort Lauderdale, Florida.

SOUNDTRACK: RCA LSP-3338

* * * * * * * * *

THE GIRL MOST LIKELY
RKO, 1957

Producer: Stanley Rubin
Director: Mitchell Leison
Screenplay: Devery Freeman
Choreography: Gower Champion
Music and Lyrics: Hugh Martin and Ralph Blane
Running time: 98 minutes, color

CAST:

Jane Powell (*Dodie*); Cliff Robertson (*Pete*); Kaye Ballard (*Marge*); Tommy Noonan (*Buzz*); Keith Andes (*Neil Patterson*); Una Merkel (*Mom*); Frank Cady (*Pop*); Judy Nugent (*Pauline*) and Kelly Brown (*Sam Kelsey*).

SONGS:

The Girl Most Likely* (*vocal by the HiLo's*); I Don't Know What I Want; We Gotta Keep Up With the Joneses; Balboa; Crazy Horse; All the Colors of the Rainbow.

music and lyrics by Nelson Riddle and Bob Russell

SYNOPSIS:

Dodie: engaged to Buzz, in love with Pete, but would like to marry millionaire Neil Patterson. What's a girl to do?

SOUNDTRACK: Capitol W-930

* * * * * * * * *

THE GIRL NEXT DOOR
20th Century Fox, 1953

Producer: Robert Bassler
Director: Richard Sale
Screenplay: Isobel Lennart; based on a story by L. Bush-Fekete and Mary Helen Fay
Choreography: Richard Barstow
Music and Lyrics: Josef Myrow and Mack Gordon
Running time: 91 minutes, color

CAST:

Dan Dailey (*Bill Carter*); June Haver (*Jeannie*); Dennis Day (*Reed Appleton*); Billy Gray (*Joe Carter*); Cara Williams (*Rosie*); Natalie Schafer (*Evelyn*); Clinton Sundberg (*Samuels*); Hayden Rorke (*Fields*) and Mary Jane Saunders (*Kitty*).

SONGS:

If I Love You a Mountain; I'm Mad About the Girl Next Door; We Girls of the Chorus; You; A Quiet Little Place in the Country; I'd Rather Have a Pal Than a Gal-Anytime; You're Doin' All Right; Nowhere Guy.

SYNOPSIS:

Jeannie, a Broadway star, buys a house next door to comic-strip illustrator Bill Carter and his son Joe--who objects when the two adults fall in love.

SOUNDTRACK: No soundtrack available

* * * * * * * * * *

THE GIRL OF THE GOLDEN WEST
Metro-Goldwyn-Mayer, 1938

Producer: William Anthony McGuire
Director: Robert Z. Leonard
Screenplay: Isabel Dawn and Boyce DeGaw; based on the play by David Belasco
Choreography: Albertina Rasch
Music and Lyrics: Sigmund Romberg and Gus Kahn
Running time: 121 minutes, B/W

CAST:

Jeanette MacDonald (*Mary Robbins*); Nelson Eddy (*Ramerez/Lt. Richard Johnson*); Walter Pidgeon (*Sheriff Jack Rance*); Leo Carillo (*"Mosquito"*); Buddy Ebsen (*"Alabama"*); Leonard Penn (*Pedro*); Priscilla Lawson (*Nina Martinez*); Bob Murphy (*"Sonora Slim"*); Olin Howland (*"Trinidad Joe"*); Cliff Edwards (*"Minstrel Joe"*); Bill Bevan (*Nick*); Brandon Trynan (*The Professor*); H.B. Warner (*Father Sienna*); Monty Woolley (*The Governor*); Charley Grapewin (*Uncle Davy*); Noah Beery, Sr. (*The General*); Bill Cody, Jr. (*Gringo*); Jeanne Ellis (*Young Mary*) and Ynez Seabury (*Wowkle*).

SONGS:

Shadows on the Moon; Soldiers of Fortune; The Wind in the Trees; Lieberstraum*; Avé Maria**; Señorita; Mariachi; The West Ain't Wild Anymore; Who Are We to Say?

 *music and lyrics by Franz Liszt and Gus Kahn
**music and lyrics by Franz Schubert

SYNOPSIS:

Mary Robbins runs a saloon called "The Polka" in California's Gold Rush country and falls in love with the notorious bandit Ramerez, incognito to her as Army lieutenant Richard Johnson. Her jealous boyfriend, sheriff Jack Rance, plans to trick Ramerez into trying to steal Mary's gold reserve so that he can capture him.

SOUNDTRACK: No soundtrack available

* * * * * * * * * *

GIRLS! GIRLS! GIRLS!
Paramount, 1962

Producer: Hal B. Wallis
Director: Norman Taurog
Screenplay: Edward Anhalt and Allan Weiss; based on a story by Allan Weiss
Choreography: Charles O'Curran
Music and Lyrics: see below with song titles
Running time: 106 minutes, color

CAST:

Elvis Presley (*Ross Carpenter*); Laurel Goodwin (*Laurel Dodge*); Stella Stevens (*Robin Gantner*); Jeremy Slate (*Wesley Johnson*); Robert Strauss (*Sam*); Benson Fong (*Kin Yung*); Guy Lee (*Chen Yung*) and Beulah Quo (*Mme. Yung*).

SONGS:

Girls! Girls! Girls! - *Jerry Leiber and Mike Stoller*
Never Let Me Go - *Ray Evans and Jay Livingston*
I Don't Wanna Be Tied - *Bill Giant, Bernie Baum and Florence Kaye*
We'll Be Together, Mama - *Charles O'Curran and Dudley Brooks*
A Boy Like Me, a Girl Like You - *Sid Tepper and Roy C. Bennett*
Earth Boy - *Sid Tepper and Roy C. Bennett*
The Nearness of You - *Ned Washington and Hoagy Carmichael*
Return to Sender - *Otis Blackwell and Winfield Scott*
Because of Love - *Ruth Batchelor and Bob Roberts*
Thanks to the Rolling Sea - *Ruth Batchelor and Bob Roberts*
Song of the Shrimp - *Sid Tepper and Roy C. Bennett*
The Walls Have Ears - *Sid Tepper and Roy C. Bennett*
We're Coming in Loaded - *Otis Blackwell and Winfield Scott*

SYNOPSIS:

Ross Carpenter, a fishing boat captain, is caught between three loves: old flame Robin, mystery girl Laurel and the *Westwind*--the sailboat he built with his late father.

SOUNDTRACK: RCA LSP-2621

* * * * * * * * *

GIVE A GIRL A BREAK
Metro-Goldwyn-Mayer, 1953

Producer: Jack Cummings
Director: Stanley Donen
Screenplay: Albert Hackett and Frances Goodrich; based on a story by Vera
        Caspary
Choreography: Stanley Donen and Gower Champion
Music and Lyrics: Burton Lane and Ira Gershwin
Running time: 81 minutes, color

CAST:

Marge Champion (*Madelyn Corlane*); Gower Champion (*Ted Sturgis*); Debbie
Reynolds (*Suzy Doolittle*); Helen Wood (*Joanna Moss*); Bob Fosse (*Bob Dowdy*);
Kurt Kasznar (*Leo Belney*); Richard Anderson (*Burton Bradshaw*); William Ching
(*Anson Pritchett*); Lurene Tuttle (*Mrs. Doolittle*); Larry Keating (*Felix Jordan*) and
Donna Martell (*Janet Hallson*).

SONGS:

Give a Girl a Break; In Our United State; It Happens Every Time; Challenge
Dance* (instrumental); Nothing is Impossible; Applause, Applause.

music by André Previn and Saul Chaplin

SYNOPSIS:

After star Janet Hallson quits her Broadway show, aspiring actresses Madelyn
Corlane, Suzy Doolittle and Joanna Moss all decide to try out for the part--with a
different member of the cast helping them along.

SOUNDTRACK: No soundtrack available

* * * * * * * * * *

GIVE MY REGARDS TO BROADWAY
20th Century Fox, 1948

Producer: Walter Morosco
Director: Lloyd Bacon
Screenplay: Samuel Hoffenstein and Elizabeth Reinhardt; based on a story by John
        Klempner
Choreography: Seymour Felix
Music and Lyrics: see below with song titles
Running time: 89 minutes, color

CAST:

Dan Dailey (*Bert Norwick*); Charles Winninger (*Albert Norwick*); Nancy Guild (*Helen Wallace*); Charlie Ruggles (*Toby Helper*); Fay Bainter (*Fay Norwick*); Barbara Lawrence (*June Norwick*); Jane Nigh (*May Norwick*); Herbert Anderson (*Frank Doty*); Charles Russell (*Arthur Waldron, Jr.*); Sig Rumann (*Dinkel*) and Howard Freeman (*Mr. Waldron*).

SONGS:

Give My Regards to Broadway - *George M. Cohan*
When Frances Dances With Me - *Benny Ryan and Sol Violinsky*
Let a Smile Be Your Umbrella - *Sammy Fain, Irving Kahal and Francis Wheeler*
Where Did You Get That Hat? - *J.W. Kelly*

SYNOPSIS:

When the death of vaudeville signals the end of the act of "Albert the Great and Family", Albert Norwick refuses to acknowledge the fact and begins to drive his family away with his obsession.

SOUNDTRACK: Caliban 6018

* * * * * * * * *

GODSPELL
Columbia, 1973

Producer: Edgar Lansbury
Director: David Greene
Screenplay: John-Michael Tebelak and David Greene; based on the stage musical
         book by John-Michael Tebelak
Choreography: Sammy Bayes
Music and Lyrics: Stephen Schwartz
Running time: 103 minutes, color

CAST:

Victor Garber (*Jesus*); David Haskell (*John/Judas*); Jerry Sroka (*Jerry*); Lynne Thigpen (*Lynne*); Katie Hanley (*Katie*); Robin Lamont (*Robin*); Gilmer McCormick (*Gilmer*); Joanne Jonas (*Joanne*); Merrell Jackson (*Merrell*) and Jeffrey Mylett (*Jeffrey*).

SONGS:

Prepare Ye The Way Of The Lord; God Save The People; Day By Day; Turn Back O Man; O, Bless The Lord My Soul; All For The Best; All Good Gifts; Light Of The World; Alas For You; By My Side*; Beautiful City; On The Willows.

*music and lyrics by Jay Hamburger and Peggy Gordon

SYNOPSIS:

The Gospel According to St. Matthew, set to music, with a group of young disciples who follow Jesus through modern-day New York City.

SOUNDTRACK: Bell 1118

* * * * * * * * * *

GOLD DIGGERS IN PARIS
Warner Bros., 1938

Producer: Sam Bischoff
Director: Ray Enright
Screenplay: Earl Baldwin and Warren Duff; based on a story by Jerry Wald, Richard Macauley and Maurice Leo, from an idea by Jerry Horwin and James Seymour
Choreography: Busby Berkeley
Music and Lyrics: Harry Warren and Al Dubin
Running time: 100 minutes, B/W

CAST:

Rudy Vallee (*Terry Moore*); Rosemary Lane (*Kay Morrow*); Hugh Herbert (*Maurice Giraud*); Allen Jenkins (*Duke Dennis*); Gloria Dickson (*Mona Moore*); Melville Cooper (*Pierre LeBrec*); Mabel Todd (*Letitia*); Fritz Feld (*Luis Leoni*); Ed Brophy (*Mike Coogan*); Curt Bois (*Padrinsky*) and Eddie "Rochester" Anderson (*Doorman*).

SONGS:

I Wanna Go Back to Bali; Listen to the Mockingbird*; Daydreaming; A Stranger in Paree; The Latin Quarter.

*music and lyrics by Richard Milburn and Septimus Winner

SYNOPSIS:

Confusion reigns when French emissary Maurice Giraud accidentally signs the dancers of the New York nightclub "Club Balleé" to perform at a dance exposition in Paris instead of the American Academy of Ballet!

SOUNDTRACK: No soundtrack available

* * * * * * * * *

GOLD DIGGERS OF 1933
Warner Bros., 1933

Producer: The Vitaphone Corporation
Director: Mervyn LeRoy
Screenplay: Erwin Gelsey, James Seymour, David Boehm and Ben Markson; based
                        on a play by Avery Hopwood
Choreography: Busby Berkeley
Music and Lyrics: Harry Warren and Al Dubin
Running time: 96 minutes, B/W

CAST:

Warren William (*J. Lawrence Bradford*); Joan Blondell (*Carol*); Aline MacMahon (*Trixie Lorraine*); Ruby Keeler (*Polly Parker*); Dick Powell (*Brad Roberts/Robert Treat Bradford*); Guy Kibbee (*Thaniel H. Peabody*); Ned Sparks (*Barney Hopkins*) and Ginger Rogers (*Fay Fortune*).

SONGS:

We're in the Money; I've Got to Sing a Torch Song; Pettin' in the Park; Remember My Forgotten Man; The Shadow Waltz.

SYNOPSIS:

Wealthy Robert Treat Bradford, incognito as struggling songwriter Brad Roberts, agrees to finance Barney Hopkins' new show if his girlfriend Polly can have a leading role in it.

SOUNDTRACK: No soundtrack available

* * * * * * * * *

GOLD DIGGERS OF 1937
Warner Bros., 1936

Producer: Hal B. Wallis
Director: Lloyd Bacon
Screenplay: Warren Duff; based on the play *Sweet Mystery of Life* by Richard
        Maibaum, Michael Wallace and George Haight
Choreography: Busby Berkeley
Music and Lyrics: Harry Warren, Al Dubin, Harold Arlen and E.Y. Harburg
Running time: 101 minutes, B/W

CAST:

Dick Powell (*Rosmer Peek*); Joan Blondell (*Norma Parry*); Glenda Farrell (*Genevieve Larkin*); Victor Moore (*J.J. Hobart*); Lee Dixon (*Boop Oglethorpe*); Osgood Perkins (*Morty Wethered*); Charles D. Brown (*John Hugo*); Rosalind Marquis (*Sally*); Irene Ware (*Irene*) and William Davidson (*Andy Callahan*).

SONGS:

The Life Insurance Song; Speaking of the Weather; With Plenty of Money and You (The Gold Diggers' Song); Let's Put Our Heads Together; All's Fair in Love and War.

SYNOPSIS:

After they imbezzle their company's funds, Morty Wethered and John Hugo get insurance agent Rosmer Peek to write a policy for ailing senior partner J.J. Hobart, a big Broadway producer--with them as the beneficiaries.

SOUNDTRACK: No soundtrack available

* * *. * * * * * * *

GOLDEN GIRL
20th Century Fox, 1951

Producer: George Jessel
Director: Lloyd Bacon
Screenplay: Walter Bullock, adaptation by Charles O'Neal and Gladys Lehman;
        based on a story by Albert Lewis and Arthur Lewis
Choreography: Seymour Felix
Music and Lyrics: see below with song titles
Running time: 108 minutes, color

124

CAST:

Mitzi Gaynor (*Lotta Crabtree*); Dale Robertson (*Tom Richmond*); Dennis Day (*Mart Taylor*); Una Merkel (*Mrs. Mary Ann Crabtree*); James Barton (*Mr. John Crabtree*); Raymond Walburn (*Cornelius*); Gene Sheldon (*Sam Jordan*) and Carmen D'Antonio (*Lola Montez*).

SONGS:

Oh, Dem Golden Slippers - *traditional*
When You and I Were Young, Maggie - *James Austin Butterfield and George W.*
                                                            Johnson
Little Brown Jug - *Joseph E. Winner*
California Moon - *Joe Cooper, George Jessel and Sam Lerner*
Beautiful Dreamer - *Stephen Foster*
De Camptown Races - *Stephen Foster*
Sunday Mornin' - *Ken Darby and Eliot Daniel*
Carry Me Back to Old Virginny - *James A. Bland*
Never - *Lionel Newman and Eliot Daniel*
When Johnny Comes Marching Home - *Patrick Sarsfield Gilmore*
Dixie - *Daniel Decatur Emmett*

SYNOPSIS:

Nineteenth century entertainer Lotta Crabtree tours the gold mining camps of California during the Civil War and falls in love with Confederate spy Tom Richmond, who is preying upon Union gold shipments disguised as "The Spaniard".

SOUNDTRACK: Caliban 6037

* * * * * * * * * *

GOODBYE, MR. CHIPS
Metro-Goldwyn-Mayer, 1969

Producer: Arthur P. Jacobs
Director: Herbert Ross
Screenplay: Terence Ratigan; based on the novel by James Hilton
Choreography: Nora Kaye
Music and Lyrics: Leslie Bricusse
Running time: 151 minutes, color

CAST:

Peter O'Toole (*Arthur Chipping*); Petula Clark (*Katherine Bridges*); Michael Redgrave (*Headmaster*); Sian Phillips (*Ursula Mossbank*); George Baker (*Lord Sutterwick*); Michael Bryant (*Max Staefel*); Jack Hedley (*William Baxter*); Alison Leggatt (*Headmaster's Wife*) and Michael Culver (*Johnny Longbridge*).

SONGS:

Fill the World With Love; Where Did My Childhood Go?; London is London; And the Sky Smiled; Apollo; When I Am Older; Walk Through the World; What Shall I Do With Today?; What a Lot of Flowers; Schooldays; When I Was Younger; You and I.

SYNOPSIS:

Arthur Chipping, a prim British schoolmaster, lives only for his "boys" until one day he meets Katherine Bridges, a chorus girl who opens his eyes to a whole new world.

SOUNDTRACK: MGM SLE-19

* * * * * * * * *

GOOD NEWS
Metro-Goldwyn-Mayer, 1947

Producer: Arthur Freed
Director: Charles Walters
Screenplay: Betty Comden and Adolph Green; based on the stage musical book by Lawrence Schwab and B.G. DeSylva
Choreography: Charles Walters
Music and Lyrics: B.G. DeSylva, Lew Brown and Ray Henderson
Running time: 95 minutes, color

CAST:

June Allyson (*Connie Lane*); Peter Lawford (*Tommy Marlowe*); Patricia Marshall (*Pat McClellan*); Joan McCracken (*Babe Dolittle*); Ray McDonald (*Bobby Turner*); Mel Tormé (*Danny*); Robert Strickland (*Peter Van Dyne III*); Connie Gilchrist (*Cora*); Clinton Sundberg (*Professor Burton Kenyon*); Lon Tindall (*Beef*) and Donald MacBride (*Coach Johnson*).

126

SONGS:

Good News (Tait College); He's a Ladies' Man; Lucky in Love; The French Lesson*; The Best Things in Life Are Free; Pass That Peace Pipe**; Just Imagine; The Varsity Drag.

*music and lyrics by Betty Comden, Adolph Green and Roger Edens
**music and lyrics by Hugh Martin, Ralph Blane and Roger Edens

SYNOPSIS:

Tait College football hero Tommy Marlowe needs to pass French in order to play in the Big Game but without Connie Lane's help he'll never make it.

SOUNDTRACK: MGM 2-SES-49ST (with *In the Good Old Summertime* and *Two Weeks With Love*)

* * * * * * * * * *

GREASE
Paramount, 1978

Producer: Robert Stigwood and Allan Carr
Director: Randal Kleiser
Screenplay: Bronte Woodard, adapted by Allan Carr; based on the stage musical
            book by Jim Jacobs and Warren Casey
Choreography: Patricia Birch
Music and Lyrics: see below with song titles
Running time: 110 minutes, color

CAST:

John Travolta (*Danny Zuko*); Olivia Newton-John (*Sandy Olson*); Stockard Channing (*Rizzo*); Jeff Conaway (*Kenickie*); Didi Conn (*Frenchy*); Dinah Manoff (*Marty*); Eve Arden (*Principal McGee*); Sid Caesar (*Coach Calhoun*); Frankie Avalon (*Teen Angel*); Alice Ghostley (*Miss Murdock*); Jamie Donnelly (*Jan*); Kelly Ward (*Putzie*); Barry Pearl (*Doody*); Michael Tucci (*Sonny*); Susan Buckner (*Patty Simcox*); Edd Byrnes (*Vince Fontaine*); Lorenzo Lamas (*Tom Chisum*); Annette Charles (*Cha-Cha*); Dennis C. Stewart (*Leo*); Dody Goodman (*Blanche*); Joan Blondell (*Vi*) and Sha-Na-Na (*Johnny Casino and the Gamblers*).

SONGS:

Grease* - *Barry Gibb*
Summer Nights - *Jim Jacobs and Warren Casey*

Look At Me, I'm Sandra Dee - *Jim Jacobs and Warren Casey*
Hopelessly Devoted to You - *John Farrar*
Greased Lightnin' - *Jim Jacobs and Warren Casey*
Beauty School Dropout - *Jim Jacobs and Warren Casey*
Rock 'n Roll is Here to Stay - *David White*
Those Magic Changes - *Jim Jacobs and Warren Casey*
Tears On My Pillow - *Sylvester Bradford and Al Lewis*
Hound Dog - *Jerry Leiber and Mike Stoller*
Born to Hand-Jive - *Jim Jacobs and Warren Casey*
Blue Moon - *Richard Rodgers and Lorenz Hart*
Sandy - *Louis St. Louis and Scott J. Simon*
There Are Worse Things I Could Do - *Jim Jacobs and Warren Casey*
You're the One That I Want - *John Farrar*
We Go Together - *Jim Jacobs and Warren Casey*

vocal by Frankie Valli

SYNOPSIS:

Australian transfer student Sandy Olson finds her romance with Rydell High's resident heartthrob Danny Zuko anything but smooth when she discovers that at school he's one of the "T-Birds".

SOUNDTRACK: PolyGram 825 095-1

* * * * * * * * *

GREASE 2
Paramount, 1982

Producer: Robert Stigwood and Allan Carr
Director: Patricia Birch
Screenplay: Ken Finkleman
Choreography: Patricia Birch
Music and Lyrics: see below with song titles
Running time: 114 minutes, color

CAST:

Maxwell Caulfield (*Michael Carrington*); Michelle Pfeiffer (*Stephanie Zinoni*); Adrian Zmed (*Johnny Nogerelli*); Lorna Luft (*Paulette Rebchuk*); Didi Conn (*Frenchy*); Eve Arden (*Principal McGee*); Sid Caesar (*Coach Calhoun*); Connie Stevens (*Miss Mason*); Tab Hunter (*Mr. Stuart*); Maureen Teefy (*Sharon Cooper*); Peter Frechette (*Louis diMucci*); Alison Price (*Rhonda Ritter*); Christopher McDonald (*"Goose"*

McKenzie); Leif Green (*Davey Jaworski*); Pamela Segall (*Dolores Rebchuk*); Dennis C. Stewart (*Balmudo*) and Dody Goodman (*Blanche*).

SONGS:

Back to School Again* - *Louis St. Louis and Howard Greenfield*
Score Tonight - *Louis St. Louis, Dominic Bugatti and Frank Musker*
Brad - *Christopher Cerf*
Cool Rider - *Dennis Linde*
Reproduction - *Dennis Linde*
Who's That Guy? - *Louis St. Louis and Howard Greenfield*
Do It For Our Country - *Rob Hegel*
Prowlin' - *Dominic Bugatti, Frank Musker and Christopher Cerf*
Charades - *Louis St. Louis and Michael Gibson*
Girl For All Seasons - *Dominic Bugatti and Frank Musker*
(Love Will) Turn Back the Hands of Time - *Louis St. Louis and Howard Greenfield*
Rock-a-Hula-Luau (Summer is Coming) - *Dominic Bugatti and Frank Musker*
We'll Be Together - *Bob Morrison and Johnny MacRae*

vocal by The Four Tops

SYNOPSIS:

The class of 1961 at Rydell High are up to their old hi-jinks as they prepare to enjoy their senior year (at the expense of the staff's sanity).

SOUNDTRACK: RSO RS-1-3803

* * * * * * * * *

THE GREAT CARUSO
Metro-Goldwyn-Mayer, 1951

Producer: Joe Pasternak
Director: Richard Thorpe
Screenplay: Sonya Levien and William Ludwig
Choreography: Peter Herman Adler
Music and Lyrics: see below with song titles
Running time: 109 minutes, color

CAST:

Mario Lanza (*Enrico Caruso*); Ann Blyth (*Dorothy Benjamin*); Dorothy Kirsten (*Louise Heggar*); Jarmila Novotna (*Maria Selka*); Richard Hageman (*Carlo Santi*);

Carl Benton Reid (*Park Benjamin*); Eduard Franz (*Giulio Gatti-Casazza*); Ludwig Donath (*Alfredo Brazzi*); Alan Napier (*Jean de Reszke*); Paul Javier (*Antonio Scotti*); Carl Milletaire (*Gino*); Shepard Menken (*Fueito*); Vincent Renno (*Tullio*); Nestor Paiva (*Egisto Barreto*); Peter Edward Price (*Enrico as a boy*); Mario Siletti (*Papa Caruso*); Angela Clarke (*Mama Caruso*); Ian Wolfe (*Hutchins*); Yvette Duguay (*Musetta*) and Argentina Brunetti (*Mrs. Barreto*).

SONGS:

Mattinata - *traditional*
The Loveliest Night of the Year - *Irving Aaronson and Paul Francis Webster*
Vesti la guibba (*Pagliacci*) - *Ruggiero Leoncavallo*
The Last Rose of Summer (*Martha*) - *Friedrich Von Flotow*
M'Appari (*Martha*) - *Friedrich Von Flotow*
Celeste Aida (*Aida*) - *Giuseppe Verdi*
Numi, Pieta (*Aida*) - *Giuseppe Verdi*
Finale (*Aida*) - *Giuseppe Verdi*
Sweethearts (*Sweethearts*) - *Victor Herbert*
Sextette (*Lucia de Lammermoor*) - *Gaetano Donizetti*
La donna è mobile (*Rigoletto*) - *Giuseppe Verdi*
Che gelida manina (*La Bohème*) - *Giacomo Puccini*
E lucevan le stelle (*Tosca*) - *Giacomo Puccini*
Avé Maria - *Franz Schubert*

SYNOPSIS:

The biography of the great opera star Enrico Caruso traces his life from his boyhood in Naples through his triumphs on the stage, his courtship amd marriage with Dorothy Benjamin and, finally, his tragic death.

SOUNDTRACK: No soundtrack available

* * * * * * * * * *

THE GREAT MUPPET CAPER
Universal, 1981

Producer: David Lazer and Frank Oz
Director: Jim Henson
Screenplay: Tom Patchett, Jay Tarses, Jerry Juhl and Jack Rose
Choreography: Anita Mann
Music and Lyrics: Joe Raposo
Running time: 95 minutes, color

CAST:

Jim Henson (*Kermit/Rowlf/Dr. Teeth/Waldorf/The Swedish Chef*); Frank Oz (*Miss Piggy/Fozzie Bear/Animal/Sam the Eagle*); Dave Goelz (*The Great Gonzo/Beauregard/Zoot/Dr. Bunsen Honeydew*); Jerry Nelson (*Floyd/Pops/Lew Zealand*); Richard Hunt (*Scooter/Statler/Sweetums/Janice/Beaker*); Steve Whitmore (*Rizzo the Rat/Lips*); Carroll Spinney (*Oscar the Grouch*); Charles Grodin (*Nicky Holiday*); Diana Rigg (*Lady Holiday*); John Cleese (*Cameo*); Robert Morley (*Cameo*); Peter Ustinov (*Cameo*) and Jack Warden (*Mike Tarkanian*).

SONGS:

Hey a Movie!; Happiness Hotel; Steppin' Out With a Star; Night Life; The First Time It Happens; Couldn't We Ride?; Piggy's Fantasy.

SYNOPSIS:

The Muppet Gang, Kermit the Frog and his friends, go to London to get the "big scoop" on a diamond robbery but soon end up implicated in the crime themselves.

SOUNDTRACK: Atlantic SD-16047

* * * * * * * * * *

GREENWICH VILLAGE
20th Century Fox, 1944

Producer: William LeBaron
Director: Walter Lang
Screenplay: Earl Baldwin and Walter Bullock, adaptation by Michael Fessier and Ernest Pagano; based on a story by Frederick Hazlitt Brennan
Choreography: Seymour Felix
Music and Lyrics: Nacio Herb Brown and Leo Robin
Running time: 82 minutes, color

CAST:

Carmen Miranda (*Princess Querida*); Don Ameche (*Kenneth Harvey*); William Bendix (*Danny O'Mara*); Vivian Blaine (*Bonnie Watson*); Felix Bressart (*Hofer*); Tony & Sally DeMarco (*Themselves*); The Revuers (*Themselves*) and B.S. Pully (*Brophy*).

SONGS:

It Goes to Your Toes; I'm Just Wild About Harry*; It's All For Art's Sake; Give Me a Bad Reputation; Whispering**.

music and lyrics by Eubie Blake and Noble Sissle
**music and lyrics by John Schonberger, Richard Coburn and Vincent Rose*

SYNOPSIS:

When composer Ken Harvey arrives in New York he goes to work as a pianist for Danny O'Mara in his Greenwich Village night club--where he falls for singer Bonnie Watson.

SOUNDTRACK: Caliban 6026

* * * * * * * * *

GUYS AND DOLLS
Metro-Goldwyn-Mayer, 1955

Producer: Samuel Goldwyn
Director: Joseph L. Mankiewicz
Screenplay: Joseph L. Mankiewicz; based on the stage musical book by Jo Swerling
　　　　　　and Abe Burrows
Choreography: Michael Kidd
Music and Lyrics: Frank Loesser
Running time: 150 minutes, color

CAST:

Marlon Brando (*Sky Masterson*); Frank Sinatra (*Nathan Detroit*); Jean Simmons (*Sarah Brown*); Vivian Blaine (*Miss Adelaide*); Robert Keith (*Lt. Brannigan*); Stubby Kaye (*Nicely-Nicely Johnson*); B.S. Pully (*Big Jule*); Johnny Silver (*Benny Southstreet*); Regis Toomey (*Arvide Abernathy*); Veda Ann Borg (*Laverne*) and Sheldon Leonard (*Harry the Horse*).

SONGS:

Fugue For Tinhorns; Follow the Fold; The Oldest, Established, Permanent, Floating Crap Game in New York; I'll Know; Pet Me, Poppa; Adelaide's Lament; Guys and Dolls; Adelaide; If I Were a Bell; A Woman in Love; Take Back Your Mink; Luck Be a Lady; Sue Me; Sit Down, You're Rockin' the Boat.

SYNOPSIS:

Damon Runyon's "musical fable" of New York City gamblers and their battles with

132

the police--and the opposite sex.

SOUNDTRACK: Motion Picture Tracks - 1 (Limited Edition)

* * * * * * * * *

GYPSY
Warner Bros., 1962

Producer: Mervyn LeRoy
Director: Mervyn LeRoy
Screenplay: Leonard Spigelgass; based on the stage musical book by Arthur Laurents
Choreography: Robert Tucker
Music and Lyrics: Jule Styne and Stephen Sondheim
Running time: 149 minutes, color

CAST:

Rosalind Russell* (*Rose Hovick*); Natalie Wood (*Rose Louise Hovick*); Karl Malden (*Herbie Sommers*); Paul Wallace (*Tulsa*); Betty Bruce (*Tessie Tura*); Parley Baer (*Mr. Kringelein*); Harry Shannon (*Grandpa*); Ann Jilliann (*June Hovick*); Suzanne Cupito (*"Baby" June*); Diane Pace (*"Baby" Louise*); Faith Dane (*Mazeppa*); Roxanne Arlen (*Electra*); Ben Lessy (*Mr. Goldstone*) and Jack Benny (*Himself*).

*vocals dubbed by Lisa Kirk

SONGS:

Small World; Some People; Baby June and Her Newsboys; Mr. Goldstone, I Love You; Little Lamb; You'll Never Get Away From Me; Dainty June and Her Farmboys; If Mama Was Married; All I Need is the Girl; Everything's Coming Up Roses; You Gotta Have a Gimmick; Let Me Entertain You; Rose's Turn.

SYNOPSIS:

From the Broadway show comes the life of Rose Louise Hovick, better known as "Gypsy Rose Lee". With the constant pushing of her frustrated stage mother, Louise and her sister June grow up in vaudeville but in its decline Louise finds a new career as a stripper in burlesque.

SOUNDTRACK: Warner Bros. 1480

H

HAIR
United Artists, 1979

Producer: Lester Persky and Michael Butler
Director: Milos Forman
Screenplay: Michael Weller; based on the stage musical book by Gerome Ragni and
           James Rado
Choreography: Twyla Tharp
Music and Lyrics: Galt MacDermot, Gerome Ragni and James Rado
Running time: 121 minutes, color

CAST:

John Savage (*Claude Bukowski*); Treat Williams (*George Berger*); Beverly D'Angelo
(*Sheila*); Annie Golden (*Jeannie*); Don Dacus (*Woof*); Dorsey Wright (*Hud*); Cheryl
Barnes (*Hud's Fiancée*); Richard Bright (*Fenton*); Nicholas Ray (*The General*); Miles
Chapin (*Steve*); Charlotte Rae (*Lady in Pink*) and Ren Woods ("*Aquarius*" *singer*).

SONGS:

(The Age of) Aquarius; Sodomy; Donna; Hashish; I'm Black; Manchester; Ain't Got
No; Colored Spade; I Got Life; Hair; LBJ; Old-Fashioned Melody; Electric Blues;
Hare Krishna; The Flesh Failures; Where Did I Go?; Black Boys/White Boys;
Walking in Space; Easy to Be Hard; 3-5-0-0; Good Morning, Starshine; Somebody to
Hold; Let the Sunshine In.

SYNOPSIS:

Claude Bukowski, a young Oklahoma farm boy on his way to his draft enlistment,
falls in with a group of New York City hippies and host of new experiences.

SOUNDTRACK: RCA CBL2-3374

* * * * * * * * *

HALF A SIXPENCE
Paramount, 1967

Producer: Charles H. Schneer and George Sidney
Director: George Sidney
Screenplay: Beverley Cross, based on his stage musical book
Choreography: Gillian Lynne

Music and Lyrics: David Heneker
Running time: 148 minutes, color

CAST:

Tommy Steele (*Arthur Kipps*); Julia Foster* (*Ann*); Cyril Ritchard (*Harry Chitterlow*); Penelope Horner (*Helen Walsingham*); Grover Dale (*Pearce*); James Villiers (*Hubert Walsingham*); Leslie Meadows (*Buggins*); Christopher Sandford (*Sid*); Aleta Morrison (*Laura Livermore*); Julia Sutton (*Flo*); Elaine Taylor (*Victoria*) and Sheila Falconer (*Kate*).

vocals dubbed by Marti Webb

SONGS:

All in the Cause of Economy; Half a Sixpence; Money to Burn; I Don't Believe a Word Of It; I'm Not Talking to You; Proper Gentleman; She's Too Far Above Me; If the Rain's Got to Fall; The Race is On; Flash, Bang, Wallop!; I Know What I Am; This is My World.

SYNOPSIS:

Arthur Kipps, a draper's assistant, suddenly inherits a fortune from his late grandfather and encounters trouble when he tries to crash society.

SOUNDTRACK: RCA LSO-1146

* * * * * * * * * *

HANS CHRISTIAN ANDERSEN
RKO, 1952

Producer: Samuel Goldwyn
Director: Charles Vidor
Screenplay: Moss Hart; based on a story by Myles Connolly
Choreography: Roland Petit
Music and Lyrics: Frank Loesser
Running time: 120 minutes, color

CAST:

Danny Kaye (*Hans Christian Andersen*); Farley Granger (*Niels*); Jeanmarie (*Doro*); Joey Walsh (*Peter*); Philip Tonge (*Otto*); Roland Petit (*The Prince*); Erik Bruhn (*The*

Hussar); John Qualen (*The Burgermaster*); John Brown (*The Schoolmaster*); Jeanne
Lafayette (*Celine*) and Peter Votrian (*Lars*).

SONGS:

The King's New Clothes; Inchworm; I'm Hans Christian Andersen; Wonderful,
Wonderful Copenhagen; Thumbelina; The Ugly Duckling; Anywhere I Wander; No
Two People.

SYNOPSIS:

A fairy tale in itself, based on the life of the Danish storyteller Hans Christian
Andersen with several of his famous fairy tales set to music.

SOUNDTRACK: No soundtrack available

* * * * * * * * *

HANSEL AND GRETEL
Cannon Films, 1987

Producer: Menahem Golan and Yoram Globus
Director: Len Talan
Screenplay: Nancy Weems and Len Talan; based on the fairy tale by the Brothers
           Grimm
Choreography: Christine Oren
Music and Lyrics: Michael Cohen, Enid Futterman and Nancy Weems, based on
                  themes from Engelbert Humperdinck
Running time: 84 minutes, color

CAST:

David Warner (*Stefan*); Cloris Leachman (*Grizelda*); Hugh Pollard (*Hansel*); Nicola
Stapleton (*Gretel*); Emily Richard (*Maria*); Susie Miller (*Marta*); Eugene Kline
(*Farmer*) and Warren M. Feigin (*Baker*).

SONGS:

Punch & Judy's Dance; The Fairy Song; Oh, What a Day; Sugar and Spice; The
Witch is Dead.

SYNOPSIS:

Classic fairy tale about two children who get lost in the woods while picking berries

136

and stumble upon a house made of gingerbread. Their delight soons turns to horror when the owner turns out to be an evil witch!

SOUNDTRACK: No soundtrack available

* * * * * * * * *

THE HAPPIEST MILLIONAIRE
Buena Vista, 1967

Producer: Walt Disney
Director: Norman Tokar
Screenplay: A.J. Carothers; based on the book and play by Kyle Crichton and Cordelia Drexl-Biddle
Choreography: Marc Breaux and Dee Dee Wood
Music and Lyrics: Richard M. Sherman and Robert B. Sherman
Running time: 164 minutes, color

CAST:

Fred MacMurray (*Anthony J. Drexl-Biddle*); Tommy Steele (*John Lawless*); Greer Garson (*Cordelia Drexl-Biddle*); Geraldine Page (*Mrs. Duke*); Gladys Cooper (*Aunt Mary*); Lesley Ann Warren (*Cordy Drexl-Biddle*); John Davidson (*Angie Duke*); Hermione Baddeley (*Mrs. Worth*); Paul Peterson (*Tony Drexl-Biddle*); Eddie Hodges (*Livingston Drexl-Biddle*) and Joyce Bulifant (*Rosemary*).

SONGS:

Fortuosity; What's Wrong With That?; Watch Your Footwork; Valentine Candy; Strengthen the Dwelling; I'll Always Be Irish; Bye-Yum Pum Pum; Are We Dancing?; Detroit; There Are Those; Let's Have a Drink On It; It Won't Be Long 'Til Christmas.

SYNOPSIS:

Anthony J. Drexl-Biddle, an eccentric Philadelphia millionaire, finds that his well-ordered but unconventional life begins to change when his daughter Cordy decides to marry the son of a stuffy New York society matron.

SOUNDTRACK: Buena Vista 5001

* * * * * * * * *

137

HAPPY LANDING
20th Century Fox, 1938

Producer: David Hempstead
Director: Roy Del Ruth
Screenplay: Milton Sperling and Boris Engster
Choreography: Harry Losee
Music and Lyrics: Sam Pokrass and Jack Yellen
Running time: 102 minutes, B/W

CAST:

Sonja Henie (*Trudy Erickson*); Don Ameche (*Jimmy Hall*); Ethel Merman (*Flo Kelly*); Cesar Romero (*Duke Sargent*); Jean Hersholt (*Herr Erickson*); Billy Gilbert (*Counter Man*); Wally Vernon (*Al Mahoney*) and El Brendel (*Yonnie*).

SONGS:

Hot and Happy; You Appeal to Me; A Gypsy Told Me; You Are the Words to the Music in My Heart; Yonnie and His Oompah.

SYNOPSIS:

In order to get Norwegian skater Trudy Erickson all to himself, Jimmy Hall must first get Duke Sargent's mind on someone else--like singer Flo Kelly.

SOUNDTRACK: No soundtrack available

* * * * * * * * * *

HARUM SCARUM
Metro-Goldwyn-Mayer, 1965

Producer: Sam Katzman
Director: Gene Nelson
Screenplay: Gerald Drayson Adams
Choreography: Earl Barton
Music and Lyrics: see below with song titles
Running time: 85 minutes, color

CAST:

Elvis Presley (*Johnny Tyrone*); Mary Ann Mobley (*Princess Shalimar*); Fran Jeffries (*Aishah*); Michael Ansara (*Prince Dragna*); Philip Reed (*King Toranshah*); Jay

Novello (*Zacha*); Theo Marcuse (*Sinan*); Billy Barty (*Baba*); Vicki Malkin (*Sari*) and Ryck Rydon (*Mustapha*).

SONGS:

My Desert Serenade - *Stanley Jay Gelber*
Go East-Young Man - *Bill Giant, Bernie Baum and Florence Kaye*
Mirage - *Bill Giant, Bernie Baum and Florence Kaye*
Kismet - *Sid Tepper and Roy C. Bennett*
Shake That Tambourine - *Bill Giant, Bernie Baum and Florence Kaye*
Hey, Little Girl - *Joy Byers*
Golden Coins - *Bill Giant, Bernie Baum and Florence Kaye*
So Close, Yet So Far (From Paradise) - *Joy Byers*
Harem Holiday - *Peter Andreoli, Vince Poncia, Jr. and Jimmie Crane*

SYNOPSIS:

On a goodwill tour in the Middle East American film star Johnny Tyrone is kidnapped by an evil prince and ordered to execute the ruling king.

SOUNDTRACK: RCA APL1-2558

* * * * * * * * *

THE HARVEY GIRLS
Metro-Goldwyn-Mayer, 1946

Producer: Arthur Freed
Director: George Sidney
Screenplay: Edmund Beloin, Nathaniel Curtis, Harry Crane, James O'Hanlon, Samson Rafaelson and Kay Van Riper; based on the novel by Samuel Hopkins
Choreography: Robert Alton
Music and Lyrics: Harry Warren and Johnny Mercer
Running time: 101 minutes, color

CAST:

Judy Garland (*Susan Bradley*); John Hodiak (*Ned Trent*); Ray Bolger (*Chris Maule*); Angela Lansbury* (*Em*); Preston Foster (*Judge Sam Purvis*); Virginia O'Brien (*Alma*); Marjorie Main (*Sonora Cassidy*); Chill Wills (*H.H. Hartsey*); Kenny Baker (*Terry O'Halloran*); Selena Royle (*Miss Bliss*); Cyd Charisse** (*Deborah*); Ruth Brady (*Ethel*); Catherine McLeod (*Louise*); Jack Lambert (*Marty Peters*); Edward Earle (*Jed Adams*); Virginia Hunter (*Jane*) and William "Bill" Phillips (*John Henry*).

*vocals dubbed by Virginia Rees
**vocals dubbed by Betty Wilson

SONGS:

In the Valley; Wait and See; On the Atchison, Topeka and the Santa Fe; The Train Must Be Fed; Oh You Kid; It's a Great Big World; The Wild Wild West; Swing Your Partner 'Round and 'Round.

SYNOPSIS:

Susan Bradley goes out West to Sand Creek, Arizona as a mail-order bride but when it falls through she decides to become a "Harvey Girl"--one of the young girls who worked as waitresses in Fred Harvey's chain of restaurants along the railways.

SOUNDTRACK: Hollywood Soundstage 5002

* * * * * * * * *

HELLO, DOLLY!
20th Century Fox, 1969

Producer: Ernest Lehman
Director: Gene Kelly
Screenplay: Ernest Lehman; based on the stage musical book by Michael Stewart
Choreography: Michael Kidd
Music and Lyrics: Jerry Herman
Running time: 146 minutes, color

CAST:

Barbra Streisand (*Dolly Levi*); Walter Matthau (*Horace Vandergelder*); Michael Crawford (*Cornelius Hackl*); Marianne McAndrew (*Irene Molloy*); Tommy Tune (*Ambrose Kemper*); Danny Lockin (*Barnaby Tucker*); E.J. Peaker (*Minnie Fay*); Joyce Ames (*Ermengarde*) and Louis Armstrong (*Louis*).

SONGS:

Just Leave Everything to Me; It Takes a Woman; Put On Your Sunday Clothes; Ribbons Down My Back; Dancing; Before the Parade Passes By; Elegance; Love is Only Love; Hello, Dolly; It Only Takes a Moment.

SYNOPSIS:

Musical version of Thornton Wilder's *The Matchmaker* has widow Dolly Levi matchmaking for everyone, including herself with wealthy but gruff Horace Vandergelder.

SOUNDTRACK: 20th Century ST-102

* * * * * * * * *

HELLO, FRISCO, HELLO
20th Century Fox, 1943

Producer: Milton Sperling
Director: Bruce Humberstone
Screenplay: Robert Ellis, Helen Logan and Richard Macauley
Choreography: Val Raset
Music and Lyrics: see below with song titles
Running time: 98 minutes, color

CAST:

Alice Faye (*Trudy Evans*); John Payne (*Johnny Cornell*); Jack Oakie (*Dan Daley*); Lynn Bari (*Bernice Croft*); June Havoc (*Beulah Clancy*); Laird Cregar (*Sam Weaver*); Ward Bond (*Sharkey*); Aubrey Mather (*Charles Cochran*); George Barbier (*Colonel Weatherby*) and John Archer (*Ned Clark*).

SONGS:

By the Watermelon Vine, Lindy Lou - *Thomas S. Allen*
Hello, Frisco, Hello - *Louis A. Hirsch and Gene Buck*
You'll Never Know - *Harry Warren and Mack Gordon*
Ragtime Cowboy Joe - *Grant Clark, Maurice Abrahams and Lewis E. Muir*
Sweet Cider Time - *Percy Wenrich and Joseph McCarthy*
Doin' the Grizzly Bear - *Irving Berlin and George Botsford*
It's Tulip Time in Holland - *Richard A. Whiting and Dave Radford*
Why Do They Always Pick On Me? - *Harry Von Tilzer and Stanley Murphy*
Bedelia - *Jean Schwartz and William Jerome*
Has Anybody Seen Kelly? - *Will Letters, C.W. Murphy and William J. McKenna*
By the Light of the Silvery Moon - *Edward Madden and Gus Edwards*
Gee, But It's Great to Meet a Friend From Your Own Home Town - *James McGavish, Fred Fisher and William G. Tracey*
Strike Up the Band, Here Comes a Sailor - *Andrew B. Sterling and Charles P. Ward*

SYNOPSIS:

San Francisco Barbary Coast entertainers Johnny Cornell and Company work their way to the top but Johnny yearns to be accepted by Nob Hill society.

SOUNDTRACK: Caliban 6005 (with *Spring Parade*)

* * * * * * * * * *

HERE COMES THE GROOM
Paramount, 1951

Producer: Frank Capra
Director: Frank Capra
Screenplay: Virginia Van Upp, Liam O'Brien and Myles Connolly; based on a story
            by Robert Riskin and Liam O'Brien
Choreography: Charles O'Curran
Music and Lyrics: Ray Evans and Jay Livingston
Running time: 113 minutes, B/W

CAST:

Bing Crosby (*Peter Garvey*); Jane Wyman (*Emmadel Jones*); Alexis Smith (*Winifred Stanley*); Franchot Tone (*Wilbur Stanley*); James Barton (*Pa Jones*); Robert Keith (*George Degnan*); Jacques Gencel (*Robert "Bobby" DuLac*); Beverly Washburn (*Suzi*); Connie Gilchrist (*Ma Jones*); Walter Catlett (*Mr. McGonigle*); Alan Reed (*Mr. Walter Godfrey*); Minna Gombell (*Mrs. Godfrey*); Howard Freeman (*Governor*); Maidel Turner (*Aunt Abby*); H.B. Warner (*Uncle Elihu*); Nicholas Joy (*Uncle Prentise*); Ian Wolfe (*Uncle Adam*); Ellen Corby (*Mrs. McGonigle*); Louis Armstrong (*Himself*); Dorothy Lamour (*Herself*); Phil Harris (*Himself*); Frank Fontaine (*Himself*) and Anna Maria Alberghetti (*Theresa*).

SONGS:

Caro Nome (*Rigoletto*)*; Your Own Little House; Misto Cristofo Columbo; In the Cool, Cool, Cool of the Evening**; Bonne Nuit.

 **music and lyrics by Giuseppe Verdi*
 ***music and lyrics by Hoagy Carmichael and Johnny Mercer*

SYNOPSIS:

Reporter Pete Garvey comes home from Paris with two war orphans, Bobby and

142

Suzi, to find that his childhood sweetheart Emmadel Jones is about to marry multi-millionaire Wilbur Stanley.

SOUNDTRACK: Decca DL-4262

* * * * * * * * * *

HERE COME THE GIRLS
Paramount, 1953

Producer: Paul Jones
Director: Claude Binyon
Screenplay: Edmund Hartmann and Hal Kanter; based on a story by Edmund
          Hartmann
Choreography: Nick Castle
Music and Lyrics: Ray Evans and Jay Livingston
Running time: 77 minutes, color

CAST:

Bob Hope (*Stanley Snodgrass*); Tony Martin (*Allen Trent*); Arlene Dahl (*Irene Bailey*); Rosemary Clooney (*Daisy Crockett*); Millard Mitchell (*Albert Snodgrass*); William Demarest (*Detective Dennis Logan*); Fred Clark (*Harry Fraser*); Robert Strauss (*"Jack the Slasher"*); Zamah Cunningham (*Mama Snodgrass*) and Frank Orth (*Mr. Hungerford*).

SONGS:

Girls Are Here to Stay/Never So Beautiful; You Got Class; Desire; When You Love Someone; Ali Baba Be My Baby; Heavenly Days; See the Circus.

SYNOPSIS:

In turn-of-the-century New York inept chorus boy Stanley Snodgrass is used as a decoy to catch crazed killer "Jack the Slasher" who's after the show's star, Irene Bailey.

SOUNDTRACK: No soundtrack available

* * * * * * * * * *

HIGHER AND HIGHER
RKO, 1943

Producer: Tim Whelan
Director: Tim Whelan
Screenplay: Jay Dratler, Ralph Spence, William Bowers and Howard Harris; based
             on the play by Gladys Hurlbut and Joshua Logan
Choreography: Ernst Matray
Music and Lyrics: Jimmy McHugh and Harold Adamson
Running time: 90 minutes, B/W

CAST:

Michele Morgan (*Millie*); Jack Haley (*Mike O'Brien*); Frank Sinatra (*Frank Sinatra*);
Leon Errol (*Cyrus Drake*); Marcy McGuire (*Mickey*); Victor Borge (*Sir Victor
Fitzroy Victor/Joe Brown*); Mary Wickes (*Sandy Brooks*); Elizabeth Risdon (*Mrs.
Georgia Keating*); Barbara Hale (*Katherine Keating*); Mel Tormé (*Marty*); Paul
Hartman (*Byngham*); Grace Hartman (*Hilda*); Dooley Wilson (*Oscar*); Rex Evans
(*Douglas Green*) and Ivy Scott (*Miss Whiffin*).

SONGS:

A Most Important Affair; Today I'm a Debutante; Disgustingly Rich*; I Couldn't
Sleep a Wink Last Night; The Music Stopped; I Saw You First; A Lovely Way to
Spend an Evening; You're On Your Own; Minuet in Boogie.

music and lyrics by Richard Rodgers and Lorenz Hart

SYNOPSIS:

Businessman Cyrus Drake is on the verge of bankruptcy so he and his household
staff decide to try and pass off Millie the scullery maid as his daughter and marry
her off to a rich man.

SOUNDTRACK: Hollywood Soundstage 411

* * * * * * * * * *

HIGH SOCIETY
Metro-Goldwyn-Mayer, 1956

Producer: Sol C. Siegel
Director: Charles Walters
Screenplay: John Patrick; based on a play by Philip Barry
Choreography: Charles Walters
Music and Lyrics: Cole Porter
Running time: 112 minutes, color

Bing Crosby (*C.K. Dexter-Haven*); Grace Kelly (*Tracy Lord*); Frank Sinatra (*Mike Connor*); Celeste Holm (*Liz Imbrie*); John Lund (*George Kittredge*); Louis Calhern (*Uncle Willie*); Sidney Blackmer (*Seth Lord*); Margalo Gillmore (*Mrs. Seth Lord*); Lydia Reed (*Carloine Lord*) and Louis Armstrong (*Himself*).

SONGS:

High Society Calypso; Little One; Who Wants to Be a Millionaire?; True Love; You're Sensational; I Love You, Samantha; Now You Has Jazz; Well, Did You Evah!; Mind If I Make Love to You?

SYNOPSIS:

Musical adaptation of *The Philadelphia Story* has wealthy socialite Tracy Lord about to be married to George Kittredge but finds things begin to get a bit complicated when her ex-husband Dexter moves back in next door.

SOUNDTRACK: Capitol SW-750

* * * * * * * * *

HIT THE DECK
Metro-Goldwyn-Mayer, 1955

Producer: Joe Pasternak
Director: Roy Rowland
Screenplay: Sonya Levien and William Ludwig; based on the stage musical book by Herbert Fields
Choreography: Hermes Pan
Music and Lyrics: see below with song titles
Running time: 113 minutes, color

CAST:

Jane Powell (*Susan Smith*); Tony Martin (*Chief Boatswain's Mate William F. "Bilge" Clark*); Debbie Reynolds (*Carol Pace*); Walter Pidgeon (*Read Admiral Daniel Xavier Smith*); Vic Damone (*Rico Ferrari*); Russ Tamblyn (*Danny Xavier Smith*); Gene Raymond (*Wendell Craig*); Ann Miller (*Ginger*); J. Carrol Naish (*Mr. Peroni*); Kay Armen (*Mrs. Ottavio Ferrari*); Richard Anderson (*Lt. Jackson*); Jane Darwell (*Jenny*); Henry Slate (*Shore Patrol Officer*) and Alan King (*Shore Patrol Officer*).

Hallelujah! - *Vincent Youmans, Leo Robin and Clifford Grey*
Keepin' Myself For You - *Vincent Youmans and Sidney Clare*
Lucky Bird - *Vincent Youmans, Leo Robin and Clifford Grey*
A Kiss or Two - *Vincent Youmans and Leo Robin*
Why, Oh, Why? - *Vincent Youmans, Leo Robin and Clifford Grey*
Sometimes I'm Happy - *Vincent Youmans and Irving Caesar*
I Know That You Know - *Vincent Youmans and Anne Caldwell*
Lady From the Bayou - *Vincent Youmans and Leo Robin*
Ciribiribin - *Alberto Pestalozza and Rudolf Thaler*
More Than You Know - *Vincent Youmans, Edward Eliscu and Billy Rose*
Join the Navy/Loo-Loo - *Vincent Youmans, Leo Robin and Clifford Grey*

SYNOPSIS:

When on leave in San Francisco, shipmates Bilge Clark, Rico Ferrari and Danny Smith try to rescue Danny's sister Susan from lecherous stage star Wendell Craig and find they must keep on the run from the Shore Patrol.

SOUNDTRACK: MGM 2-SES-43ST (with *The Pirate* and *Pagan Love Song*)

* * * * * * * * *

HOLIDAY IN MEXICO
Metro-Goldwyn-Mayer, 1946

Producer: Joe Pasternak
Director: George Sidney
Screenplay: Isobel Lennart; based on a story by William Kozlenko
Choreography: Stanley Donen
Music and Lyrics: see below with song titles
Running time: 127 minutes, color

CAST:

Walter Pidgeon (*Jeffrey Evans*); José Iturbi (*Himself*); Roddy McDowall (*Stanley Owen*); Jane Powell (*Christine Evans*); Ilona Massey (*Countess Toni Karpathy*); Xavier Cugat (*Himself*); Hugo Haas (*Angus*); Mikhail Rasumny (*Mr. Baranga*) and Helene Stanley (*Yvette Baranga*).

SONGS:

Holiday in Mexico - *Ralph Freed and Sammy Fain*

Italian Street Song (*Naughty Marietta*) - *Victor Herbert and Rida Johnson Young*
Goodnight Sweetheart - *Ray Noble, James Campbell and Reg Connelly*
The Music Goes 'Round and 'Round - *Red Hodgson, Ed Farley and Michael Riley*
You, So It's You - *Nacio Herb Brown and Earl Brent*
And Dreams Remain - *Ralph Freed and Raoul Soler*
I Think Of You - *Sergei Rachmaninoff, Jack Elliott and Don Marcotte*
Avé Maria - *Franz Schubert*

SYNOPSIS:

Christine Evans, daughter of U.S. Ambassador to Mexico Jeffrey Evans, is upset over her widowed father's involvement with Toni Karpathy, a singer with Xavier Cugat's orchestra. In her confusion she imagines that she is in love with José Iturbi--much to the chagrin of her boyfriend Stanley.

SOUNDTRACK: No soundtrack available

* * * * * * * * *

HOLIDAY INN
Paramount, 1942

Producer: Mark Sandrich
Director: Mark Sandrich
Screenplay: Claude Binyon, adaptation by Elmer Rice; based on an idea by Irving Berlin
Choreography: Danny Dare
Music and Lyrics: Irving Berlin
Running time: 100 minutes, B/W

CAST:

Bing Crosby (*Jim Hardy*); Fred Astaire (*Ted Hanover*); Marjorie Reynolds (*Linda Mason*); Virginia Dale (*Lila Dixon*); Walter Abel (*Danny Reid*); Louise Beavers (*Mamie*); Irving Bacon (*Gus*); Marek Windheim (*François*); James Bell (*Dunbar*); John Gallaudet (*Parker*); Shelby Bacon (*Vanderbilt*) and Joan Arnold (*Daphne*).

SONGS:

I'll Capture Her Heart; Lazy; You're Easy to Dance With; White Christmas; Happy Holidays; Holiday Inn; Let's Start the New Year Right; Abraham, Abraham; It's My Heart; I Gotta Say I Love You Cause I Can't Tell a Lie; Easter Parade; Let's Say It With Firecrackers; Plenty to Be Thankful For.

Song-and-dance man Jim Hardy decides to open his Connecticut farm as a country inn that will only be open on holidays--fifteen of them. But soon his star--and girlfriend--Linda Mason is being lured away by Jim's former partner, Ted Hanover, with the promise of a Hollywood film contract.

SOUNDTRACK: Sountrak 112

* * * * * * * * *

HOLLYWOOD OR BUST
Paramount, 1956

Producer: Hal B. Wallis
Director: Frank Tashlin
Screenplay: Erna Lazarus, based on her story
Choreography: Charles O'Curran
Music and Lyrics: Sammy Fain and Paul Francis Webster
Running time: 94 minutes, color

CAST:

Dean Martin (*Steve Wiley*); Jerry Lewis (*Malcolm Smith*); Anita Ekberg (*Herself*); Pat Crowley (*Terry*); Maxie Rosenbloom (*Bookie Benny*); Willard Waterman (*Neville*) and Jack McElroy (*Stupid Sam*).

SONGS:

Hollywood or Bust; The Wild and Woolly West; Let's Be Friendly; A Day in the Country; It Looks Like Love.

SYNOPSIS:

Malcolm Smith desperately wants to go to Hollywood to meet his idol, Anita Ekberg, so his pal Steve gets the idea to forge some lottery tickets that allow them to win a car and travel cross-country to the movie capitol.

SOUNDTRACK: No soundtrack available

* * * * * * * * *

148

HOUND-DOG MAN
20th Century Fox, 1959

Producer: Jerry Wald
Director: Don Siegel
Screenplay: Fred Gipson and Winston Miller; based on the novel by Fred Gipson
Choreography: Josephine Earl
Music and Lyrics: Ken Darby, Frankie Avalon, Sol Ponti, Robert Macucci, Pete De Angelis, Doc Pomus and Mort Shuman
Running time: 87 minutes, color

CAST:

Fabian (*Clint McKinney*); Carol Lynley (*Dony Waller*); Stuart Whitman (*Blackie Scantling*); Arthur O'Connell (*Aaron McKinney*); Dodie Stevens (*Nita Stringer*); Betty Field (*Cora McKinney*); Royal Dano (*"Fiddling Tom" Waller*); Margo Moore (*Susie Bell*); Claude Akins (*Hog Peyson*); Edgar Buchanan (*Doc Cole*); Jane Darwell (*Grandma Wilson*); Dennis Holmes (*Spud McKinney*); L.Q. Jones (*Dave Wilson*) and Virginia Gregg (*Amy Waller*).

SONGS:

Hound-Dog Man; I'm Growin' Up; Single; This Friendly World; Pretty Little Girl; What Big Boy?

SYNOPSIS:

Farm boy Clint McKinney wants to be a "hound-dog man" like his best friend Blackie Scantling but he soon comes to see that the free-and-easy lifestyle is not for him.

SOUNDTRACK: No soundtrack available

* * * * * * * * *

HOW TO SUCCEED IN BUSINESS WITHOUT REALLY TRYING
United Artists, 1967

Producer: David Swift
Director: David Swift
Screenplay: David Swift; based on the stage musical book by Abe Burrows
Choreography: Dale Moreda
Music and Lyrics: Frank Loesser
Running time: 121 minutes, color

CAST:

Robert Morse (*J. Pierrepont Finch*); Michele Lee (*Rosemary Pilkington*); Rudy Vallee (*J.B. Biggley*); Anthony Teague (*Bud Frump*); Maureen Arthur (*Hedy LaRue*); Murray Matheson (*Benjamin Ovington*); Kay Reynolds (*Smitty*); John Myhers (*Mr. Bratt*); Sammy Smith (*Mr. Twimble/Wally Womper*); Robert Q. Lewis (*Mr. Tackaberry*); Ruth Kobart (*Miss Jones*); Anne Seymour (*Mrs. Biggley*); Dan Tobin (*Mr. Johnson*); John Holland (*Mr. Matthews*); Paul Hartman (*Mr. Toynbee*) and Justin Smith (*Mr. Jenkins*).

SONGS:

How To; Coffee Break; The Company Way; A Secretary is Not a Toy; Been a Long Day; I Believe in You; Grand Old Ivy; Rosemary; Gotta Stop That Man; Brotherhood of Man.

SYNOPSIS:

J. Pierrepont Finch is an ambitious young man who, with the help of a book entitled *How to Succeed in Business Without Really Trying*, manages to rise to the head of World Wide Wicket Corporation with astonishing speed.

SOUNDTRACK: United Artists 5151

* * * * * * * * *

HUCKLEBERRY FINN
United Artists, 1974

Producer: Arthur P. Jacobs
Director: J. Lee Thompson
Screenplay: Richard M. Sherman and Robert B. Sherman; based on the novel by
         Mark Twain
Choreography: Marc Breaux
Music and Lyrics: Richard M. Sherman and Robert B. Sherman
Running time: 117 minutes, color

CAST:

Jeff East (*Huckleberry Finn*); Paul Winfield (*Jim*); Harvey Korman (*"The King"*); David Wayne (*"The Duke"*); Arthur O'Connell (*Colonel Grangerford*); Gary Merrill (*Pap*); Natalie Trundy (*Mrs. Loftus*); Lucille Benson (*Widder Douglas*); Kim O'Brien (*Maryjane*); Jean Fay (*Susan*); Ruby Leftwich (*Miss Watson*) and Odessa Cleveland (*Jim's Wife*).

SONGS:

Freedom*; Huckleberry Finn; Someday, Honey Darlin'; Cairo, Illinois; A Rose in a Bottle; Royalty; The Royal Nonesuch; What's Right-What's Wrong?; Rotten Luck.

*vocal by Roberta Flack

SYNOPSIS:

Musical version of Mark Twain's tale of orphan Huckleberry Finn and his adventures on the Mississippi River with runaway slave Jim.

SOUNDTRACK: United Artists LA-229-F

I

ICELAND
20th Century Fox, 1942

Producer: William LeBaron
Director: Bruce Humberstone
Screenplay: Robert Ellis and Helen Logan
Choreography: James Gonzales
Music and Lyrics: Harry Warren and Mack Gordon
Running time: 79 minutes, B/W

CAST:

Sonja Henie (*Katine Jonsdottir*); John Payne (*Corporal James Murfin*); Jack Oakie (*Slip Riggs*); Felix Bressart (*Papa*); Osa Massen (*Helga Jonsdottir*); Joan Morrill (*Adele Wynn*); Fritz Feld (*Tegnar*); Sterling Holloway (*Sverdrup Svenson*); Adeline deWalt Reynolds (*Grandma*); Ludwig Stossel (*Valtyr's Father*); Duke Adlon (*Valtyr*); Ilka Grunig (*Aunt Sophie*) and Sammy Kaye (*Himself*).

SONGS:

You Can't Say No to a Soldier; Lovers' Knot; Let's Bring New Glory to Old Glory; There Will Never Be Another You; I Like a Military Tune.

SYNOPSIS:

Marine corporal Jim Murfin is posted to Reykjevik, Iceland and decides to make a play for pretty Katine Jonsdottir--and is shocked to discover that they are now considered to be engaged!

SOUNDTRACK: No soundtrack available

* * * * * * * * *

I COULD GO ON SINGING
United Artists, 1963

Producer: Stuart Millar and Lawrence Turman
Director: Ronald Neame
Screenplay: Mayo Simon; based on a story by Robert Dozier
Music and Lyrics: see below with song titles
Running time: 99 minutes, color

CAST:

Judy Garland (*Jenny Bowman*); Dirk Bogarde (*Dr. David Donne*); Jack Klugman (*George Kogan*); Aline MacMahon (*Ida*); Gregory Phillips (*Matt Donne*) and Pauline Jameson (*Miss Plimpton*).

SONGS:

I Am the Monarch of the Sea (*H.M.S. Pinafore*) - *Sir Arthur Sullivan and Sir William Gilbert*
Hello Bluebird - *Cliff Friend*
It Never Was You - *Kurt Weill and Maxwell Anderson*
By Myself - *Arthur Schwartz and Howard Dietz*
I Could Go On Singing - *Harold Arlen and E.Y. Harburg*

SYNOPSIS:

Singer Jenny Bowman is in London for an engagement at the Palladium and seeks out her ex-lover David Donne and the son, Matt, she gave him to raise in favor of her career.

SOUNDTRACK: Capitol SW-1861

* * * * * * * * *

I DREAM TOO MUCH
RKO, 1935

Producer: Pandro S. Berman
Director: John Cromwell
Screenplay: Edmund North and James Gow; based on a story by Elsie Finn and David G. Wittels
Choreography: Hermes Pan
Music and Lyrics: Jerome Kern and Dorothy Fields
Running time: 95 minutes, B/W

CAST:

Lily Pons (*Annette Monard Street*); Henry Fonda (*Jonathan Street*); Eric Blore (*Roger Briggs*); Osgood Perkins (*Paul Darcy*); Lucien Littlefield (*Hubert Dilley*); Esther Dale (*Mrs. Dilley*); Lucille Ball (*Gwendolyn Dilley*); Mischa Auer (*Pianist*); Paul Porcasi (*Tito*) and Scotty Beckett (*Boy on Merry-Go-Round*).

SONGS:

The Bell Song (*Lakme*)*; The Jockey on the Carousel; I Got Love; I'm the Echo; I Dream Too Much; Caro Nome (*Rigoletto*)*.

 **music and lyrics by Leo Delibes*
 ***music and lyrics by Giuseppe Verdi*

SYNOPSIS:

Struggling composer Jonathan Street decides to help his wife Annette become an opera star while she does her best to get his music published.

SOUNDTRACK: Grapon 15 (with *One Night of Love*)

* * * * * * * * * *

I'LL GET BY
20th Century Fox, 1950

Producer: William Perlberg
Director: Richard Sale
Screenplay: Richard Sale and Mary Loos; based on a story by Robert Ellis, Helen
          Logan and Pamela Harris
Choreography: Larry Ceballos
Music and Lyrics: see below with song titles·
Running time: 82 minutes, color

CAST:

June Haver (*Liza Martin*); William Lundigan (*William Spencer*); Gloria De Haven (*Terry Martin*); Dennis Day (*Freddy Lee*); Harry James (*Himself*); Thelma Ritter (*Miss Murphy*); Steve Allen (*Peter Pepper*); Danny Davenport (*Chester Dooley*); Jeanne Crain (*Herself*); Victor Mature (*Himself*); Reginald Gardiner (*Himself*) and Dan Dailey (*Himself*).

SONGS:

Deep in the Heart of Texas - *Don Swander and June Hershey*
Taking a Chance on Love - *Vernon Duke, John LaTouche and Ted Fetter*
I'll Get By - *Fred Ahlert and Roy Turk*
There Will Never Be Another You - *Harry Warren and Mack Gordon*
MacNamara's Band - *Shamus O'Connor, John J. Stamford, Red Latham, Wamp
          Carlson and Guy Bonham*

154

I've Got the World on a String - *Harold Arlen and Ted Koehler*
You Make Me Feel So Young - *Josef Myrow and Mack Gordon*
Yankee Doodle Blues - *George Gershwin, Irving Caesar and B.G. DeSylva*
Fifth Avenue - *Harry Warren and Mack Gordon*
No Love, No Nothin' - *Harry Warren and Leo Robin*
It's Been a Long, Long Time - *Jule Styne and Sammy Cahn*

SYNOPSIS:

Remake of *Tin Pan Alley* finds song publishers Bill Spencer and Freddy Lee convincing Liza and Terry Martin to help plug their songs.

SOUNDTRACK: Titania 504 (with *Look For the Silver Lining*)

* * * * * * * * *

I'LL SEE YOU IN MY DREAMS
Warner Bros., 1952

Producer: Louis F. Edelman
Director: Michael Curtiz
Screenplay: Melville Shavelson and Jack Rose
Choreography: LeRoy Prinz
Music and Lyrics: Gus Kahn (collaborator listed below with song titles)
Running time: 113 minutes, color

CAST:

Doris Day (*Grace LeBoy Kahn*); Danny Thomas (*Gus Kahn*); Frank Lovejoy (*Walter Donaldson*); Patrice Wymore (*Gloria Knight*); James Gleason (*Fred Thompson*); Mary Wickes (*Anna*); Julie Oshins (*Johnny Martin*); Jim Backus (*Sam Harris*); Minna Gombell (*Mrs. LeBoy*); Harry Antrim (*Mr. LeBoy*); William Forrest (*Florenz Ziegfeld*); Dick Simmons (*Egbert Van Alstyne*); Ray Kellogg (*John McCormack*); Christy Olson (*Donald Kahn, age 5*); Robert Lyden (*Donald Kahn, age 8*); Mimi Gibson (*Irene Kahn, age 3*) and Bunny Lewbel (*Irene Kahn, age 6*).

SONGS:

I Wish I Had a Girl - *with Grace LeBoy*
Memories - *with Egbert Van Alstyne*
Pretty Baby - *with Egbert Van Alstyne and Tony Jackson*
The One I Love Belongs to Somebody Else - *with Isham Jones*
Nobody's Sweetheart - *with Ernie Erdman, Billy Meyers and Elmer Schoebel*
My Buddy - *with Walter Donaldson*

Toot Toot Tootsie - *with Ernie Erdman and Dan Russo*
It Had to Be You - *with Isham Jones*
Yes Sir, That's My Baby - *with Walter Donaldson*
Swingin' Down the Lane - *with Isham Jones*
Carolina in the Morning - *with Walter Donaldson*
Love Me or Leave Me - *with Walter Donaldson*
Making Whoopee - *with Walter Donaldson*
No, No, Nora - *with Ernie Erdman and Ted Fiorito*
Your Eyes Have Told Me So - *with Walter Blaufuss and Egbert Van Alstyne*
Ukelele Lady - *with Richard A. Whiting*
I'll See You in My Dreams - *with Isham Jones*

SYNOPSIS:

The biography of songwriter Gus Kahn with focus on his courtship and marriage with Grace LeBoy and his relationships with co-writers Walter Donaldson and Egbert Van Alstyne.

SOUNDTRACK: Caliban 6008 (with *Lullaby of Broadway*)

* * * * * * * * *

I LOVE MELVIN
Metro-Goldwyn-Mayer, 1953

Producer: George Wells
Director: Don Weis
Screenplay: George Wells and Ruth Brooks Flippen; based on a story by Laslo Vadnay
Choreography: Robert Alton
Music and Lyrics: Mack Gordon and Josef Myrow
Running time: 76 minutes, color

CAST:

Donald O'Connor (*Melvin Hoover*); Debbie Reynolds (*Judy LeRoy*); Una Merkel (*Mom Schneider*); Richard Anderson (*Harry Flack*); Allyn Joslyn (*Pop Schneider*); Jim Backus (*Mr. Mergo*); Noreen Corcoran (*Clarabelle*) and Les Tremayne (*Mr. Hennenman*).

SONGS:

A Lady Loves; We Have Never Met As Yet; Saturday Afternoon Before the Game; Where Did You Learn to Dance?; Life Has Its Funny Little Ups and Downs; I

156

Wanna Wander; And There You Are (instrumental).

SYNOPSIS:

Aspiring actress Judy LeRoy asks her photographer boyfriend Melvin to get her on the cover of *LOOK* magazine but trouble starts when he gets a fake cover to make her happy.

SOUNDTRACK: MGM 2-SES-52ST (with *Summer Stock* and *Everything I Have is Yours*)

* * * * * * * * *

I MARRIED AN ANGEL
Metro-Goldwyn-Mayer, 1942

Producer: Hunt Stromberg
Director: W.S. Van Dyke II
Screenplay: Anita Loos; based on the stage musical book by Richard Rodgers and Lorenz Hart
Choreography: Ernst Matray
Music and Lyrics: Richard Rodgers, Lorenz Hart, Robert Wright and George Forrest
Running time: 84 minutes, B/W

CAST:

Jeanette MacDonald (*Anna Zador/Briggitta*); Nelson Eddy (*Count Willie Palaffi*); Binnie Barnes (*Peggy*); Edward Everett Horton (*Peter*); Reginald Owen (*"Whiskers" Rothbart*); Mona Maris (*Marika Szabo*); Janice Carter (*Sufi*); Inez Cooper (*Iren*); Douglass Dumbrille (*Baron Szigethy*); Leonid Kinskey (*Zinski*); Anne Jeffreys (*Polly*) and Marion Rosamond (*Dolly*).

SONGS:

Tira Lira La; Now You've Met the Angel; I Married an Angel; I'll Tell the Man in the Street; Spring is Here; May I Present the Girl?; A Twinkle in Your Eye; Chanson boheme (*Carmen*)*; Anges purs (*Faust*)**; Aloha Oe***.

  **music and lyrics by Georges Bizet*
 ***music and lyrics by Charles Gounod*
****music and lyrics by Queen Liliuokalani*

SYNOPSIS:

Budapest playboy millionaire Willie Palaffi has a dream on his 35th birthday that he marries an angel--and wakes up to find that she looks just like his secretary Anna Zador.

SOUNDTRACK: Caliban 6004 (with *Balalaika*)

* * * * * * * * *

THE INSPECTOR GENERAL
Warner Bros., 1949

Producer: Jerry Wald
Director: Henry Koster
Screenplay: Philip Rapp and Harry Kurnitz; based on the play by Nikolai Gogol
Choreography: Eugene Loring
Music and Lyrics: Sylvia Fine
Running time: 102 minutes, color

CAST:

Danny Kaye (*Georgi*); Walter Slezak (*Yakov Gourys*); Barbara Bates (*Leza*); Elsa Lanchester (*Maria*); Gene Lockhart (*The Mayor*); Alan Hale (*Kovatch*); Walter Catlett (*Colonel Castine*); Rhys Williams (*The Inspector General*); Benny Baker (*Telecki*); Norman Leavitt (*Laszlo*); Sam Hearn (*Gizzick*) and Lew Hearn (*Izzick*).

SONGS:

The Medicine Show; Brodny; The Inspector General (Soliloquy For Three Heads); Happy Times; The Gypsy Drinking Song.

SYNOPSIS:

Georgi, the bumbling helper in Yakov Gourys' traveling medicine show, is mistaken by the corrupt officials of the town of Brodny for an emissary of the emperor Napoleon--the Inspector General. As such he is treated as if he were royalty despite the fact that he can neither read nor write.

SOUNDTRACK: No soundtrack available

* * * * * * * * *

IN THE GOOD OLD SUMMERTIME
Metro-Goldwyn-Mayer, 1949

Producer: Joe Pasternak
Director: Robert Z. Leonard
Screenplay: Albert Hackett, Frances Goodrich and Ivan Tors; based on the play *The Shop Around the Corner* by Miklos Laszlo
Choreography: Robert Alton
Music and Lyrics: see below with song titles
Running time: 104 minutes, color

CAST:

Judy Garland (*Veronica Fisher*); Van Johnson (*Andrew Delby Larkin*); S.Z. Sakall (*Otto Oberkugen*); Spring Byington (*Nellie Burke*); Buster Keaton (*Hickey*); Clinton Sundberg (*Rudy Hansen*); Marcia Van Dyke (*Louise Parkson*) and Lillian Bronson (*Aunt Addie*).

SONGS:

In the Good Old Summertime - *George Evans and Ren Shields*
Meet Me Tonight in Dreamland - *Leo Friedman and Beth Slater Wilson*
Put Your Arms Around Me, Honey - *Albert Von Tilzer and Junie McCree*
I Don't Care - *Harry Sutton and Jean Lenox*
Merry Christmas - *Fred Spielman and Janice Torre*

SYNOPSIS:

Mr. Oberkugen's music store in turn-of-the-century Chicago is where Andy Larkin works but when Veronica Fisher gets a job there the two soon become rivals with Andy secretly wishing she could be more like his ideal girl--his pen-pal.

SOUNDTRACK: MGM 2-SES-49ST (with *Good News* and *Two Weeks With Love*)

* * * * * * * * * *

IRISH EYES ARE SMILING
20th Century Fox, 1944

Producer: Damon Runyon
Director: Gregory Ratoff
Screenplay: Earl Baldwin and John Tucker Battle; based on a story by E.A. Ellington
Choreography: Hermes Pan
Music and Lyrics: see below with song titles
Running time: 90 minutes, color

CAST:

Monty Woolley (*Edgar Brawley*); June Haver (*Mary "Irish" O'Brien*); Dick Haymes (*Ernest R. Ball*); Anthony Quinn (*Al Jackson*); Beverly Whitney (*Lucille Lacey*); Maxie Rosenbloom (*Stanley Ketchel*); Veda Ann Borg (*Belle La Tour*) and Clarence Kolb (*Leo Betz*).

SONGS:

Be My Little Baby Bumble Bee - *Stanley Murphy and Henry I. Marshall*
I'll Forget You - *Ernest R. Ball and Annalu Burns*
Dear Little Boy of Mine - *Ernest R. Ball and J. Keirn Brennan*
I Don't Want a Million Dollars - *Mack Gordon and James V. Monaco*
Let the Rest of the World Go By - *Ernest R. Ball and J. Keirn Brennan*
Mother Machree - *Ernest R. Ball, Chauncey Olcott and George Graff*
A Little Bit of Heaven (Shure They Call It Ireland) - *Ernest R. Ball and J. Keirn Brennan*
When Irish Eyes Are Smiling - *Ernest R. Ball, Chauncey Olcott and George Graff*
Strut Miss Lizzie - *Henry Creamer and Turner Layton*
Bessie in a Bustle - *Mack Gordon and James V. Monaco*
Love Me and the World is Mine - *Ernest R. Ball and Dave Read, Jr.*

SYNOPSIS:

The life of Irish-American Ernest R. Ball provides the background for the story of the young composer's rise to fame in pre-WWI New York and his love for beautiful aspiring singer Mary "Irish" O'Neill.

SOUNDTRACK: No soundtrack available

* * * * * * * * * *

IT HAPPENED AT THE WORLD'S FAIR
Metro-Goldwyn-Mayer, 1963

Producer: Ted Richmond
Director: Norman Taurog
Screenplay: Si Rose and Seaman Jacobs
Choreography: Jack Baker
Music and Lyrics: see below with song titles
Running time: 105 minutes, color

160

CAST:

Elvis Presley (*Mike Edwards*); Joan O'Brien (*Diane Warren*); Gary Lockwood (*Danny Burke*); Vicky Tiu (*Sue-Lin*); Yvonne Craig (*Dorothy Johnson*); Kam Tong (*Walter Ling*) and H.M. Wynant (*Vince Bradley*).

SONGS:

Beyond the Bend - *Ben Weisman, Fred Wise and Dolores Fuller*
Relax - *Sid Tepper and Roy C. Bennett*
Take Me to the Fair - *Sid Tepper and Roy C. Bennett*
They Remind Me Too Much of You - *Don Robertson*
One Broken Heart For Sale - *Otis Blackwell and Winfield Scott*
I'm Falling in Love Tonight - *Don Robertson*
Cotton Candy Land - *Ruth Batchelor and Bob Roberts*
A World Of Our Own - *Bill Giant, Bernie Baum and Florence Kaye*
How Would You Like To Be? - *Ben Raleigh and Mark Barkan*
Happy Ending - *Sid Wayne and Ben Weisman*

SYNOPSIS:

Mike Edwards and Danny Burke are crop dusters who have had their plane impounded for lack of back payments and end up babysitting a little girl, Sue-Lin, at the 1962 Seattle World's Fair.

SOUNDTRACK: RCA APL1-2568

* * * * * * * * *

IT HAPPENED IN BROOKLYN
Metro-Goldwyn-Mayer, 1947

Producer: Jack Cummings
Director: Richard Whorf
Screenplay: Isobel Lennart; based on a story by John McGowan
Choreography: Jack Donohue
Music and Lyrics: Jule Styne and Sammy Cahn
Running time: 104 minutes, B/W

CAST:

Frank Sinatra (*Danny Webson Miller*); Kathryn Grayson (*Anne Fielding*); Peter Lawford (*Jamie Shellgrove*); Jimmy Durante (*Nick Lombardi*); Gloria Grahame

(*Army Nurse*); Marcy McGuire (*Rae Jakobi*); Aubrey Mather (*Digby John*); Tamara Shayne (*Mrs. Kardos*); Billy Roy (*Leo Kardos*) and Bobby Long (*Johnny O'Brien*).

SONGS:

Brooklyn Bridge; I Believe; Time After Time; The Song's Gotta Come From the Heart; La ci darem la mano (*Don Giovanni*)*; It's the Same Old Dream; Whose Baby Are You?; The Bell Song (*Lakme*)*.

 **music and lyrics by Wolfgang Amadeus Mozart*
***music and lyrics by Leo Delibes*

SYNOPSIS:

Eager to get back to his home in Brooklyn after his discharge from the Army, Danny Miller soon finds that life is not quite as rosy as he remembered it.

SOUNDTRACK: Caliban 6006 (with *On Moonlight Bay* and *Three Smart Girls*)

* * * * * * * * * *

IT'S A GREAT FEELING
Warner Bros., 1949

Producer: Alex Gottlieb
Director: David Butler
Screenplay: Jack Rose and Melville Shavelson; based on a story by I.A.L. Diamond
Choreography: LeRoy Prinz
Music and Lyrics: Jule Styne and Sammy Cahn
Running time: 85 minutes, color

CAST:

Dennis Morgan (*Himself*); Doris Day (*Judy Adams*); Jack Carson (*Himself*); Bill Goodwin (*Arthur Trent*); Irving Bacon (*Information Clerk*); Claire Carleton (*Grace*); Harlan Wade (*Publicity Man*); Jacqueline de Wit (*Secretary*); Wilfred Lucas (*Mr. Adams*); Pat Flaherty (*Gate Guard*) and Errol Flynn (*Jeffrey Bushdinkle*).

SONGS:

It's a Great Feeling; Give Me a Song With a Beautiful Melody; Blame My Absent-Minded Heart; Big Fat Lie; Fiddle-Dee-Dee; Café Rendezvous; There's Nothing Rougher Than Love.

162

SYNOPSIS:

After all the directors on the Warner Bros. lot refuse to work with Jack Carson on his new film with Dennis Morgan he decides to direct the film himself. Upon learning the news, Morgan pulls out and Carson is forced to hire waitress Judy Adams to pose as his pregnant wife to force Morgan back to work.

SOUNDTRACK: Caliban 6015 (with *Romance on the High Seas*)

* * * * * * * * * *

IT'S ALWAYS FAIR WEATHER
Metro-Goldwyn-Mayer, 1955

Producer: Arthur Freed
Director: Gene Kelly and Stanley Donen
Screenplay: Betty Comden and Adolph Green, based on their story
Choreography: Gene Kelly and Stanley Donen
Music and Lyrics: André Previn, Betty Comden and Adolph Green
Running time: 102 minutes, color

CAST:

Gene Kelly (*Ted Riley*); Dan Dailey (*Doug Hallerton*); Cyd Charisse (*Jackie Leighton*); Dolores Gray (*Madeline Bradbille*); Michael Kidd (*Angie Valentine*); David Burns (*Tim*); Jay C. Flippen (*Charles Z. Culloran*); Steve Mitchell (*Kid Mariacchi*) and Hal March (*Rocky Heldon*).

SONGS:

March, March; The Time For Parting; Blue Danube (Why Are We Here?); Music is Better Than Words*; Stillman's Gym; Baby, You Knock Me Out; Once Upon a Time; Situation Wise; I Like Myself; Thanks a Lot But No Thanks.

**music and lyrics by André Previn, Betty Comden, Adolph Green and Roger Edens*

SYNOPSIS:

Three WWII Army buddies--Ted, Doug and Angie--decide to have a reunion 10 years to the day of their discharge (October 11th) but when the appointed day arrives they find that they don't have anything in common anymore.

SOUNDTRACK: MCA 25018

* * * * * * * * * *

I WONDER WHO'S KISSING HER NOW?

20th Century Fox, 1947

Producer: George Jessel
Director: Lloyd Bacon
Screenplay: Lewis R. Foster and Marion Turk
Choreography: Hermes Pan
Music and Lyrics: see below with song titles
Running time: 105 minutes, color

CAST:

June Haver (*Katie McCullum*); Mark Stevens* (*Joseph E. Howard*); Martha Stewart (*Lulu Madison*); Reginald Gardiner (*Will Hough*); Lenore Aubert (*Fritzi Barrington*); William Frawley (*Jim Mason*); Gene Nelson (*Tommy*) and Truman Bradley (*Martin Webb*).

**vocals dubbed by Buddy Clark*

SONGS:

In the Sweet Bye and Bye - *Harry Von Tilzer and Vincent P. Bryan*
Wait 'Til the Sun Shines, Nellie - *Harry Von Tilzer and Andrew B. Sterling*
Hello! Ma Baby - *Joseph E. Howard and Ida Emerson*
Oh, Gee, Be Sweet to Me Kid - *Joseph E. Howard*
Goodbye, My Lady Love - *Joseph E. Howard*
Honeymoon - *Joseph E. Howard, Will M. Hough, Frank Adams, George Jessel and Charles Henderson*
What's the Use of Dreaming? - *Joseph E. Howard*
Glow Worm - *Paul Lincke and Lilla Cayley Robinson*
I Wonder Who's Kissing Her Now? - *Joseph E. Howard, Will M. Hough, Frank Adams, George Jessel and Charles Henderson*

SYNOPSIS:

The story of composer Joe Howard who wrote many songs at the turn-of-the-century and his "sister" Katie who does her best to keep him out of the clutches of singers Lulu Madison and Fritzi Barrington--and to herself.

SOUNDTRACK: Titania 502 (with *Oh, You Beautiful Doll!*)

164

J

JAILHOUSE ROCK
Metro-Goldwyn-Mayer, 1957

Producer: Pandro S. Berman
Director: Richard Thorpe
Screenplay: Guy Trosper; based on a story by Ned Young
Music and Lyrics: Mike Stoller, Jerry Leiber, Roy C. Bennett, Abner Silver, Ben
                 Weisman, Aaron Schroeder and Sid Tepper
Running time: 96 minutes, B/W (has been colorized)

CAST:

Elvis Presley (*Vince Everett*); Judy Tyler (*Peggy Van Alden*); Mickey Shaughnessy
(*Hunk Houghton*); Jennifer Holden (*Sherry Wilson*); Dean Jones (*Teddy Talbot*);
Anne Neyland (*Laury Jackson*); Hugh Sanders (*Warden*); Vaughn Taylor (*Mr.
Shores*); Grandon Rhodes (*Professor August Van Alden*); Katharine Warren (*Mrs.
Van Alden*); Percy Helton (*Sam Brewster*); Peter Adams (*Jack Lease*); Robert Bice
(*Mr. Bardeman*); Tom McKee (*Mr. Drummond*) and Francis DeSales (*Doctor*).

SONGS:

One More Day; Young and Beautiful; I Wanna Be Free; Don't Leave Me Now;
Treat Me Nice; Jailhouse Rock; Baby, I Don't Care.

SYNOPSIS:

Sentenced to prison for manslaughter after killing a man in a barroom brawl, Vince
Everett is groomed to become a singing star by his cellmate Hunk. After he is
paroled he goes on to become a big, although egocentric, star.

SOUNDTRACK: Pirate PR-101

* * * * * * * * *

THE JAZZ SINGER
Warner Bros., 1953

Producer: Louis F. Edelman
Director: Michael Curtiz
Screenplay: Frank Davis, Leonard Stern and Lewis Meltzer; based on the play by
           Samson Raphaelson
Choreography: LeRoy Prinz

Music and Lyrics: see below with song titles
Running time: 106 minutes, color

CAST:

Danny Thomas (*Jerry Golding*); Eduard Franz (*Cantor Golding*); Peggy Lee (*Judy Lane*); Mildred Dunnock (*Mrs. Golding*); Alex Gerry (*Uncle Louie*); Allyn Joslyn (*George Miller*); Tom Tully (*McGurney*); Harold Gordon (*Rabbi Roth*) and Hal Ross (*Joseph*).

SONGS:

Just One of Those Things - *Cole Porter*
Lover - *Richard Rodgers and Lorenz Hart*
I Hear the Music Now - *Sammy Fain and Jerry Seelen*
Living the Life I Love - *Sammy Fain and Jerry Seelen*
I'm Looking Over a Four Leaf Clover - *Harry Woods and Mort Dixon*
I'll String Along With You - *Harry Warren and Al Dubin*
Breezin' Along With the Breeze - *Richard A. Whiting, Seymour Simons and Haven Gillespie*
If I Could Be With You One Hour Tonight - *Henry Creamer and Jimmy P. Johnson*
This is a Very Special Day - *Peggy Lee*
All's Well That Ends Well - *Sammy Fain and Jerry Seelen*
What Are New Yorkers Made Of? - *Sammy Fain and Jerry Seelen*
The Birth of the Blues - *B.G. DeSylva, Lew Brown and Ray Henderson*
Oh, Moon - *Sammy Fain and Jerry Seelen*
Hush-a-Bye - *Sammy Fain and Jerry Seelen*

SYNOPSIS:

Sgt. Jerry Golding returns to his family home in Philadelphia from Army service in Korea and announces that he intends to seek a career on the Broadway stage--even though his father wants him to take over as the cantor in their synagogue.

SOUNDTRACK: No soundtrack available

* * * * * * * * *

THE JAZZ SINGER
Associated Films, 1980

Producer: Jerry Leider
Director: Richard Fleischer

Screenplay: Herbert Baker, adaptation by Stephen H. Foreman; based on the play
    by Samson Raphaelson
Choreography: Don McKayle
Music and Lyrics: Neil Diamond, Gilbert Becaud, Alan Lindgren and Richard
    Bennett
Running time: 115 minutes, color

CAST:

Neil Diamond (*Jess Robin*); Laurence Olivier (*Cantor Rabinovitch*); Lucie Arnaz
(*Molly Bell*); Catlin Adams (*Rivka Rabinovitch*); Franklyn Ajaye (*Bubba*); Paul
Nicholas (*Keith Lennox*); Sully Boyar (*Eddie Gibbs*) and Mike Kellin (*Leo*).

SONGS:

You Baby; Havam Nagilam*; Love on the Rocks; On the Robert E. Lee; Hello
Again; Amazed and Confused; Summerlove; Hey Louise; Jerusalem; Songs of Life;
You Are My Sunshine**; Kol Nidre*.

traditional
***music and lyrics by Jimmie Davis and Charles Mitchell*

SYNOPSIS:

Second remake of the original Al Jolson talkie is the story of a cantor's son who
would rather pursue a career as a popular singer and songwriter rather than follow
in his father's footsteps.

SOUNDTRACK: Capitol SWAV-12120

* * * * * * * * *

JESUS CHRIST, SUPERSTAR
Universal, 1973

Producer: Norman Jewison and Robert Stigwood
Director: Norman Jewison
Screenplay: Melvyn Bragg and Norman Jewison; based on the stage musical book
    by Tim Rice
Choreography: Rob Iscove
Music and Lyrics: Andrew Lloyd Webber and Tim Rice
Running time: 103 minutes, color

CAST:

Ted Neeley (*Jesus Christ*); Carl Anderson (*Judas Iscariot*); Yvonne Elliman (*Mary Magdalene*); Barry Dennen (*Pontius Pilate*); Joshua Mostel (*King Herod*); Larry T. Marshall (*Simon Zealotes*); Bob Bingham (*Caiaphas*); Kurt Yahgjian (*Annas*) and Philip Toubus (*Peter*).

SONGS:

Heaven On Their Minds; What's the Buzz?; Strange Thing Mystifying; Then We Are Decided; Everything's Alright; This Jesus Must Die; Hosanna; Simon Zealotes; Poor Jerusalem; Pilate's Dream; The Temple; I Don't Know How to Love Him; Damned For All Time/Blood Money; The Last Supper; Gethsemane (I Only Want to Say); The Arrest; Peter's Denial; Pilate and Christ; King Herod's Song; Could We Start Again, Please?; Judas' Death; Trial Before Pilate; Superstar; The Crucifixion; John Nineteen Forty-One.

SYNOPSIS:

Rock opera based on the last seven days in the life of Jesus Christ.

SOUNDTRACK: MCA 2-11000

* * * * * * * * *

THE JOKER IS WILD
Paramount, 1957

Producer: Samuel J. Briskin
Director: Charles Vidor
Screenplay: Oscar Saul; based on the book *The Life of Joe E. Lewis* by Art Cohn
Choreography: Josephine Earl
Music and Lyrics: see below with song titles
Running time: 126 minutes, B/W

CAST:

Frank Sinatra (*Joe E. Lewis*); Mitzi Gaynor (*Martha Stewart*); Jeanne Crain (*Letty Page*); Eddie Albert (*Austin Mack*); Beverly Garland (*Cassie Mack*); Jackie Coogan (*Swifty Morgan*); Barry Kelley (*Capt. Hugh McCarthy*); Ted de Corsia (*Georgie Parker*); Leonard Graves (*Tim Coogan*) and Valerie Allen (*Flora*).

SONGS:

All the Way - *James Van Heusen and Sammy Cahn*
At Sundown - *Walter Donaldson*
I Cried For You - *Nacio Herb Brown and Arthur Freed*
If I Could Be With You - *Jimmy Johnson and Henry Creamer*
Out of Nowhere - *John Green and Harry Harris*
Swinging On a Star - *James Van Heusen and Harry Harris*
Naturally (*Martha*) - *Friedrich Von Flotow, new lyrics by Harry Harris*
June in January - *Leo Robin and Ralph Rainger*
Chicago - *Fred Fisher*

SYNOPSIS:

The life of entertainer Joe E. Lewis that follows his rise as a comic after a run-in with a pair of thugs during Prohibition destroys his singing voice. He soon falls into an alcoholic descent and drives all of his family and friends away before beginning his recovery.

SOUNDTRACK: No soundtrack available

* * * * * * * * *

JOLSON SINGS AGAIN
Columbia, 1949

Producer: Sidney Buchman
Director: Henry Levin
Screenplay: Sidney Buchman
Choreography: Audrene Brier
Music and Lyrics: see below with song titles
Running time: 96 minutes, color

CAST:

Larry Parks* (*Al Jolson/Himself*); Barbara Hale (*Ellen Clark*); William Demarest (*Steve Martin*); Ludwig Donath (*Cantor Yoelson*); Bill Goodwin (*Tom Baron*); Myron McCormick (*Ralph Bryant*); Tamara Shayne (*Mrs. Yoelson*); Eric Wilton (*Henry*) and Robert Emmett Keane (*Charlie*).

vocals dubbed by Al Jolson

SONGS:

Rock-a-Bye Your Baby With a Dixie Melody - *Jean Schwartz, Sam M. Lewis and Joe Young*

Is It True What They Say About Dixie? - *Sammy Lerner, Irving Caesar and Gerald Marks*

For Me and My Gal - *Edgar Leslie, E. Ray Goetz and George W. Meyer*

Back in Your Own Backyard - *Al Jolson, Billy Rose and Dave Dreyer*

I'm Looking Over a Four Leaf Clover - *Harry Woods and Mort Dixon*

When the Red, Red Robin Comes Bob, Bob, Bobbin' Along - *Harry Woods*

I'm Just Wild About Harry - *Eubie Blake and Noble Sissle*

Chinatown, My Chinatown - *Jean Schwartz and William Jerome*

Baby Face - *Benny Davis and Harry Akst*

After You've Gone - *Harry Creamer and Turner Layton*

I Only Have Eyes For You - *Harry Warren and Al Dubin*

Sonny Boy - *B.G. DeSylva, Lew Brown, Ray Henderson and Al Jolson*

Toot Toot Tootsie - *Gus Kahn, Ernie Erdman and Dan Russo*

California, Here I Come - *Al Jolson, B.G. DeSylva and Joseph Meyer*

You Made Me Love You - *Joseph McCarthy and James V. Monaco*

Let Me Sing and I'm Happy - *Irving Berlin*

Ma Blushin' Rose - *John Stromberg and Edgar Smith*

My Mammy - *Walter Donaldson, Sam M. Lewis and Joe Young*

Swanee - *George Gershwin and Irving Caesar*

The Spaniard Who Blighted My Life - *Billy Myerson*

About a Quarter to Nine - *Harry Warren and Al Dubin*

The Anniversary Song - *Al Jolson, Saul Chaplin and J. Ivanovici*

Waitin' For the Robert E. Lee - *L. Wolfe Gilbert and Lewis F. Muir*

April Showers - *B.G. DeSylva and Louis Silvers*

Pretty Baby - *Egbert Van Alstyne and Gus Kahn*

Carolina in the Morning - *Gus Kahn and Walter Donaldson*

SYNOPSIS:

The life of singer Al Jolson picks up where *The Jolson Story* left off and continues through his second marriage to Ellen Clark, a nurse he met in a hospital in New York during WWII, and his coaching of actor Larry Parks for *The Jolson Story*.

SOUNDTRACK: No soundtrack available

* * * * * * * * *

THE JOLSON STORY
Columbia, 1946

170

Producer: Sidney Skolsky
Director: Alfred E. Green
Screenplay: Stephen Longstreet, adaptation by Harry Chandlee and Andrew Solt
Choreography: Jack Cole
Music and Lyrics: see below with song titles
Running time: 128 minutes, color

CAST:

Larry Parks* (*Al Jolson*); Evelyn Keyes (*Julie Benson*); William Demarest (*Steve Martin*); Bill Goodwin (*Tom Baron*); Ludwig Donath (*Cantor Yoelson*); Scotty Beckett (*Jolson as a boy*); Tamara Shayne (*Mrs. Yoelson*); Jo-Carroll Dennison (*Ann Murray*); John Alexander (*Lew Dockstader*); Ernest Cossart (*Father McGee*); Edwin Maxwell (*Oscar Hammerstein*); Emmett Vogan (*Jonesy*); Eddie Kane (*Florenz Ziegfeld*) and William Forrest (*Dick Glenn*).

vocals dubbed by Al Jolson

SONGS:

Let Me Sing and I'm Happy - *Irving Berlin*
On the Banks of the Wabash - *Paul Dresser*
Avé Maria - *Franz Schubert*
When You Were Sweet Sixteen - *James Thornton*
After the Ball - *Charles K. Harris*
By the Light of the Silvery Moon - *Edward Madden and Gus Edwards*
Blue Bell - *Theodore F. Morse, Edward Madden and Dolly Morse*
Ma Blushin' Rose - *John Stromberg and Edgar Smith*
I Want a Girl Just Like the Girl That Married Dear Old Dad - *William Dillon and*
Harry Von Tilzer
My Mammy - *Walter Donaldson, Sam M. Lewis and Joe Young*
I'm Sitting on the Top of the World - *Ray Henderson, Sam M. Lewis and Joe Young*
You Made Me Love You - *Joseph McCarthy and James V. Monaco*
Swanee - *George Gershwin and Irving Caesar*
Toot Toot Tootsie - *Gus Kahn, Ernie Erdman and Dan Russo*
The Spaniard Who Blighted My Life - *Billy Myerson*
April Showers - *B.G. DeSylva and Louis Silvers*
California, Here I Come - *Al Jolson, B.G. DeSylva and Joseph Meyer*
Liza - *George Gershwin, Ira Gershwin and Gus Kahn*
There's a Rainbow Round My Shoulder - *Al Jolson, Billy Rose and Dave Dreyer*
A Latin From Manhattan - *Harry Warren and Al Dubin*
About a Quarter to Nine - *Harry Warren and Al Dubin*
The Anniversary Song - *Al Jolson, Saul Chaplin and J. Ivanovici*
Waitin' For the Robert E. Lee - *L. Wolfe Gilbert and Lewis F. Muir*

Rock-a-Bye Your Baby With a Dixie Melody - *Jean Schwartz, Sam M. Lewis and Joe Young*

SYNOPSIS:

The biography of singer Al Jolson (born Asa Yoelson) from his childhood in Washington, D.C. through his marriage to dancer Julie Benson (a.k.a. Ruby Keeler).

SOUNDTRACK: No soundtrack available

* * * * * * * * *

THE JUNGLE BOOK
Buena Vista, 1967

Producer: Walt Disney
Director: Wolfgang Reitherman
Screenplay: Larry Clemmons, Ralph Wright, Ken Anderson and Vance Gerry; based on the stories by Rudyard Kipling
Music and Lyrics: Richard M. Sherman and Robert B. Sherman
Running time: 78 minutes, color

VOCAL TALENTS:

Phil Harris (*Baloo*); Sebastian Cabot (*Bagheera*); Louis Prima (*King Louie*); George Sanders (*Shere Khan*); Sterling Holloway (*Kaa*); J. Pat O'Malley (*Colonel Hathi/Vulture*); Bruce Reitherman (*Mowgli*); Verna Felton (*Winifred*); Clint Howard (*Junior*); Chad Stuart (*Vulture*); Lord Tim Hudson (*Vulture*) and Darleen Carr (*Girl from village*).

SONGS:

Colonel Hathi's March; Kaa's Song; The Bare Necessities*; I Wanna Be Like You; That's What Friends Are For; My Own Home.

*music and lyrics by Terry Gilkyson

SYNOPSIS:

Animated tale about a wolf-pack that has raised Mowgli, the "man-cub", since infancy and now that he is almost grown decides that he must be returned to the village so they entrust him to the care of Bagheera to see him safely on his way.

SOUNDTRACK: Buena Vista 4041

172

* * * * * * * * * *

JUPITER'S DARLING
Metro-Goldwyn-Mayer, 1955

Producer: George Wells
Director: George Sidney
Screenplay: Dorothy Kingsley; based on the play *Road to Rome* by Robert E.
                Sherwood
Choreography: Hermes Pan
Music and Lyrics: Burton Lane and Harold Adamson
Running time: 96 minutes, color

CAST:

Howard Keel (*Hannibal*); Esther Williams (*Amytis*); George Sanders (*Fabius Maximus*); Marge Champion (*Meta*); Gower Champion (*Varius*); Richard Haydn (*Horatio*); Norma Varden (*Fabia*); William Demarest (*Mago*); Douglass Dumbrille (*Scipio*) and Michael Ansara (*Maharbal*).

SONGS:

Horatio's Narration*; If This Be Slav'ry; I Have a Dream; Hannibal's Victory March; I Never Trust a Woman; Don't Let This Night Get Away; The Life of an Elephant.

music and lyrics by Saul Chaplin, George Wells and Harold Adamson

SYNOPSIS:

Fictionalized account of Hannibal's attempt to conquer Rome and how a pretty Roman girl named Amytis tries seduction to distract him from his intended plan.

SOUNDTRACK: No soundtrack available

* * * * * * * * * *

JUST AROUND THE CORNER
20th Century Fox, 1938

Producer: Darryl F. Zanuck
Director: Irving Cummings
Screenplay: Ethel Hill, J.P. McEvoy and Darrell Ware; based on a story by Paul
                Gerard Smith
Choreography: Bill Robinson

Music and Lyrics: Walter Bullock and Harold Spina
Running time: 70 minutes, B/W

CAST:

Shirley Temple (*Penny Hale*); Charles Farrell (*Jeff Hale*); Joan Davis (*Kitty*); Amanda Duff (*Lola Ramsby*); Bill Robinson (*Corporal Jones*); Bert Lahr (*Gus*); Franklin Pangborn (*Mr. Waters*); Cora Witherspoon (*Julia Ramsby*); Claude Gillingwater, Sr. (*Samuel G. Henshaw*) and Bennie Bartlett (*Milton Ramsby*).

SONGS:

Just Around the Corner; This is a Happy Little Ditty; Brass Buttons and Epaulets; I Love to Walk in the Rain.

SYNOPSIS:

Financial difficulties during the Depression force architect Jeff Hale to give up his penthouse apartment and become the building's engineer so his daughter Penny and her friend Milton decide to stage a benefit to convince his uncle, Samuel Henshaw, to give Jeff back his job.

SOUNDTRACK: No soundtrack available

* * * * * * * * *

JUST FOR YOU
Paramount, 1952

Producer: Pat Duggan
Director: Elliot Nugent
Screenplay: Robert Carson; based on a story by Stephen Vincent Benét
Choreography: Helen Tamiris
Music and Lyrics: Harry Warren and Leo Robin
Running time: 104 minutes, color

CAST:

Bing Crosby (*Jordan Blake*); Jane Wyman (*Carolina Hill*); Ethel Barrymore (*Allida de Bronkhart*); Natalie Wood (*Barbara Blake*); Bob Arthur (*Jerry Blake*); Cora Witherspoon (*Mrs. Angevine*); Ben Lessy (*Georgie Polansky*) and Regis Toomey (*Hodges*).

174

SONGS:

Zing a Little Zong; He's Just Crazy For Me; The Live Oak Tree; A Flight of Fancy; I'll Si-Si Ya in Bahia; On the 10:10 (From Ten-Ten-Tennessee); Just For You.

SYNOPSIS:

Entertainer Jordan Blake, a widower, has a tendancy to ignore his two children until singer Carolina Hill makes him see the light.

SOUNDTRACK: No soundtrack available

K

THE KID FROM BROOKLYN
RKO, 1946

Producer: Samuel Goldwyn
Director: Norman Z. McLeod
Screenplay: Don Hartman and Melville Shavelson; based on the screenplay *The Milky Way* by Grover Jones, Frank Butler and Richard Connell
Choreography: Bernard Pearce
Music and Lyrics: Jule Styne and Sammy Cahn
Running time: 113 minutes, color

CAST:

Danny Kaye (*Burleigh Sullivan*); Virginia Mayo* (*Polly Pringle*); Vera-Ellen** (*Susie Sullivan*); Steve Cochran (*Speed MacFarlane*); Walter Abel (*Gabby Sloan*); Eve Arden (*Ann Westley*); Lionel Stander (*Spider Schultz*); Fay Bainter (*Mrs. E. Winthrop LeMoyne*); Clarence Kolb (*Mr. Austin*) and Victor Cutler (*Photographer*).

 vocals dubbed by Dorothy Ellers
**vocals dubbed by Betty Russell*

SONGS:

The Sunflower Song; Hey! What's Your Name?; You're the Cause Of It All; I Love an Old-Fashioned Song; Josie; Pavlova*.

music and lyrics by Sylvia Fine and Max Liebman

SYNOPSIS:

Musical remake of *The Milky Way* has timid milkman Burleigh Sullivan accidentally knocking out middleweight boxing champion Speed MacFarlane and being hailed as the new champ.

SOUNDTRACK: No soundtrack available

* * * * * * * * *

THE KID FROM SPAIN
United Artists, 1932

Producer: Samuel Goldwyn
Director: Leo McCarey
Screenplay: William Anthony McGuire, Bert Kalmar and Harry Ruby
Choreography: Busby Berkeley
Music and Lyrics: Harry Ruby and Bert Kalmar
Running time: 118 minutes, B/W

CAST:

Eddie Cantor (*Edward Williams*); Lyda Roberti (*Rosalie*); Robert Young (*Ricardo*); Ruth Hall (*Anita Gomez*); John Miljan (*Pancho*); Noah Beery (*Alonzo Gomez*); J. Carrol Naish (*Pedro*); Robert Emmet O'Connor (*Detective Crawford*); Stanley Fields (*José*); Paul Porcasi (*Gonzales*); Sidney Franklin (*American Matador*) and Theresa Maxwell Conover (*Martha Oliver*).

SONGS:

The College Song; In the Moonlight; Look What You've Done; What a Perfect Combination.

SYNOPSIS:

Eddie Williams follows his friend Ricardo to his home in Mexico after he is mistaken for the getaway driver of a group of bank robbers.

SOUNDTRACK: Pelican 134

* * * * * * * * *

KID GALAHAD
United Artists, 1962

Producer: David Weisbart
Director: Phil Karlson
Screenplay: William Fay; based on the novel by Francis Wallace
Music and Lyrics: see below with song titles
Running time: 95 minutes, color

CAST:

Elvis Presley (*Walter Gulick*); Gig Young (*Willy Grogan*); Lola Albright (*Dolly Fletcher*); Joan Blackman (*Rose Grogan*); Charles Bronson (*Lew Nyack*); Ned Glass (*Max "Shangri-La" Lieberman*); Robert Emhardt (*Maynard*); David Lewis (*Otto*

Danzig); Liam Redmond (*Father Higgins*); Judson Pratt (*Zimmerman*); George Mitchell (*Harry Sperling*); Roy Roberts (*Jerry*); Michael Dante (*Joie Shakes*); Richard Devon (*Marvin*); Jeffrey Morris (*Ralphie*) and Ed Asner (*Frank Gurson*).

SONGS:

King of the Whole Wide World - *Ruth Batchelor and Bob Roberts*
This is Living - *Fred Wise and Ben Weisman*
Riding the Rainbow - *Fred Wise and Ben Weisman*
Home is Where the Heart Is - *Sherman Edwards and Hal David*
I Got Lucky - *Dee Fuller, Fred Wise and Ben Weisman*
A Whistling Tune - *Sherman Edwards and Hal David*

SYNOPSIS:

Just out of the Army, Walter Gulick finds unlikely employment as a fledgling boxer (under the name "Kid Galahad") with Willy Grogan, at Grogan's training camp in Cream Valley, New York.

SOUNDTRACK: RCA EPA-4380

* * * * * * * * * *

KID MILLIONS
United Artists, 1934

Producer: Samuel Goldwyn
Director: Roy Del Ruth
Screenplay: Arthur Sheekman, Nat Perrin and Nunnally Johnson
Choreography: Seymour Felix
Music and Lyrics: Walter Donaldson and Gus Kahn
Running time: 90 minutes, B/W and color

CAST:

Eddie Cantor (*Edward Grant Wilson, Jr.*); Ann Sothern (*Joan Larrabee*); Ethel Merman (*Dot Clark*); George Murphy (*Gerald Lane*); Jesse Black (*Ben Ali*); Eve Sully (*Fanya*); Berton Churchill (*Colonel Harry Larrabee*); Warren Hymer (*Louie*); Paul Harvey (*Sheik Mulhulla*); Otto Hoffman (*Khoot*); Doris Davenport (*Toots*); Stanley Fields (*Oscar*) and Edgar Kennedy (*Herman*).

SONGS:

An Earful of Music; When My Ship Comes In; I Want to Be Your Minstrel Man*;

Mandy**; Your Head On My Shoulder*; Okay, Toots; Ice Cream Fantasy.

*music and lyrics by Burton Lane and Harold Adamson
**music and lyrics by Irving Berlin

SYNOPSIS:

Archeologist Edward Grant Wilson dies in Egypt, leaving an estate of $77 million to his only child, Eddie, Jr., but a number of other people claim they are the ones who are entitled to the fortune.

SOUNDTRACK: Classic International Filmusicals 3007 (with *Roman Scandals*)

* * * * * * * * *

THE KING AND I
20th Century Fox, 1956

Producer: Charles Brackett
Director: Walter Lang
Screenplay: Ernest Lehman; based on the stage musical book by Oscar Hammerstein
          II
Choreography: Jerome Robbins
Music and Lyrics: Richard Rodgers and Oscar Hammerstein II
Running time: 133 minutes, color

CAST:

Deborah Kerr* (*Anna Leonowens*); Yul Brynner (*The King*); Rita Moreno (*Tuptim*); Terry Saunders (*Lady Thiang*); Carlos Rivas** (*Lun Tha*); Martin Benson (*The Kralahome*); Alan Mowbray (*British Ambassador*); Patrick Adiarte (*Prince Chulalongkorn*) and Rex Thompson (*Louis Leonowens*).

*vocals dubbed by Marni Nixon
**vocals dubbed by Reuben Fuentes

SONGS:

I Whistle a Happy Tune; My Lord and Master; Hello, Young Lovers; The March of the Siamese Children (instrumental); A Puzzlement; Getting to Know You; We Kiss in a Shadow; Shall I Tell You What I Think Of You?; Something Wonderful; I Have Dreamed; Song of the King; Shall We Dance?

SYNOPSIS:

In 1862, Mrs. Anna Leonowens, an English widow, arrives in Bangkok, Siam, to be the schoolteacher to the many children of the King. She eventually becomes his friend and confidant even though they disagree on many subjects.

SOUNDTRACK: Capitol SW-740

* * * * * * * * *

KING CREOLE
Paramount, 1958

Producer: Hal B. Wallis
Director: Michael Curtiz
Screenplay: Herbert Baker and Michael Vincente Gazzo; based on the novel *A Stone For Danny Fisher* by Harold Robbins
Choreography: Charles O'Curran
Music and Lyrics: see below with song titles
Running time: 115 minutes, B/W

CAST:

Elvis Presley (*Danny Fisher*); Carolyn Jones (*Ronnie*); Walter Matthau (*Maxie Fields*); Dolores Hart (*Nellie*); Dean Jagger (*Mr. Fisher*); Liliane Montevecchi ("*Forty*" *Nina*); Vic Morrow (*Shark*); Paul Stewart (*Charlie LeGrand*); Jan Shepard (*Mimi Fisher*); Brian Hutton (*Sal*); Jack Grinnage (*Dummy*); Dick Winslow (*Eddie Burton*) and Raymond Bailey (*Mr. Evans*).

SONGS:

Crawfish - *Fred Wise and Ben Weisman*
Steadfast, Loyal and True - *Jerry Leiber and Mike Stoller*
Lover Doll - *Sid Wayne and Abner Silver*
Trouble - *Jerry Leiber and Mike Stoller*
Dixieland Rock - *Aaron Schroeder and Rachel Frank*
Young Dreams - *Martin Kalmanoff and Aaron Schroeder*
New Orleans - *Sid Tepper and Roy C. Bennett*
Hard-Headed Woman - *Claude DeMetrius*
King Creole - *Jerry Leiber and Mike Stoller*
Don't Ask Me Why - *Fred Wise and Ben Weisman*
As Long As I Have You - *Fred Wise and Ben Weisman*

180

SYNOPSIS:

New Orleans teenager Danny Fisher wants something better in life than what he now has and soon finds himself in over his head with local mobster Maxie Fields.

SOUNDTRACK: RCA LSP-1884(e)

* * * * * * * * *

KISMET
Metro-Goldwyn-Mayer, 1955

Producer: Arthur Freed
Director: Vincente Minelli
Screenplay: Charles Lederer and Luther Davis, based on their stage musical book
Choreography: Jack Cole
Music and Lyrics: Robert Wright and George Forrest, based on themes from
                  Alexander Borodin
Running time: 113 minutes, color

CAST:

Howard Keel (*The Poet/"Haaj"*); Ann Blyth (*Marsinah*); Dolores Gray (*Lalume*); Vic Damone (*The Caliph*); Monty Woolley (*Omar*); Sebastian Cabot (*The Wazir*); Jay C. Flippen (*Jawan*); Mike Mazurki (*Chief Policeman*); Jack Elam (*Hassan-Ben*) and Ted de Corsia (*Police Subaltern*).

SONGS:

Fate; Not Since Nineveh; Baubles, Bangles and Beads; Stranger in Paradise; Gesticulate; Night of My Nights; Bored; The Olive Tree; And This is My Beloved; Sands of Time.

SYNOPSIS:

In old Baghdad, a street poet finds himself involved with the wicked Wazir of Police while his daughter falls in love with the young Caliph.

SOUNDTRACK: MGM Select 2353-057

* * * * * * * * *

KISSIN' COUSINS
Metro-Goldwyn-Mayer, 1964

Producer: Sam Katzman
Director: Gene Nelson
Screenplay: Gerald Drayson Adams and Gene Nelson; based on a story by Gerald
            Drayson Adams
Choreography: Hal Belfer
Music and Lyrics: see below with song titles
Running time: 96 minutes, color

CAST:

Elvis Presley (*Lt. Josh Morgan/Jody Tatum*); Arthur O'Connell (*Pappy Tatum*); Jack
Albertson (*Capt. Robert Salbo*); Glenda Farrell (*Ma Tatum*); Pam Austin (*Selena
Tatum*); Yvonne Craig (*Azalea Tatum*); Cynthia Pepper (*PFC Midge Riley*); Tommy
Farrell (*Master Sgt. George Bailey*); Beverly Powers (*Trudy*) and Donald Woods
(*General Alvin Donford*).

SONGS:

Smokey Mountain Boy - *Lenore Rosenblatt and Victor Millrose*
There's Gold in the Mountains - *Bill Giant, Bernie Baum and Florence Kaye*
One Boy, Two Little Girls - *Bill Giant, Bernie Baum and Florence Kaye*
Catchin' On Fast - *Bill Giant, Bernie Baum and Florence Kaye*
Tender Feeling - *Bill Giant, Bernie Baum and Florence Kaye*
Barefoot Ballad - *Dolores Fuller and Lee Morris*
Once is Enough - *Sid Tepper and Roy C. Bennett*
Kissin' Cousins - *Bill Giant, Bernie Baum and Florence Kaye*

SYNOPSIS:

Air Force lieutenant Josh Morgan receives orders to aid Capt. Salbo in securing a
lease on a Tennessee mountain top for a new missile base. He soon finds the
hillbillies there are distant cousins with Jody Tatum his exact lookalike.

SOUNDTRACK: RCA LSP-2894

* * * * * * * * * *

THE KISSING BANDIT
Metro-Goldwyn-Mayer, 1948

Producer: Joe Pasternak
Director: Laslo Benedek
Screenplay: Isobel Lennart and John Briard Harding
Choreography: Stanley Donen and Robert Alton

Music and Lyrics: Nacio Herb Brown, Earl Brent and Edward Heyman
Running time: 102 minutes, color

CAST:

Frank Sinatra (*Ricardo*); Kathryn Grayson (*Teresa*); J. Carrol Naish (*Chico*); Mildred Natwick (*Aunt Isabella*); Mikhail Rasumny (*Don José*); Billy Gilbert (*General Torro*); Sono Osato (*Bianca*); Clinton Sundberg (*Colonel Gomez*); Edna Skinner (*Juanita*); Carlton Young (*Count Belmonte*); Ricardo Montalban (*Fiesta Dancer*); Cyd Charisse (*Fiesta Dancer*) and Ann Miller (*Fiesta Dancer*).

SONGS:

Tomorrow Means Romance; What's Wrong With Me?; If I Steal a Kiss; I Like You; Siesta; Dance of Fury (instrumental); Señorita; Love is Where You Find It.

SYNOPSIS:

Shy Ricardo returns to Old California to take over his late father's old business. He thinks it's keeping an inn--but his father was really "The Kissing Bandit"!

SOUNDTRACK: No soundtrack available

* * * * * * * * *

KISS ME, KATE!
Metro-Goldwyn-Mayer, 1953

Producer: Jack Cummings
Director: George Sidney
Screenplay: Dorothy Kingsley; based on the stage musical book by Samuel Spewack
         and Bella Spewack
Choreography: Hermes Pan
Music and Lyrics: Cole Porter
Running time: 109 minutes, color

CAST:

Howard Keel (*Fred Graham/"Petruchio"*); Kathryn Grayson (*Lilli Vanessi/"Katharine"*); Ann Miller (*Lois Lane/"Bianca"*); Tommy Rall (*Bill Calhoun/"Lucentio"*); Bobby Van (*"Gremio"*); Bob Fosse (*"Hortensio"*); Kurt Kasznar (*"Baptista"*); Ron Randell (*Cole Porter*); Willard Parker (*Tex Callaway*); Keenan Wynn (*Lippy*); James Whitmore (*Slug*); Dave O'Brien (*Ralph*); Claud Allister (*Paul*) and Ann Codee (*Suzanne*).

<u>SONGS</u>:

So in Love; Too Darn Hot; Why Can't You Behave?; Wunderbar; We Open in Venice; Tom, Dick or Harry; I've Come to Wive It Wealthily in Padua; I Hate Men; Were Thine That Special Face; Where is the Life That Late I Led?; Always True to You in My Fashion; Brush Up Your Shakespeare; From This Moment On; Kiss Me, Kate!

<u>SYNOPSIS</u>:

Literally a show within a show about a group of actors trying to stage a production of Cole Porter's *Kiss Me, Kate*! Originally filmed in 3-D.

SOUNDTRACK: MGM 2-SES-44ST (with *The Bandwagon*)

L

LADY AND THE TRAMP
Buena Vista, 1955

Producer: Walt Disney
Director: Hamilton Luske, Clyde Geronimi and Wilfred Jackson
Screenplay: Erdman Penner, Joe Rinaldi, Ralph Wright and Don DaGradi; based on
        a story by Ward Greene
Music and Lyrics: Sonny Burke and Peggy Lee
Running time: 75 minutes, color

VOCAL TALENTS:

Peggy Lee (*Darling/Peg/Si & Am*); Barbara Luddy (*Lady*); Larry Roberts (*Tramp*);
Bill Thompson (*Jock/Bull/Dachsie*); Bill Baucon (*Trusty*); Stan Freberg (*Beaver*);
Verna Felton (*Aunt Sarah*); Lee Millar (*Jim Dear*); Alan Reed (*Boris*); George Givot
(*Tony*) and Dallas McKennon (*Toughy/Professor*).

SONGS:

Peace on Earth; La-La-Loo; Siamese Cat Song; Bella Notte; He's a Tramp.

SYNOPSIS:

Disney animated tale about a pedigreed cocker spaniel named Lady who accidentally
meets up with a mongrel dog-about-town named Tramp.

SOUNDTRACK: Disneyland DQ-1231

* * * * * * * * *

LES GIRLS
Metro-Goldwyn-Mayer, 1957

Producer: Sol C. Siegel
Director: George Cukor
Screenplay: John Patrick; based on a story by Vera Caspary
Choreography: Jack Cole
Music and Lyrics: Cole Porter
Running time: 114 minutes, color

CAST:

Gene Kelly (*Barry Nichols*); Kay Kendall (*Lady Sybil Wren*); Mitzi Gaynor (*Joy Henderson*); Taina Elg (*Angele Ducros*); Jacques Bergerac (*Pierre Ducros*); Leslie Phillips (*Sir Gerald Wren*); Patrick Macnee (*Sir Percy*) and Henry Daniell (*Judge*).

SONGS:

Les Girls; Ça, C'est L'amour; Ladies in Waiting; Habañera (*Carmen*)*; You're Just Too, Too; Why Am I So Gone About That Gal?

*music and lyrics by Georges Bizet

SYNOPSIS:

When Angele Ducros brings suit against Lady Sybil Wren for libel with regards to her newly published memoirs, *Les Girls*, the resulting testimony by both women reveals two very different versions of the same story--when they were both part of a stage act with Barry Nichols.

SOUNDTRACK: MGM 2-SES-51ST (with *Silk Stockings* and *The Barkleys of Broadway*)

* * * * * * * * *

LET'S DANCE
Paramount, 1950

Producer: Robert Fellows
Director: Norman Z. McLeod
Screenplay: Allan Scott and Dane Lussier; based on a story by Maurice Zolotow
Choreography: Hermes Pan
Music and Lyrics: Frank Loesser
Running time: 112 minutes, color

CAST:

Betty Hutton (*Kitty McNeil*); Fred Astaire (*Donald Elwood*); Roland Young (*Mr. Edmund Pohlwhistle*); Ruth Warrick (*Carola Everett*); Lucile Watson (*Serena Everett*); Gregory Moffett (*Richard Everett VII*); Barton MacLane (*Larry Channock*); Sheppard Strudwick (*Timothy Bryant*); Melville Cooper (*Mr. Charles Wagstaffe*); Harold Huber (*Marcel*); George Zucco (*Judge*); Peggy Badey (*Bubbles Malone*) and Virginia Toland (*Elsie*).

186

SONGS:

Can't Stop Talking About Him; Piano Dance (instrumental); Jack and the Beanstalk; Oh, Them Dudes; Why Fight the Feeling?; The Tunnel of Love.

SYNOPSIS:

WWII widow Kitty McNeil decides to run away with her son from her staid Boston lifestyle and joins her former partner Don Elwood on the stage but soon she finds herself in a custody battle with her late husband's grandmother.

SOUNDTRACK: No soundtrack available

* * * * * * * * *

LET'S MAKE LOVE
20th Century Fox, 1960

Producer: Jerry Wald
Director: George Cukor
Screenplay: Norman Krasna and Hal Kanter
Choreography: Jack Cole
Music and Lyrics: James Van Heusen and Sammy Cahn
Running time: 118 minutes, color

CAST:

Marilyn Monroe (*Amanda Dell*); Yves Montand (*Jean-Marc Clement*); Tony Randall (*Alexander Kaufman*); Frankie Vaughan (*Tony Danton*); Wilfrid Hyde-White (*George Wales*); David Burns (*Oliver Burton*); Michael David (*Dave Kerry*); Dennis King, Jr. (*Abe Miller*); Mara Lynn (*Lily*); Joe Besser (*Charlie Lamont*); Ray Foster (*Jimmy*); Madge Kennedy (*Miss Manners*); Richard Haydn (*Narrator*); Milton Berle (*Himself*); Bing Crosby (*Himself*) and Gene Kelly (*Himself*).

SONGS:

My Heart Belongs to Daddy*; Gimme a Song That Sells; You With the Crazy Eyes; Specialization; Let's Make Love; Incurably Romantic.

**music and lyrics by Cole Porter*

SYNOPSIS:

After billionaire Jean-Marc Clement discovers that there is an off-Broadway show in production that parodies him he decides to audition (anonymously) for the part--and gets it! He then falls for leading lady Amanda Dell who doesn't like rich men and thinks that struggling actor "Alexander Dumas" is just what she wants.

SOUNDTRACK: Columbia CS-8327

* * * * * * * * *

LI'L ABNER
Paramount, 1959

Producer: Norman Panama
Director: Melvin Frank
Screenplay: Norman Panama and Melvin Frank, based on their stage musical book
Choreography: Dee Dee Wood and Michael Kidd
Music and Lyrics: Gene DePaul and Johnny Mercer
Running time: 113 minutes, color

CAST:

Peter Palmer (*Li'l Abner*); Leslie Parrish (*Daisy Mae*); Stubby Kaye (*Marryin' Sam*); Julie Newmar (*Stupefyin' Jones*); Howard St. John (*General Bullmoose*); Stella Stevens (*Appassionata Von Climax*); Billie Hayes (*Mammy Yokum*); Joe E. Marks (*Pappy Yokum*); Bern Hoffman (*Earthquake McGoon*); Al Nesor (*Evil Eye Fleagle*); Robert Strauss (*Romeo Scragg*); William Lanteau (*Available Jones*); Ted Thurston (*Senator Jack S. Phogbound*); Carmen Alvarez (*Moonbeam McSwine*); Alan Carney (*Mayor Dawgmeat*); Stanley Simmonds (*Rasmussen T. Finsdale*); Diki Lerner (*Lonesome Polecat*) and Joe Ploski (*Hairless Joe*).

SONGS:

A Typical Day; If I Had My Druthers; Jubilation T. Cornpone; Don't Take That Rag Off'n the Bush; Namely You; The Country's in the Very Best of Hands; Matrimonial Stomp (instrumental); I'm Past My Prime; Put 'Em Back the Way They Wuz; I Wish It Could Be Otherwise.

SYNOPSIS:

Based on Al Capp's comic strip is the story of the hillbilly folk in the town of Dogpatch, U.S.A. and what happens when they find that they will all have to move when the government decides to turn their town into an A-bomb test site.

SOUNDTRACK: Columbia OS-2021

* * * * * * * * *

THE LITTLE MERMAID
Walt Disney, 1989

Producer: Howard Ashman and John Musker
Director: Ron Clements and John Musker
Screenplay: Ron Clements and John Musker; based on the fairy tale by Hans
                Christian Andersen
Music and Lyrics: Alan Menken and Howard Ashman
Running time: 82 minutes, color

VOCAL TALENTS:

Jodi Benson (*Ariel*); Christopher Daniel Barnes (*Prince Eric*); Pat Carroll (*Ursula*);
Buddy Hackett (*Scuttle*); Samuel E. Wright (*Sebastian*); Rene Auberjonois (*Louie*);
Kenneth Mars (*King Triton*); Ben Wright (*Grimsby*); Edie McClurg (*Carlotta*); Paddi
Edwards (*Flotsam/Jetsam*); Will Ryan (*Seahorse*) and Jason Marin (*Flounder*).

SONGS:

Fathoms Below; Daughters of Triton; Part of Your World; Under the Sea; Poor
Unfortunate Souls; Les Poissons; Kiss the Girl.

SYNOPSIS:

Animated story about a little mermaid, Ariel, who defies her father King Triton and
makes a deal with the evil sea witch Ursula to receive a pair of legs--in order to win
the heart of Prince Eric.

SOUNDTRACK: Walt Disney Records CD-018 (compact disc)

* * * * * * * * *

LITTLE MISS BROADWAY
20th Century Fox, 1938

Producer: Darryl F. Zanuck
Director: Irving Cummings
Screenplay: Harry Tugend and Jack Yellen
Choreography: Nick Castle and Geneva Sawyer
Music and Lyrics: Walter Bullock and Harold Spina
Running time: 70 minutes, B/W (has been colorized)

CAST:

Shirley Temple (*Betsy Brown*); George Murphy (*Roger Wendling*); Jimmy Durante (*Jimmy Clayton*); Phyllis Brooks (*Barbara Shea*); Edna May Oliver (*Sarah Wendling*); George Barbier (*Fiske*); Edward Ellis (*Pop Shea*); Jane Darwell (*Miss Hutchins*); El Brendel (*Ole*); Donald Meek (*Willoughby Wendling*); Patricia Wilder (*Flossie*); Claude Gillingwater, Sr. (*Judge*); Charles Williams (*Mike Brody*); Charles Coleman (*Simmons*); Russell Hicks (*Perry*); Claire DuBrey (*Miss Blodgett*); Robert Gleckler (*Detective*); C. Montague Shaw (*Miles*) and Frank Dae (*Pool*).

SONGS:

Be Optimistic; Auld Lang Syne*; How Can I Thank You?; We Should Be Together; If All the World Were Paper; When You Were Sweet Sixteen**; Thank You For the Use of the Hall; Swing Me an Old-Fashioned Song; Little Miss Broadway.

 *traditional
**music and lyrics by James Thornton

SYNOPSIS:

Betsy Brown is an orphan who, after being adopted by Pop Shea and his daughter Barbara, moves into the Hotel Variety managed by the pair. But when their pompous landlady Sarah Wendling decides to throw them out for back rent and send Betsy back to the orphanage her nephew Roger tries to help them raise the necessary funds.

SOUNDTRACK: No soundtrack available

* * * * * * * * *

LITTLE NELLIE KELLY
Metro-Goldwyn-Mayer, 1940

Producer: Arthur Freed
Director: Norman Taurog
Screenplay: Jack McGowan; based on the stage musical book by George M. Cohan
Music and Lyrics: see below with song titles
Running time: 100 minutes, B/W

CAST:

Judy Garland (*Nellie Kelly/Little Nellie Kelly*); George Murphy (*Jerry Kelly*); Charles Winninger (*Michael Noonan*); Arthur Shields (*Timothy Fogarty*); Douglas McPhail

(*Dennis Fogarty*); Forrester Harvey (*Moriarity*); Rita Page (*Mary Fogarty*) and James Burke (*Sergeant McGowan*).

SONGS:

Nellie is a Darlin' - *arranged by Roger Edens*
It's a Great Day For the Irish - *Roger Edens*
A Pretty Girl Milking Her Cow - *arranged by Roger Edens*
Singin' in the Rain - *Nacio Herb Brown and Arthur Freed*
Nellie Kelly, I Love You - *George M. Cohan*

SYNOPSIS:

The ups and downs of widowed New York City police captain Jerry Kelly and his crusty father-in-law Michael Noonan are woven around their love for Jerry's daughter, Little Nellie Kelly.

SOUNDTRACK: Cheerio 5000 (with *Thousands Cheer*)

* * * * * * * * *

A LITTLE NIGHT MUSIC
New World, 1978

Producer: Elliott Kastner
Director: Harold Prince
Screenplay: Hugh Wheeler, based on his stage musical book
Choreography: Patricia Birch
Music and Lyrics: Stephen Sondheim
Running time: 124 minutes, color

CAST:

Elizabeth Taylor (*Desirée Armfeldt*); Len Cariou (*Frederick Egerman*); Diana Rigg (*Countess Charlotte Mittelheim*); Lesley-Anne Down (*Ann Egerman*); Hermione Gingold (*Mme. Armfeldt*); Laurence Guittard (*Count Carl-Magnus Mittelheim*); Christopher Guard (*Erich Egerman*); Lesley Dunlop (*Petra*) and Chloe Franks (*Fredericka Armfeldt*).

SONGS:

Love Takes Time (Night Waltz); The Glamourous Life; Now/Soon/Later; You Must Meet My Wife; Every Day a Little Death; A Weekend in the Country; It Would Have Been Wonderful; Send in the Clowns.

Based on Ingmar Bergman's *Smiles of a Summer Night* is the story of stage actress Desirée Armfeldt who gathers her lovers, old and new, for a weekend in the country at her mother's villa.

SOUNDTRACK: Columbia 35333

* * * * * * * * * *

THE LITTLE PRINCE
Paramount, 1974

Producer: Stanley Donen
Director: Stanley Donen
Screenplay: Alan Jay Lerner; based on the book by Antoine de Saint-Exupéry
Choreography: Ronn Forella and Bob Fosse
Music and Lyrics: Frederick Loewe and Alan Jay Lerner
Running time: 88 minutes, color

CAST:

Richard Kiley (*The Pilot*); Bob Fosse (*The Snake*); Gene Wilder (*The Fox*); Clive Revill (*The Businessman*); Joss Ackland (*The King*); Victor Spinetti (*The Historian*); Donna McKechnie (*The Rose*); Graham Crowden (*The General*) and Steven Warner (*The Little Prince*).

SONGS:

I Need Air; I'm On Your Side; Be Happy; You're a Child; I Never Met a Rose; Why is the Desert?; A Snake in the Grass; Closer and Closer and Closer; Little Prince.

SYNOPSIS:

Based on the well-known children's story about an aviator who counsels and guides a little boy--from another planet--who yearns to learn about life.

SOUNDTRACK: ABC Records ABDP-854

* * * * * * * * * *

LITTLE SHOP OF HORRORS
Warner Bros., 1986

Producer: David Geffen
Director: Frank Oz
Screenplay: Howard Ashman, based on his stage musical book
Choreography: Pat Garrett
Music and Lyrics: Alan Menken and Howard Ashman
Running time: 94 minutes, color

CAST:

Rick Moranis (*Seymour Krelborn*); Ellen Greene (*Audrey*); Vincent Gardenia (*Mushnik*); Steve Martin (*Orin Scrivello, D.D.S.*); Tichina Arnold (*Crystal*); Michelle Weeks (*Ronette*); Tisha Campbell (*Chiffon*); James Belushi (*Patrick Martin*); John Candy (*Wink Wilkinson*); Christopher Guest (*First Customer*); Bill Murray (*Arthur Denton*) and Levi Stubbs (*voice of "Audrey II"*).

SONGS:

Little Shop of Horrors; Skid Row (Downtown); Grow For Me; Somewhere That's Green; Some Fun Now; Dentist!; Feed Me (Git It); Suddenly, Seymour; Suppertime; The Meek Shall Inherit; Mean Green Mother From Outer Space.

SYNOPSIS:

After a total eclipse meek Seymour Krelborn finds an unusual plant, and it soon becomes the top attraction at Mushnik's Skid Row florist shop, making him a botanical hero. A problem arises when Seymour discovers that "Audrey II" requires human blood to survive!

SOUNDTRACK: Geffen GHS-24125

* * * * * * * * *

LIVE A LITTLE, LOVE A LITTLE
Metro-Goldwyn-Mayer, 1968

Producer: Douglas Laurence
Director: Norman Taurog
Screenplay: Michael A. Hoey and Dan Greenburg; based on the novel *Kiss My
        Firm But Pliant Lips* by Dan Greenburg
Choreography: Jack Regas and Jack Baker
Music and Lyrics: see below with song titles
Running time: 89 minutes, color

CAST:

Elvis Presley (*Greg Nolan*); Michele Carey (*Bernice*); Rudy Vallee (*Louis Penlow*); Don Porter (*Mike Lansdowne*); Dick Sargent (*Harry*); Sterling Holloway (*Milkman*); Celeste Yarnall (*Ellen*); Eddie Hodges (*Delivery Boy*); Joan Shawlee (*Robbie's Mother*) and Mary Grover (*Miss Selfridge*).

SONGS:

Wonderful World - *Bill Giant, Bernie Baum and Florence Kaye*
Edge of Reality - *Bill Giant, Bernie Baum and Florence Kaye*
A Little Less Conversation - *Billy Strange and Scott Davis*
Almost in Love - *Randy Starr and Luiz Bonfa*

SYNOPSIS:

Photographer Greg Nolan has his life turned upside-down (and loses his job) when he meets a kooky girl named Bernice on the beach. He soon finds employment with two firms: a men's magazine and a prestigious advertising firm.

SOUNDTRACK: Camden CAS-2440

* * * * * * * * *

LIVING IT UP
Paramount, 1954

Producer: Paul Jones
Director: Norman Taurog
Screenplay: Jack Rose and Melville Shavelson; based on the stage musical *Hazel Flagg* by Ben Hecht
Choreography: Nick Castle
Music and Lyrics: Jule Styne and Bob Merrill
Running time: 94 minutes, color

CAST:

Dean Martin (*Steve Harris*); Jerry Lewis (*Homer Flagg*); Janet Leigh (*Wally Cook*); Fred Clark (*Oliver Stone*); Edward Arnold (*The Mayor*); Sheree North (*Jitterbug Dancer*); Sammy White (*Waiter*); Sid Tomack (*Master of Ceremonies*); Sig Ruman (*Dr. Egelhofer*) and Richard Loo (*Dr. Lee*).

SONGS:

That's What I Like; You're Gonna Dance With Me, Baby; Champagne and Wedding Cake; How Do You Speak to an Angel?; Money Burns a Hole in My Pocket; Every Street's a Boulevard in Old New York.

SYNOPSIS:

Musical remake of the film *Nothing's Sacred* has Homer Flagg a supposed victim of radiation poisoning who gets a chance to live it up in New York City when reporter Wally Cook hears of his "condition".

SOUNDTRACK: No soundtrack available

* * * * * * * * *

LOOK FOR THE SILVER LINING
Warner Bros., 1949

Producer: William Jacobs
Director: David Butler
Screenplay: Phoebe Ephron, Henry Ephron and Marian Spitzer; based on a story by
             Bert Kalmar and Harry Ruby
Choreography: LeRoy Prinz
Music and Lyrics: see below with song titles
Running time: 106 minutes, color

CAST:

June Haver (*Marilyn Miller*); Ray Bolger (*Jack Donohue*); Gordon MacRae (*Frank Carter*); Charles Ruggles (*Pop Miller*); Rosemary De Camp (*Mom Miller*); Lee Wilde (*Claire Miller*); Lyn Wilde (*Ruth Miller*); S.Z. Sakall (*Shendorff*); Walter Catlett (*Himself*); Lillian Yarbo (*Violet*); Paul E. Burns (*Mr. Beeman*) and Douglas Kennedy (*Doctor*).

SONGS:

Look For the Silver Lining - *Jerome Kern and B.G. DeSylva*
Time On My Hands - *Vincent Youmans, Harold Adamson and Mack Gordon*
Who - *Jerome Kern and Oscar Hammerstein II*
Sunny - *Jerome Kern and Oscar Hammerstein II*
A Kiss in the Dark - *Victor Herbert and B.G. DeSylva*
Wild Rose - *Jerome Kern and Clifford Grey*

Biography of entertainer Marilyn Miller and her rise from vaudeville to the Broadway stage as told by her friend and mentor Jack Donohue.

SOUNDTRACK: Titania 504 (with *I'll Get By*)

* * * * * * * * * *

LOOKING FOR LOVE

Metro-Goldwyn-Mayer, 1964

Producer: Joe Pasternak
Director: Don Weis
Screenplay: Ruth Brooks Flippen
Choreography: Robert Sidney
Music and Lyrics: see below with song titles
Running time: 83 minutes, color

CAST:

Connie Francis (*Libby Caruso*); Jim Hutton (*Paul Davis*); Susan Oliver (*Jan McNair*); Joby Baker (*Cuz Rickover*); Jesse White (*Tiger Shay*); Jay C. Flippen (*Ralph Front*); Johnny Carson (*Himself*); Danny Thomas (*Himself*); George Hamilton (*Himself*); Barbara Nichols (*Gaye Swinger*); Joan Marshall (*Miss Devine*); Charles Lane (*Director*); Paula Prentiss (*Society Matron*) and Yvette Mimieux (*Society Matron*).

SONGS:

Let's Have a Party - *Hank Hunter and Stan Vincent*
When the Clock Strikes Midnight - *Hank Hunter and Stan Vincent*
This is My Happiest Moment - *Ted Murray and Benny Davis*
Be My Love - *Nicholas Brodsky and Sammy Cahn*
I Can't Believe That You're in Love With Me - *Clarence Gaskill and Jimmy McHugh*
Looking For Love - *Hank Hunter and Stan Vincent*
Whoever You Are, I Love You - *Gary Geld and Peter Udell*

SYNOPSIS:

Libby Caruso invents a clothes rack she calls "The Lady Valet" but when she goes on Johnny Carson's talk show to promote it she finds that her singing gets more attention than her invention.

SOUNDTRACK: MGM SE-4229

196

LOST HORIZON
Columbia, 1973

Producer: Ross Hunter
Director: Charles Jarrott
Screenplay: Larry Kramer; based on the novel by James Hilton
Choreography: Hermes Pan
Music and Lyrics: Burt Bacharach and Hal David
Running time: 143 minutes, color

CAST:

Peter Finch (*Richard Conway*); Liv Ullmann (*Catherine*); Sally Kellerman (*Sally Hughes*); George Kennedy (*Sam Cornelius*); Michael York (*George Conway*); Olivia Hussey (*Maria*); Bobby Van (*Harry Lovett*); James Shigeta (*Brother To-Len*); John Gielgud (*Chang*) and Charles Boyer (*The High Lama*).

SONGS:

Lost Horizon*; Share the Joy; The World is a Circle; Living Together, Growing Together; I Might Frighten Her Away; The Things I Will Not Miss; Reflections; Question Me an Answer.

vocal by Shawn Phillips

SYNOPSIS:

The Himalayan monastery of Shangri-La is the setting for a group of hijacked refugees from an Asian rebellion. Their destinies seem to lie in the magical land where old age and sickness are practically unknown.

SOUNDTRACK: Bell 1300

* * * * * * * * *

LOUISIANA PURCHASE
Paramount, 1941

Producer: B.G. DeSylva and Harold Wilson
Director: Irving Cummings
Screenplay: Jerome Chodorov and Joseph Fields; based on the stage musical book
        by Morrie Ryskind and B.G. DeSylva

Music and Lyrics: Irving Berlin
Running time: 98 minutes, color

CAST:

Bob Hope (*Jim Taylor*); Vera Zorina (*Marina Van Linden*); Victor Moore (*Senator Oliver P. Loganberry*); Irene Bordoni (*Mme. Yvonne Bordelaise*); Dona Drake (*Beatrice*); Raymond Walburn (*Colonel Davis, Sr.*) and Maxie Rosenbloom (*"The Shadow"*).

SONGS:

Before the Picture Starts; Dance With Me (at the Mardi Gras); You're Lonely and I'm Lonely; Louisiana Purchase; It's a Lovely Day Tomorrow.

SYNOPSIS:

Senator Loganberry goes to New Orleans to investigate the reportedly shady dealings of the Louisiana Purchasing Company. When he arrives, the scapegoat president of the firm, Jim Taylor, tries to set him up with various ladies in order to discredit his findings.

SOUNDTRACK: No soundtrack available

* * * * * * * * *

LOVELY TO LOOK AT
Metro-Goldwyn-Mayer, 1952

Producer: Jack Cummings
Director: Mervyn LeRoy and Vincente Minelli
Screenplay: George Wells, Harry Ruby and Andrew Solt; based on the stage musical
        Roberta by Otto A. Harbach
Choreography: Hermes Pan
Music and Lyrics: Jerome Kern, Otto A. Harbach and Dorothy Fields
Running time: 105 minutes, color

CAST:

Kathryn Grayson (*Stephanie*); Howard Keel (*Tony Naylor*); Red Skelton (*Al Marsh*); Marge Champion (*Clarisse*); Gower Champion (*Jerry Ralby*); Ann Miller (*Bubbles Cassidy*); Zsa Zsa Gabor (*Zsa Zsa*); Kurt Kasznar (*Max "Mox" Fogelsby*); Marcel Dalio (*Pierre*) and Diane Cassidy (*Diane*).

SONGS:

Opening Night; I'll Be Hard to Handle; Lafayette; Yesterdays; I Won't Dance; You're Devastating; Lovely to Look At; Smoke Gets in Your Eyes; The Touch of Your Hand.

SYNOPSIS:

Remake of the film *Roberta* has Al Marsh inheriting half of a dress shop, "Roberta's", in Paris but when he goes to sell his half he finds himself enchanted by the other owner, Stephanie.

SOUNDTRACK: MGM 2-SES-50ST (with *Brigadoon*)

* * * * * * * * * *

LOVE ME OR LEAVE ME
Metro-Goldwyn-Mayer, 1955

Producer: Joe Pasternak
Director: Charles Vidor
Screenplay: Daniel Fuchs and Isobel Lennart; based on a story by Daniel Fuchs
Choreography: Alex Romero
Music and Lyrics: see below with song titles
Running time: 122 minutes, color

CAST:

Doris Day (*Ruth Etting*); James Cagney (*Martin Snyder*); Cameron Mitchell (*Johnny Alderman*); Robert Keith (*Bernard V. Loomis*); Tom Tully (*Frobisher*); Harry Bellaver (*Georgie*); Richard Gaines (*Paul Hunter*); Peter Leeds (*Fred Taylor*) and Claude Stroud (*Eddie Fulton*).

SONGS:

I'm Sitting On the Top of the World - *Sam M. Lewis, Joe Young and Ray Henderson*
You Made Me Love You - *Joseph McCarthy and James V. Monaco*
Stay On the Right Side, Sister - *Ted Koehler and Rube Bloom*
Everybody Loves My Baby - *Jack Palmer and Spencer Williams*
Mean to Me - *Roy Turk and Fred Ahlert*
Sam, the Old Accordian Man - *Walter Donaldson*
Shaking the Blues Away - *Irving Berlin*
After I Say I'm Sorry - *Walter Donaldson and Abe Lyman*
I Cried For You - *Arthur Freed, Gus Arnheim and Abe Lyman*

My Blue Heaven - *Walter Donaldson and George Whiting*
Ten Cents a Dance - *Richard Rodgers and Lorenz Hart*
I'll Never Stop Loving You - *Nicholas Brodsky and Sammy Cahn*
Never Look Back - *Chilton Price*
At Sundown - *Walter Donaldson*
Love Me or Leave Me - *Walter Donaldson and Gus Kahn*

SYNOPSIS:

Based on the life of Ruth Etting, torch singer of the 1920's, who finds her life complicated by her relationship with her manager, and later husband, small-time hood Marty "The Gimp" Snyder.

SOUNDTRACK: Columbia CL-710

* * * * * * * * *

LOVE ME TONIGHT
Paramount, 1932

Producer: Rouben Mamoulian
Director: Rouben Mamoulian
Screenplay: Samuel Hoffenstein, Waldemar Young and George Marion, Jr.; based
                on a play by Leopold Marchand and Paul Armont
Music and Lyrics: Richard Rodgers and Lorenz Hart
Running time: 104 minutes, B/W

CAST:

Maurice Chevalier (*Maurice Courtelin*); Jeanette MacDonald (*Princess Jeanette*); Charlie Ruggles (*Vicomte Gilbert de Vareze*); Charles Butterworth (*Count de Savignac*); Myrna Loy (*Countess Valentine*); C. Aubrey Smith (*The Duke*) and Joseph Cawthorne (*Dr. Armand de Fontinac*).

SONGS:

The Song of Paree; How Are You?; Isn't It Romantic?; Lover; Mimi; A Woman Needs Something Like That; Poor Apache; Love Me Tonight; The Son-of-a-Gun is Nothing But a Tailor.

SYNOPSIS:

Tailor Maurice Courtelin goes to the family chateau of the Vicomte de Vareze to collect the money owed to him and his friends for their work and while there falls

200

in love with the Vicomte's cousin, the Princess Jeanette.

SOUNDTRACK: No soundtrack available

* * * * * * * * *

THE LOVE PARADE
Paramount, 1929

Producer: Ernst Lubitsch
Director: Ernst Lubitsch
Screenplay: Ernst Vajda and Guy Bolton; based on the play *The Prince Consort* by
                Leon Xanrof and Jules Chancel
Music and Lyrics: Victor Schertzinger and Clifford Grey
Running time: 110 minutes, B/W

CAST:

Maurice Chevalier (*Count Alfred Renard*); Jeanette MacDonald (*Queen Louise*);
Lupino Lane (*Jacques*); Lillian Roth (*Lulu*); Edgar Norton (*Master of Ceremonies*);
Lionel Belmore (*Prime Minister*); Albert Roccardi (*Foreign Minister*); Carl Stockdale
(*Admiral*); Eugene Pallette (*Minister of War*) and E.H. Calvert (*Sylvanian
Ambassador*).

SONGS:

Oo-La-La-La; Paris, Stay the Same; Dream Lover; Anything to Please the Queen; My
Love Parade; Let's Be Common; March of the Grenadiers; Nobody's Using It Now;
The Queen is Always Right.

SYNOPSIS:

With her ministers of state constantly nagging her to marry, Queen Louise of
Sylvania decides to wed the only man who interests her--a Navy officer named Count
Alfred Renard, who is not happy to be the new Prince Consort.

SOUNDTRACK: La Nadine 260 (with *The Merry Widow*/1934)

* * * * * * * * *

LOVING YOU
Paramount, 1957

Producer: Hal B. Wallis
Director: Hal Kanter
Screenplay: Herbert Baker and Hal Kanter; based on a story by Mary Agnes
          Thompson
Choreography: Charles O'Curran
Music and Lyrics: see below with song titles
Running time: 102 minutes, color

CAST:

Elvis Presley (*Deke Rivers*); Lizabeth Scott (*Glenda Markle*); Wendell Corey (*Walter "Tex" Warner*); Dolores Hart (*Susan Jessup*); James Gleason (*Carl Meade*); Paul Smith (*Skeeter*); Ken Becker (*Wayne*) and Jana Lund (*Daisy Bricker*).

SONGS:

Got a Lot of Livin' to Do - *Aaron Schroeder and Ben Weisman*
Party - *Jessie Mae Robinson*
Lonesome Cowboy - *Sid Tepper and Roy C. Bennett*
Hot Dog - *Jerry Leiber and Mike Stoller*
Mean Woman Blues - *Claude DeMetrius*
Teddy Bear - *Karl Mann and Bernie Lowe*
Loving You - *Jerry Leiber and Mike Stoller*

SYNOPSIS:

Small town boy Deke Rivers is discovered by press agent Glenda Markle and is soon catapulted into the stardom he is ill-equipped to handle.

SOUNDTRACK: RCA LSP-1515(e)

* * * * * * * * *

LUCKY ME
Warner Bros., 1954

Producer: Henry Blanke
Director: Jack Donohue
Screenplay: James O'Hanlon, Robert O'Brien and Irving Elinson; based on a story
          by James O'Hanlon
Choreography: Jack Donohue
Music and Lyrics: Sammy Fain and Paul Francis Webster
Running time: 99 minutes, color

CAST:

Doris Day (*Candy Williams*); Robert Cummings (*Dick Carson*); Phil Silvers (*Hap Snyder*); Eddie Foy, Jr. (*Duke McGee*); Nancy Walker (*Flo Neely*); Martha Hyer (*Lorraine Thayer*); Bill Goodwin (*Otis Thayer*); Marcel Dalio (*Anton*); Hayden Rorke (*Tommy Arthur*); James Burke (*Officer Mahoney*); Herb Vigran (*Theatre Manager*) and George Sherwood (*Smith*).

SONGS:

Lucky Me; Superstition Song; Take a Memo to the Moon; Men; Parisian Pretties; High Hopes; I Speak to the Stars; Bluebells of Broadway; Love You Dearly; Wanna Sing Like an Angel.

SYNOPSIS:

Entertainers Hap Snyder and his troupe get stranded in Miami but when lead singer Candy Williams gets a chance for a part in Dick Carson's new show she finds that producer Otis Thayer's daughter Lorraine has other ideas.

SOUNDTRACK: Athena LM1B-9 (with *Incendiary Blonde*)

* * * * * * * * *

LULLABY OF BROADWAY
Warner Bros., 1951

Producer: William Jacobs
Director: David Butler
Screenplay: Earl Baldwin, based on his story *My Irish Molly O*
Choreography: Al White and Eddie Prinz
Music and Lyrics: see below with song titles
Running time: 91 minutes, color

CAST:

Doris Day (*Melinda Howard*); Gene Nelson (*Tom Farnham*); S.Z. Sakall (*Adolph Hubbell*); Billy DeWolfe (*Lefty Mack*); Gladys George (*Jessica Howard*); Florence Bates (*Mrs. Hubbell*); Anne Triole (*Gloria Davis*) and Hanley Stafford (*George Ferndel*).

SONGS:

Just One of Those Things - *Cole Porter*

In a Shanty in Old Shanty Town - *Little Jack Little, John Siras and Joe Young*
You're Dependable - *Sy Miller and Jerry Seelen*
Zing! Went the Strings of My Heart - *James F. Hanley*
You're Getting to Be a Habit With Me - *Harry Warren and Al Dubin*
Somebody Loves Me - *George Gershwin and Ira Gershwin*
I Love the Way You Say Goodnight - *Eddie Pela and George Wyle*
Please Don't Talk About Me When I'm Gone - *Sam H. Stept and Sidney Clare*
We'd Like to Go On a Trip - *Sy Miller and Jerry Seelen*
Lullaby of Broadway - *Harry Warren and Al Dubin*

SYNOPSIS:

Melinda Howard returns to New York from Europe expecting to find her mother Jessica a big stage star but she is now an alcoholic Greenwich Village torch singer and her old pals Lefty and Gloria team up to keep Melinda from finding out the truth.

SOUNDTRACK: Caliban 6008 (with *I'll See You in My Dreams*)

* * * * * * * * * *

LUXURY LINER
Metro-Goldwyn-Mayer, 1948

Producer: Joe Pasternak
Director: Richard Whorf
Screenplay: Gladys Lehman and Richard Connell
Music and Lyrics: see below with song titles
Running time: 97 minutes, color

CAST:

George Brent (*Captain Jeremy Bradford*); Jane Powell (*Polly Bradford*); Lauritz Melchior (*Olaf Eriksen*); Frances Gifford (*Laura Dene*); Marina Koshetz (*Zita Romanka*); Xavier Cugat (*Himself*); Thomas E. Breen (*Denis Mulvy*); Richard Derr (*Charles G.K. Worton*); John Ridgely (*Chief Officer Carver*); Connie Gilchrist (*Bertha*) and the Pied Pipers (*Themselves*).

SONGS:

Spring Came Back to Vienna - *Janice Torre, Fred Spielman and Fritz Rotter*
Alouette - *traditional French-Canadian folksong*
Yes! We Have No Bananas - *Frank Silver and Irving Cohn*
Gavotte (*Manon*) - *Jules Massenet*

204

Con Maracas - *Xavier Cugat and Candido Dimanlig*
The Peanut Vendor - *L. Wolfe Gilbert, Marion Sunshine and Moises Simons*
I've Got You Under My Skin - *Cole Porter*
M'Appari (*Martha*) - *Friedrich Von Flotow*

<u>SYNOPSIS</u>:

Schoolgirl Polly Bradford stows away on her widowed father's cruise ship and soon begins matchmaking for him with passenger Laura Dene while trying to further her operatic career with passenger Olaf Eriksen, a Metropolitan Opera star.

SOUNDTRACK: No soundtrack available

M

MAME
Warner Bros., 1974

Producer: Robert Fryer and James Cresson
Director: Gene Saks
Screenplay: Paul Zindel; based on the stage musical book by Jerome Lawrence and
        Robert E. Lee
Choreography: Onna White
Music and Lyrics: Jerry Herman
Running time: 131 minutes, color

CAST:

Lucille Ball (*Mame Dennis*); Beatrice Arthur (*Vera Charles*); Robert Preston
(*Beauregard Jackson Pickett Burnside*); Bruce Davison (*Patrick Dennis*); Joyce Van
Patten (*Sally Cato*); Jane Connell (*Agnes Gooch*); Kirby Furlong (*Patrick as a child*);
John McGiver (*Mr. Babcock*) and Don Porter (*Claude Upson*).

SONGS:

St. Bridget; It's Today; Open a New Window; The Man in the Moon; My Best Girl;
We Need a Little Christmas; Mame; Loving You; The Letter; Bosom Buddies;
Gooch's Song; If He Walked Into My Life.

SYNOPSIS:

Upon the death of his father Patrick Dennis is sent to live with his flamboyant
Auntie Mame whose outlook on life is in direct contrast with that of his trustee, Mr.
Babcock.

SOUNDTRACK: Warner Bros. 2773

* * * * * * * * *

MAMMY
Warner Bros., 1930

Producer: Walter Morosco
Director: Michael Curtiz
Screenplay: Joseph Jackson and Gordon Rigby; based on the play *Mr. Bones* by
        Irving Berlin

Music and Lyrics: see below with song titles
Running time: 83 minutes, B/W

CAST:

Al Jolson (*Al Fuller*); Lois Moran (*Nora Meadows*); Louise Dresser (*Mrs. Fuller*); Lowell Sherman (*Bill "Westy" West*); Hobart Bosworth (*Mr. Meadows*); Tully Marshall (*Slats*); Mitchell Lewis (*Tambo*) and Jack Curtis (*Sheriff Trimble*).

SONGS:

Here We Are, Here We Are, Here We Are Again - *Charles Knight and Kenneth Lyle*
Let Me Sing and I'm Happy - *Irving Berlin*
Who Paid the Rent For Mrs. Rip Van Winkle? - *Fred Fisher and Alfred Bryan*
Yes! We Have No Bananas - *Giuseppe Verdi, Frank Silver and Irving Cohn*
Looking at You - *Irving Berlin*
Oh, Dem Golden Slippers - *traditional*
Why Do They All Take the Night Boat to Albany? - *Jean Schwartz, Joe Young and Sam M. Lewis*
The Old Folks at Home - *Stephen Foster*
My Mammy - *Walter Donaldson, Sam M. Lewis and Joe Young*

SYNOPSIS:

Al Fuller is a member of Meadows' Merry Minstrels traveling show who tries to help Mr. Meadows daughter Nora regain her boyfriend Westy even though he's in love with her himself.

SOUNDTRACK: Milloball 34031 (with *Twenty Million Sweethearts*)

* * * * * * * * *

MAN OF LA MANCHA
United Artists, 1972

Producer: Arthur Hiller
Director: Arthur Hiller
Screenplay: Dale Wasserman, based on his stage musical book
Choreography: Gillian Lynne
Music and Lyrics: Mitch Leigh and Joe Darion
Running time: 130 minutes, color

CAST:

Peter O'Toole* (*Miguel de Cervantes/Alonso Quijana/Don Quixote de la Mancha*);
Sophia Loren (*Aldonza/Dulcinea*); James Coco (*Manservant/Sancho Panza*); Harry
Andrews (*Governor/Innkeeper*); John Castle (*Duke/Dr. Carras/Black Knight/Knight
of the Mirrors*); Brian Blessed (*Pedro*); Ian Richardson (*Padre*); Rosalie Crutchley
(*Housekeeper*) and Julie Gregg (*Antonia/Lady in White*).

vocals dubbed by Simon Gilbert

SONGS:

Man of La Mancha (I, Don Quixote); It's All the Same; Dulcinea; I'm Only Thinking
Of Him; I Really Like Him; Barber's Song/Golden Helmet of Mambrino; Little Bird,
Little Bird; The Impossible Dream (The Quest); The Dubbing; Life As It Really Is
(Soliloquy); Aldonza; A Little Gossip; The Psalm.

SYNOPSIS:

While in prison awaiting the Spanish Inquisition, author Miguel de Cervantes passes
the time by acting out his condemned plays for, and with, his fellow prisoners.

SOUNDTRACK: United Artists 9906

* * * * * * * * * *

MARDI GRAS
20th Century Fox, 1958

Producer: Jerry Wald
Director: Edmund Goulding
Screenplay: Winston Miller and Hal Kanter; based on a story by Curtis Harrington
Choreography: Bill Foster
Music and Lyrics: Sammy Fain and Paul Francis Webster
Running time: 107 minutes, color

CAST:

Pat Boone (*Pat Newell*); Christine Carere (*Michelle Marton*); Tommy Sands (*Barry
Denton*); Sheree North (*Eadie*); Gary Crosby (*Tony*); Fred Clark (*Curtis*); Richard
Sargent (*Dick Saglon*); Barrie Chase (*Torchy*); Geraldine Wall (*Ann Harris*) and
Jennifer West (*Sylvia*).

Loyalty; Stonewall Jackson; Bourbon Street Blues; That Man Can Sell Me the Brooklyn Bridge; I'll Remember Tonight; A Fiddle, a Rifle, an Axe and a Bible.

SYNOPSIS:

The cadets of Virginia Military Institute go to the Mardi Gras in New Orleans to perform with their school band and while there Pat Newell falls in love with singer Michelle Marton.

SOUNDTRACK: No soundtrack available

* * * * * * * * *

MARY POPPINS
Buena Vista, 1964

Producer: Walt Disney
Director: Robert Stevenson
Screenplay: Bill Walsh and Don DaGradi; based on the books by P.L. Travers
Choreography: Marc Breaux and Dee Dee Wood
Music and Lyrics: Richard M. Sherman and Robert B. Sherman
Running time: 140 minutes, color

CAST:

Julie Andrews (*Mary Poppins*); Dick Van Dyke (*Bert/Mr. Dawes, Sr.*); David Tomlinson (*George Banks*); Glynis Johns (*Winifred Banks*); Hermione Baddeley (*Ellen*); Reta Shaw (*Mrs. Brill*); Elsa Lanchester (*Katie Nanna*); Arthur Treacher (*Constable Jones*); Reginald Owen (*Admiral Boom*); Jane Darwell (*The Bird Woman*); Arthur Malet (*Mr. Dawes, Jr.*); Karen Dotrice (*Jane Banks*); Matthew Garber (*Michael Banks*) and Ed Wynn (*Uncle Albert*).

SONGS:

Sister Suffragette; The Life I Lead; The Perfect Nanny; A Spoonful of Sugar; Jolly Holiday; Supercalifragilisticexpialidocious; Stay Awake; I Love to Laugh; Feed the Birds (Tuppence a Bag); Fidelity Fiduciary Bank; Chim-Chim-Cheree; Step in Time; Let's Go Fly a Kite.

SYNOPSIS:

P.L. Travers' magical nanny, Mary Poppins, arrives in 1910 London to help care for the children of George Banks.

SOUNDTRACK: Buena Vista 5005

* * * * * * * * *

MAYTIME
Metro-Goldwyn-Mayer, 1937

Producer: Hunt Stromberg
Director: Robert Z. Leonard and William Von Wymetal
Screenplay: Noel Langley; based on the stage musical book by Rida Johnson Young
Choreography: Val Raset
Music and Lyrics: Sigmund Romberg and Rida Johnson Young
Running time: 132 minutes, B/W

CAST:

Jeanette MacDonald (*Marcia Mornay/Miss Morrison*); Nelson Eddy (*Paul Allison*); John Barrymore (*Nicolai Nazaroff*); Herman Bing (*Augustus Archipenko*); Tom Brown (*Kip Stuart*); Lynne Carver (*Barbara Roberts*); Rafaela Ottiano (*Ellen*); Charles Judels (*Cabby*); Paul Porcasi (*Trentini*) and Sig Rumann (*Fanchon*).

SONGS:

Summer is a-Comin' In; Sombre Meuse; Stein Song (Students' Drinking Song)*; Vive l'Opera**; Virginia Eggs and Ham**; Carry Me Back to Old Virginny***; Sweetheart, Will You Remember This Day in May?

   *music and lyrics by Herbert Stothart
  **music and lyrics by Herbert Stothart, Robert Wright and George Forrest
***music and lyrics by James A. Bland

SYNOPSIS:

Aging opera star Marcia Mornay thinks back upon her youth, career and love with fellow opera star Paul Allison--and its tragic consequences--as she advises aspiring singer Barbara Roberts.

SOUNDTRACK: Sandy Hook SH-2008

* * * * * * * * *

210

MEET ME AFTER THE SHOW
20th Century Fox, 1951

Producer: George Jessel
Director: Richard Sale
Screenplay: Mary Loos and Richard Sale; based on a story by Erna Lazarus and W.
          Scott Darling
Choreography: Jack Cole
Music and Lyrics: Jule Styne and Leo Robin
Running time: 86 minutes, color

CAST:

Betty Grable (*Delilah*); Macdonald Carey (*Jeff*); Rory Calhoun (*David Hemingway*);
Eddie Albert (*Christopher Leeds*); Fred Clark (*Tim*); Lois Andrews (*Gloria Carstairs*);
Irene Ryan (*Tillie*); Arthur Walge (*Joe*) and Edwin Max (*Charlie*).

SONGS:

Meet Me After the Show; Bettin' On a Man; (Every Day is Like) A Day in
Maytime; It's a Hot Night in Alaska; No Talent Joe; I Feel Like Dancing.

SYNOPSIS:

Discovering that her husband Jeff is fooling around with other women Delilah runs
off to Miami and pretends to have lost her memory while performing her old night
club routine.

SOUNDTRACK: Caliban 6012 (with *Painting the Clouds With Sunshine*)

* * * * * * * * * *

MEET ME AT THE FAIR
Universal, 1952

Producer: Albert J. Cohen
Director: Douglas Sirk
Screenplay: Irving Wallace, adaptation by Martin Berkeley; based on the novel *The
          Great Companions* by Gene Markey
Choreography: Kenny Williams
Music and Lyrics: see below with song titles
Running time: 87 minutes, color

211

CAST:

Dan Dailey (*"Doc" Tilbee*); Diana Lynn (*Zerelda Wing*); Chet Allen (*Tad Bayliss*); Benjamin "Scatman" Crothers (*Enoch Jones*); Hugh O'Brien (*Chilton Corr*); Carole Matthews (*Clara Brink*); Rhys Williams (*Pete McCoy*); Thomas E. Jackson (*Billy Gray*); Russell Simpson (*Sheriff Evans*); George Chandler (*Deputy Sheriff Leach*); Virginia Brissac (*Mrs. Spooner*); Doris Packer (*Mrs. Swaile*); Edna Holland (*Miss Burghey*) and George L. Spaulding (*Governor*).

SONGS:

Oh Susannah! - *Stephen Foster*
Ezekial Saw De Wheel - *traditional Black American spiritual*
All God's Chillun Got Shoes - *traditional Black American spiritual*
I Was There - *F.E. Miller and Benjamin "Scatman" Crothers*
Remember the Time - *Kenny Williams and Marvin Wright*
Meet Me at the Fair - *Milton Rosen and Frederick Herbert*
Avé Maria - *Franz Schubert*
I Got the Shiniest Mouth in Town - *Stan Freberg*
Bill Bailey, Won't You Please Come Home? - *Hughie Cannon*
Sweet Genevieve - *George Cooper and Henry Tucker*

SYNOPSIS:

After running away from the local orphanage Tad Bayliss joins the travelling carnival show of "medicine man" Doctor Tilbee.

SOUNDTRACK: No soundtrack available

* * * * * * * * *

MEET ME IN ST. LOUIS
Metro-Goldwyn-Mayer, 1944

Producer: Arthur Freed
Director: Vincente Minelli
Screenplay: Irving Brecher and Fred F. Finklehoffe; based on the book by Sally Benson
Choreography: Charles Walters
Music and Lyrics: see below with song titles
Running time: 114 minutes, color

212

CAST:

Judy Garland (*Esther Smith*); Margaret O'Brien (*"Tootie Smith"*); Mary Astor* (*Mrs. Anna Smith*); Lucille Bremer (*Rose Smith*); June Lockhart (*Lucille Ballard*); Tom Drake (*John Truett*); Marjorie Main (*Katie*); Harry Davenport (*Grandpa Prophater*); Leon Ames** (*Mr. Alonzo Smith*); Henry H. Daniels, Jr. (*Lon Smith, Jr.*); Joan Carroll (*Agnes Smith*); Hugh Marlowe (*Colonel Darby*); Robert Sully (*Warren Sheffield*) and Chill Wills (*Mr. Neely*).

vocals dubbed by D. Markas
**vocals dubbed by Arthur Freed*

SONGS:

Meet Me in St. Louis - *Kerry Mills and Andrew B. Sterling*
The Boy Next Door - *Hugh Martin and Ralph Blane*
Skip to My Lou - *Hugh Martin and Ralph Blane*
Under the Bamboo Tree - *J. Rosamond Johnson and Bob Cole*
The Trolley Song - *Hugh Martin and Ralph Blane*
Have Yourself a Merry Little Christmas - *Hugh Martin and Ralph Blane*
You and I - *Nacio Herb Brown and Arthur Freed*

SYNOPSIS:

The 1904 Louisiana Purchase Exposition in St. Louis, Missouri is the focal event of the year and the Smith children just might miss it if Mr. Alonzo Smith takes a new job offer in New York City.

SOUNDTRACK: Hollywood Soundstage HS-5007

* * * * * * * * *

MELODY CRUISE
RKO, 1933

Producer: Merian C. Cooper
Director: Mark Sandrich
Screenplay: Ben Holmes and Mark Sandrich
Choreography: Dave Gould
Music and Lyrics: Will Jason and Val Burton
Running time: 76 minutes, B/W

CAST:

Charles Ruggles (*Peter Wells*); Phil Harris (*Alan Chandler*); Helen Mack (*Laurie Marlowe*); Greta Nissen (*Elsa Von Rader*); Chick Chandler (*Hickey*); June Brewster (*Zoe*); Shirley Chambers (*Vera*); Florence Roberts (*Miss Potts*) and Marjorie Gateson (*Mrs. Grace Wells*).

SONGS:

I Met Her at a Party; He's Not the Marrying Kind; This is the Hour; Isn't This a Night For Love?

SYNOPSIS:

On a cruise ship from New York to California businessman Pete Wells is desperate to keep his buddy Alan from marrying--*anyone*--because if he does then Pete's wife will get a *very* enlightening letter about his business trips.

SOUNDTRACK: No soundtrack available

* * * * * * * * * *

MERRY ANDREW
Metro-Goldwyn-Mayer, 1958

Producer: Sol C. Siegel
Director: Michael Kidd
Screenplay: Isobel Lennart and I.A.L. Diamond; based on a story by Paul Gallico
Choreography: Michael Kidd
Music and Lyrics: Saul Chaplin and Johnny Mercer
Running time: 103 minutes, color

CAST:

Danny Kaye (*Andrew Larrabee*); Pier Angeli* (*Selena*); Baccaloni (*Antonio Gallini*); Robert Coote (*Dudley Larrabee*); Noel Purcell (*Matthew Larrabee*); Patricia Cutts (*Letitia Fairchild*); Rex Evans (*Gregory Larrabee*); Walter Kingsford (*Mr. Fairchild*) and Tommy Rall (*Giacomo Gallini*).

**vocals dubbed by Betty Wand*

SONGS:

The Pipes of Pan; Chin Up Stout Fellows; Everything is Tickety-Boo; Salud/Here's Cheers; The Square of the Hypotenuse; You Can't Always Have What You Want.

SYNOPSIS:

British schoolmaster Andrew Larrabee would really rather be an archeologist but is intimidated by the headmaster--his father--so he meekly acceeds to his wishes to carry on the family tradition in the school.

SOUNDTRACK: Capitol T-1016

* * * * * * * * *

THE MERRY WIDOW
Metro-Goldwyn-Mayer, 1934

Producer: Irving Thalberg
Director: Ernst Lubitsch
Screenplay: Ernst Vajda and Samson Raphaelson; based on the stage musical book
                by Victor Leon and Leo Stein
Choreography: Albertina Rasch
Music and Lyrics: Franz Lehar, Lorenz Hart, Richard Rodgers and Gus Kahn
Running time: 99 minutes, B/W

CAST:

Maurice Chevalier (*Count Danilo*); Jeanette MacDonald (*Mme. Sonia*); Edward Everett Horton (*Ambassador Popoff*); Una Merkel (*Queen Dolores*); George Barbier (*King Achmed*); Minna Gombell (*Marcelle*); Ruth Channing (*Lulu*) and Sterling Holloway (*Mischka*).

SONGS:

Girls, Girls, Girls; Vilia; Tonight Will Teach Me to Forget; Melody of Laughter; Maxim's; The Girls at Maxim's; The Merry Widow Waltz; If Widows Are Rich; Russian Dance (instrumental).

SYNOPSIS:

In the tiny Eastern European country of Marshovia, in 1895, the richest widow in the land--Mme. Sonia-- has decided to pack her things and moved to paris to escape her restrictive lifestyle. But when King Achmed finds that his country is on the of bankruptcy without her he sends the rakish Captain of the Guard, Count Danilo, to woo her back.

SOUNDTRACK: La Nadine 260 (with *The Love Parade*)

* * * * * * * * * *

THE MERRY WIDOW
Metro-Goldwyn-Mayer, 1952

Producer: Joe Pasternak
Director: Curtis Bernhardt
Screenplay: Sonya Levien and William Ludwig; based on the stage musical book by
              Victor Leon and Leo Stein
Choreography: Jack Cole
Music and Lyrics: Franz Lehar and Paul Francis Webster
Running time: 105 minutes, color

CAST:

Lana Turner* (*Crystal Radek*); Fernando Lamas (*Count Danilo*); Una Merkel (*Kitty Riley*); Richard Haydn (*Baron Popoff*); Thomas Gomez (*King Herman*); John Abbott (*Marshovian Ambassador*); Marcel Dalio (*Police Sergeant*); King Donovan (*Nitki*); Robert Coote (*Marquis de Crillon*); Sujata (*Gypsy Girl*); Lisa Ferraday (*Marcella*); Shepard Menken (*Kunjany*); Ludwig Stossel (*Major Domo*) and Dave Willock (*Attaché*).

*vocals dubbed by Trudy Erwin

SONGS:

Girls, Girls, Girls; Vilia; Night; I'm Going to Maxim's; The Merry Widow Waltz.

SYNOPSIS:

Remake of the operetta this time has wealthy widow Crystal Radek being wooed by playboy Count Danilo, nephew of King Herman II of Marshovia, in order to get her to bail the country out of its huge debt.

SOUNDTRACK: No soundtrack available

* * * * * * * * *

216

MR. IMPERIUM
Metro-Goldwyn-Mayer, 1951

Producer: Edwin H. Knopf
Director: Don Hartman
Screenplay: Don Hartman and Edwin H. Knopf; based on a play by Edwin H. Knopf
Music and Lyrics: Harold Arlen and Dorothy Fields
Running time: 87 minutes, color

CAST:

Lana Turner* (*Fredda Barlo*); Ezio Pinza (*Alexi/"Mr. Imperium"*); Sir Cedric Hardwicke (*Prime Minister Bernand*); Barry Sullivan (*Paul Hunter*); Marjorie Main (*Mrs. Mary Cabot*); Debbie Reynolds (*Gwen*) and Ann Codee (*Anna Pelan*).

vocals dubbed by Trudy Erwin

SONGS:

My Love and My Mule; Let Me Look At You; Andiamo; You Belong to My Heart*.

music and lyrics by Ray Gilbert and Agustin Lara

SYNOPSIS:

While working in Italy, singer Fredda Barlo falls in love with Crown Prince Alexi (incognito as "Mr. Imperium") but when the Prime Minister breaks up the romance she decides to pursue a film career in Hollywood.

SOUNDTRACK: No soundtrack available

* * * * * * * * *

MR. MUSIC
Paramount, 1950

Producer: Robert L. Welch
Director: Richard Haydn
Screenplay: Arthur Sheekman; based on a play by Samson Raphaelson
Choreography: Gower Champion
Music and Lyrics: James Van Heusen and Johnny Burke
Running time: 113 minutes, B/W

CAST:

Bing Crosby (*Paul Merrick*); Nancy Olson (*Katherine Holbrook*); Charles Coburn (*Alex Conway*); Robert Stack (*Jefferson Blake*); Ruth Hussey (*Lorna Marvis*); Tom Ewell (*Haggerty*); Ida Moore (*Aunt Amy*); Charles Kemper (*Danforth*); Donald Woods (*Tippy Carpenter*); Gower Champion (*Himself*); Marge Champion (*Herself*); Groucho Marx (*Himself*); Peggy Lee (*Herself*); Dorothy Kirsten (*Herself*); The Merry Macs (*Themselves*) and Claud Curdle (*Jerome Thisby*).

SONGS:

Once More; Milady; Then You'll Be Home; High On the List; Wouldn't It Be Funny?; Accidents Will Happen; Life is So Peculiar; Mr. Music.

SYNOPSIS:

Songwriter Paul Merrick would rather play golf than work but producer Alex Conway needs him for his new show and hires Katherine Holbrook as a secretary to see that he does indeed work.

SOUNDTRACK: No soundtrack available

* * * * * * * * *

MOON OVER MIAMI
20th Century Fox, 1941

Producer: Harry Joe Brown
Director: Walter Lang
Screenplay: Vincent Lawrence and Brown Holmes, adaptation by George Seaton and
            Lynn Starling; based on a play by Stephen Powys
Choreography: Hermes Pan
Music and Lyrics: Leo Robin and Ralph Rainger
Running time: 91 minutes, color

CAST:

Don Ameche (*Phil O'Neil*); Betty Grable (*Kay Latimer*); Robert Cummings (*Jeffrey Bolton III*); Carole Landis (*Barbara Latimer*); Jack Haley (*Jack O'Hara*); Charlotte Greenwood (*Susan Latimer*); Cobina Wright, Jr. (*Connie Fentress*); George Lessey (*William Bolton*); Robert Conway (*Mr. Lester*) and Robert Grieg (*Brearley*).

SONGS:

What Can I Do For You?; Oh Me, Oh Mi-Am-Mi; You Started Something; I've Got You All to Myself; Is That Good?; Loneliness and Love; Kindergarten Conga; Solitary Seminole.

SYNOPSIS:

Sisters Kay and Barbara Latimer along with their Aunt Susan head for Miami in order to land rich husbands by pretending to be rich themselves.

SOUNDTRACK: Caliban 6001 (with *Coney Island*)

* * * * * * * * *

MOTHER WORE TIGHTS
20th Century Fox, 1947

Producer: Lamar Trotti
Director: Walter Lang
Screenplay: Lamar Trotti; based on the book by Miriam Young
Choreography: Seymour Felix and Kenny Williams
Music and Lyrics: see below with song titles
Running time: 107 minutes, color

CAST:

Betty Grable (*Myrtle McKinley Burt*); Dan Dailey (*Frank Burt*); Mona Freeman (*Iris Burt*); Connie Marshall (*Mikie Burt*); Vanessa Brown (*Bessie*); Robert Arthur (*Bob Clarkman*); Sara Allgood (*Grandmother McKinley*); William Frawley (*Mr. Schneider*); Ruth Nelson (*Miss Ridgeway*); Anabel Shaw (*Alice Flemmerhammer*); George Cleveland (*Grandfather McKinley*); Veda Ann Borg (*Rosemary Olcott*); Sig Rumann (*Papa*) and Anne Baxter (*Narrator*).

SONGS:

Burlington Bertie From Bow - *William Hargreaves*
You Do - *Mack Gordon and Josef Myrow*
This is My Favorite City - *Mack Gordon and Josef Myrow*
Kokomo, Indiana - *Mack Gordon and Josef Myrow*
Silent Night - *Joseph Mohr and Franz Gruber*
Choo'n Gum - *Mann Curtis and Vic Mizzy*
Lily of the Valley - *L. Wolfe Gilbert and Anatole Friedland*
Stumbling - *Zez Confrey*

There's Nothing Like a Song - *Mack Gordon and Josef Myrow*
Rolling Down to Bowling Green - *Mack Gordon and Josef Myrow*
Fare-Thee-Well Dear Alma Mater - *Mack Gordon and Josef Myrow*

SYNOPSIS:

The story of husband and wife vaudeville team Myrtle and Frank Burt in the early 1900's as told by their daughter Mikie.

SOUNDTRACK: Classic International Filmusicals 3008 (with *The Shocking Miss Pilgrim*)

* * * * * * * * *

THE MUPPET MOVIE
Associated Films, 1979

Producer: Jim Henson
Director: James Frawley
Screenplay: Jerry Juhl and Jack Burns
Music and Lyrics: Paul Williams and Kenny Ascher
Running time: 96 minutes, color

CAST:

Jim Henson (*Kermit the Frog/Rowlf/Dr. Teeth/Waldorf*); Frank Oz (*Miss Piggy/Fozzie Bear/Animal/Sam the Eagle*); Jerry Nelson (*Floyd Pepper/Crazy Harry/Robin/Lew Zealand*); Richard Hunt (*Scooter/Statler/Janice/Sweetums/Beaker*); Dave Goelz (*The Great Gonzo/Zoot/Dr. Bunsen Honeydew*); Carroll Spinney (*Big Bird*); Charles Durning (*Doc Hopper*); Austin Pendleton (*Max*); Scott Walker (*"The Frog Killer"*); Mel Brooks (*Professor Krassman*); Edgar Bergen (*Himself*); Milton Berle (*"Mad Mooney"*); James Coburn (*Saloon Owner*); Dom DeLuise (*Bernie the Agent*); Elliot Gould (*Beauty Contest Emcee*); Bob Hope (*Ice Cream Vendor*); Madeline Kahn (*Girl in Saloon*); Carol Kane (*Girl with Lisp*); Cloris Leachman (*Lord's Secretary*); Steve Martin (*Waiter*); Richard Pryor (*Balloon Vendor*); Telly Savalas (*Man in Saloon*); Paul Williams (*Piano Player*) and Orson Welles (*Lew Lord*).

SONGS:

Rainbow Connection; Movin' Right Along; Can You Picture That?; Never Before, Never Again; I Hope That Somethin' Better Comes Along; I'm Going to Go Back There Someday; The Magic Store.

SYNOPSIS:

First film for Jim Henson's Muppets charts Kermit the Frog's odyssey as he seeks fame and fortune in Hollywood--far from his Georgia swamp home.

SOUNDTRACK: Atlantic SD-16001

* * * * * * * * *

THE MUPPETS TAKE MANHATTAN
Tri-Star, 1984

Producer: David Lazer
Director: Frank Oz
Screenplay: Frank Oz, Tom Patchett and Jay Tarses; based on a story by Tom
            Patchett and Jay Tarses
Choreography: Chris Chadman
Music and Lyrics: Jeff Moss
Running time: 94 minutes, color

CAST:

Jim Henson (*Kermit the Frog/Dr. Teeth/Rowlf/Waldorf/The Swedish Chef*); Frank Oz (*Miss Piggy/Fozzie Bear/Animal*); Steve Whitmore (*Rizzo the Rat/Gil*); Dave Goelz (*The Great Gonzo/Chester/Rat/Bill/Zoot*); Jerry Nelson (*Camilla/Lew Zealand/Floyd*); Richard Hunt (*Scooter/Janice/Statler*); Karen Prell (*Yolanda*); Juliana Donald (*Jenny*); Lonny Price (*Ronnie Crawford*); Louis Zorich (*Pete*); Art Carney (*Bernard Crawford*); James Coco (*Mr. Skeffington*); Dabney Coleman (*Martin Price/Murray Plotsky*); Gregory Hines (*Roller Skater*); Linda Lavin (*Doctor*); Joan Rivers (*Saleswoman*); Elliot Gould (*Policeman*); Liza Minelli (*Herself*); Brooke Shields (*Diner*); Frances Bergen (*Winesop's Secretary*); Edward I. Koch (*Himself*); Vincent Sardi (*Himself*) and John Landis (*Leonard Winesop*).

SONGS:

Together Again; You Can't Take "No" For an Answer; Saying Goodbye; Rat Scat; I'm Gonna Always Love You; Right Where I Belong.

SYNOPSIS:

Kermit the Frog and his college friends try to take their senior variety show, "Manhattan Melodies", to New York to get it produced on Broadway but find their way often difficult.

221

SOUNDTRACK: Warner Bros. WB 25114-1

* * * * * * * * *

THE MUSIC MAN
Warner Bros., 1962

Producer: Morton DaCosta
Director: Morton DaCosta
Screenplay: Marion Hargrove; based on the stage musical book by Meredith Willson
Choreography: Onna White
Music and Lyrics: Meredith Willson
Running time: 151 minutes, color

CAST:

Robert Preston (*Professor Harold Hill*); Shirley Jones (*Marian Paroo*); Buddy Hackett (*Marcellus Washburne*); Hermione Gingold (*Eulalie McKechnie Shinn*); Paul Ford (*Mayor George Shinn*); Ronnie Howard (*Winthrop Paroo*); Timmy Everett (*Tommy Djilas*); Susan Luckey (*Zaneeta Shinn*); Harry Hickox (*Charlie Cowell*); Pert Kelton (*Mrs. Paroo*) and the Buffalo Bills (*The Town Council*).

SONGS:

Rock Island; Iowa Stubborn; Ya Got Trouble; Goodnight, My Someone; Seventy-Six Trombones; Sincere; The Sadder-But-Wiser Girl; Pick-a-Little, Talk-a-Little/Goodnight Ladies; Marian the Librarian; Being in Love; Gary, Indiana; The Wells Fargo Wagon; Lida Rose/Will I Ever Tell You?; Shipoopi; 'Til There Was You.

SYNOPSIS:

Con-man Prof. Harold Hill discovers that he's the one who's been conned when he arrives in River City, Iowa trying to sell a boys' band.

SOUNDTRACK: Warner Bros. 1459

* * * * * * * * *

MY BLUE HEAVEN
20th Century Fox, 1950

Producer: Sol C. Siegel
Director: Henry Koster
Screenplay: Lamar Trotti and Claude Binyon; based on a story by S.K. Lauren

222

Choreography: Billy Daniel and Seymour Felix
Music and Lyrics: Ralph Blane and Harold Arlen
Running time: 96 minutes, color

CAST:

Betty Grable (*Kitty Moran*); Dan Dailey (*Jack Moran*); David Wayne (*Walter Pringle*); Jane Wyatt (*Janet Pringle*); Mitzi Gaynor (*Gloria Adams*); Una Merkel (*Miss Gilbert*); Louise Beavers (*Selma*); Laura Pierpont (*Mrs. Johnson*) and Larry Keating (*Doctor*).

SONGS:

My Blue Heaven*; It's Deductible; What a Man!; Halloween; I Love a New Yorker; Live Hard, Work Hard, Love Hard; Friendly Islands; Don't Rock the Boat, Dear.

*music and lyrics by Walter Donaldson and George Whiting

SYNOPSIS:

After losing their unborn child in an auto accident, husband and wife entertainers Kitty and Jack Moran decide to adopt a baby but find their way often blocked by prejudice against their profession.

SOUNDTRACK: Titania 503 (with *You Were Meant For Me*)

* * * * * * * * * *

MY DREAM IS YOURS
Warner Bros., 1949

Producer: Michael Curtiz
Director: Michael Curtiz
Screenplay: Harry Kurnitz, Dane Lussier, Allen Rivkin and Laura Kerr
Choreography: LeRoy Prinz
Music and Lyrics: see below with song titles
Running time: 99 minutes, color

CAST:

Jack Carson (*Doug Blake*); Doris Day (*Martha Gibson*); Lee Bowman (*Gary Mitchell*); Adolphe Menjou (*Thomas Hutchins*); Eve Arden (*Vivian Martin*); S.Z. Sakall (*Felix Hofer*); Selena Royle (*Freda Hofer*); Edgar Kennedy (*Uncle Charlie*);

Sheldon Leonard (*Fred Grimes*); Franklin Pangborn (*"Sourpuss"*); Ada Leonard (*Herself*); Duncan Robertson (*Freddie*) and Mel Blanc (*voice of "Bugs Bunny"*).

SONGS:

Love Finds a Way - *Harry Warren and Ralph Blane*
Canadian Capers - *Gus Chandler, Bert White and Henry Cohen*
With Plenty of Money and You - *Harry Warren and Al Dubin*
My Dream is Yours - *Harry Warren and Ralph Blane*
Tic, Tic, Tic - *Harry Warren and Ralph Blane*
You Must Have Been a Beautiful Baby - *Harry Warren and Johnny Mercer*
I'll String Along With You - *Harry Warren and Al Dubin*
Someone Like You - *Harry Warren and Ralph Blane*
Freddie Get Ready - *Franz Liszt, Harry Warren and Ralph Blane*

SYNOPSIS:

Talent scout Doug Blake tries to make a star out of Martha Gibson when his client Gary Mitchell decides that he is too important for Doug's management.

SOUNDTRACK: Titania 501 (with *The West Point Story*)

* * * * * * * * *

MY FAIR LADY
Warner Bros., 1964

Producer: Jack L. Warner
Director: George Cukor
Screenplay: Alan Jay Lerner, based on his stage musical book
Choreography: Hermes Pan
Music and Lyrics: Frederick Loewe and Alan Jay Lerner
Running time: 170 minutes, color

CAST:

Rex Harrison (*Professor Henry Higgins*); Audrey Hepburn* (*Eliza Doolittle*); Stanley Holloway (*Alfred P. Doolittle*); Wilfrid Hyde-White (*Colonel Hugh Pickering*); Gladys Cooper (*Mrs. Higgins*); Jeremy Brett (*Freddy Eynsford-Hill*); Theodore Bikel (*Zoltan Karpathy*); Isobel Elsom (*Mrs. Eynsford-Hill*) and Mona Washbourne (*Mrs. Pearce*).

*vocals dubbed by Marni Nixon

224

SONGS:

Why Can't the English?; Wouldn't It Be Loverly?; I'm Just an Ordinary Man; With a Little Bit of Luck; Just You Wait; The Rain in Spain; I Could Have Danced All Night; Ascot Gavotte; On the Street Where You Live; You Did It; Show Me; Get Me to the Church On Time; A Hymn to Him; Without You; I've Grown Accustomed to Her Face.

SYNOPSIS:

George Bernard Shaw's *Pygmalion* set to music is the story of a Cockney flower girl named Eliza Doolittle who wants to become a lady with a little help from speech expert Prof. Henry Higgins.

SOUNDTRACK: Columbia 2600

* * * * * * * * * *

MY GAL SAL
20th Century Fox, 1942

Producer: Robert Bessler
Director: Irving Cummings
Screenplay: Seton I. Miller, Darrell Ware and Karl Tunberg; based on the book *My Brother Paul* by Theodore Dreiser
Choreography: Hermes Pan and Val Raset
Music and Lyrics: Paul Dresser
Running time: 103 minutes, color

CAST:

Rita Hayworth* (*Sally Elliott*); Victor Mature (*Paul Dresser*); John Sutton (*Fred Haviland*); Carole Landis (*Mae Collins*); James Gleason (*Pat Howley*); Phil Silvers (*Wiley*); Walter Catlett (*Colonel Truckee*); Mona Maris (*Countess Mariana Rossini*); Frank Orth (*McGuinness*); Stanley Andrews (*Mr. Dreiser*); Margaret Moffat (*Mrs. Dreiser*); John Kelly (*John L. Sullivan*) and Barry Downing (*Theodore Dreiser*).

vocals dubbed by Nan Wynn

SONGS:

On the Gay White Way*; Come Tell Me What's Your Answer (Yes or No?); Oh, the Pity Of It All*; Here You Are*; The Convict and the Bird; On the Banks of the Wabash; Me and My Fella and a Big Umbrella*; My Gal Sal.

music and lyrics by Leo Robin and Ralph Rainger

SYNOPSIS:

The life of songwriter Paul Dresser, brother of author Theodore Dreiser, follow his career from his early days in a travelling medicine show to his successes on Tin Pin Alley.

SOUNDTRACK: Caliban 6035

* * * * * * * * *

MY SISTER EILEEN
Columbia, 1955

Producer: Fred Kohlmar
Director: Richard Quine
Screenplay: Blake Edwards and Richard Quine; based on the play by Joseph Fields and Jerome Chodorov
Choreography: Bob Fosse
Music and Lyrics: Jule Styne and Leo Robin
Running time: 108 minutes, color

CAST:

Betty Garrett (*Ruth Sherwood*); Jack Lemmon (*Robert Baker*); Janet Leigh (*Eileen Sherwood*); Bob Fosse (*Frank Lippencott*); Kurt Kasznar (*"Papa" Appopolous*); Tommy Rall (*Chick Clark*); Dick York (*Ted "The Wreck" Loomis*); Richard Deacon (*George*); Lucy Marlow (*Helen*) and Horace McMahon (*Policeman*).

SONGS:

Atmosphere; As Soon As They See Eileen; I'm Great!; There's Nothing Like Love; Give Me a Band and My Baby; It's Bigger Than You and Me; Conga.

SYNOPSIS:

Ruth and Eileen Sherwood, two sisters from Ohio, arrive in New York City to seek their fortunes--Ruth as a writer and Eileen as an actress.

SOUNDTRACK: No soundtrack available

N

NANCY GOES TO RIO
Metro-Goldwyn-Mayer, 1950

Producer: Joe Pasternak
Director: Robert Z. Leonard
Screenplay: Sidney Sheldon; based on a story by Jane Hall, Frederick Kohner and Ralph Block
Choreography: Nick Castle
Music and Lyrics: see below with song titles
Running time: 99 minutes, color

CAST:

Jane Powell (*Nancy Barclay*); Ann Sothern (*Frances Elliott*); Barry Sullivan (*Paul Berten*); Carmen Miranda (*Marina Rodrigues*); Louis Calhern (*Gregory Elliott*); Scotty Beckett (*Scotty Sheldon*); Fortunio Bonanova (*Ricardo Domingos*); Glenn Anders (*Arthur Barrett*); Nella Walker (*Mrs. Harrison*); Hans Conried (*Alfredo*) and Frank Fontaine (*Masher*).

SONGS:

Time and Time Again - *Earl Brent and Fred Spielman*
Shine On, Harvest Moon - *Jack Norworth and Nora Bayes*
Magic is the Moonlight - *Charles Pasquale and Maria Grever*
Nancy Goes to Rio - *George Stoll and Earl Brent*
Yipsee-I-O - *Ray Gilbert*
Love is Like This - *Jay Gilbert*
Cha-Boom-Pa-Pa - *Ray Gilbert*
Musetta's Waltz (*La Bo'hème*) - *Giacomo Puccini*

SYNOPSIS:

Young Nancy Barclay and her mother, stage star Frances Elliott, are both vying for the same part in Ricardo Domingos' new play--and the same man, Paul Berten.

SOUNDTRACK: MGM 2-SES-53ST (with *Royal Wedding* and *Rich, Young and Pretty*)

* * * * * * * * *

NAUGHTY BUT NICE
Warner Bros., 1939

Producer: Sam Bischoff
Director: Ray Enright
Screenplay: Richard Macauley and Jerry Wald
Music and Lyrics: Harry Warren and Johnny Mercer
Running time: 90 minutes, B/W

CAST:

Ann Sheridan (*Zelda Manion*); Dick Powell (*Professor Donald Hardwick*); Gale Page (*Linda McKay*); Helen Broderick (*Aunt Martha*); Ronald Reagan (*Ed Clark*); ZaSu Pitts (*Aunt Penelope*); Allen Jenkins (*Joe Dirk*); Maxie Rosenbloom (*"Killer"*); Jerry Colonna (*Allie Gray*); Vera Lewis (*Aunt Annabella*); Elizabeth Dunne (*Aunt Henrietta*) and Luis Alberni (*Stanislaus Pysinski*).

SONGS:

Hooray For Spinach; Happy About the Whole Thing; In a Moment of Weakness; Corn Pickin'; I Don't Believe in Signs.

SYNOPSIS:

Donald Hardwicke is a classical music professor who finds that the rhapsody he is trying to get published is being adapted for "swing"!

SOUNDTRACK: No soundtrack available

* * * * * * * * * *

NAUGHTY MARIETTA
Metro-Goldwyn-Mayer, 1935

Producer: Hunt Stromberg
Director: W.S. Van Dyke II
Screenplay: John Lee Mahin, Frances Goodrich and Albert Hackett; based on the stage musical book by Rida Johnson Young
Music and Lyrics: Victor Herbert, Rida Johnson Young and Gus Kahn
Running time: 106 minutes, B/W

CAST:

Jeanette MacDonald (*Princess Marie/"Marietta"*); Nelson Eddy (*Capt. Richard Warrington*); Frank Morgan (*Governor d'Annard*); Elsa Lanchester (*Mme. d'Annard*); Douglass Dumbrille (*Uncle*); Joseph Cawthorne (*Herr Schuman*); Cecelia Parker

(*Julie*); Walter Kingsford (*Don Carlos*); Greta Meyer (*Frau Schuman*); Akim Tamiroff (*Rudolpho*); Harold Huber (*Abe*) and Edward Brophy (*Zeke*).

SONGS:

Chansonette; Antoinette and Anatole; Live For Today; Tramp, Tramp, Tramp; The Owl and the Polecat; 'Neath the Southern Moon; Italian Street Song; Dance of the Marionettes; I'm Falling in Love With Someone; Ah! Sweet Mystery of Life.

SYNOPSIS:

To escape an arranged marriage with the drunken Don Carlos, Princess Marie trades places with her maid Marietta and takes passage to New Orleans on a ship of contract brides.

SOUNDTRACK: Hollywood Soundstage 413

* * * * * * * * *

NAVY BLUES
Warner Bros., 1941

Producer: Hal B. Wallis
Director: Lloyd Bacon
Screenplay: Jerry Walk, Richard Macauley, Arthur T. Horman and Sam Perrin;
     based on a story by Arthur T. Horman
Choreography: Seymour Felix
Music and Lyrics: Arthur Schwartz and Johnny Mercer
Running time: 108 minutes, B/W

CAST:

Ann Sheridan (*Margie Jordan*); Jack Oakie (*Cake O'Hara*); Jack Haley (*Powerhouse Bolton*); Martha Raye (*Lilibelle Bolton*); Herbert Anderson (*Homer Matthews*); Jack Carson (*Buttons Johnson*); Jackie Gleason (*Tubby*); William T. Orr (*Mac*) and Richard Lane (*Rocky Anderson*).

SONGS:

Navy Blues; When Are We Gonna Land Abroad?; In Waikiki; You're a Natural.

SYNOPSIS:

While on shore leave in Waikiki, Navy buddies Cake O'Hara and Powerhouse Bolton try to raise money for an upcoming gunnery contest only to doscover that their top contender's enlistment is up two days before the event.

SOUNDTRACK: No soundtrack available

* * * * * * * * *

NEPTUNE'S DAUGHTER
Metro-Goldwyn-Mayer, 1949

Producer: Jack Cummings
Director: Edward Buzzell
Screenplay: Dorothy Kingsley, Ray Singer and Dick Chevillat
Choreography: Jack Donohue
Music and Lyrics: Frank Loesser
Running time: 93 minutes, color

CAST:

Esther Williams (*Eve Barrett*); Red Skelton (*Jack Spratt*); Ricardo Montalban (*José O'Rourke*); Betty Garrett (*Betty Barrett*); Keenan Wynn (*Joe Beckett*); Xavier Cugat (*Himself*); Ted de Corsia (*Lukie Luzette*); Mike Mazurki (*Mac Mazolla*) and Mel Blanc (*Julio*).

SONGS:

I Love Those Men; My Heart Beats Faster; Baby, It's Cold Outside.

SYNOPSIS:

After swimsuit manufacturer Eve Barrett finds her younger sister Betty infactuated with South American polo star José O'Rourke she decides to break up the romance but falls for him herself.

SOUNDTRACK: No soundtrack available

* * * * * * * * *

NEVER STEAL ANYTHING SMALL
Universal, 1959

Producer: Aaron Rosenberg
Director: Charles Lederer

230

Screenplay: Charles Lederer; based on the play *The Devil's Hornpipe* by Maxwell Anderson and Rouben Mamoulian
Choreography: Hermes Pan
Music and Lyrics: Allie Wrubel and Maxwell Anderson
Running time: 94 minutes, color

CAST:

James Cagney (*Jake MacIllaney*); Shirley Jones (*Linda Cabot*); Roger Smith (*Dan Cabot*); Cara Williams (*Winnipeg*); Nehemiah Persoff (*Pinelli*); Royal Dano (*Words Cannon*); Anthony Caruso (*Lt. Trevis*); Horace McMahon (*O.K. Merritt*); Virginia Vincent (*Ginger*) and Jack Albertson (*Sleep-Out Charlie*).

SONGS:

Helping Out Friends; I Haven't Got a Thing to Wear; I'm Sorry, I Want a Ferrari; It Takes Love to Make a Home; Never Steal Anything Small.

SYNOPSIS:

Crooked union leader Jake MacIllaney has his eye on his lawyer Dan Cabot's wife Linda so he sets up Dan on a phoney larceny charge but soon begins to doubt himself.

SOUNDTRACK: No soundtrack available

* * * * * * * * *

NEW MOON
Metro-Goldwyn-Mayer, 1940

Producer: Robert Z. Leonard
Director: Robert Z. Leonard
Screenplay: Jacques Deval and Robert Arthur; based on the stage musical book by Oscar Hammerstein II, Frank Mandel and Lawrence Schwab
Choreography: Val Raset
Music and Lyrics: Sigmund Romberg and Oscar Hammerstein II
Running time: 105 minutes, B/W

CAST:

Jeanette MacDonald (*Marianne de Beaumanoir*); Nelson Eddy (*Charles Mission/Duc de Villiers*); Mary Boland (*Valerie de Rossac*); George Zucco (*Vicomte de Ribaud*);

H.B. Warner (*Father Michel*); Grant Mitchell (*Governor of New Orleans*); Stanley Fields (*Tambour*); Richard Purcell (*Alexander*); Bunty Cutler (*Julie*); John Miljan (*Pierre Brugnon*) and Ivan Simpson (*Guizot*).

SONGS:

Dance Your Cares Away; Stranger in Paris; Shoes; Softly, as in a Morning Sunrise; One Kiss; Troubles of the World; Wanting You; Lover, Come Back to Me; Stouthearted Men; Marianne.

SYNOPSIS:

New Orleans, 1795: To escape execution by the King of France the Duc de Villiers disguises himself as a bondsman named Charles Mission and then engineers a plan to aid in the escape of all the bondsmen in New Orleans.

SOUNDTRACK: Pelican 103 (with *I Married an Angel*)

* * * * * * * * * *

NEW YORK, NEW YORK
United Artists, 1977

Producer: Irwin Winkler and Robert Chartoff
Director: Martin Scorsese
Screenplay: Earl MacRauch and Mardik Martin; based on a story by Earl MacRauch
Choreography: Ron Field
Music and Lyrics: see below with song titles
Running time: 137 minutes, color

CAST:

Liza Minelli (*Francine Evans*); Robert De Niro (*Jimmy Doyle*); Lionel Stander (*Tony Harwell*); Georgie Auld (*Frankie Harte*); Mary Kay Place (*Bernice*); George Memmoli (*Nicky*); Barry Primus (*Paul Wilson*); Dick Miller (*Palm Club Owner*); Diahnne Abbott (*Harlem Club Singer*) and Larry Kert (*Singer*).

SONGS:

You Brought a New Kind of Love to Me - *Sammy Fain, Irving Kahal and Pierre*
Norman Connor
Flip the Dip - *Georgie Auld*
Once in a While - *Bud Green and Michael Edwards*
You Are My Lucky Star - *Nacio Herb Brown and Arthur Freed*

Game Over - *Georgie Auld*
The Man I Love - *George Gershwin and Ira Gershwin*
Just You, Just Me - *Raymond Klages and Jesse Greer*
There Goes the Ball Game - *John Kander and Fred Ebb*
Blue Moon - *Richard Rodgers and Lorenz Hart*
Happy Endings - *John Kander and Fred Ebb*
But the World Goes 'Round - *John Kander and Fred Ebb*
Honeysuckle Rose - *Thomas "Fats" Waller and Andy Razaf*
South America, Take It Away - *Harold J. Rome*
Taking a Chance On Love - *Vernon Duke, John LaTouche and Ted Fetter*
Once Again Right Away - *Ralph Burns*
New York, New York - *John Kander and Fred Ebb*

SYNOPSIS:

In the Big Band era, saxophone player Jimmy Doyle and singer Francine Evans alternately love and fight each other as they struggle for happiness and recognition.

SOUNDTRACK: United Artists LA750-L2

O

OH, YOU BEAUTIFUL DOLL!
20th Century Fox, 1949

Producer: George Jessel
Director: John M. Stahl
Screenplay: Albert Lewis and Arthur Lewis
Choreography: Seymour Felix
Music and Lyrics: see below with song titles
Running time: 93 minutes, color

CAST:

Mark Stevens* (*Larry Kelly*); June Haver (*Doris Breitenbach*); S.Z. Sakall (*Fred Fisher/Alfred Breitenbach*); Charlotte Greenwood (*Anna Breitenbach*); Gale Robbins (*Marie Carle*); Jay C. Flippen (*Lippy Brannigan*); Andrew Tombes (*Ted Held*); Eduard Franz (*Gottfried Steiner*); Eula Morgan (*Mme. Zaubel*) and Nestor Paiva (*Lucca*).

vocals dubbed by Bill Shirley

SONGS:

Oh, You Beautiful Doll! - *Fred Fisher and Alfred Bryan*
Come Josephine in My Flying Machine - *Fred Fisher and Alfred Bryan*
Ireland Must Be Heaven For My Mother Came From There - *Joseph McCarthy, Fred Fisher and Howard Johnson*
I Want You to Want Me to Want You - *Bob Schafer, Alfred Bryan and Fred Fisher*
When I Get You Alone Tonight - *Joseph McCarthy, Fred Fisher and Joe Goodwin*
Peg 'O My Heart - *Fred Fisher and Alfred Bryan*
There's a Broken Heart For Every Light On Broadway - *Fred Fisher and Howard Johnson*
Who Paid the Rent For Mrs. Rip Van Winkle? - *Fred Fisher and Alfred Bryan*
Daddy, You've Been More Than a Mother To Me - *Fred Fisher*
Dardanella - *Felix Bernard, Johnny S. Black and Fred Fisher*
Chicago - *Fred Fisher*

SYNOPSIS:

The biography of Tin Pan Alley songwriter Fred Fisher who for years wrote his popular songs incognito (his real name was Alfred Breitenbach) because he wanted to be accepted as a serious musician.

SOUNDTRACK: Titania 502 (with *I Wonder Who's Kissing Her Now*)

* * * * * * * * *

OKLAHOMA!
20th Century Fox, 1955

Producer: Arthur Hornblow, Jr.
Director: Fred Zinnemann
Screenplay: Oscar Hammerstein II, based on his stage musical book
Choreography: Agnes DeMille
Music and Lyrics: Richard Rodgers and Oscar Hammerstein II
Running time: 145 minutes, color

CAST:

Gordon MacRae (*Curly*); Shirley Jones (*Laurey*); Gloria Grahame (*Ado Annie*); Gene Nelson (*Will*); Charlotte Greenwood (*Aunt Eller*); Rod Steiger (*Jud Fry*); Jay C. Flippen (*Mr. Skidmore*); Barbara Lawrence (*Gerty*); James Whitmore (*Mr. Carnes*) and Eddie Albert (*Ali Hakim*).

SONGS:

Oh, What a Beautiful Mornin'; The Surrey With the Fringe On Top; Kansas City; I Cain't Say No; Many a New Day; People Will Say We're in Love; Poor Jud is Dead; Out Of My Dreams; The Farmer and the Cowman; All 'Er Nothin'; Oklahoma!

SYNOPSIS:

Romantic triangles and cowman/farmer rivalries abound in this story set in turn-of-the-century Oklahoma Territory.

SOUNDTRACK: Capitol SWA-0595

* * * * * * * * *

THE OLD CURIOSITY SHOP
Readers' Digest, 1975

Producer: Helen M. Strauss
Director: Michael Tuchner
Screenplay: Louis Kamp and Irene Kamp; based on the novel by Charles Dickens
Choreography: Gillian Lynne

Music and Lyrics: Anthony Newley
Running time: 118 minutes, color

CAST:

Anthony Newley (*Daniel Quilp*); David Hemmings (*Richard Swiveller*); David Warner (*Sampson Brass*); Jill Bennett (*Sally Brass*); Peter Duncan (*Christopher "Kit" Nubbles*); Michael Hordern (*Edward Trent*); Mona Washbourne (*Mrs. Jarley*); Paul Rogers (*Henry Trent*); Yvonna Antrobus (*Bessie Quilp*); Sarah Webb (*"Duchess"*) and Sarah Jane Varley (*Nell Trent*).

SONGS:

Quilp; When a Felon Needs a Friend; Happiness Pie; Somewhere; The Sport of Kings; Love Has the Longest Memory.

SYNOPSIS:

London, 1840: The villianous hunchback Daniel Quilp forecloses on the Old Curiosity Shop belonging to Edward Trent and his granddaughter Nell forcing them to become wandering vagrants while Quilp and his evil associates search for them and their supposed hidden treasures. Formerly titled *Mr. Quilp*.

SOUNDTRACK: Chap 12574

* * * * * * * * *

OLIVER!
Columbia, 1968

Producer: John Woolf
Director: Carol Reed
Screenplay: Vernon Harris; based on the stage musical book by Lionel Bart
Choreography: Onna White
Music and Lyrics: Lionel Bart
Running time: 153 minutes, color

CAST:

Ron Moody (*Fagin*); Oliver Reed (*Bill Sikes*); Shani Wallis (*Nancy*); Harry Secombe (*Mr. Bumble*); Jack Wild (*The Artful Dodger*); Hugh Griffith (*The Magistrate*); Peggy Mount (*Widow Corney*); Sheila White (*Bet*) and Mark Lester (*Oliver Twist*).

236

SONGS:

SONGS:

Food, Glorious Food; Oliver!; Boy For Sale; Where is Love?; Consider Yourself; Pick a Pocket Or Two; I'd Do Anything; Be Back Soon; As Long As He Needs Me; Who Will Buy?; It's a Fine Life; Reviewing the Situation; Oom-Pah-Pah.

SYNOPSIS:

Charles Dickens' classic about an orphan named Oliver Twist who escapes from a workhouse only to fall in with a band of thieves led by the wily Fagin.

SOUNDTRACK: Colgems 5501

* * * * * * * * * *

ON A CLEAR DAY YOU CAN SEE FOREVER
Paramount, 1970

Producer: Howard W. Koch
Director: Vincente Minelli
Screenplay: Alan Jay Lerner, based on his stage musical book
Choreography: Howard Jeffrey
Music and Lyrics: Burton Lane and Alan Jay Lerner
Running time: 129 minutes, color

CAST:

Barbra Streisand (*Daisy Gamble*); Yves Montand (*Dr. Marc Chabot*); Larry Blyden (*Warren Pratt*); Simon Oakland (*Dr. Conrad Fuller*); Bob Newhart (*Dr. Mason Hume*); Jack Nicholson (*Tad Pringle*); Laurie Main (*Lord Percy Moorpark*) and John Richardson (*Sir Robert Tentrees*).

SONGS:

Hurry! It's Lovely Up Here; Love With All the Trimmings; Melinda; Go to Sleep; He Isn't You; What Did I Have That I Don't Have?; Come Back To Me; On a Clear Day.

SYNOPSIS:

While undergoing hypnosis to quit smoking, Daisy Gamble reveals that she has had several previous lives--all much more interesting than her present one prompting her psychiatrist to question his own sanity.

237

SOUNDTRACK: Columbia 30086

* * * * * * * * * *

ON AN ISLAND WITH YOU
Metro-Goldwyn-Mayer, 1948

Producer: Joe Pasternak
Director: Richard Thorpe
Screenplay: Dorothy Kingsley, Dorothy Cooper, Charles Martin and Hans Wilhelm;
        based on a story by Charles Martin and Hans Wilhelm
Choreography: Jack Donohue

Music and Lyrics: Nacio Herb Brown and Edward Heyman
Running time: 107 minutes, color

CAST:

Esther Williams (*Rosalind Reynolds*); Peter Lawford (*Lt. Lawrence Y. Kingslee*); Ricardo Montalban (*Ricardo Montez*); Jimmy Durante (*Buckley*); Cyd Charisse (*Yvonne Terro*); Xavier Cugat (*Himself*); Leon Ames (*Commander Harrison*); Kathryn Beaumont (*Penelope Peabody*); Dick Simmons (*George Blaine*) and Marie Wilson (*Jane*).

SONGS:

On an Island With You; My Little Chihuahua; I Can Do Without Broadway*; I'm Taking Miss Mary to the Ball; If I Were You; I'll Do the Strut-away in My Cutaway*; Start Out Each Day With a Song.

**music and lyrics by Jimmy Durante*

SYNOPSIS:

While acting as technical advisor on Rosalind Reynolds' new film in the tropics, Lt. Larry Kingslee decides to "kidnap" her and fly her to the island where he first met her during WWII.

SOUNDTRACK: No soundtrack available

* * * * * * * * * *

THE ONE AND ONLY, GENUINE, ORIGINAL FAMILY BAND
Buena Vista, 1968

Producer: Bill Anderson
Director: Michael O'Herlihy
Screenplay: Lowell Hawley; based on the book by Laura Bower Van Nuys
Choreography: Hugh Lambert
Music and Lyrics: Richard M. Sherman and Robert B. Sherman
Running time: 117 minutes, color

CAST:

Walter Brennan (*Grandpa Bower*); Buddy Ebsen (*Calvin Bower*); Lesley Ann Warren (*Alice Bower*); John Davidson (*Joe Carder*); Janet Blair (*Katie Bower*); Wally Cox (*Mr. Wampler*); Richard Deacon (*Charlie Wren*); Kurt Russell (*Sidney Bower*); Goldie Jeanne Hawn (*Giggly Girl*); Steve Harmon (*Ernie Stubbins*); Bobby Riha (*Mayo Bower*) and Pam Ferdin (*Laura Bower*).

SONGS:

The One and Only, Genuine, Original Family Band; The Happiest Girl Alive; Let's Put It Over With Grover; Ten Feet Off the Ground; Dakota; 'Bout Time; Drummin', Drummin', Drummin'; West O' the Wide Missouri; Oh, Benjamin Harrison.

SYNOPSIS:

The Presidential election of 1888 between Grover Cleveland and Benjamin Harrison and the fight for Dakota statehood form the backdrop for a performing family's divided loyalties.

SOUNDTRACK: Buena Vista 5002

* * * * * * * * *

ONE HOUR WITH YOU
Paramount, 1932

Producer: Ernst Lubitsch
Director: Ernst Lubitsch and George Cukor
Screenplay: Samson Raphaelson; based on the play *Nur ein Traum* by Lothar
         Schmidt
Music and Lyrics: Oscar Straus, Richard A. Whiting and Leo Robin
Running time: 75 minutes, B/W

CAST:

Maurice Chevalier (*Dr. André Bertier*); Jeanette MacDonald (*Colette Bertier*);

239

Genevieve Tobin (*Mitzi Olivier*); Charles Ruggles (*Dr. Adolph*); Roland Young (*Professor Olivier*); George Barbier (*Police Commissioner*); Josephine Dunn (*Mlle. Martel*); Richard Carle (*Detective*) and Charles Judels (*Policeman*).

SONGS:

One Hour With You; We Will Always Be Sweethearts; What Would You Do?; What a Little Thing Like a Wedding Ring Can Do; Oh, That Mitzi; Three Times a Day; It Was Only a Dream Kiss.

SYNOPSIS:

Dr. André Bertier has a roving eye and when his wife Colette suspects him of having an affair with her best friend Mitzi she retaliates by flirting with Adolph.

SOUNDTRACK: Caliban 6011 (with *Do You Love Me?*)

* * * * * * * * * *

ONE IN A MILLION
20th Century Fox, 1936

Producer: Darryl F. Zanuck
Director: Sidney Lanfield
Screenplay: Leonard Praskins and Mark Kelly
Choreography: Jack Haskell
Music and Lyrics: Sidney D. Mitchell and Lew Pollack
Running time: 95 minutes, B/W

CAST:

Sonja Henie (*Greta Muller*); Adolphe Menjou (*Thaddeus "Tad" Spencer*); Don Ameche (*Bob Harris*); Ned Sparks (*Danny Simpson*); Jean Hersholt (*Heinrich Muller*); The Ritz Brothers (*Themselves*); Arline Judge (*Billie Spencer*); Dixie Dunbar (*Goldie*); Borrah Minevitch (*Adolph*) and Montagu Love (*Ratoffsky/Sir Frederick Brooks*).

SONGS:

One in a Million; The Moonlight Waltz (instrumental); We're Back in Circulation Again; The Horror Boys From Hollywood; Who's Afraid of Love?; Lovely Lady in White (instrumental).

SYNOPSIS:

Tad Spencer and his troupe are stranded in a Swiss hotel and discover that the daughter of the owner, Greta, is a skating star who is being groomed for the 1936 Munich Olympics. When Tad decides to exploit her talents reporter Bob Harris tries to stop him from endangering her amateur status.

SOUNDTRACK: No soundtrack available

* * * * * * * * *

ONE NIGHT OF LOVE
Columbia, 1934

Producer: Harry Cohn
Director: Victor Schertzinger
Screenplay: S.K. Lauren, James Gow and Edmund North; based on a story by
     Dorothy Speare and Charles Beahan
Music and Lyrics: see below with song titles
Running time: 82 minutes, B/W

CAST:

Grace Moore (*Mary Barrett*); Tullio Carminati (*Giulio Monteverdi*); Lyle Talbot (*Bill Houston*); Mona Barrie (*Lally*); Nydia Westman (*Muriel*); Jessie Ralph (*Angelina*); Luis Alberni (*Giovanni*); Andres De Segurola (*Caluppi*); Rosemary Glosz (*Frappazini*); William Burress (*Mary's Father*) and Jane Darwell (*Mary's Mother*).

SONGS:

Sextette (*Lucia di Lammermoor*) - *Gaetano Donizetti*
The Last Rose of Summer (*Martha*) - *Friedrich Von Flotow*
One Night of Love - *Gus Kahn and Victor Schertzinger*
Ciribiribin - *Alberto Pestalozza and Rudolf Thaler*
Sempre libera (*La Traviata*) - *Giuseppe Verdi*
Habañera (*Carmen*) - *Georges Bizet*
Un bel di (*Madama Butterfly*) - *Giacomo Puccini*

SYNOPSIS:

Mary Barrett is a struggling opera singer in Italy who impresses impressario Giulio Monteverdi in a small cabaret where she is singing. He is soon helplessly in love with her but promises himself that as she is his pupil any romance between them is out of the question.

SOUNDTRACK: Grapon 15 (with *I Dream Too Much*)

* * * * * * * * * *

ONE SUNDAY AFTERNOON
Warner Bros., 1948

Producer: Jerry Wald
Director: Raoul Walsh
Screenplay: Robert L. Richards; based on the play by James Hagan
Choreography: LeRoy Prinz
Music and Lyrics: Ralph Blane
Running time: 90 minutes, color

CAST:

Dennis Morgan (*Timothy "Biff" Grimes*); Janis Paige (*Virginia Brush*); Don DeFore (*Hugo Barnstead*); Dorothy Malone (*Amy Lind*); Ben Blue (*Nick*); Oscar O'Shea (*Toby*); Alan Hale, Jr. (*Marty*) and George Neise (*Chauncey*).

SONGS:

One Sunday Afternoon; Some Day; Johnny and Lucille; In My Merry Oldsmobile*; Daisy Bell**; Sweet Corner Girl; Girls Were Made to Take Care of Boys; Amy, You're a Little Bit Old-Fashioned***.

music and lyrics by Vincent Bryan and Gus Edwards
**music and lyrics by Harry Dacre*
***music and lyrics by Marion Sunshine and Henry I. Marshall*

SYNOPSIS:

Biff Grimes and Hugo Barnstead are rivals in business and love--for Virginia Brush--in the Gay Nineties but when Hugo's shady business dealings send Biff to prison it's Amy Lind who stands by him.

SOUNDTRACK: No soundtrack available

* * * * * * * * * *

ON MOONLIGHT BAY
Warner Bros., 1951

242

Producer: William Jacobs
Director: Roy Del Ruth
Screenplay: Jack Rose and Melville Shavelson; based on the *Penrod* stories by Booth Tarkington
Choreography: LeRoy Prinz
Music and Lyrics: see below with song titles
Running time: 94 minutes, color

CAST:

Doris Day (*Marjorie Winfield*); Gordon MacRae (*William Sherman*); Jack Smith (*Hubert Wakely*); Leon Ames (*George Winfield*); Rosemary De Camp (*Mrs. Winfield*); Billy Gray (*Wesley Winfield*); Mary Wickes (*Stella*); Ellen Corby (*Miss Stevens*); Jeffrey Stevens (*Jim Sherman*); Esther Dale (*Aunt Martha*) and Suzanne Whitney (*Cora*).

SONGS:

On Moonlight Bay - *Percy Wenrich and Edward Madden*
Love Ya - *Charles Tobias and Peter DeRose*
Cuddle Up a Little Closer, Lovey Mine - *Karl Hoschna and Otto Harbach*
Tell Me - *Max Kortlander and J. Will Callahan*
I'm Forever Blowing Bubbles - *Jean Kenbrovin and John W. Kellette*
Every Little Movement - *Karl Hoschna and Otto Harbach*
Pack Up Your Troubles - *George Asaf and Felix Powell*
Till We Meet Again - *Richard A. Whiting and Raymond B. Egan*
Christmas Story - *Pauline Walsh*
Yoo-Hoo - *Al Jolson and B.G. DeSylva*

SYNOPSIS:

Tomboy Marjorie Winfield is more interested in baseball than boys but soon changes her mind when she meets handsome William Sherman.

SOUNDTRACK: Caliban 6006 (with *It Happened in Brooklyn* and *Three Smart Girls*)

* * * * * * * * *

ON THE AVENUE
20th Century Fox, 1937

Producer: Darryl F. Zanuck
Director: Roy Del Ruth
Screenplay: Gene Markey and William Conselman

Choreography: Seymour Felix
Music and Lyrics: Irving Berlin
Running time: 90 minutes, B/W

CAST:

Dick Powell (*Gary Blake*); Madeleine Carroll (*Mimi Caraway*); Alice Faye (*Mona Merrick*); The Ritz Brothers (*Themselves*); George Barbier (*Commodore Caraway*); Alan Mowbray (*Frederick Sims*); Cora Witherspoon (*Aunt Fritz Peters*); Walter Catlett (*Jake Dribble*); Douglas Fowley (*Eddie Eads*); Joan Davis (*Miss Katz*); Sig Rumann (*Herr Hanfstangel*) and Billy Gilbert (*Joe Papaloupas*).

SONGS:

This Year's Kisses; You're Laughing At Me; I've Got My Love to Keep Me Warm; Slumming On Park Avenue; He Ain't Got Rhythm; The Girl on the Police Gazette.

SYNOPSIS:

Broadway producer Gary Blake puts on a new show that satirizes wealthy socialite Mimi Caraway but soon he is hopelessly in love with her--much to the chagrin of his girlfriend Mona.

SOUNDTRACK: Hollywood Soundstage 401

* * * * * * * * *

ON THE RIVIERA
20th Century Fox, 1951

Producer: Sol C. Siegel
Director: Walter Lang
Screenplay: Valentine Davies, Phoebe Ephron and Henry Ephron; based on a play
            by Rudolph Lothar and Hans Adler
Choreography: Jack Cole
Music and Lyrics: Sylvia Fine
Running time: 89 minutes, color

CAST:

Danny Kaye (*Henri Duran/Jack Martin*); Gene Tierney (*Lilli*); Corinne Calvet (*Colette*); Marcel Dalio (*Philippe Lebrix*); Jean Murat (*Periton*); Henri Letondal (*Louis Forel*); Clinton Sundberg (*Antoine*); Sig Rumann (*Capeaux*); Joyce MacKenzie

(*Mimi*); Monique Chantal (*Minette*); Marina Koshetz (*Mme. Cornet*); Ann Codee (*Mme. Periton*) and Mari Blanchard (*Eugenie*).

SONGS:

On the Riviera; Popo the Puppet; Ballin' the Jack*; The Rhythm of a New Romance; Happy Ending.

music and lyrics by Chris Smith and James Henry Burris

SYNOPSIS:

Night club entertainer Jack Martin is asked to impersonate playboy businessman Henri Duran while he goes abroad to secure a loan for his floundering company. Remake of *That Night in Rio*.

SOUNDTRACK: No soundtrack available

* * * * * * * * *

ON THE TOWN
Metro-Goldwyn-Mayer, 1949

Producer: Arthur Freed
Director: Gene Kelly and Stanley Donen
Screenplay: Betty Comden and Adolph Green, based on their stage musical book
Choreography: Gene Kelly and Stanley Donen
Music and Lyrics: Leonard Bernstein, Betty Comden and Adolph Green
Running time: 98 minutes, color

CAST:

Gene Kelly (*Gabey*); Frank Sinatra (*Chip*); Betty Garrett (*Brunhilde Esterhazy*); Ann Miller (*Claire Hudson*); Jules Munshin (*Ozzie*); Vera-Ellen (*Ivy Smith*); Florence Bates (*Mme. Dilyovska*); Alice Pearce (*Lucy Schmeeler*); George Meader (*Professor*); Bern Hoffman (*Dock Worker*); Hans Conried (*François*) and Bea Benaderet (*Working Girl*).

SONGS:

I Feel Like I'm Not Out of Bed Yet; New York, New York; Miss Turnstiles' Dance (instrumental); Pre-Historic Man*; Come Up to My Place; Main Street*; You're Awful*; On the Town*; You Can Count On Me*; A Day in New York Ballet (instrumental); Pearl of the Persian Sea*;

music and lyrics by Roger Edens, Betty Comden and Adolph Green

SYNOPSIS:

Gabey, Chip and Ozzie are three sailors with a 24-hour leave in New York City and their first order of business is to find girls and soon, with Hildy Esterhazy and Claire Huson, they are helping search for Gabey's dream girl--"Miss Turnstiles", Ivy Smith.

SOUNDTRACK: Show Biz Records 5603

* * * * * * * * *

THE OPPOSITE SEX
Metro-Goldwyn-Mayer, 1956

Producer: Joe Pasternak
Director: David Miller
Screenplay: Fay Kanin and Michael Kanin; based on the play *The Women* by Clare
       Boothe
Choreography: Robert Sidney
Music and Lyrics: Nicholas Brodsky, Sammy Cahn, George Stoll and Ralph Freed
Running time: 117 minutes, color

CAST:

June Allyson (*Kay Hilliard*); Joan Collins (*Crystal Allen*); Dolores Gray (*Sylvia Fowler*); Ann Sheridan (*Amanda Penrose*); Ann Miller (*Gloria Dell*); Leslie Nielsen (*Steven Hilliard*); Jeff Richards (*Buck Winston*); Agnes Moorehead (*Countess*); Sam Levene (*Mike Pearl*); Charlotte Greenwood (*Lucy*); Joan Blondell (*Edith Potter*); Carolyn Jones (*Pat*); Alice Pearce (*Olga*); Sandy Descher (*Debbie Hilliard*); Barbara Jo Allen (*Dolly*); Dick Shawn (*Himself*) and Harry James (*Himself*).

SONGS:

Dere's Yellow Gold On De Trees (De Banana); Young Man With a Horn; A Perfect Love; The Opposite Sex; Now! Baby, Now!; Rock and Roll Tumbleweed.

SYNOPSIS:

When Kay and Steven Hilliard's marriage is broken up by wily starlet Crystal Allen Kay finds a mixture of solace and spite from her circle of friends.

SOUNDTRACK: No soundtrack available

246

P

PAGAN LOVE SONG
Metro-Goldwyn-Mayer, 1950

Producer: Arthur Freed
Director: Robert Alton
Screenplay: Robert Nathan and Jerry Davis; based on the book *Tahiti Landfall* by
        William S. Stone
Choreography: Robert Alton
Music and Lyrics: Harry Warren and Arthur Freed
Running time: 76 minutes, color

CAST:

Esther Williams (*Mimi Bennett*); Howard Keel (*Hazard Endicott*); Minna Gombell
(*Kate Bennett*); Charles Mauu (*Tavae*); Rita Moreno (*Teuru*); Philip Costa (*Manu*);
Dione Leilani (*Tani*); Charles Freund (*Papera*); Marcella Corday (*Countess Mariani*);
Sam Maikai (*Tua*); Helen Rapoza (*Angele*); Birdie DeBolt (*Mama Ruau*); Bill Kaliloa
(*Mata*) and Carlo Cook (*Monsieur Bouchet*).

SONGS:

Pagan Love Song*; Tahiti; Singing in the Sun; Etiquette; Why is Love So Crazy?;
The House of the Singing Bamboo; The Sea of the Moon.

music and lyrics by Nacio Herb Brown and Arthur Freed

SYNOPSIS:

Schoolteacher Hazard Endicott goes to Tahiti to take over a plantation willed to him
by his uncle and falls in love with Mimi Bennett, a wealthy islander.

SOUNDTRACK: MGM 2-SES-43ST (with *The Pirate* and *Hit the Deck*)

* * * * * * * * * *

PAINT YOUR WAGON
Paramount, 1969

Producer: Alan Jay Lerner
Director: Joshua Logan
Screenplay: Alan Jay Lerner, adaptation by Paddy Chayefsky; based on the stage
        musical book by Alan Jay Lerner

Choreography: Jack Baker
Music and Lyrics: Frederick Loewe and Alan Jay Lerner
Running time: 166 minutes, color

CAST:

Lee Marvin (*Ben Rumson*); Clint Eastwood (*"Pardner"*); Jean Seberg (*Elizabeth*); Harve Presnell (*"Rotten Luck Willie"*); Ray Walston (*"Mad Jack" Duncan*); Tom Ligon (*Horton Fenty*); Alan Dexter (*Parson*); William O'Connell (*Horace Tabor*); H.B. Haggerty (*Steve Bull*); Robert Easton (*Ezra Atwell*); Terry Jenkins (*Joe Mooney*); Karl Bruck (*Schermerhorn*) and John Mitchum (*Jacob Woodling*).

SONGS:

I'm On My Way; I Still See Elisa; The First Thing You Know*; Hand Me Down That Can O' Beans; They Call the Wind Maria; A Million Miles Away Behind the Door*; There's a Coach Comin' In; Whoop-Ti-Ay! (Shivaree); I Talk to the Trees; The Gospel of No-Name City*; Best Things*; Wand'rin' Star; Gold Fever*.

music and lyrics by André Previn and Alan Jay Lerner

SYNOPSIS:

California's Gold Rush lures miners by the hundreds and two of them, Ben Rumson and his new partner--"Pardner"--decide that due to the extreme shortage of women that they will just have to share Ben's new bride Elizabeth!

SOUNDTRACK: Paramount 1001

* * * * * * * * * *

THE PAJAMA GAME
Warner Bros., 1957

Producer: George Abbott and Stanley Donen
Director: George Abbott and Stanley Donen
Screenplay: George Abbott and Richard Bissell, based on their stage musical book
Choreography: Bob Fosse
Music and Lyrics: Richard Adler and Jerry Ross
Running time: 101 minutes, color

CAST:

Doris Day (*Kate "Babe" Williams*); John Raitt (*Sid Sorokin*); Carol Haney (*Gladys*

Hotchkiss); Eddie Foy, Jr. (*Vernon Hines*); Reta Shaw (*Mabel*); Barbara Nichols (*Poopsie*); Ralph Dunn (*Mr. Hasler*); Thelma Pelish (*Mae*); Franklyn Fox (*Pop Williams*) and Jack Straw (*Prez*).

SONGS:

The Pajama Game; Racing With the Clock; I'm Not At All in Love; I'll Never Be Jealous Again; Hey, There; Once-a-Year Day; Small Talk; There Once Was a Man; Steam Heat; Hernando's Hideaway; 7½ Cents.

SYNOPSIS:

When new supervisor Sid Sorokin takes over the pajama factory he falls for Babe, but when she leads the workers in a strike for a pay raise their romance becomes rocky.

SOUNDTRACK: Columbia AOL-5210

* * * * * * * * * *

PAL JOEY
Columbia, 1957

Producer: Fred Kohlmar
Director: George Sidney
Screenplay: Dorothy Kingsley; based on the stage musical book by John O'Hara
Choreography: Hermes Pan
Music and Lyrics: Richard Rodgers and Lorenz Hart
Running time: 111 minutes, color

CAST:

Rita Hayworth* (*Vera Simpson*); Frank Sinatra (*Joey Evans*); Kim Novak** (*Linda English*); Barbara Nichols (*Gladys*); Bobby Sherwood (*Ned Galvin*); Hank Henry (*Mike*); Elizabeth Patterson (*Mrs. Casey*); Frank Wilcox (*Colonel Langley*) and Pierre Watkin (*Mr. Forsythe*).

 *vocals dubbed by Jo Ann Greer
**vocals dubbed by Trudy Erwin

SONGS:

A Great Big Town; I Could Write a Book; That Terrific Rainbow; Happy Hunting Horn; Bewitched; Pal Joey (What Do I Care For a Dame?); Zip; Plant You Now,

Dig You Later; Do It the Hard Way; Take Him; There's a Small Hotel; I Didn't Know What Time It Was; My Funny Valentine; The Lady is a Tramp.

SYNOPSIS:

Joey Evans is a night club singer whose ambitions are put to the test when wealthy society widow Vera Simpson offers him his own club--on the provision that he give up his girlfriend Linda.

SOUNDTRACK: Capitol W-912

* * * * * * * * *

PANAMA HATTIE
Metro-Goldwyn-Mayer, 1942

Producer: Arthur Freed
Director: Norman McLeod and Vincente Minelli
Screenplay: Jack McGowan and Wilkie Mahoney; based on the stage musical book
            by Herbert Fields and B.G. DeSylva
Choreography: Danny Dare
Music and Lyrics: Cole Porter
Running time: 85 minutes, B/W

CAST:

Ann Sothern (*Hattie Maloney*); Dan Dailey (*Dick Bulliet*); Red Skelton (*"Red"*); Marsha Hunt (*Leila Tree*); Virginia O'Brien (*Flo Foster*); "Rags" Ragland (*"Rags"*); Alan Mowbray (*Jay Jerkins*); Ben Blue (*"Rowdy"*); Jackie Horner (*Geraldine Bulliet*); Carl Esmond (*Lucas Kefler*) and Lena Horne (*Singer*).

SONGS:

Hattie From Panama*; Fresh as a Daisy; I'll Do Anything For You*; Good Neighbors*; Let's Be Buddies; I've Still Got My Health; Just One Of Those Things; Make It Another Old-Fashioned, Please; Did I Get Stinkin' at the Club Savoy**; The Son-of-a-Gun Who Picks On Uncle Sam*.

 *music and lyrics by Burton Lane, Roger Edens and E.Y. Harburg
**music and lyrics by Walter Donaldson

SYNOPSIS:

Hattie Maloney runs a night club in Panama City where she meets Dick Bulliet, a

250

well-to-do widower from Philadelphia. They decide to marry but first must overcome his daughter Geraldine's hostility towards Hattie.

SOUNDTRACK: No soundtrack available

* * * * * * * * *

PARADISE, HAWAIIAN STYLE
Paramount, 1966

Producer: Hal B. Wallis
Director: Michael Moore
Screenplay: Allan Weiss and Anthony Lawrence; based on a story by Allan Weiss
Choreography: Jack Regas
Music and Lyrics: see below with song titles
Running time: 91 minutes, color

CAST:

Elvis Presley (*Rick Richards*); James Shigeta (*Danny Kohana*); Suzanna Leigh (*Judy "Friday" Hudson*); Donna Butterworth (*Jan Kohana*); Marianna Hill (*Lani Kaimana*); Julie Parrish (*Joanna*); Philip Ahn (*Moke Kaimana*); Jan Shepard (*Betty Kohana*); Irene Tsu (*Pua*); Linda Wong (*Lehua Kawena*) and John Doucette (*Donald Belden*).

SONGS:

Paradise, Hawaiian Style - *Bill Giant, Bernie Baum and Florence Kaye*
Queenie Wahine's Papaya - *Bill Giant, Bernie Baum and Florence Kaye*
Scratch My Back (Then I'll Scratch Yours) - *Bill Giant, Bernie Baum and Florence Kaye*
Drums of the Islands - *Sid Tepper, Roy C. Bennett and the Polynesian Cultural Center*
A Dog's Life - *Sid Wayne and Ben Weisman*
Datin' - *Fred Wise and Randy Starr*
House of Sand - *Bill Giant, Bernie Baum and Florence Kaye*
Bill Bailey, Won't You Please Come Home? - *Hughie Cannon*
Stop Where You Are - *Bill Giant, Bernie Baum and Florence Kaye*
This is My Heaven - *Bill Giant, Bernie Baum and Florence Kaye*

SYNOPSIS:

Rick Richards and his partner Danny Kohana run an air charter service in Hawaii, relying on Rick's many girlfriends (on different islands--*of course*) as contacts for potentials clients.

251

* * * * * * * * * *

THE PERILS OF PAULINE
Paramount, 1947

Producer: Sol C. Siegel
Director: George Marshall
Screenplay: P.J. Wolfson and Frank Butler; based on a story by P.J. Wolfson
Choreography: Billy Daniel
Music and Lyrics: Frank Loesser
Running time: 96 minutes, color

CAST:

Betty Hutton (*Pearl White*); John Lund (*Michael Farrington*); Billy DeWolfe (*Timmie*); William Demarest (*George McGuire*); Constance Collier (*Julia Gibbs*); Frank Faylen (*Joe Gurt*); Paul Panzer (*Man in Drawing Room*); William Farnum (*Hero in Saloon*); Chester Conklin (*Chef Comic*); Snub Pollard (*Propman in Saloon*); James Finlayson (*Chef Comic*); Creighton Hale (*Leading Man*); Hank Mann (*Chef Comic*); Francis McDonald (*Heavy in Saloon*); Bert Roach (*Bartender in Saloon*) and Heinie Conklin (*Studio Cop*).

SONGS:

The Sewing Machine; Rumble; I Wish I Didn't Love You So; Poor Pauline*; Poppa, Don't Preach to Me.

**music and lyrics by Charles McCarron and Raymond Walker*

SYNOPSIS:

The life and times (and misadventures) of silent screen star Pearl White from her job as a sweatshop seamstress to her triumph on the Paris musical stage.

SOUNDTRACK: Verdette 8702

* * * * * * * * * *

PETER PAN
RKO, 1953

Producer: Walt Disney
Director: Hamilton Luske, Clyde Geronimi and Wilfred Jackson
Screenplay: Ted Sears, Bill Peet, Joe Rinaldi, Erdman Penner, Winston Hibler, Milt
            Banta and Ralph Wright; based on the play by Sir James M. Barrie
Music and Lyrics: see below with song titles
Running time: 77 minutes, color

VOCAL TALENTS:

Bobby Driscoll (*Peter Pan*); Kathryn Beaumont (*Wendy*); Hans Conried (*Captain Hook/Mr. Darling*); Bill Thompson (*Mr. Smee*); Heather Angel (*Mrs. Darling*); Paul Collins (*Michael*); Tommy Luske (*John*); Candy Candido (*Indian Chief*) and Tom Conway (*Narrator*).

SONGS:

You Can Fly! You Can Fly! You Can Fly! - *Sammy Fain and Sammy Cahn*
A Pirate's Life - *Oliver Wallace and Erdman Penner*
Following the Leader (Tee-Dum, Tee-Dee) - *Oliver Wallace, Ted Sears and Winston
                                          Hibler*
Your Mother and Mine - *Sammy Fain and Sammy Cahn*
The Elegant Captain Hook - *Sammy Fain and Sammy Cahn*
Never Smile at a Crocodile - *Frank Churchill and Jack Lawrence*
What Makes the Red Man Red? - *Sammy Fain and Sammy Cahn*

SYNOPSIS:

Animated version of the Sir James Barrie tale of three London children who take a trip to Never-Never-Land with the boy who refused to grow up and his pixie Tinkerbell.

SOUNDTRACK: Disneyland 1206

* * * * * * * * * *

PETE'S DRAGON
Buena Vista, 1977

Producer: Ron Miller and Jerome Courtland
Director: Don Chaffey
Screenplay: Malcolm Mamorstein; based on a story by Seton I. Miller and S.S. Field
Choreography: Onna White
Music and Lyrics: Al Kasha and Joel Hirschhorn
Running time: 134 minutes, color

CAST:

Helen Reddy (*Nora*); Jim Dale (*Dr. Terminus*); Mickey Rooney (*Lampie*); Red Buttons (*Hoagy*); Shelley Winters (*Lena Gogan*); Sean Marshall (*Pete*); Jane Kean (*Miss Taylor*); Jim Backus (*Mayor*); Charles Tyner (*Merle Gogan*); Gary Morgan (*Grover Gogan*); Jeff Conaway (*Willie Gogan*); Cal Bartlett (*Paul*) and Charlie Callas (*voice of "Elliott"*).

SONGS:

The Happiest Home in These Hills; Boo Bop Bopbop Bop (I Love You Too); I Saw a Dragon; It's Not Easy; Passamashloddy; Candle on the Water; There's Room For Everyone; Every Little Piece; Brazzle Dazzle Day; Bill of Sale.

SYNOPSIS:

With the help of his friend Elliott (a giant flying green dragon) orphan Pete manages to run away from the evil Gogans to find a new life with Lampie, a lighthouse keeper in Maine, and his daughter Nora.

SOUNDTRACK: Capitol SW-11704

* * * * * * * * * *

THE PHANTOM OF THE OPERA
Universal, 1943

Producer: George Waggner
Director: Arthur Lubin
Screenplay: Eric Taylor and Samuel Hoffenstein; based on the novel by Gaston Leroux
Choreography: William Von Wymetal and Lester Horton
Music and Lyrics: see below with song titles
Running time: 93 minutes, color

CAST:

Nelson Eddy (*Anatole Garron*); Susanna Foster (*Christine DuBois*); Claude Rains (*Erique Claudin*); Edgar Barrier (*Inspector Raoul de Chagny*); Leo Carillo (*Signor Feretti*); Jane Farrar (*Biancarolli*); J. Edward Bromberg (*Amiot*); Fritz Feld (*Lecours*) and Fritz Leiber (*Franz Liszt*).

SONGS:

The Porter Lied (*Martha*) - *Friedrich Von Flotow*
Third Act Finale (*Martha*) - *Friedrich Von Flotow*
Lullaby of the Bells - *Edward Ward and George Waggner*
Amour et Gloire - *Frederick Chopin and William Von Wymetal*
Nocturne in E Flat - *Frederick Chopin*
Le Prince de Caucasie - *Peter Tchaikovsky and George Waggner*

SYNOPSIS:

Musical remake of the Gaston Leroux novel has middle-aged, third-rate violinist Erique Claudin secretly paying for singing lessons for young soprano Christine DuBois and she is in turn courted by both Paris Opéra baritone Anatole Garron and Sûreté policeman Raoul de Chagny. When an altercation leads to a disfiguring accident for Claudin he kidnaps the girl taking her deep beneath the vast opera house.

SOUNDTRACK: Sountrak 114

* * * * * * * * *

PHANTOM OF THE PARADISE
20th Century Fox, 1974

Producer: Edward R. Pressman
Director: Brian De Palma
Screenplay: Brian De Palma
Choreography: Harold Oblong and William Shepherd
Music and Lyrics: Paul Williams and George Aliceson Tipten
Running time: 92 minutes, color

CAST:

Paul Williams (*Swan*); William Finley (*Winslow Leach/"The Phantom"*); Jessica Harper (*Phoenix*); George Memmoli (*Philbin*); Gerrit Graham (*Beef*); Archie Hahn (*Rock Singer*); Jeffrey Comanor (*Rock Singer*) and Harold Oblong (*Rock Singer*).

SONGS:

Goodbye, Eddie, Goodbye; Faust; Upholstery; Special To Me; The Phantom's Theme (Beauty and the Beast); Somebody Super Like You; Life at Last*; Old Souls; The Hell Of It.

*vocal by Ray Kennedy

<u>SYNOPSIS</u>:

Satire about a songwriter, horribly maimed in an accident, who sells his soul to the powerful impressario who destroyed him so that his rock opera can be performed by the young singer, Phoenix, he adores from afar.

SOUNDTRACK: A&M SP-3653

* * * * * * * * *

PINOCCHIO
RKO, 1940

Producer: Walt Disney
Director: Ben Sharpsteen and Hamilton Luske
Screenplay: Ted Sears, Otto Englander, Webb Smith, William Cottrell, Joseph Sabo, Erdman Penner and Aurelius Battaglia; based on the story by Collodi
Music and Lyrics: Leigh Harline, Ned Washington and Paul J. Smith
Running time: 88 minutes, color

VOCAL TALENTS:

Dickie Jones (*Pinocchio*); Cliff Edwards (*Jiminy Cricket*); Christian Rub (*Geppetto*); Evelyn Venable (*The Blue Fairy*); Walter Catlett (*J. Worthington Foulfellow*); Frankie Darro (*Lampwick*) and Charles Judels (*Stromboli/The Coachman*).

SONGS:

Little Woodenhead; When You Wish Upon a Star; Give a Little Whistle; Hi Diddle Dee Dee (An Actor's Life For Me); I've Got No Strings.

SYNOPSIS:

Animated story, based on the classic fairy tale, about a wood carver named Geppetto who longs for a little boy of his own. Thanks to the magic of the Blue Fairy his wish is granted--the puppet Pinocchio comes to life but then he must earn the right to be a real little boy (with the help of his conscience, Jiminy Cricket).

SOUNDTRACK: Disneyland 4002

* * * * * * * * *

PIN UP GIRL
20th Century Fox, 1944

Producer: William LeBaron
Director: Bruce Humberstone
Screenplay: Robert Ellis, Helen Logan and Earl Baldwin; based on a story by Libbie
    Block
Choreography: Hermes Pan and Alice Sullivan
Music and Lyrics: Mack Gordon and James V. Monaco
Running time: 83 minutes, color

CAST:

Betty Grable (*Laurie Jones/Laura Lorraine*); John Harvey (*Tommy Dooley*); Martha
Raye (*Molly McKay*); Joe E. Brown (*Eddie Hall*); Eugene Pallette (*Barney Briggs*);
Dorothea Kent (*Kay Bridges*); Dave Willock (*Dud Miller*); Roger Clark (*George
Davis*) and Charlie Spivak (*Himself*).

SONGS:

You're My Little Pin Up Girl; Time Alone Will Tell; Red Robins, Bob Whites and
Blue Birds; Don't Carry Tales Out of School; Yankee Doodle Hayride; Once Too
Often; The Story of the Very Merry Widow; I'll Be Marching to a Love Song.

SYNOPSIS:

Laurie Jones is a "pin up" girl in Missoula who goes to Washington, D.C. to be a
civilian stenographer for the Navy. On her way there she soon finds herself
pretending to be a New York musical star named Laura Lorraine--and engaged to
Guadalcanal hero Tommy Dooley.

SOUNDTRACK: No soundtrack available

* * * * * * * * * *

PIPPIN
U.S.A. Home Video, 1981

Producer: David Sheehan
Director: Bob Fosse and David Sheehan
Book: Roger O. Hirson
Choreography: Bob Fosse and Kathryn Doby
Music and Lyrics: Stephen Schwartz
Running time: 120 minutes, color

CAST:

Ben Vereen (*The Leading Player*); William Katt (*Pippin*); Martha Raye (*Berthe*); Leslie Denniston (*Catherine*); Benjamin Rayson (*Charlemagne*) and Chita Rivera (*Fastrada*).

SONGS:

Magic to Do; Corner of the Sky; War is a Science; Glory; Simple Joys; No Time At All; With You; Spread a Little Sunshine; Morning Glow; On the Right Track; Kind of Woman; Extraordinary; Love Song; I Guess I'll Miss the Man.

SYNOPSIS:

The life of Pippin, the illegitimate son of the emperor Charlemagne, is chronicled in this slightly irreverent musical.

SOUNDTRACK: Motown 760

* * * * * * * * * *

THE PIRATE
Metro-Goldwyn-Mayer, 1948

Producer: Arthur Freed
Director: Vincente Minelli
Screenplay: Albert Hackett and Frances Goodrich; based on a play by S.N. Behrman
Choreography: Robert Alton and Gene Kelly
Music and Lyrics: Cole Porter
Running time: 102 minutes, color

CAST:

Judy Garland (*Manuela*); Gene Kelly (*Serafin*); Walter Slezak (*Don Pedro Vargas*); Gladys Cooper (*Aunt Inez*); Reginald Owen (*The Advocate*); George Zucco (*The Viceroy*); Lester Allen (*Uncle Capucho*); Jean Dean (*Casilda*); Lola Deem (*Isabella*); Ellen Ross (*Mercedes*); Mary Jo Ellis (*Lizarda*); Marion Murray (*Eloise*); Ben Lessy (*Gumbo*) and the Nicholas Brothers (*Acrobatic Dancers*).

SONGS:

Mack the Black; Nina; You Can Do No Wrong; The Pirate Ballet (instrumental): Love Of My Life; Be a Clown.

<u>SYNOPSIS</u>:

The Caribbean of the 1830's is where Manuela lives with her aunt and uncle and where they have arranged her marriage to the town mayor--the much older (and duller) Don Pedro Vargas. However, Manuela yearns for more excitement in her life, especially in the form of Black Macoco--"Mack the Black"--the infamous pirate.

SOUNDTRACK: MGM 2-SES-43ST (with *Hit the Deck* and *Pagan Love Song*)

* * * * * * * * * *

THE PIRATES OF PENZANCE
Universal, 1983

Producer: Joseph Papp
Director: Wilford Leach
Screenplay: Wilford Leach; based on the stage musical book by Sir William Gilbert
Choreography: Graciela Daniele
Music and Lyrics: Sir Arthur Sullivan and Sir William Gilbert
Running time: 112 minutes, color

<u>CAST</u>:

Kevin Kline (*The Pirate King*); Angela Lansbury (*Ruth*); Linda Ronstadt (*Mabel*); George Rose (*Major-General Stanley*); Rex Smith (*Frederic*); Tony Azito (*Sergeant*); David Hatton* (*Samuel*); Louise Gold** (*Edith*) and Teresa Codling*** (*Kate*).

   *vocals dubbed by Stephen Hanan
  **vocals dubbed by Alexandra Kerey
 ***vocals dubbed by Marcia Shaw

<u>SONGS</u>:

Pour, O Pour the Pirate Sherry; When Frederic Was a Little Lad; Oh, Better Far to Live and Die; Oh False One, You Have Deceived Me!; Climbing Over Rocky Mountain; Stop, Ladies, Pray; Oh, Is There Not One Maiden Breast?; Poor Wandering One!; What Ought We to Do?; Stay, We Must Not Lose Our Senses; Hold, Monsters!; I Am the Very Model of a Modern Major-General; Oh, Men of Dark and Dismal Fate; Oh, Dry the Glist'ning Tear; Then, Frederic, Let Your Escort Lion-Hearted; When the Foreman Bears His Steel; Now For the Pirates' Lair; When You Had Left Our Pirate Fold; My Eyes Are Fully Open; Away, Away! My Heart's On Fire; Stay, Frederic, Stay!; No, I Am Brave!; When a Felon's Not Engaged in His Employment; With Cat-Like Tread, Upon Our Prey We Steal; Hush, Hush! Not a Word; Sighing Softly to the River.

SYNOPSIS:

Gilbert and Sullivan operetta about a young apprentice pirate named Frederic who falls in love with Mabel, the daughter of a major-general.

SOUNDTRACK: Elektra VE-601

* * * * * * * * * *

POOR LITTLE RICH GIRL
20th Century Fox, 1936

Producer: Darryl F. Zanuck
Director: Irving Cummings
Screenplay: Sam Hellman, Gladys Lehman and Harry Tugend; based on stories by Eleanor Gates and Ralph Spence
Choreography: Jack Haskell and Ralph Cooper
Music and Lyrics: Harry Revel and Mack Gordon
Running time: 72 minutes, B/W

CAST:

Shirley Temple (*Barbara Barry*); Alice Faye (*Jerry Dolan*); Gloria Stuart (*Margaret Allen*); Jack Haley (*Jimmy Dolan*); Michael Whalen (*Richard Barry*); Sara Haden (*Collins*); Jane Darwell (*Woodward*); Claude Gillingwater, Sr. (*Simon Peck*); Henry Armetta (*Tony*); Arthur Hoyt (*Percival Gooch*); Paul Stanton (*George Hathaway*); Charles Coleman (*Stebbins*); John Wray (*Flagin*); Tyler Brooke (*Dan Ward*) and Mathilde Comont (*Tony's wife*).

SONGS:

Oh My Goodness; Buy a Bar of Barry's; When I'm With You; But Definitely; Wash Your Necks With a Cake of Peck's; You've Gotta Eat Your Spinach, Baby; A Military Man.

SYNOPSIS:

After an accident on the way to boarding school leaves her all alone at a railway station, Barbara Barry pretends that she is an orphan and joins husband-and-wife vaudevillians Jerry and Jimmy Dolan in their act.

SOUNDTRACK: No soundtrack available

* * * * * * * * * *

260

POPEYE
Paramount/Walt Disney, 1980

Producer: Robert Evans
Director: Robert Altman
Screenplay: Jules Feiffer
Choreography: Sharon Kinney, Hovey Burgess and Lou Wills
Music and Lyrics: Harry Nilsson
Running time: 114 minutes, color

CAST:

Robin Williams (*Popeye*); Shelley Duvall (*Olive Oyl*); Ray Walston (*Poopdeck Pappy*); Paul Smith (*Bluto*); Paul Dooley (*Wimpy*); Richard Libertini (*Geezil*); Donovan Scott (*Castor Oyl*); Donald Moffat (*The Taxman*); MacIntyre Dixon (*Cole Oyl*); Roberta Maxwell (*Nana Oyl*); Allan Nicholls (*Rough House*) and Wesley Ivan Hurt (*Swee'Pea*).

SONGS:

Sweethaven; Blow Me Down; Food; He's Large; I'm Mean; Sailin'; I Yam What I Yam; He Needs Me; Swee'Pea's Lullaby; It's Not Easy Being Me; Kids; Popeye the Sailor Man*.

**music and lyrics by Sammy Lerner*

SYNOPSIS:

The life and times of Popeye, the sailor man including his rivalry with Bluto, romance (?) with Olive Oyl and his finding the orphaned infant Swee'Pea.

SOUNDTRACK: Boardwalk SW-36880

* * * * * * * * * *

PORGY AND BESS
Columbia, 1959

Producer: Samuel Goldwyn
Director: Otto Preminger
Screenplay: N. Richard Nash; based on the stage musical book by DuBose Heyward
Choreography: Hermes Pan
Music and Lyrics: George Gershwin, Ira Gershwin and DuBose Heyward
Running time: 138 minutes, color

261

CAST:

Sidney Poitier* (*Porgy*); Dorothy Dandridge** (*Bess*); Sammy Davis, Jr. (*Sportin'
Life*); Pearl Bailey (*Maria*); Brock Peters (*Crown*); Leslie Scott (*Jake*); Diahann
Carroll*** (*Clara*); Ruth Attaway**** (*Serena*); Clarence Muse (*Peter*); Everdine
Wilson (*Annie*); Joel Fluellen (*Robbins*); Earl Jackson (*Mingo*); Moses LaMarr
(*Nelson*); Margaret Hairston (*Lily*); Ivan Dixon (*Jim*) and Antoine Durousseau
(*Scipio*).

   *vocals dubbed by Robert McFerrin
  **vocals dubbed by Adele Addison
 ***vocals dubbed by Loulie Jean Norman
****vocals dubbed by Inez Matthews

SONGS:

Summertime; A Woman is a Sometime Thing; Gone, Gone, Gone/Porgy's Prayer; My
Man's Gone Now; I Got Plenty O' Nuttin'; Bess, You is My Woman Now;
Morning/Catfish Row; Oh, I Can't Sit Down; It Ain't Necessarily So; I Ain't Got No
Shame; What You Want With Bess?; Strawberry Woman/Crab Man; I Love You,
Porgy; A Red-Headed Woman; Clara, Clara; There's a Boat Dat's Leavin' Soon For
New York; Oh, Where's My Bess?; I'm On My Way.

SYNOPSIS:

Folk opera about the lives of the people who live on a street called Catfish Row in
Charleston, South Carolina.

SOUNDTRACK: Columbia OL-5410

* * * * * * * * *

PRESENTING LILY MARS
Metro-Goldwyn-Mayer, 1943

Producer: Joe Pasternak
Director: Norman Taurog
Screenplay: Richard Connell and Gladys Lehman; based on the book by Booth
            Tarkington
Choreography: Ernst Matray
Music and Lyrics: see below with song titles
Running time: 105 minutes, B/W

262

<u>CAST</u>:

Van Heflin (*John Thornway*); Judy Garland (*Lily Mars*); Fay Bainter (*Mrs. Thornway*); Richard Carlson (*Owen Vail*); Marta Eggerth (*Isobel Rekay*); Spring Byington (*Mrs. Flora Mars*); Connie Gilchrist (*Frankie*); Leonid Kinskey (*Leo*); Bob Crosby (*Himself*) and Tommy Dorsey (*Himself*).

<u>SONGS</u>:

Is It Love? - *Paul Francis Webster and Walter Jurmann*
Tom, Tom, the Piper's Son - *Burton Lane and E.Y. Harburg*
Every Little Movement Has a Meaning Of Its Own - *Otto Harbach and Karl*
Hoschna
When I Look At You - *Paul Francis Webster and Walter Jurmann*
Kulebaika - *Paul Francis Webster and Walter Jurmann*
Where There's Music - *Roger Edens*
Three O'Clock in the Morning - *Julian Robledo and Dorothy Terriss*
Broadway Rhythm - *Nacio Herb Brown and Arthur Freed*

<u>SYNOPSIS</u>:

Lily Mars is a stage-struck teenager who is determined to get a part in John Thornway's new show and when star Isobel Rekay quits in a temper she sees her chance.

SOUNDTRACK: Sountrak 117

* * * * * * * * *

PUSS IN BOOTS
Cannon Films, 1987

Producer: Menahem Golan and Yoram Globus
Director: Eugene Marner
Screenplay: Carole Lucia Satrina; based on the fairy tale by Charles Perrault
Choreography: Christine Oren
Music and Lyrics: Michael Abbott and Anne Croswell
Running time: 90 minutes, color

<u>CAST</u>:

Christopher Walken (*Puss in Boots*); Jason Connery* (*Corin*); Carmela Marner (*Princess Vera*); Yossi Graber (*The King*); Elki Jacobs (*Lady Clara*); Amnon Meskin (*Great Ogre*); Yaakov Ben Sura (*Prime Minister*) and Michael Schneider (*Tailor*).

vocals dubbed by Nick Curtis

SONGS:

Happy Cat; Cat's Lullaby; Marquis of Carabas; Love at First Sight; To Be Genteel; Stick Your Neck Out.

SYNOPSIS:

In his will Corin's father left him only the family cat, Puss, who assumes a human form in order to give Corin all the things he desires--including the Princess Vera as a wife.

SOUNDTRACK: No soundtrack available

R

READY, WILLING AND ABLE
Warner Bros., 1937

Producer: Sam Bischoff
Director: Ray Enright
Screenplay: Jerry Wald, Sid Herzig and Warren Duff; based on a story by Richard Macauley
Choreography: Bobby Connolly
Music and Lyrics: Johnny Mercer and Richard A. Whiting
Running time: 95 minutes, B/W

CAST:

Ruby Keeler (*Jane Clarke*); Ross Alexander* (*Barry Granville*); Lee Dixon (*Pinky Blair*); Allen Jenkins (*J. Van Courtland*); Carol Hughes (*Angie*); Louise Fazenda (*Clara Heineman*); Hugh O'Connell (*Truman Hardy*); Addison Richards (*Edward McNeil*) and Wini Shaw (*English Jane Clarke*).

*vocals dubbed by James Newill

SONGS:

Ready, Willing and Able; The World is My Apple; There's a Little Old House; Handy With Your Feet; Just a Quiet Evening; Sentimental and Melancholy; Too Marvelous For Words.

SYNOPSIS:

It's a case of mistaken identity when eager Broadway producer Barry Granville and songwriter Pinky Blair sign unknown Jane Clarke to a big new show thinking that she is a famous English stage star.

SOUNDTRACK: No soundtrack available

* * * * * * * * *

REBECCA OF SUNNYBROOK FARM
20th Century Fox, 1938

Producer: Darryl F. Zanuck
Director: Allan Dwan

Screenplay: Karl Tunberg and Don Ettlinger; based on the novel by Kate Douglas
    Wiggin
Choreography: Nick Castle and Geneva Sawyer
Music and lyrics: see below with song titles
Running time: 80 minutes, B/W

CAST:

Shirley Temple (*Rebecca Winstead*); Randolph Scott (*Anthony Kent*); Jack Haley
(*Orville Smithers*); Gloria Stuart (*Gwen Warren*); Phyllis Brooks (*Lola Lee*); Helen
Westley (*Aunt Miranda Wilkins*); Slim Summerville (*Homer Busby*); Bill Robinson
(*Aloysius*); J. Edward Bromberg (*Dr. Hill*); Alan Dinehart (*Purvis*); Dixie Dunbar
(*Receptionist*); Paul Hurst (*Mug*); William Demarest (*Henry Kipper*); Ruth Gillette
(*Melba*); Paul Harvey (*Cyrus Bartlett*); Franklin Pangborn (*Hamilton Montmarcy*);
William Wagner (*Reverend Turner*); Eily Malyon (*Mrs. Turner*) and Mary McCarty
(*Florabelle*).

SONGS:

Happy Ending - *Sidney D. Mitchell and Lew Pollack*
An Old Straw Hat - *Harry Revel and Mack Gordon*
Crackly Grain Flakes - *Sidney D. Mitchell and Lew Pollack*
Alone With You - *Sidney D. Mitchell and Lew Pollack*
Come and Get Your Happiness - *Jack Yellen and Samuel Pokrass*
Parade of the Wooden Soldiers - *Sidney D. Mitchell, Lew Pollack and Raymond
    Scott*

SYNOPSIS:

Rebecca Winstead goes to live with her aunt, Miranda Wilkins, on Sunnybrook Farm
after she thinks she fails at a radio audition. But when the man next door turns out
to be Tony Kent, the show's director, her chance for a career is met with resistance
by Aunt Miranda.

SOUNDTRACK: No soundtrack available

* * * * * * * * *

RED GARTERS
Paramount, 1954

Producer: Pat Duggan
Director: George Marshall
Screenplay: Michael Fessier

Choreography: Nick Castle
Music and Lyrics: Jay Livingston and Ray Evans
Running time: 91 minutes, color

CAST:

Rosemary Clooney (*Calaveras Kate*); Jack Carson (*Jason Carberry*); Guy Mitchell (*Reb Randall*); Pat Crowley (*Susana Martinez de la Cruz*); Joanne Gilbert (*Sheila Winthrop*); Gene Barry (*Rafael Moreno*); Cass Daley (*Minnie Redwing*); Frank Faylen (*Billy Buckett*); Reginald Owen (*Judge Winthrop*); Buddy Ebsen (*Ginger Pete*) and Richard Hale (*Dr. J. Pott Troy*).

SONGS:

A Dime and a Dollar; Big Doin's; Man and Woman; Lady Killer; Red Garters; Good Intentions; Vaquero; Bad News; Brave Men; Meet a Happy Guy; This is Greater Than I Thought.

SYNOPSIS:

Reb Randall goes to Paradise Lost, California to avenge the death of his brother but soon falls in love with pretty saloon owner-performer Calaveras Kate.

SOUNDTRACK: No soundtrack available

* * * * * * * * * *

RED RIDING HOOD
Cannon Films, 1987

Producer: Menahem Golan and Yoram Globus
Director: Adam Brooks
Screenplay: Carole Lucia Satrina; based on the fairy tale by the Brothers Grimm
Choreography: Barbara Allen
Music and Lyrics: Stephen Lawrence and Michael Korie
Running time: 84 minutes, color

CAST:

Craig T. Nelson (*Sir Percival/Sir Godfrey*); Isabella Rossellini (*Lady Jean*); Amelia Shankley (*Linet*); Rocco Sisto (*Dagger*); Helen Elazary (*Nanny Bess*); Linda Kaye (*Badger Kate*); Amnon Meskin (*Great Peter*) and Julian Joy-Chagrin (*Allan Owen*).

SONGS:

Lost in the Woods; Good at Being Bad; You Won't Be Here in the Morning; In the Blue; Man Without a Heart; Never Talk to Strangers.

SYNOPSIS:

With his brother away at the wars for the past seven years, evil Sir Godfrey uses his power to transform his aide Dagger into a wolf to spy on the villagers. But when his niece Linet refuses to fear him he arranges for her to be destroyed by the wolf.

SOUNDTRACK: No soundtrack available

* * * * * * * * *

RICH, YOUNG AND PRETTY
Metro-Goldwyn-Mayer, 1951

Producer: Joe Pasternak
Director: Norman Taurog
Screenplay: Sidney Sheldon and Dorothy Cooper; based on a story by Dorothy Cooper
Choreography: Nick Castle
Music and Lyrics: Nicholas Brodsky and Sammy Cahn
Running time: 95 minutes, color

CAST:

Jane Powell (*Elizabeth Rogers*); Danielle Darrieux (*Marie Devarone*); Wendell Corey (*Jim Stauton Rogers*); Vic Damone (*André Milan*); Fernando Lamas (*Paul Sarnac*); Marcel Dalio (*Claude Duval*); Una Merkel (*Glynnie*); Richard Anderson (*Bob Lennart*); Jean Murat (*Henri Milan*) and Hans Conried (*Jean*).

SONGS:

Paris; Deep in the Heart of Texas*; L'Amour Toujours (Tonight For Sure); There's Danger in Your Eyes, Chérie**; Wonder Why; I Can See You; We Never Talk Much; Dark is the Night; The Old Piano Roll Blues***; How Do You Like Your Eggs in the Morning?

*music and lyrics by June Hershey and Don Swander
**music and lyrics by Jack Meskill and Pete Wendling
***music and lyrics by Cy Coben

SYNOPSIS:

On a State Department trip to Paris with her father, Jim, Liz Rogers meets her mother Marie who had abandoned her when she was just a baby.

SOUNDTRACK: MGM 2-SES-53ST (with *Royal Wedding* and *Nancy Goes to Rio*)

* * * * * * * * *

RIDING HIGH
Paramount, 1950

Producer: Frank Capra
Director: Frank Capra
Screenplay: Robert Riskin, Melville Shavelson and Jack Rose; based on the story *Broadway Bill* by Mark Hellinger
Music and Lyrics: James Van Heusen and Johnny Burke
Running time: 112 minutes, B/W

CAST:

Bing Crosby (*Dan Brooks*); Coleen Gray (*Alice Higgins*); Charles Bickford (*J.L. Higgins*); Frances Gifford (*Margaret Higgins*); William Demarest (*Happy McGuire*); Raymond Walburn (*Professor Pettigrew*); James Gleason (*Racing Secretary*); Ward Bond (*Lee*); Clarence Muse (*Whitey*); Percy Kilbride (*Pop Jones*); Harry Davenport (*Johnson*); Margaret Hamilton (*Edna*); Paul Harvey (*Whitehall*); Douglass Dumbrille (*Eddie Howard*) and Gene Lockhart (*J.P. Chase*).

SONGS:

We've Got a Sure Thing; Someplace On Anywhere Road; The Whiffenpoof Song*; Sunshine Cake; The Horse Told Me; De Camptown Races**.

 **music and lyrics by Tod B. Galloway, George S. Pomeroy and Meade Minnigerode*
***music and lyrics by Stephen Foster*

SYNOPSIS:

Dan Brooks is a small-time horse trainer who believes his horse, "Broadway Bill", has a chance to win the big race.

SOUNDTRACK: Decca DL-4261

* * * * * * * * *

ROAD TO BALI
Paramount, 1952

Producer: Harry Tugend
Director: Hal Walker
Screenplay: Frank Butler, Hal Kanter and William Morrow; based on a story by
          Frank Butler and Harry Tugend
Choreography: Charles O'Curran
Music and Lyrics: James Van Heusen and Johnny Burke
Running time: 90 minutes, color

CAST:

Bob Hope (*Harold Gridley*); Bing Crosby (*George Cochran*); Dorothy Lamour (*Lalah*); Murvyn Vye (*Ken Arok*); Peter Coe (*Gung*); Ralph Moody (*Bhoma Da*); Leon Askin (*Ramayana*); Bob Crosby (*Himself*) and Jane Russell (*Herself*).

SONGS:

Chicago Style; The Whiffenpoof Song*; Moonflowers; Hoots Mon; To See You; The Merry-Go-Runaround.

music and lyrics by Tod B. Galloway, George S. Pomeroy and Meade Minnigerode

SYNOPSIS:

On the run from a pair of irate fathers in Australia, entertainers George and Harold take jobs as deep-sea divers and are soon at a South Seas island where they try and help pretty Lalah save her fortune in jewels from evil Arok.

SOUNDTRACK: No soundtrack available

* * * * * * * * *

ROAD TO RIO
Paramount, 1947

Producer: Daniel Dare
Director: Norman Z. McLeod
Screenplay: Edmund Beloin and Jack Rose
Choreography: Bernard Pearce and Billy Daniel
Music and Lyrics: James Van Heusen and Johnny Burke
Running time: 100 minutes, B/W

270

CAST:

Bing Crosby (*Scat Sweeney*); Bob Hope (*Hot Lips Barton*); Dorothy Lamour (*Lucia Maria de Andrade*); Gale Sondergaard (*Mrs. Catherine Vail*); Frank Faylen (*Harry*); Joseph Vitale (*Tony*); Frank Puglia (*Rodrigues*); Nestor Paiva (*Cardoso*); Robert Barrat (*Johnson*); George Meeker (*Sherman Mallory*); The Wiere Brothers (*Brazilian Musicians*); Jerry Colonna (*Cavalry Captain*); Stanley Andrews (*Captain Harmon*); Harry Woods (*Ship's Purser*) and the Andrews Sisters (*Themselves*).

SONGS:

Apalachicola; But Beautiful; You Don't Have to Know the Language; Experience; Brazil*.

*music and lyrics by Ary Barroso and Bob Russell

SYNOPSIS:

On the run from a fire they inadvertently caused in a carnival, Scat Sweeney and Hot Lips Barton stow away on a ship bound for Rio de Janeiro where they meet a young woman, Lucia, who is being forced into a marriage (by hypnosis) by her evil guardian, Catherine Vail.

SOUNDTRACK: No soundtrack available

* * * * * * * * *

ROAD TO SINGAPORE
Paramount, 1940

Producer: Harlan Thompson
Director: Victor Schertzinger
Screenplay: Don Hartman and Frank Butler; based on a story by Harry Harvey
Choreography: LeRoy Prinz
Music and Lyrics: James Van Heusen and Johnny Burke
Running time: 84 minutes, B/W

CAST:

Bing Crosby (*Josh Mallon*); Dorothy Lamour (*Mima*); Bob Hope (*Ace Lannigan*); Charles Coburn (*Joshua Mallon IV*); Judith Barrett (*Gloria Wycott*); Anthony Quinn (*Caesar*); Jerry Colonna (*Achilles Bombanassa*); Johnny Arthur (*Timothy Willow*) and Pierre Watkin (*Morgan Wycott*).

271

SONGS:

Captain Custard*; Kaigoon; Too Romantic; The Moon and the Willow Tree*; Sweet Potato Piper.

*music and lyrics by Victor Schertzinger and Johnny Burke

SYNOPSIS:

Tired of trying to live up to his father's expectations of him Josh Mallon heads for Singapore with his best friend Ace Lannigan and once there engage pretty Mima as their housekkeeper--creating a romantic triangle.

SOUNDTRACK: No soundtrack available

* * * * * * * * *

ROAD TO UTOPIA
Paramount, 1945

Producer: Paul Jones
Director: Hal Walker
Screenplay: Norman Panama and Melvin Frank
Choreography: Danny Dare
Music and Lyrics: James Van Heusen and Johnny Burke
Running time: 90 minutes, B/W

CAST:

Bing Crosby (*Duke Johnson/Junior Hooten*); Bob Hope (*Chester Hooten*); Dorothy Lamour (*Sal Van Hoyden*); Hillary Brooke (*Kate*); Douglass Dumbrille (*Ace Larson*); Jack LaRue (*LeBec*); Robert Barrat (*Sperry*); Nestor Paiva (*McGurk*); Will Wright (*Mr. Latimer*) and Robert Benchley (*Narrator*).

SONGS:

Good-Time Charley; It's Anybody's Spring; Personality; Welcome to My Dreams; Put It There, Pal; Would You?

SYNOPSIS:

On the run from a scam gone bad in San Francisco, Duke Johnson and Chester Hooten flee to Alaska with a deed to a gold mine they lifted from a pair of murderers, Sperry and McGurk. In the Golden Rail saloon they meet Sal Van

272

Hoyden who tries to seduce both of them--in an attempt to get the deed for herself--which had originally belonged to her father.

SOUNDTRACK: No soundtrack available

* * * * * * * * *

ROAD TO ZANZIBAR
Paramount, 1941

Producer: Paul Jones
Director: Victor Schertzinger
Screenplay: Frank Butler and Don Hartman; based on a story by Don Hartman and
             Sy Bartlett
Choreography: LeRoy Prinz
Music and Lyrics: James Van Heusen and Johnny Burke
Running time: 92 minutes, B/W

CAST:

Bing Crosby (*Chuck Reardon*); Bob Hope (*Hubert "Fearless" Frazier*); Dorothy Lamour (*Donna Latour*); Una Merkel (*Julia Quimby*); Eric Blore (*Charles Kimble*); Iris Adrian (*Soubrette*); Lionel Royce (*Monsieur LeBec*); Buck Woods (*Thonga*); Leigh Whipper (*Scarface*); Ernest Whitman (*Whiteface*); Norma Varden (*Clara Kimble*) and Joan Marsh (*Dimples*).

SONGS:

Birds of a Feather; African Etude; On the Road to Zanzibar; It's Always You; You're Dangerous; You Lucky People.

SYNOPSIS:

After gangster LeBec comes "looking" for them, Chuck Reardon and Fearless Frazier head for Zanzibar where they meet Donna LaTour and Julia Quimby who are supposedly searching for Donna's lost brother.

SOUNDTRACK: No soundtrack available

* * * * * * * * *

ROBERTA
RKO, 1935

Producer: Pandro S. Berman
Director: William A. Seiter
Screenplay: Jane Murfin, Sam Mintz and Allan Scott; based on the stage musical
           book by Otto Harbach
Choreography: Fred Astaire and Hermes Pan
Music and Lyrics: Jerome Kern, Otto Harbach, Dorothy Fields and Jimmy McHugh
Running time: 105 minutes, B/W

CAST:

Irene Dunne (*Stephanie*); Fred Astaire (*Huck Haines*); Ginger Rogers (*Countess Scharwenka/Lizzie Gatz*); Randolph Scott (*John Kent*); Helen Westley (*Roberta/Aunt Minnie*); Victor Varconi (*Ladislaw*); Claire Todd (*Sophie*); Luis Alberni (*Voyda*); Ferdinand Munier (*Lord Henry*); Torben Meyer (*Albert*); Adrian Rosley (*Professor*) and Bodil Rosing (*Fernando*).

SONGS:

Let's Begin; The Touch of Your Hand; I'll Be Hard to Handle; Yesterdays; I Won't Dance; Smoke Gets in Your Eyes; Lovely to Look At.

SYNOPSIS:

High school football coach John Kent goes to Paris with his buddy Huck and ends up helping to run Roberta's--the dress shop his late aunt left him--with Stephanie, the head designer.

SOUNDTRACK: Classic International Filmusicals 3011

* * * * * * * * *

ROBIN AND THE SEVEN HOODS
Warner Bros., 1964

Producer: Frank Sinatra
Director: Gordon Douglas
Screenplay: David R. Schwartz
Choreography: Jack Baker
Music and Lyrics: James Van Heusen and Sammy Cahn
Running time: 123 minutes, color

CAST:

Frank Sinatra (*Robbo*); Dean Martin (*Little John*); Sammy Davis, Jr. (*Will*); Peter

Falk (*Guy Gisborne*); Barbara Rush (*Marian Stephens*); Victor Buono (*Deputy Sheriff Alvin Potts*); Bing Crosby (*Allen A. Dale*); Hank Henry (*Six Seconds*); Allen Jenkins (*Vermin*); Jack LaRue (*Tomatoes*); Robert Foulk (*Sheriff Octavius Glick*); Phil Crosby (*Robbo's Hood*); Robert Carricart (*Blue Jaw*); Phil Arnold (*Hatrack*); Sonny King (*Robbo's Hood*); Richard Simmons (*Prosecutor*); Harry Swoger (*Soupmeat*); Harry Wilson (*Gisborne's Hood*); Richard Bakalyan (*Robbo's Hood*); Bernard Fein (*Charlie Bananas*); Caryl Lee Hill (*Cocktail Waitress*); Joseph Ruskin (*Twitch*); Hans Conried (*Mr. Ricks*); Al Silvani (*Robbo's Hood*) and Edward G. Robinson (*Big Jim*).

SONGS:

All For One; Any Man Who Loves His Mother; Bang Bang; Style; Charlotte Couldn't Charleston; Mr. Booze; Don't Be a Do-Badder; My Kind of Town (Chicago Is).

SYNOPSIS:

In 1920's Prohibition Chicago two rival gangs, led by Robbo and Guy Gisborne, are vying for control of the city and when Robbo donates $50,000 to the Blessed Shelter Orphanage, run by Allen A. Dale, he's hailed as a modern-day Robin Hood.

SOUNDTRACK: Reprise 2021

* * * * * * * * *

ROBIN HOOD
Buena Vista, 1973

Producer: Wolfgang Reitherman
Director: Wolfgang Reitherman
Screenplay: Larry Clemmons; based on a story by Ken Anderson
Music and Lyrics: see below with song titles
Running time: 83 minutes, color

VOCAL TALENTS:

Brian Bedford (*Robin Hood*); Phil Harris (*Little John*); Peter Ustinov (*Prince John/King Richard*); Andy Devine (*Friar Tuck*); Pat Buttram (*The Sheriff of Nottingham*); Roger Miller (*Allan-a-Dale*); Monica Evans (*Maid Marian*); Carole Shelley (*Lady Kluck*); George Lindsay (*Trigger*); Ken Curtis (*Nutsy*) and Terry-Thomas (*Sir Hiss*).

SONGS:

Whistle Stop - *Roger Miller*

Oo-de-Lally - *Roger Miller*
Love* - *Floyd Huddleston and George Bruns*
The Phony King of England - *Johnny Mercer*
Not in Nottingham - *Roger Miller*

vocal by Nancy Adams

SYNOPSIS:

Robin Hood of Sherwood Forest turns out to be a fox--*literally*--in this animated version by Disney of the bandit who robs from the rich to give to the poor.

SOUNDTRACK: Disneyland 3810

* * * * * * * * *

ROCK-A-BYE BABY
Paramount, 1958

Producer: Jerry Lewis
Director: Frank Tashlin
Screenplay: Frank Tashlin; based on a story by Preston Sturgess
Choreography: Nick Castle
Music and Lyrics: Harry Warren and Sammy Cahn
Running time: 103 minutes, color

CAST:

Jerry Lewis (*Clayton Poole*); Marilyn Maxwell (*Carla Naples*); Baccaloni (*Papa Naples*); Reginald Gardiner (*Henry Herman*); Connie Stevens (*Sandy Naples*); Hans Conried (*Mr. Wright*); Ida Moore (*Miss Bessie Polk*); Isobel Elsom (*Mrs. Van Cleve*); Alex Gerry (*Judge Jenkins*); James Gleason (*Dr. Simkins*) and Gary Lewis (*Clayton as a boy*).

SONGS:

Rock-a-Bye My Baby; In the Land of La La La; Love is a Lonely Thing; Dormi, Dormi, Dormi; Why Can't He Care For Me?; The White Virgin of the Nile.

SYNOPSIS:

When Clayton Poole secretly agrees to care for the infant triplets of his old girlfriend, movie star Carla Naples, everyone thinks that they were just left on his doorstep and should not be put up for adoption.

276

SOUNDTRACK: No soundtrack available

* * * * * * * * *

THE ROCKY HORROR PICTURE SHOW
20th Century Fox, 1975

Producer: Michael White and John Goldstone
Director: Jim Sharman
Screenplay: Jim Sharman and Richard O'Brien; based on the stage musical book by Richard O'Brien
Choreography: David Toguri
Music and Lyrics: Richard O'Brien
Running time: 100 minutes, color

CAST:

Tim Curry (*Dr. Frank N. Furter*); Susan Sarandon (*Janet Weiss*); Barry Bostwick (*Brad Majors*); Richard O'Brien (*Riff Raff*); Jonathan Adams (*Dr. Everett Scott*); Nell Campbell (*Columbia*); Peter Hinwood (*Rocky Horror*); Patricia Quinn (*Magenta*); Meat Loaf (*Eddie*) and Charles Gray (*Criminologist*).

SONGS:

Science Fiction Double Feature; Over at the Frankenstein Place; Sweet Transvestite; Time Warp; The Sword of Damocles; Charles Atlas Song; What Ever Happened to Saturday Night?; Touch-a Touch Me; Eddie's Teddy; Planet Schmanet; Going Home; Super-Heroes; It Was Great When It All Began.

SYNOPSIS:

Camp film about a young couple, Janet and Brad, who seek shelter from a storm at a creepy old house when their car breaks down. They soon discover that the house is inhabited by a strange and motley crew from the planet Transylvania--led by the transvestite Dr. Frank N. Furter.

SOUNDTRACK: Ode SP-77031

* * * * * * * * *

ROMANCE ON THE HIGH SEAS
Warner Bros., 1948

Producer: Alex Gottlieb
Director: Michael Curtiz
Screenplay: Julius Epstein, Philip G. Epstein and I.A.L. Diamond; based on a story
by Sixto Pondal Rios and Carlos A. Olivari
Choreography: Busby Berkeley
Music and Lyrics: Jule Styne and Sammy Cahn
Running time: 99 minutes, color

CAST:

Jack Carson (*Peter Virgil*); Janis Paige (*Elvira Kent*); Don DeFore (*Michael Kent*);
Doris Day (*Georgia Garrett*); Oscar Levant (*Oscar Farrar*); S.Z. Sakall (*Uncle Lazlo*);
Fortunio Bonanova (*Plinio*); Eric Blore (*Ship's Doctor*) and Leslie Brooks (*Miss
Medwick*).

SONGS:

I'm in Love; It's You or No One; It's Magic; Put 'Em in a Box, Tie 'Em With a
Ribbon and Throw 'Em in the Deep Blue Sea; Run, Run, Run.

SYNOPSIS:

New York socialite Elvira Kent thinks her husband Michael is having an affair with
his secretary so she sends young singer Georgia Garrett in her place on a vacation
cruise so she can spy on him--while her husband hires private detective Peter Virgil
to follow her!

SOUNDTRACK: Caliban 6015 (with *It's a Great Feeling*)

* * * * * * * * *

ROMAN SCANDALS
United Artists, 1933

Producer: Samuel Goldwyn
Director: Frank Tuttle
Screenplay: George S. Kaufman, Robert E. Sherwood, George Oppenheimer, Arthur
Sheekman and Nat Perrin, adaptation by William Anthony McGuire
Choreography: Busby Berkeley
Music and Lyrics: Harry Warren and Al Dubin
Running time: 93 minutes, B/W

CAST:

Eddie Cantor (*Eddie*); Ruth Etting (*Olga*); Gloria Stuart (*Princess Sylvia*); David Manners (*Josephus*); Veree Teasdale (*Empress Agrippa*); Edward Arnold (*Emperor Valerius*); Alan Mowbray (*Majordomo*); Jack Rutherford (*Manius*); Grace Poggi (*Slave Dancer*); Willard Robertson (*Warren F. Cooper*); Harry Holman (*Mayor of West Rome*) and Stanley Fields (*Slave Auctioneer*).

SONGS:

Build a Little Home; No More Love; Keep Young and Beautiful; Don't Put a Tax on Love*.

music and lyrics by Harry Warren and L. Wolfe Gilbert

SYNOPSIS:

A delivery boy in West Rome, Oklahoma falls asleep and suddenly finds himself a slave in Ancient Rome.

SOUNDTRACK: Classic International Filmusicals 3007 (with *Roman Scandals*)

* * * * * * * * *

ROSALIE
Metro-Goldwyn-Mayer, 1937

Producer: William Anthony McGuire
Director: W.S. Van Dyke II
Screenplay: William Anthony McGuire; based on the play by William Anthony
           McGuire and Guy Bolton
Choreography: Albertina Rasch
Music and Lyrics: Cole Porter
Running time: 123 minutes, B/W

CAST:

Nelson Eddy (*Dick Thorpe*); Eleanor Powell (*Rosalie Romanikoff*); Ray Bolger (*Bill Delroy*); Frank Morgan (*King Frederic Romanikoff*); Ilona Massey (*Countess Brenda*); Edna May Oliver (*Queen*); Billy Gilbert (*Oloff*); Reginald Owen (*Chancellor*); George Zucco (*General Maroff*); Virginia Grey (*Mary Callahan*); Tom Rutherford (*Prince Paul*); Clay Clement (*Captain Banner*); Oscar O'Shea (*Mr. Callahan*); Janet Beecher (*Miss Baker*); William Demarest (*Army Football Coach*); Tommy Bond (*Mickey*) and Jerry Colonna (*Joseph*).

The Caissons Go Rolling Along*; Anchors Aweigh**; Who Knows?; I've Got a Strange New Rhythm in My Heart; M'Appari (*Martha*)***; Rosalie; Why Should I Care?; Spring Love is in the Air; In the Still Of the Night; It's All Over But the Shouting; To Love or Not to Love.

music and lyrics by Edmund L. Gruber
**music and lyrics by Charles A. Zimmerman, Alfred Hart Miles and Royal Lovell*
***music and lyrics by Friedrich Von Flotow*

SYNOPSIS:

Incognito princess Rosalie is a Vassar student who reluctantly falls in love with West Point cadet Dick Thorpe--even though her father, King Frederic, has promised her hand to Prince Paul.

SOUNDTRACK: No soundtrack available

* * * * * * * * *

THE ROSE
20th Century Fox, 1979

Producer: Marvin Worth and Aaron Russo
Director: Mark Rydell
Screenplay: Bo Goldman and William Kerby; based on a story by William Kerby
Choreography: Toni Basil
Music and Lyrics: see below with song titles
Running time: 134 minutes, color

CAST:

Bette Midler (*Rose*); Alan Bates (*Rudge Campbell*); Frederic Forrest (*Houston Dyer*); Harry Dean Stanton (*Billy Ray*); Barry Primus (*Dennis*); David Keith (*Mal*); Sandra McCabe (*Sarah Willingham*); Will Hare (*Mr. Leonard*); Rudy Bond (*Monty*); Don Calfa (*Don Frank*); James Keane (*Dealer*); Doris Roberts (*Rose's Mother*) and Sandy Ward (*Rose's Father*).

SONGS:

Whose Side Are You On? - *Kenny Hopkins and Charley Williams*
Midnight in Memphis - *Tony Johnson*
When a Man Loves a Woman - *C. Lewis and A. Wright*

Fire Down Below - *Bob Segar*
Let Me Call You Sweetheart - *Leo Friedman and Beth Slater Whitson*
Keep On Rockin' - *Sammy Hagar and John Carter*
Sold My Soul to Rock 'n Roll - *Gene Pistilli*
Stay With Me - *Jerry Ragavoy and George Weiss*
The Rose - *Amanda McBroom*

SYNOPSIS:

Biography of a fictitious 1960's rock and roll singer named "The Rose" and the emotional rollercoaster life she leads that ultimately ends in tragedy.

SOUNDTRACK: Atlantic SD-16010

* * * * * * * * *

ROSE-MARIE
Metro-Goldwyn-Mayer, 1936

Producer: Hunt Stromberg
Director: W.S. Van Dyke II
Screenplay: Frances Goodrich, Albert Hackett and Alice Duer Miller; based on the
            stage musical book by Otto Harbach and Oscar Hammerstein II
Choreography: Chester Hale and William Von Wymetal
Music and Lyrics: see below with song titles
Running time: 110 minutes, B/W

CAST:

Jeanette MacDonald (*Marie de Flor*); Nelson Eddy (*Sergeant Bruce*); James Stewart (*John Flower*); Reginald Owen (*Myerson*); George Regas (*Boniface*); Robert Grieg (*Café Manager*); Una O'Connor (*Anna*); Dorothy Gray (*Edith*); David Nivens (*Teddy*); Allan Jones ("*Romeo*"/"*Mario Cavaradossi*"); Alan Mowbray (*Premier*); Aileen Carlyle (*Susan*); Gilda Gray (*Belle*) and Mary Anita Loos (*Corn Queen*).

SONGS:

Pardon Me, Madame - *Herbert Stothart and Gus Kahn*
The Mounties - *Rudolf Friml, Herbert Stothart, Otto Harbach and Oscar
               Hammerstein II*
Dinah - *Harry Akst, Sam M. Lewis and Joe Young*
Some of These Days - *Shelton Brooks*
Rose-Marie - *Rudolf Friml, Otto Harbach and Oscar Hammerstein II*

Totem Tom Tom - *Rudolf Friml, Herbert Stothart, Otto Harbach and Oscar
     Hammerstein II*
Just For You - *Rudolf Friml, Herbert Stothart and Gus Kahn*
Three Blind Mice - *traditional*
Indian Love Call - *Rudolf Friml, Otto Harbach and Oscar Hammerstein II*

SYNOPSIS:

Opera singer Marie de Flor goes to Canada to aid her brother, John Flower, on the
run after killing a Mountie. Once there, she falls in love with Sgt. Bruce, the
Mountie assigned to bring her brother in.

SOUNDTRACK: Hollywood Soundstage 414

* * * * * * * * * *

ROSE-MARIE
Metro-Goldwyn-Mayer, 1954

Producer: Mervyn LeRoy
Director: Mervyn LeRoy
Screenplay: Ronald Miller and George Froeschel; based on the stage musical book
     by Otto Harbach and Oscar Hammerstein II
Choreography: Busby Berkeley
Music and Lyrics: see below with song titles
Running time: 115 minutes, color

CAST:

Ann Blyth (*Rose-Marie Lemaitre*); Howard Keel (*Mike Malone*); Fernando Lamas
(*James Severn Duval*); Bert Lahr (*Barney McGorkle*); Marjorie Main (*Lady Jane
Dunstock*); Joan Taylor (*Wanda*); Roy Collins (*Inspector Appleby*) and Chief
Yowlachie (*Black Eagle*).

SONGS:

Rose-Marie - *Rudolf Friml, Otto Harbach and Oscar Hammerstein II*
Free To Be Free - *Rudolf Friml and Paul Francis Webster*
The Right Place For a Girl - *Rudolf Friml and Paul Francis Webster*
Love and Kisses - *Rudolf Friml and Paul Francis Webster*
The Mounties - *Rudolf Friml, Herbert Stothart, Otto Harbach and Oscar
     Hammerstein II*
I Have the Love - *Rudolf Friml and Paul Francis Webster*
The Mountie Who Never Got His Man - *George Stoll and Herbert Baker*

Totem Tom Tom - *Rudolf Friml, Herbert Stothart, Otto Harbach and Oscar Hammerstein II*
Indian Love Call - *Rudolf Friml, Otto Harbach and Oscar Hammerstein II*

SYNOPSIS:

Rose-Marie Lemaitre is being watched over by Royal Canadian Mountie Mike Malone to make sure she becomes a lady but she falls in love with trapper James Duval triggering a love triangle between the three.

SOUNDTRACK: MGM 2-SES-41ST (with *Seven Brides For Seven Brothers*)

* * * * * * * * *

ROSE OF WASHINGTON SQUARE
20th Century Fox, 1939

Producer: Darryl F. Zanuck
Director: Gregory Ratoff
Screenplay: Nunnally Johnson; based on a story by John Larkin and Jerry Horwin
Choreography: Seymour Felix
Music and Lyrics: see below with song titles
Running time: 90 minutes, B/W

CAST:

Tyrone Power (*Bert Clinton*); Alice Faye (*Rose Sargent*); Al Jolson (*Ted Cotter*); William Frawley (*Harry Long*); Joyce Compton (*Peggy*); Hobart Cavanaugh (*Whitey Boone*) and Moroni Olsen (*Buck Russell*).

SONGS:

I Never Knew Heaven Could Speak - *Mack Gordon and Harry Revel*
Rose of Washington Square - *James Hanley and Ballard MacDonald*
My Man - *Maurice Yvoin and Channing Pollock*
Toot Toot Tootsie - *Gus Kahn, Ernie Erdman and Dan Russo*
The Vamp - *Byron Gay*
Ja-Da - *Bob Carleton*
I'm Always Chasing Rainbows - *Frederick Chopin, Harry Carroll and Joseph McCarthy*
Rock-a-Bye Your Baby With a Dixie Melody - *Jean Schwartz, Sam M. Lewis and Joe Young*
California, Here I Come - *B.G. DeSylva, Al Jolson and Joseph Meyer*
April Showers - *B.G. DeSylva and Louis Silvers*

I'm Just Wild About Harry - *Eubie Blake and Noble Sissle*
Everybody Loves My Baby - *Jack Palmer and Spencer Williams*
My Mammy - *Walter Donaldson, Sam M. Lewis and Joe Young*
Avalon - *Al Jolson, B.G. DeSylva and Vincent Rose*
I'm Sorry I Made You Cry - *N.J. Clesi*
The Curse of an Aching Heart - *Al Piantadosi and Henry Fink*

SYNOPSIS:

Singer Rose Sargent tries her best to keep her boyfriend Bert out of jail and when she finally makes it to the "big time"--a Ziegfeld show--she vows to stand by him even after he's sent to prison.

SOUNDTRACK: Caliban 6002 (with *Footlight Serenade*)

* * * * * * * * *

ROUSTABOUT
Paramount, 1964

Producer: Hal B. Wallis
Director: John Rich
Screenplay: Anthony Lawrence and Allan Weiss; based on a story by Allan Weiss
Choreography: Earl Barton
Music and Lyrics: see below with song titles
Running time: 101 minutes, color

CAST:

Elvis Presley (*Charlie Rogers*); Barbara Stanwyck (*Maggie Morgan*); Joan Freeman (*Cathy Lean*); Leif Erickson (*Joe Lean*); Sue Ane Langdon (*Madame Mijanou*); Pat Buttram (*Harry Carver*); Joan Staley (*Marge*); Dabbs Greer (*Arthur Nielsen*); Steve Brodie (*Fred*); Norman Grabowski (*Sam*); Jack Albertson (*Lou*); Jane Dulo (*Hazel*); Joel Fluellen (*Cody Marsh*) and Wilda Taylor (*"Little Egypt"*).

SONGS:

Roustabout - *Bill Giant, Bernie Baum and Florence Kaye*
Poison Ivy League - *Bill Giant, Bernie Baum and Florence Kaye*
Wheels On My Heels - *Sid Tepper and Roy C. Bennett*
It's a Wonderful World - *Sid Tepper and Roy C. Bennett*
It's Carnival Time - *Ben Weisman and Sid Wayne*
Carny Town - *Fred Wise and Randy Starr*
One Track Heart - *Bill Giant, Bernie Baum and Florence Kaye*

Hard Knocks - *Joy Byers*
Little Egypt - *Jerry Leiber and Mike Stoller*
Big Love, Big Heartache - *Dolores Fuller, Lee Morris and Sonny Hendrix*
There's a Brand New Day on the Horizon - *Joy Byers*

SYNOPSIS:

Drifter Charlie Rogers goes to work for Maggie Morgan's carnival when his motorcycle is wrecked but soon runs afoul of Joe Lean who doesn't want Charlie dating his daughter Cathy.

SOUNDTRACK: RCA LSP-2999

* * * * * * * * *

ROYAL WEDDING
Metro-Goldwyn-Mayer, 1951

Producer: Arthur Freed
Director: Stanley Donen
Screenplay: Alan Jay Lerner, based on his story
Choreography: Nick Castle
Music and Lyrics: Burton Lane and Alan Jay Lerner
Running time: 93 minutes, color

CAST:

Fred Astaire (*Tom Bowen*); Jane Powell (*Ellen Bowen*); Peter Lawford (*Lord John Brindale*); Sarah Churchill (*Anne Ashmond*); Keenan Wynn (*Irving & Edgar Klinger*); Albert Sharpe (*Jamie Ashmond*) and Viola Roache (*Sarah Ashmond*).

SONGS:

Ev'ry Night at Seven; Sunday Jumps (instrumental); Open Your Eyes; The Happiest Day of My Life; How Could You Believe Me When I Said I Loved You When You Know I've Been a Liar All My Life?; Too Late Now; You're All the World to Me; I Left My Hat in Haiti; What a Lovely Day For a Wedding.

SYNOPSIS:

Brother and sister dance team Tom and Ellen Bowen are invited to London to open their new show at the time of the royal wedding--Princess Elizabeth to Prince Philip.

SOUNDTRACK: MGM 2-SES-53ST (with *Nancy Goes to Rio* and *Rich, Young and Pretty*)

* * * * * * * * *

RUMPLESTILTSKIN
Cannon Films, 1987

Producer: Menahem Golan and Yoram Globus
Director: David Irving
Screenplay: David Irving; based on the fairy tale by the Brothers Grimm
Choreography: Dari Shai
Music and Lyrics: Max Robert
Running time: 85 minutes, color

CAST:

Amy Irving (*Katie*); Billy Barty (*Rumplestiltskin*); John Moulder-Brown* (*Prince Henry*); Clive Revill (*King Mezzer*); Priscilla Pointer (*Queen Grizelda*); Yael Uziely (*Emily*) and Robert Symonds (*Victor*).

**vocals dubbed by Stuart Zagnit*

SONGS:

When I'm Queen of the Castle; I Need a Miracle; I'm Greedy; I Love the Miller's Daughter*; One Little Name; My Name is Rumplestiltskin**.

 **music and lyrics by Max Robert and Jules Irving*
***music and lyrics by Max Robert and David Irving*

SYNOPSIS:

After Victor the miller brags that his daughter Katie can actually spin straw into gold she is brought before the king to be put to the test--if she is successful she is to marry the prince but if she fails she will be executed. In desperation, she makes a deal with an evil dwarf--he will spin the gold in exchange for her first-born child.

SOUNDTRACK: Kid Stuff CMT-6620 (cassette only)

S

SAY ONE FOR ME
20th Century Fox, 1959

Producer: Frank Tashlin
Director: Frank Tashlin
Screenplay: Robert O'Brien
Choreography: Alex Romero
Music and Lyrics: James Van Heusen and Sammy Cahn
Running time: 119 minutes, color

CAST:

Bing Crosby (*Father Conroy*); Debbie Reynolds (*Holly*); Robert Wagner (*Tony Vincent*); Ray Walston (*Phil Stanley*); Les Tremayne (*Harry LaMaise*); Connie Gilchrist (*Mary Manning*); Frank McHugh (*Jim Dugan*); Joe Besser (*Joe Greb*); Alena Murray (*Sunny*); June Harriet (*June January*) and Sebastian Cabot (*Monsignor*).

SONGS:

Say One For Me; You Can't Love 'Em All; The Girl Most Likely to Succeed; I Couldn't Care Less; The Night That Rock and Roll Died (Almost); Chico's Choo-Choo; The Secret of Christmas.

SYNOPSIS:

Father Conroy's parish is in the theatrical district of New York City and he decides to help produce a charity show to raise money for his sometimes out-of-work parishoners.

SOUNDTRACK: Columbia CL-1337

* * * * * * * * *

SCROOGE
Cinema Center Films, 1970

Producer: Robert H. Solo
Director: Ronald Neame
Screenplay: Leslie Bricusse; based on the book *A Christmas Carol* by Charles
            Dickens
Choreography: Paddy Stone

287

Music and Lyrics: Leslie Bricusse
Running time: 115 minutes, color

CAST:

Albert Finney (*Ebeneezer Scrooge*); Alec Guinness (*Jacob Marley's Ghost*); Edith Evans (*Ghost of Christmas Past*); Kenneth More (*Ghost of Christmas Present*); Laurence Naismith (*Fezziwig*); Richard Beaumont (*Tiny Tim*); David Collings (*Bob Crachit*); Frances Cuka (*Mrs. Crachit*); Anton Rodgers (*Tom Jenkins*); Kay Walsh (*Mrs. Fezziwig*); Michael Medwin (*Nephew*) and Suzanne Neve (*Isabel*).

SONGS:

Christmas Children; I Hate People; Farver Chris'mas; See the Phantoms; A Christmas Carol; December the 25th; You . . . You . . .; Happiness; I Like Life; The Beautiful Day; Thank You Very Much; I'll Begin Again.

SYNOPSIS:

Based on Charles Dickens' classic tale it's the story of Ebeneezer Scrooge and that special Christmas Eve when the visitations of three spirits enlightened him about his miserable lifestyle.

SOUNDTRACK: Columbia S-30258

* * * * * * * * *

SECOND CHORUS
Paramount, 1940

Producer: Boris Morros
Director: H.C. Potter
Screenplay: Elaine Ryan, Ian McLellan Hunter and Johnny Mercer; based on a story
             by Frank Cavett
Choreography: Hermes Pan
Music and Lyrics: see below with song titles
Running time: 83 minutes, B/W (has been colorized)

CAST:

Fred Astaire (*Danny O'Neill*); Paulette Goddard (*Ellen Miller*); Burgess Meredith (*Hank Taylor*); Charles Butterworth (*Mr. Chisholm*); Artie Shaw (*Himself*); Frank Melton (*Stu*) and Jimmy Conlon (*Mr. Dunn*).

SONGS:

Dig It - *Hal Borne and Johnny Mercer*
Sweet Sue (instrumental) - *Will Harris and Victor Young*
Would You Like to Be the Love of My Life? - *Artie Shaw and Johnny Mercer*
I'm Yours - *Johnny Mercer and E.Y. Harburg*
Poor Mr. Chisholm - *Bernie Hanighan and Johnny Mercer*

SYNOPSIS:

Danny O'Neill's college dance band is known as "The Perennials" because they only stay in school in order to make money on their engagements, but they soon abandon college for a chance to join Artie Shaw's orchestra.

SOUNDTRACK: Hollywood Soundstage 404

* * * * * * * * *

SECOND FIDDLE
20th Century Fox, 1939

Producer: Darryl F. Zanuck
Director: Sidney Lanfield
Screenplay: Harry Tugend; based on a story by George Bradshaw
Choreography: Harry Losee
Music and Lyrics: Irving Berlin
Running time: 87 minutes, B/W

CAST:

Sonja Henie (*Greta Hovland*); Tyrone Power (*Jimmy Sutton*); Rudy Vallee (*Roger Maxwell*); Edna May Oliver (*Aunt Phoebe*); Mary Healy (*Jean Varick*); Lyle Talbot (*Willy Hogger*); Alan Dinehart (*Whit*); Minna Gombell (*Jenny*) and Spencer Charters (*Joe Clayton*).

SONGS:

Sorry For Myself; Back to Back; If Winter Comes; An Old-Fashioned Tune Always is New; I Poured My Heart Into a Song; Song of the Metronome.

SYNOPSIS:

Studio publicist Jimmy Sutton discovers Greta Hovland, a skating star, on a trip to her native Minnesota. He persuades her to accompany him back to Hollywood but has second thoughts when he arranges a romance for her with studio heartthrob Roger Maxwell.

SOUNDTRACK: No soundtrack available

* * * * * * * * *

SEVEN BRIDES FOR SEVEN BROTHERS
Metro-Goldwyn-Mayer, 1954

Producer: Jack Cummings
Director: Stanley Donen
Screenplay: Albert Hackett, Frances Goodrich and Dorothy Kingsley; based on a story by Stephen Vincent Benét
Choreography: Michael Kidd
Music and Lyrics: Gene DePaul and Johnny Mercer
Running time: 103 minutes, color

CAST:

Howard Keel (*Adam Pontipee*); Jane Powell (*Milly*); Jeff Richards (*Benjamin*); Julie Newmeyer (*Dorcas*); Matt Mattox* (*Caleb*); Ruta Kilmonis (*Ruth*); Marc Platt (*Daniel*); Norma Doggett (*Martha*); Jacques d'Amboise (*Ephraim*); Betty Carr (*Sarah*); Tommy Rall (*Frank*); Virginia Gibson (*Liza*); Russ Tamblyn (*Gideon*); Nancy Kilgas (*Alice*); Ian Wolfe (*Rev. Elcott*); Howard Petrie (*Pete Perkins*) and Kelly Brown (*Carl*).

vocals dubbed by Bill Lee

SONGS:

Bless Yore Beautiful Hide; Wonderful, Wonderful Day; When You're in Love; Goin' Co'tin'; Barn-raising Ballet (instrumental); Lonesome Polecat (Lament); Sobbin' Women; June Bride; Spring, Spring, Spring.

SYNOPSIS:

When Adam Pontipee goes to town to get supplies for his farm, his list also includes a wife! He persuades Milly to become his bride and soon his six brothers decide that they want to get married as well.

SOUNDTRACK: MGM 2-SES-41ST (with *Rose-Marie*/1954)

* * * * * * * * *

SEVEN DAYS' LEAVE
RKO, 1942

Producer: Tim Whelan
Director: Tim Whelan
Screenplay: William Bowers, Ralph Spence, Curtis Kenyon and Kenneth Earl
Choreography: Charles Walters
Music and Lyrics: Frank Loesser and Jimmy McHugh
Running time: 87 minutes, B/W

CAST:

Victor Mature (*Pvt. Johnny Gray*); Lucille Ball (*Terry Allen*); Harold Peary (*"The Great Gildersleeve"*); Mapy Cortes (*Mapy*); Ginny Simms (*Herself*); Marcy McGuire (*Mickey Allen*); Peter Lind Hayes (*Pvt. Jackson*); Walter Reed (*Ralph Bell*); Wallace Ford (*Sgt. Mead*); Arnold Stang (*Bitsy*); Buddy Clark (*Clarky*); King Kennedy (*Gifford*); Harry Holman (*Judge Gildersleeve*) and Addison Richards (*Captain Collins*).

SONGS:

Please Won't You Leave My Girl Alone?; Baby, You Speak My Language; A Touch of Texas; I Get the Neck of the Chicken; Can't Get Out of This Mood.

SYNOPSIS:

Under the terms of his ancestor's will, Pvt. Johnny Gray will have to forfeit his inheritance unless he can persude socialite Terry Allen to marry him in one week.

SOUNDTRACK: No soundtrack available

* * * * * * * * *

THE SEVEN HILLS OF ROME
Metro-Goldwyn-Mayer, 1958

Producer: Lester Welch
Director: Roy Rowland
Screenplay: Art Cohn and Giorgio Prosperi; based on a story by Giuseppe Amato
Choreography: Paul Steffen
Music and Lyrics: see below with song titles
Running time: 107 minutes, color

CAST:

Mario Lanza (*Marc Revere*); Renato Rascel (*Pepe Bonelli*); Marisa Allasio (*Rafaella Marini*); Peggie Castle (*Carol Ralston*); Clelia Matania (*Beatrice*); Amos Davoli (*Carlo*); Rossella Como (*Anita*) and Guido Celano (*Luigi*).

SONGS:

There's Gonna Be a Party Tonight (Calypso Italiano) - *George Stoll*
Come Dance With Me - *George Blake and Dick Leibart*
Arrivederci Roma - *Renato Rascel*
Temptation - *Nacio Herb Brown and Arthur Freed*
Jezebel - *Wayne Shanklin*
Memories Are Made Of This - *Terry Gilkyson, Richard Dehr and Frank Miller*
When the Saints Go Marching In - *James M. Black and Katharine E. Purvis*
Never Till Now - *Paul Francis Webster and John Green*
The Seven Hills of Rome - *Victor Young and Harold Adamson*

SYNOPSIS:

Singer Marc Revere follows his girlfriend Carol to Europe but after losing her en route he ends up in Rome at his cousin Pepe's. When he finally finds Carol he discovers that he is torn between her and his new friend Rafaella.

SOUNDTRACK: No soundtrack available

* * * * * * * * *

THE SEVEN LITTLE FOYS
Paramount, 1955

Producer: Jack Rose
Director: Melville Shavelson
Screenplay: Melville Shavelson and Jack Rose
Choreography: Nick Castle
Music and Lyrics: see below with song titles
Running time: 95 minutes, color

CAST:

Bob Hope (*Eddie Foy, Sr.*); James Cagney (*George M. Cohan*); Milly Vitale (*Madeleine Morando Foy*); George Tobias (*Barney Green*); Angela Clarke (*Clara Morando*); Herbert Heyes (*Judge Dooney*); Richard Shannon (*Stage Manager*); Billy Gray (*Bryan Foy*); Lee Erickson (*Charley Foy*); Paul DeRolf (*Richard Foy*); Lydia

Reed (*Mary Foy*); Linda Bennett (*Madeleine Foy*); Jimmy Baird (*Eddie Foy, Jr.*); Tommy Duran (*Irving Foy*) and Charley Foy (*Narrator*).

SONGS:

Nobody - *Bert Williams and Alex Rogers*
I'm Tired - *William Jerome and Jean Schwartz*
Yankee Doodle Dandy (instrumental) - *George M. Cohan*
Mary is a Grand Old Name (instrumental) - *George M. Cohan*
Row, Row, Row - *William Jerome and James V. Monaco*
Chinatown, My Chinatown - *William Jerome and Jean Schwartz*
I'm the Greatest Father of Them All - *William Jerome, Joseph J. Lilley and Eddie Foy, Sr.*

SYNOPSIS:

The biography of Eddie Foy, Sr. and his seven children that he takes into his vaudeville act with him after his wife dies.

SOUNDTRACK: No soundtrack available

* * * * * * * * *

SEVEN SWEETHEARTS
Metro-Goldwyn-Mayer, 1942

Producer: Joe Pasternak
Director: Frank Borzage
Screenplay: Walter Reisch and Leo Townsend
Choreography: Ernst Matray
Music and Lyrics: Paul Francis Webster and Walter Jurmann
Running time: 98 minutes, B/W

CAST:

Kathryn Grayson (*Billy Van Maaster*); Van Heflin (*Henry Taggart*); S.Z. Sakall (*Mr. Van Maaster*); Marsha Hunt (*Regina*); Carl Esmond (*Karl Randall*); Isobel Elsom (*Abigail Robbins*); Cecilia Parker (*Victor*); Peggy Moran (*Albert*); Frances Rafferty (*George*); Dorothy Morris (*Peter*); Frances Raeburn (*Cornelius*) and Louise Beavers (*Petunia*).

SONGS:

All Your Dreams Will Come True (Cradle Song)*; You and the Waltz and I; Little

Tingle Tangle Toes; Tulip Time.

*music and lyrics by Wolfgang Amadeus Mozart

SYNOPSIS:

Tulip time in Little Delft, Michigan is the assignment for photojournalist Henry Taggart, but Mr. Van Maaster and his seven daughters are something he didn't expect.

SOUNDTRACK: Azel 101

* * * * * * * * *

1776
Columbia, 1972

Producer: Jack L. Warner
Director: Peter H. Hunt
Screenplay: Peter Stone, based on his stage musical book
Choreography: Onna White
Music and Lyrics: Sherman Edwards
Running time: 141 minutes, color

CAST:

William Daniels (*John Adams*); Howard da Silva (*Benjamin Franklin*); Ken Howard (*Thomas Jefferson*); Blythe Danner (*Martha Jefferson*); John Cullum (*Edward Rutledge*); Donald Madden (*John Dickinson*); David Ford (*John Hancock*); Roy Poole (*Stephen Hopkins*); Ronald Holgate (*Richard Henry Lee*); John Myhers (*Robert Livingston*); Rex Robbins (*Roger Sherman*); Jonathan Moore (*Dr. Lyman Hall*); William Hansen (*Caesar Rodney*); Emory Bass (*James Wilson*); Howard Caine (*Lewis Morris*); Ralston Hill (*Charles Thomson*); William Duell (*Andrew McNair*); Stephen Nathan (*Courier*); Mark Montgomery (*Leather Apron*) and Virginia Vestoff (*Abigail Adams*).

SONGS:

Sit Down, John; Piddle, Twiddle and Resolve; Till Then; The Lees of Old Virginia; But, Mr. Adams; Yours, Yours, Yours; He Plays the Violin; Momma Look Sharp; The Egg; Molasses to Rum; Is Anybody There?

SYNOPSIS:

During a hot, humid summer in Philadelphia in 1776, the Second Continental Congress is meeting to decide whether or not to openly declare its independence from Great Britain.

SOUNDTRACK: Columbia S-31741

* * * * * * * * *

SEXTETTE
Crown International, 1977

Producer: Daniel Briggs and Robert Sullivan
Director: Ken Hughes
Screenplay: Herbert Baker; based on the play by Mae West
Choreography: Marc Breaux
Music and Lyrics: see below with song titles
Running time: 91 minutes, color

CAST:

Mae West (*Marlo Manners*); Timothy Dalton (*Sir Michael Barrington*); Dom DeLuise (*Dan Turner*); Tony Curtis (*Alexei Karansky*); Ringo Starr (*Laslo Karolny*); George Hamilton (*Vance*); Alice Cooper (*Waiter*); Walter Pidgeon (*The Chairman*); Van McCoy (*Delegate*); Keith Moon (*Dress Designer*); Richard Peel (*English Chef*) and Keith Allison (*Waiter in Alexei's Suite*).

SONGS:

Marlo's Theme - *Van McCoy*
Hooray For Hollywood - *Johnny Mercer and Richard A. Whiting*
Love Will Keep Us Together - *Neil Sedaka and Howard Greenfield*
Honey Pie - *John Lennon and Paul McCartney*
After You've Gone - *Henry Creamer and Turner Layton*
Happy Birthday, Sweet Sixteen - *Neil Sedaka, Howard Greenfield and Ian Whitcomb*
Baby Face - *Harry Akst and Benny Davis*
Next Next - *Van McCoy*

SYNOPSIS:

Movie queen (and government agent) Marlo Manners is about to begin her honeymoon with her sixth husband, Sir Michael Barrington, when her assistant Dan Turner informs her that she has a new secret mission from the State Department.

SOUNDTRACK: No soundtrack available

* * * * * * * * *

SHALL WE DANCE?
RKO, 1937

Producer: Pandro S. Berman
Director: Mark Sandrich
Screenplay: Allan Scott, Ernest Pagano and P.J. Wolfson; based on a story by Lee
              Loeb and Harold Buchman
Choreography: Hermes Pan and Harry Losee
Music and Lyrics: George Gershwin and Ira Gershwin
Running time: 116 minutes, B/W

CAST:

Fred Astaire (*"Petrov"/Pete Peters*); Ginger Rogers (*Linda Keene*); Edward Everett
Horton (*Jeffrey Baird*); Eric Blore (*Cecil Flintridge*); Jerome Cowan (*Arthur Miller*);
Ketti Gallian (*Lady Tarrington*); William Brisbane (*Jim Montgomery*) and Ann
Shoemaker (*Mrs. Fitzgerald*).

SONGS:

Slap That Bass; I've Got Beginner's Luck; They All Laughed; Let's Call the Whole
Thing Off; They Can't Take That Away From Me; Shall We Dance?

SYNOPSIS:

Ballet dancer Petrov (a.k.a. Pete Peters) longs for a career as a popular dancer--and
pretty Linda Keene--and is soon rumored to be married to her.

SOUNDTRACK: Sountrak 106 (with *Swing Time*)

* * * * * * * * *

SHE'S BACK ON BROADWAY
Warner Bros., 1953

Producer: Henry Blanke
Director: Gordon Douglas
Screenplay: Orin Jannings
Choreography: LeRoy Prinz

Music and Lyrics: Carl Sigman and Bob Hilliard
Running time: 95 minutes, color

CAST:

Virginia Mayo (*Catherine Terris*); Gene Nelson (*Gordon Evans*); Frank Lovejoy (*John Webber*); Steve Cochran (*Rick Sommers*); Patrice Wymore (*Karen Keene*); Virginia Gibson (*Angela Korinna*); Larry Keating (*Mitchell Parks*); Paul Picerni (*Jud Kellogg*); Ned Young (*Rafferty*); Jacqueline de Wit (*Lisa Kramer*) and Paul Bryar (*Ned Golby*).

SONGS:

I Think You're Wonderful; One Step Ahead of Everybody; I'll Take You As You Are; The Ties That Bind; Breakfast in Bed; Behind the Mask.

SYNOPSIS:

Catherine Terris needs a boost for her sagging film career and Rick Sommers' new Broadway show seems to be the answer.

SOUNDTRACK: Caliban 6032

* * * * *. * * * *

SHE'S WORKING HER WAY THROUGH COLLEGE
Warner Bros., 1952

Producer: William Jacobs
Director: Bruce Humberstone
Screenplay: Peter Milne; based on the play *The Male Animal* by James Thurber and
             Elliott Nugent
Choreography: LeRoy Prinz
Music and Lyrics: Vernon Duke and Sammy Cahn
Running time: 104 minutes, color

CAST:

Virginia Mayo (*Angela Gardner*); Ronald Reagan (*John Palmer*); Gene Nelson (*Don Weston*); Don DeFore (*Shep Slade*); Phyllis Thaxter (*Helen Palmer*); Patrice Wymore (*Ivy Williams*); Raymond Greenleaf (*Dean Rogers*); Roland Winters (*Fred Copeland*); Hope Sansbury (*Mrs. Rogers*) and Henrietta Taylor (*Mrs. Copeland*).

SONGS:

With Plenty of Money and You*; All Hail Midwest State; She's Working Her Way
Through College; I'll Be Loving You; Rally; The Stuff That Dreams Are Made Of;
Love is Still For Free; Am I in Love?*; Give 'Em What They Want.

*music and lyrics by Harry Warren and Al Dubin

SYNOPSIS:

Burlesque performer "Hot Garters Gertie" decides her mind needs improving so she
enters college under her real name--Angela Gardner. But when she takes part in a
school show and football star Don Weston falls for her, his jealous girlfriend Ivy tells
the authorities who she really is.

SOUNDTRACK: No soundtrack available

* * * * * * * * *

SHINE ON, HARVEST MOON
Warner Bros., 1944

Producer: William Jacobs
Director: David Butler
Screenplay: Sam Hellman, Richard Weil, Francis Swann and James Kern; based on
              a story by Richard Weil
Choreography: LeRoy Prinz
Music and Lyrics: see below with song titles
Running time: 111 minutes, B/W and color

CAST:

Ann Sheridan (*Nora Bayes*); Dennis Morgan (*Jack Norworth*); Jack Carson (*"The
Great Georgetti"*); Irene Manning (*Blanche Mallory*); S.Z. Sakall (*Poppa Karl*); Marie
Wilson (*Margie*); Robert Shayne (*Dan Costello*); Bob Murphy (*Police Sergeant*);
William B. Davidson (*Tim Donovan*); James Bush (*William Fowler*) and Joseph
Crehan (*Harry Miller*).

SONGS:

Be My Little Baby Bumble Bee - *Stanley Murphy and Henry I. Marshall*
My Own United States - *Julian Edwards and Stanislaus Stange*
Time Waits For No One - *Cliff Friend and Charles Tobias*
It Looks Like a Big Night Tonight - *Egbert Van Alstyne and Harry Williams*

298

When It's Apple Blossom Time in Normandy - *Harry Gifford, Huntley Trevor and Tom Mellor*

Take Me Out to the Ball Game - *Jack Norworth and Albert Von Tilzer*

Along With the Breeze - *Haven Gillespie, Seymour B. Simons and Richard Whiting*

So Dumb But So Beautiful - *M.K. Jerome and Kim Gannon*

Every Little Movement Has a Meaning Of Its Own - *Otto Harbach and Karl Hoschna*

I Go For You - *M.K. Jerome and Kim Gannon*

Just Like a Gypsy - *Seymour B. Simons and Nora Bayes*

Shine On, Harvest Moon - *Jack Norworth and Nora Bayes*

SYNOPSIS:

The biography of entertainers (and songwriters) Jack Norworth and Nora Bayes chronicles their struggles against a black-balling by a powerful and jealous rival, Dan Costello.

SOUNDTRACK: No soundtrack available

* * * * * * * * *

SHIPMATES FOREVER
Warner Bros., 1935

Producer: Frank Borzage
Director: Frank Borzage
Screenplay: Delmar Daves, based on his story
Choreography: Bobby Connolly
Music and Lyrics: Harry Warren and Al Dubin
Running time: 109 minutes, B/W

CAST:

Dick Powell (*Richard John Melville III*); Ruby Keeler (*June Blackburn*); Lewis Stone (*Admiral Richard Melville*); Ross Alexander ("*Sparks*" *Brown*); Eddie Acuff ("*Cowboy*" *Lincoln*); Dick Foran (*Gifford*); John Arledge (*Coxswain Johnny Lawrence*); Robert Light (*Ted Sterling*); Joseph King (*Commander Douglas*); Frederick Burton (*Admiral Fred Gates*); Mary Treen (*Cowboy's Girl*) and Henry Kolker (*Doctor*).

SONGS:

Don't Give Up the Ship; I'd Love to Take Orders From You; Abdul Abubul Amir*; I'd Rather Listen to Your Eyes.

music and lyrics by Frank Crumit

SYNOPSIS:

Crooner Dick Melville only enters the Naval Academy at Annapolis to prove to his father, Admiral Melville, that he's not afraid of the entrance exam but he has no plans to accept his commission.

SOUNDTRACK: No soundtrack available

* * * * * * * * *

THE SHOCKING MISS PILGRIM
20th Century Fox, 1947

Producer: William Perlberg
Director: George Seaton
Screenplay: George Seaton; based on a story by Ernest Maas and Frederic Maas
Choreography: Hermes Pan
Music and Lyrics: George Gershwin and Ira Gershwin
Running time: 87 minutes, color

CAST:

Betty Grable (*Cynthia Pilgrim*); Dick Haymes (*John Pritchard*); Anne Revere (*Alice Pritchard*); Allyn Joslyn (*Leander Woolsey*); Gene Lockhart (*Saxon*); Elizabeth Patterson (*Catherine Dennison*); Elisabeth Risdon (*Mrs. Pritchard*); Arthur Shields (*Michael Michael*); Charles Kemper (*Herbert Jothan*); Roy Roberts (*Mr. Foster*); Stanley Prager (*Lookout in Office*); Ed Laughton (*Quincy*); Hal K. Dawson (*Peabody*) and Lillian Bronson (*Viola Simmons*).

SONGS:

But Not in Boston; For You, For Me, For Evermore; Sweet Packard; Stand Up and Fight; Changing My Tune; Aren't You Kind Of Glad We Did?; One, Two, Three; Waltzing is Better Sitting Down; Waltz Me No Waltzes.

SYNOPSIS:

When Cynthia Pilgrim, a typist for a shipping firm in Boston, falls for her boss John Pritchard they find their romance rocky due to her advocation of women's rights.

SOUNDTRACK: Classic International Filmusicals 3008 (with *Mother Wore Tights*)

300

* * * * * * * * *

SHOW BOAT
Universal, 1936

Producer: Carl Laemmle, Jr.
Director: James Whale
Screenplay: Oscar Hammerstein II, based on his stage musical book
Choreography: LeRoy Prinz
Music and Lyrics: Jerome Kern and Oscar Hammerstein II
Running time: 110 minutes, B/W

CAST:

Irene Dunne (*Magnolia Hawks*); Allan Jones (*Gaylord Ravenal*); Charles Winninger (*Captain Andy Hawks*); Helen Westley (*Parthy Hawks*); Paul Robeson (*Joe*); Helen Morgan (*Julie LaVerne*); Donald Cook (*Steve Baker*); Sammy White (*Frank Schultz*); Queenie Smith (*Elly May Shipley*); J. Farrell MacDonald (*Windy McClain*); Arthur Hohl (*Pete Gavin*); Hattie McDaniel (*Queenie*); Charles Middleton (*Sheriff Vallon*) and Sunnie O'Dea (*Kim Ravenal as an adult*).

SONGS:

Cotton Blossom; Cap'n Andy's Ballyhoo; Where's the Mate For Me?; Make Believe; Ol' Man River; Can't Help Lovin' Dat Man; I Have the Room Above; Gallivantin' Around; You Are Love; Ah Still Suits Me; Bill*; Goodbye, My Lady Love**; After the Ball***.

  **music and lyrics by Jerome Kern, Oscar Hammerstein II and P.G. Wodehouse*
 ***music and lyrics by Joseph E. Howard*
****music and lyrics by Charles K. Harris*

SYNOPSIS:

Capt. Andy Hawks' show boat travels the length of the mississippi providing entertainment for the population along the river and drama aboard for its inhabitants.

SOUNDTRACK: Xeno 251

* * * * * * * * *

SHOW BOAT
Metro-Goldwyn-Mayer, 1951

Producer: Arthur Freed
Director: George Sidney
Screenplay: John Lee Mahin; based on the stage musical book by Oscar
              Hammerstein II
Choreography: Robert Alton
Music and Lyrics: Jerome Kern and Oscar Hammerstein II
Running time: 115 minutes, color

CAST:

Kathryn Grayson (*Magnolia Hawks*); Howard Keel (*Gaylord Ravenal*); Ava Gardner*
(*Julie LaVerne*); Joe E. Brown (*Captain Andy Hawks*); Marge Champion (*Ellie May
Shipley*); Gower Champion (*Frank Schultz*); Agnes Moorehead (*Parthy Hawks*);
William Warfield (*Joe*); Robert Sterling (*Steve Baker*); Lief Erickson (*Pete*); Frances
Williams (*Queenie*); Owen McGivney (*Windy McClain*); Regis Toomey (*Sheriff*) and
Sheila Clark (*Kim Ravenal*).

vocals dubbed by Annette Warren

SONGS:

Cotton Blossom; Where's the Mate For Me?; Make Believe; Can't Help Lovin' Dat
Man; I Might Fall Back On You; Ol' Man River; You Are Love; Why Do I Love
You?; Bill*; Life Upon the Wicked Stage; After the Ball**.

 music and lyrics by Jerome Kern, Oscar Hammerstein II and P.G. Wodehouse
**music and lyrics by Charles K. Harris*

SYNOPSIS:

Remake of the musical about life on a turn-of-the-century Mississippi River show
boat provides the setting for the romance of Magnolia Hawks and Gaylord Ravenal.

SOUNDTRACK: MGM 2-SES-42ST (with *Annie Get Your Gun*)

* * * * * * * * *

SHOW BUSINESS
RKO, 1944

Producer: Eddie Cantor
Director: Edwin L. Marin
Screenplay: Joseph Quillan, Dorothy Bennett and Irving Elinson; based on a story
              by Bert Granet

Choreography: Nick Castle
Music and Lyrics: see below with song titles
Running time: 92 minutes, B/W

CAST:

Eddie Cantor (*Eddie Martin*); George Murphy (*George Doane*); Joan Davis (*Joan Mason*); Nancy Kelly (*Nancy Gaye*); Constance Moore (*Constance Ford*); Don Douglas (*Charles Lucas*); Forbes Murray (*Director*) and Bert Moorhouse (*Desk Clerk*).

SONGS:

They're Wearing 'Em Higher in Hawaii - *Joe Goodwin and Halsay H. Mohr*
The Curse of an Aching Heart - *Henry Fink and Al Rantadosi*
It Had to Be You - *Gus Kahn and Isham Jones*
I Want a Girl (Just Like the Girl Who Married Dear Old Dad) - *Harry Von Tilzer and Will Dillon*
Alabamy Bound - *B.G. DeSylva, Ray Henderson and Bud Green*
Dinah - *Harry Akst, Sam M. Lewis and Joe Young*
I Don't Want to Get Well - *Howard Johnson, Harry Pease and Harry Jentes*
You May Not Remember - *George Jessel and Ben Oakland*
Why Am I Blue? - *Gus Kahn and Isham Jones*
Making Whoopee - *Gus Kahn and Walter Donaldson*

SYNOPSIS:

Semi-autobiographical account of four young performers and their experiences in the world of burlesque and vaudeville.

SOUNDTRACK: Caliban 6034

* * * * * * * * *

SILK STOCKINGS
Metro-Goldwyn-Mayer, 1957

Producer: Arthur Freed
Director: Rouben Mamoulian
Screenplay: Leonard Gershe and Leonard Spigelgass; based on the stage musical
          book by George S. Kaufman, Leueen McGrath and Abe Burrows
Choreography: Hermes Pan and Eugene Loring
Music and Lyrics: Cole Porter
Running time: 118 minutes, color

CAST:

Fred Astaire (*Steve Canfield*); Cyd Charisse* (*Nina "Ninotchka" Yoshenko*); Janis Paige (*Peggy Dayton*); Peter Lorre (*Comrade Brankov*); Jules Munshin (*Comrade Bibinski*); Joseph Buloff (*Comrade Ivanov*); George Tobias (*Commissar Vassili Markovich*) and Wim Sonneveld (*Peter Ilyitch Boroff*).

vocals dubbed by Carole Richards

SONGS:

Too Bad; Paris Loves Lovers; Stereophonic Sound; Chemical Reaction; All Of You; Satin and Silk; Without Love; Fated To Be Mated; Josephine; Siberia; Red Blues; The Ritz Roll 'n Rock.

SYNOPSIS:

After American film producer Steve Canfield woos Russian composer Peter Boroff into writing the score for his new movie in Paris, the Soviet government sends Comrade Yoshenko to find out why the musician would agree to do such a thing.

SOUNDTRACK: MGM 2-SES-51ST (with *The Barkleys of Broadway* and *Les Girls*)

* * * * * * * * *

THE SINGING NUN
Metro-Goldwyn-Mayer, 1966

Producer: John Beck
Director: Henry Koster
Screenplay: Sally Benson and John Furia, Jr.; based on a story by John Furia, Jr.
Choreography: Robert Sidney
Music and Lyrics: Soeur Sourire and Randy Sparks
Running time: 98 minutes, color

CAST:

Debbie Reynolds (*Sister Ann*); Ricardo Montalban (*Father Clementi*); Greer Garson (*Mother Prioress*); Agnes Moorehead (*Sister Cluny*); Chad Everett (*Robert Gerarde*); Katharine Ross (*Nicole Arlien*); Ed Sullivan (*Himself*); Juanita Moore (*Sister Mary*); Ricky Cordell (*Dominic Cordell*); Anne Wakefield (*Sister Brigitte*); Michael Pate (*Mr. Arlien*); Monique Montaigne (*Sister Michelle*) and Tom Drake (*Mr. Fitzpatrick*).

304

SONGS:

Brother John; Sister Adele; Beyond the Stars; Avec Toi; Je Voudrais; Mets Ton Joli Jupon; Lovely; Aleluia; Raindrops; It's a Miracle; Dominique; A Pied Piper's Song.

SYNOPSIS:

Based on the true-life story of a Belgian Dominican nun who finds herself torn between her love of music and the duty she feels to God.

SOUNDTRACK: MGM S1E-7

* * * * * * * * *

SINGIN' IN THE RAIN
Metro-Goldwyn-Mayer, 1952

Producer: Arthur Freed
Director: Gene Kelly and Stanley Donen
Screenplay: Betty Comden and Adolph Green
Choreography: Gene Kelly and Stanley Donen
Music and Lyrics: Nacio Herb Brown and Arthur Freed
Running time: 103 minutes, color

CAST:

Gene Kelly (*Don Lockwood*); Donald O'Connor (*Cosmo Brown*); Debbie Reynolds (*Kathy Selden*); Jean Hagen (*Lina Lamont*); Douglas Fowley (*Roscoe Dexter*); Millard Mitchell (*R.F. Simpson*); Cyd Charisse (*"Broadway Ballet" dancer*); Rita Moreno (*Zelda Zanders*); Madge Blake (*Dora Bailey*); King Donovan (*Rod*); Kathleen Freeman (*Phoebe Dinsmore*) and Jimmy Thompson (*Singer*).

SONGS:

Fit as a Fiddle (And Ready For Love)*; All I Do is Dream of You; Make 'Em Laugh; I've Got a Feelin' You're Foolin'; The Wedding of the Painted Doll; Should I?; Beautiful Girl; You Were Meant For Me; Moses Supposes**; Good Morning; Singin' in the Rain; Broadway Melody; Broadway Rhythm; You Are My Lucky Star.

 music and lyrics by Al Hoffman, Al Goodhart and Arthur Freed
 **music and lyrics by Betty Comden, Adolph Green and Roger Edens*

SYNOPSIS:

The advent of talking pictures spells disaster for Monumental Pictures top starring team of Don Lockwood and Lina Lamont unless a substitute voice can be found to dub Lina's (which resembles fingernails on a blackboard!)

SOUNDTRACK: MGM 2-SES-40ST (with *Easter Parade*)

* * * * * * * * *

SKIRTS AHOY!
Metro-Goldwyn-Mayer, 1952

Producer: Joe Pasternak
Director: Sidney Lanfield
Screenplay: Isobel Lennart
Choreography: Nick Castle
Music and Lyrics: Harry Warren and Ralph Blane
Running time: 109 minutes, color

CAST:

Esther Williams (*Whitney Young*); Joan Evans (*Mary Kate Yarborough*); Vivian Blaine (*Una Yancy*); Barry Sullivan (*Lt. Cmdr. Paul Elcott*); Keefe Brasselle (*Dick Hallson*); Dean Miller (*Archie O'Conovan*); Margalo Gillmore (*Lt. Cmdr. Stauton*); Jeff Donnell (*Chief Giff*); Thurston Hall (*Thatcher Kinston*); Roy Roberts (*Capt. Graymont*); Billy Eckstine (*Himself*); Debbie Reynolds (*Herself*); Bobby Van (*Himself*); Keenan Wynn (*Himself*); The DeMarco Sisters (*The Williams Sisters*); Russell Tongay (*Little Boy*); Kathy Tongay (*Little Girl*); Hayden Rorke (*Doctor*) and Emmett Lynn (*"Pop"*).

SONGS:

Skirts Ahoy!; Glad to Have You Aboard; What Makes a WAVE?; What Good is a Gal Without a Guy?; Hold Me Close to You; Oh By Jingo*; I Get a Funny Feeling; The Navy Waltz.

*music and lyrics by Lew Brown and Albert Von Tilzer

SYNOPSIS:

Whitney Young, Mary Kate Yarborough and Una Yancy all decide to join the Navy to try and find a new direction in life and end up finding something new about themselves.

306

SOUNDTRACK: No soundtrack available

* * * * * * * * *

SLEEPING BEAUTY
Buena Vista, 1959

Producer: Walt Disney
Director: Clyde Geronimi
Screenplay: Erdman Penner, Joe Rinaldi, Winston Hibler, Bill Peet, Ted Sears,
      Ralph Wright and Milt Banta; based on the fairy tale by Charles
      Perrault
Music and Lyrics: see below with song titles
Running time: 75 minutes, color

VOCAL TALENTS:

Mary Costa (*Princess Aurora*); Bill Shirley (*Prince Philip*); Eleanor Audley
(*Maleficent*); Verna Felton (*Flora*); Barbara Jo Allen (*Fauna*); Barbara Luddy
(*Merryweather*); Taylor Holmes (*King Stefan*) and Bill Thompson (*King Hubert*).

SONGS:

Hail the Princess Aurora - *George Bruns and Tom Adair*
I Wonder - *George Bruns, Winston Hibler and Ted Sears*
Once Upon a Dream - *Sammy Fain and Jack Lawrence*
The Skump Song - *George Bruns, Tom Adair and Erdman Penner*
The Sleeping Beauty Song - *George Bruns and Tom Adair*

SYNOPSIS:

Animated fairy tale about how three good fairies--Flora, Fauna and Merryweather--
-attempt to save the baby Princess Aurora from the evil Maleficent. When she
outwits them they amend her curse so that a kiss from a prince will be her salvation.

SOUNDTRACK: Disneyland 4018

* * * * * * * * *

SLEEPING BEAUTY
Cannon Films, 1987

Producer: Menahem Golan and Yoram Globus
Director: David Irving

Screenplay: Michael Berz; based on the fairy tale by Charles Perrault
Choreography: Yaacov Kalusky
Music and Lyrics: see below with song titles
Running time: 90 minutes, color

CAST:

Morgan Fairchild* (*The Queen*); Tahnee Welch** (*Rosebud*); Nicholas Clay*** (*Prince*); Sylvia Miles (*The Red Fairy*); Kenny Baker (*The Elf*); David Holliday (*The King*); Jane Wiedlin (*The White Fairy*); Shai K. Ophir (*The Master Elf*); Julian Joy-Chagrin (*The Advisor*) and Orna Porat (*Nana*).

   vocals dubbed by Anat Ben Yehoshua
  **vocals dubbed by Linda Lopresti*
 ***vocals dubbed by Nick Curtis*

SONGS:

Spin, Spin, Spin - *Michael Berz, Susan Berlin and Dovis Miller*
The Queen's Lament - *Michael Berz*
How Good It Is - *Michael Berz*
Life Looks Rosier Today - *Michael Berz and Max Robert*
Rip - *Michael Berz*
Dare Me - *Michael Berz, Anat Ben Yehoshua and Dovis Miller*
All to Sleep - *Michael Berz*
Slumber - *Max Robert*

SYNOPSIS:

Angry at having been excluded from baby Princess Rosebud's christening, the evil Red Fairy places a curse on the girl but the White Fairy amends it to a sleep that will last for one hundred years--to be awakened by a kiss from a prince.

SOUNDTRACK: Kid Stuff CMT-6621 (cassette only)

* * * * * * * * * *

THE SLIPPER AND THE ROSE
Universal, 1976

Producer: Stuart Lyons
Director: Bryan Forbes
Screenplay: Bryan Forbes, Richard M. Sherman and Robert B. Sherman
Choreography: Marc Breaux

308

Music and Lyrics: Richard M. Sherman and Robert B. Sherman
Running time: 128 minutes, color

CAST:

Richard Chamberlain (*Prince Edward*); Gemma Craven (*Cinderella*); Annette Crosbie (*Fairy Godmother*); Kenneth More (*Lord Chamberlain*); Michael Hordern (*The King*); Margaret Lockwood (*Stepmother*); Lally Bowers (*The Queen*); Julian Orchard (*Duke of Montague*); Christopher Gable (*John*); Polly Williams (*Lady Caroline*) and Edith Evans (*The Dowager Queen*).

SONGS:

Why Can't I Be Two People?; Once I Was Loved; What a Comforting Thing to Know; Protocoligorically Correct; A Bride-Finding Ball; Suddenly It Happens; Secret Kingdom; He Danced With Me-She Danced With Me (The Slipper and the Rose Waltz); Position and Positioning; Tell Him Anything (But Not That I Loved Him).

SYNOPSIS:

The story of Cinderella, the young girl forced to work as a maid for her wicked stepmother, who one night becomes a beautiful princess (with the help of her overworked fairy godmother) and captures a prince's heart.

SOUNDTRACK: MCA 2097

* * * * * * * * *

SMALL TOWN GIRL
Metro-Goldwyn-Mayer, 1953

Producer: Joe Pasternak
Director: Leslie Kardos
Screenplay: Dorothy Cooper and Dorothy Kingsley; based on a story by Dorothy Cooper
Choreography: Busby Berkeley
Music and Lyrics: Nicholas Brodsky and Leo Robin
Running time: 93 minutes, color

CAST:

Jane Powell (*Cindy Kimbell*); Farley Granger (*Richard Belrow Livingston III*); Ann Miller (*Lisa Bellmount*); S.Z. Sakall (*Eric "Papa" Schlemmer*); Robert Keith (*Judge Gordon Kimbell*); Bobby Van (*Ludwig Schlemmer*); Billie Burke (*Mrs. Livingston*);

Fay Wray (*Mrs. Kimbell*); Chill Wills (*Happy*); Bobby Hyatt (*Dennis Kimbell*) and Nat King Cole (*Himself*).

SONGS:

Lullaby of the Lord; Fine, Fine, Fine; Small Towns Are Smile Towns; Take Me to Broadway; The Fellow I'd Follow; I've Got to Hear That Beat; My Flaming Heart; My Gaucho.

SYNOPSIS:

When he is caught speeding through Duck Creek, Connecticut wealthy Rick Belrow Livingston is sentenced to 30 days in jail by Judge Kimbell so he decides to try to get a pardon by romancing the judge's daughter, Cindy.

SOUNDTRACK: No soundtrack available

* * * * * * * * *

SMILIN' THROUGH
Metro-Goldwyn-Mayer, 1941

Producer: Victor Saville
Director: Frank Borzage
Screenplay: Donald Ogden Stewart and John Balderston; based on the play by Jane
            Cowl and Jane Murfin
Music and Lyrics: see below with song titles
Running time: 100 minutes, color

CAST:

Jeanette MacDonald (*Kathleen Clare/Moonyean Clare*); Brian Aherne (*Sir John Carteret*); Gene Raymond (*Kenneth Wayne/Jeremy Wayne*); Ian Hunter (*Rev. Owen Harding*); Jackie Horner (*Kathleen as a child*); Frances Robinson (*Ellen*); Patrick O'Moore (*Willie*) and Eric Lonsdale (*Charles*).

SONGS:

Land of Hope and Glory - *Sir Edward Elgard and A.C. Benson*
The Kerry Dance - *L.J. Molloy*
Drink to Me Only With Thine Eyes - *Ben Johnson*
A Little Love, a Little Kiss - *Leo Silesu and Adrian Ross*
Ouvre ton coeur - *Georges Bizet*
Smilin' Through - *Arthur Penn*

310

There's a Long, Long Trail A-Winding - *Alonzo Elliott and Stoddard King*
Recessional - *Reginald de Koven and Rudyard Kipling*

SYNOPSIS:

Elderly bachelor Sir John Carteret, still bitter over the death of his fiancée Moonyean Clare on their wedding day, reluctantly takes in his orphaned niece Kathleen--who looks exactly like Moonyean.

SOUNDTRACK: No soundtrack available

* * * * * * * * *

SNOW WHITE
Cannon Films, 1987

Producer: Menahem Golan and Yoram Globus
Director: Michael Berz
Screenplay: Michael Berz; based on the fairy tale by the Brothers Grimm
Choreography: Yaacov Kalusky
Music and Lyrics: Arik Rudich and Michael Berz
Running time: 87 minutes, color

CAST:

Diana Rigg (*The Evil Queen*); Billy Barty (*Iddy*); Sarah Patterson* (*Snow White*); Nicola Stapleton (*Snow White as a child*); Mike Edmunds (*Biddy*); Ricardo Gil (*Kiddy*); Malcolm Dixon (*Diddy*); Gary Friedkin (*Fiddy*); Arturo Gil (*Giddy*); Tony Cooper (*Liddy*); Douglas Sheldon (*The King*); Dorit Adi (*The Good Queen*); Ian James Wright** (*The Prince*); Amnon Meskin (*The Hunter*) and Azaria Rapoport (*Prince's Father*).

 vocals dubbed by Jan Harvash
**vocals dubbed by Simon Green*

SONGS:

Where Am I Going?*; Let It Snow*; Daddy's Knee; Lovely Hair; Bed Song; Iddy, Biddy Names; Every Day**.

 music and lyrics by Michael Berz
***music and lyrics by Michael Abbott, Sarah Weeks, Arik Rudich and Michael Berz*

311

SYNOPSIS:

When the Evil Queen order her death, the princess Snow White runs away to the forest home of seven dwarves who try and protect "the fairest of them all."

SOUNDTRACK: No soundtrack available

* * * * * * * * * *

SNOW WHITE AND THE SEVEN DWARFS
RKO, 1937

Producer: Walt Disney
Director: David Hand
Screenplay: Ted Sears, Otto Englander, Earl Hurd, Dorothy Ann Blank, Richard Creedon, Dick Richard, Merrill De Maris and Webb Smith; based on the fairy tale by the Brothers Grimm
Music and Lyrics: Frank Churchill and Larry Morey
Running time: 83 minutes, color

VOCAL TALENTS:

Adriana Caselotti (*Snow White*); Harry Stockwell (*The Prince*); Lucille LaVerne (*The Queen*); Scotty Matthews (*Bashful*); Roy Atwell (*Doc*); Pinto Colvig (*Grumpy/Sleepy*); Otis Harlan (*Happy*); Billy Gilbert (*Sneezy*); Moroni Olsen (*The Magic Mirror*) and Stuart Buchanan (*Humbert*).

SONGS:

With a Smile and a Song; Dig-a-Dig-Dig; Heigh Ho; I'm Wishing; One Song; Whistle While You Work; Dwarfs' Yodel Song; Someday My Prince Will Come.

SYNOPSIS:

Disney's first full-length animated musical about the beautiful young girl--"the fairest of them all"--who seeks refuge with a group of forest dwarfs when her wicked stepmother, the Queen, orders her death.

SOUNDTRACK: Disneyland 1201

* * * * * * * * * *

SNOW WHITE AND THE THREE STOOGES
20th Century Fox, 1961

Producer: Charles Wick
Director: Walter Lang
Screenplay: Noel Langley and Elwood Ullmann; based on a story by Charles Wick,
            adapted from the fairy tale by the Brothers Grimm
Choreography: Ron Fletcher
Music and Lyrics: Harry Harris and Earl Brent
Running time: 107 minutes, color

CAST:

Carol Heiss (*Snow White*); The Three Stooges (*Themselves*); Edson Stroll (*Prince Charming*); Patricia Medina (*The Evil Queen*); Guy Rolfe (*Count Olga*); Michael David (*Rolf*); Edgar Barrier (*King Augustus*) and Buddy Baer (*The Hunter*).

SONGS:

A Place Called Happiness; A Day Like This; Lookin' For People, Lookin' For Fun; Because I'm in Love; I Said It Then, I Say It Now.

SYNOPSIS:

The classic Grimm Brothers fairy tale about a beautiful young girl who runs away from her castle home when her wicked stepmother orders her death. But instead of seven forest dwarves, Snow White discovers the cottage of the Three Stooges!

SOUNDTRACK: Columbia ACS-8450

* * * * * * * * *

SO DEAR TO MY HEART
RKO, 1948

Producer: Walt Disney
Director: Harold Schuster
Screenplay: John Tucker Battle; based on the book *Midnight and Jeremiah* by
            Sterling North
Music and Lyrics: see below with song titles
Running time: 84 minutes, color

CAST:

Burl Ives (*Uncle Hiram*); Beulah Bondi (*Granny Kincaid*); Harry Carey (*Judge*); Luana Patten (*Tildy*); Bobby Driscoll (*Jeremiah Kincaid*); Raymond Bond (*Storekeeper*) and Mat Willis (*Horse Trainer*).

Ol' Dan Patch - *Eliot Daniel and Larry Morey*
So Dear To My Heart - *Ticker Freeman and Irving Taylor*
It's Whatcha Do With Whatcha Got - *Don Raye and Gene DePaul*
Stick-to-it-ivity - *Eliot Daniel and Larry Morey*
Lavender Blue (Dilly Dilly) - *Eliot Daniel and Larry Morey*
County Fair - *Robert Wells and Mel Tormé*

SYNOPSIS:

Jeremiah Kincaid names his pet black lamb "Danny" after the famous sulky horse "Dan Patch" and with the help of blacksmith Hiram decides to raise him for show in the county fair.

SOUNDTRACK: Disneyland 1255

* * * * * * * * *

SOMEBODY LOVES ME
Paramount, 1952

Producer: William Perlberg and George Seaton
Director: Irving Brecher
Screenplay: Irving Brecher
Choreography: Charles O'Curran
Music and Lyrics: see below with song titles
Running time: 97 minutes, color

CAST:

Betty Hutton (*Blossom Seeley*); Ralph Meeker (*Benny Fields*); Robert Keith (*Sam Doyle*); Adele Jergens (*Nola Beach*); Billie Bird (*Essie*); Henry Slate (*Forrest*); Sid Tomack (*Harry Lake*); Ludwig Stossel (*Mr. Grauman*) and Jack Benny (*Himself*).

SONGS:

Teasing Rag - *Joe Jordan*
I Can't Tell You Why I Love You - *Will J. Cobb and Gus Edwards*
Honey, Oh, My Honey - *Ray Evans and Jay Livingston*
Toddling the Todalo - *E. Ray Goetz and A. Baldwin Sloane*
June Night - *Cliff Friend and Abel Baer*
On San Francisco Bay - *Vincent Bryan and Gertrude Hoffman*
Smiles - *J. Will Callahan and Lee M. Roberts*

I Cried For You - *Arthur Freed, Gus Arnheim and Abe Lyman*
Rose Room - *Harry Williams and Art Hickman*
Way Down Yonder in New Orleans - *Henry Creamer and Turner Layton*
Wang Wang Blues - *Gus Mueller, Buster Johnson and Henry Busse*
Somebody Loves Me - *George Gershwin and B.G. DeSylva*
Jealous - *Jack Little, Tommy Malie and Dick Finch*
Love Him - *Ray Evans and Jay Livingston*
Dixie Dreams - *Arthur Johnston, George W. Meyer, Grant Clark and Roy Turk*
Thanks to You - *Ray Evans and Jay Livingston*

SYNOPSIS:

The life of vaudevillian Blossom Seeley and her husband Benny Fields from
Blossom's beginnings at the time of the 1906 San Francisco earthquake through to
her retirement and her husband's solo career.

SOUNDTRACK: No soundtrack available

* * * * * * * * *

SOMETHING FOR THE BOYS
20th Century Fox, 1944

Producer: Irving Starr
Director: Lewis Seiter
Screenplay: Robert Ellis, Helen Logan and Frank Gabrielson; based on the stage
            musical book by Herbert Fields and Dorothy Fields
Choreography: Nick Castle
Music and Lyrics: Harold Adamson and Jimmy McHugh
Running time: 78 minutes, color

CAST:

Carmen Miranda (*Chiquita Hart*); Michael O'Shea (*Staff Sgt. Rocky Fulton*); Vivian
Blaine (*Blossom Hart*); Phil Silvers (*Harry Hart*); Perry Como (*Sgt. Laddie Green*);
Glenn Langan (*Lt. Ashley Crothers*); Cara Williams (*Secretary*); Thurston Hall
(*Colonel Jefferson L. Calhoun*) and Clarence Kolb (*Colonel Grubbs*).

SONGS:

Boom-Barachee-Boom; Eighty Miles Outside of Atlanta; I Wish I Didn't Have to Say
Good Night; In the Middle of Nowhere; Wouldn't It Be Nice?

Cousins Chiquita, Blossom and Harry Hart inherit a bankrupt plantation and decide to turn it into a home for the wives of servicemen and keep it funded by putting on a variety of shows.

SOUNDTRACK: No soundtrack available

* * * * * * * * * *

SONG OF NORWAY
Cinerama, 1970

Producer: Andrew L. Stone and Virginia Stone
Director: Andrew L. Stone
Screenplay: Andrew L. Stone; based on the stage musical book by Milton Lazarus
Choreography: Lee Theodore
Music and Lyrics: Robert Wright and George Forrest; based on themes from Edvard
                   Grieg
Running time: 138 minutes, color

CAST:

Toralv Maurstad (*Edvard Grieg*); Florence Henderson (*Nina Hagerup Grieg*); Christina Schollin (*Therese Berg*); Frank Porretta (*Rikaard Nordraack*); Harry Secombe (*Mr. Bjornson*); Robert Morley (*Mr. Berg*); Edward G. Robinson (*Mr. Krogstad*); Elizabeth Larner (*Mrs. Bjornson*); Oscar Homolka (*Mr. Engstrand*); Frederick Jaeger (*Henrik Ibsen*); Henry Gilbert (*Franz Liszt*); Richard Wordsworth (*Hans Christian Andersen*); Bernard Archard (*Rikaard's Father*); John Barrie (*Mr. Hagerup*) and Wenke Foss (*Mrs. Hagerup*).

SONGS:

Sorry for the Life of a Wife of a Sailor; Midsummer's Eve; Freddy and His Fiddle; Strange Music; The Song of Norway; A Rhyme and a Reason; The Little House; Hill of Dreams; I Love You; Be a Boy Again; Three There Were; The Solitary Wanderer; At Christmastime; The Toast (Welcome); Sugar Apples and Candy Canes; Wrong to Dream.

SYNOPSIS:

A biography of Norwegian composer Edvard Grieg which focuses on his love for his wife Nina, his friendship with fellow Norwegian composer Rikaard Nordraack and their desire for recognition for writing true Norwegian music.

316

SOUNDTRACK: ABC Records SOC-14

* * * * * * * * *

SONG OF THE ISLANDS
20th Century Fox, 1942

Producer: William LeBaron
Director: Walter Lang
Screenplay: Joseph Schrank, Robert Pirosh, Robert Ellis and Helen Logan
Choreography: Hermes Pan
Music and Lyrics: Mack Gordon and Harry Owens
Running time: 76 minutes, color

CAST:

Betty Grable (*Eileen O'Brien*); Victor Mature (*Jefferson Harper*); Jack Oakie (*Rusty Smith*); Thomas Mitchell (*Dennis O'Brien*); George Barbier (*Harper*); Billy Gilbert (*Paloloa's Father*); Hilo Hattie (*Palola*); Lillian Porter (*Palola's Cousin*) and Hal K. Dawson (*John Rodney*).

SONGS:

Hawaiian War Chant*; Blue Shadows and White Gardenias; Sing Me a Song of the Islands; Down On Ami, Ami, Oni, Oni Isle; Maluna, Malolo, Mawaena; What's Buzzin' Cousin?; Cockeyed Mayor of Kaunakakai**; O'Brien Has Gone Hawaiian.

 *music and lyrics by Prince Leleiohaku, Johnny Noble and Ralph Freed
**music and lyrics by R. Alex Anderson and Al Stillman

SYNOPSIS:

On a small Hawaiian island cattle baron Mr. Harper wants to acquire beachcomber Dennis O'Brien's deep-water harbour to build a pier in order to load his cows. He sends his son Jeff to try and make the deal but O'Brien's pretty daughter Eileen side-tracks him.

SOUNDTRACK: Caliban 6009 (with *Pin Up Girl*)

* * * * * * * * *

SONG OF THE SOUTH
RKO, 1946

317

Producer: Walt Disney
Director: Wilfred Jackson and Harve Foster
Screenplay: Dalton Raymond, Morton Grant and Maurice Rapf; based on the book
      Tales of Uncle Remus by Joel Chandler Harris
Music and Lyrics: see below with song titles
Running time: 94 minutes, color

CAST:

Ruth Warrick (*Sally*); James Baskett (*Uncle Remus/voice of "Brer Fox"*); Bobby Driscoll (*Johnny*); Luana Patten (*Ginny Favers*); Lucille Watson (*Grandmother*); Hattie McDaniel (*Aunt Tempy*); Glenn Leedy (*Toby*); Erik Rolf (*John*); Mary Fields (*Mrs. Favers*); Anita Brown (*Maid*); Johnny Lee (*voice of "Brer Rabbit"*) and Nicodemus Stewart (*voice of "Brer Bear"*).

SONGS:

Sound of the South - *Sam Coslow and Arthur Jackson*
Sooner or Later - *Charles Wolcott and Ray Gilbert*
Zip-a-dee Doo-Dah - *Allie Wrubel and Ray Gilbert*
That's What Uncle Remus Said - *Eliot Daniel, Hy Heath and Johnny Lange*
How Do You Do? - *Robert MacGimsey*
Let the Rain Pour Down - *Foster Carling*
Everybody's Got a Laughing Place - *Allie Wrubel and Ray Gilbert*
Who Wants to Live Like That? - *Foster Carling*
You'll Always Be the One I Love - *Sunny Skylar and Ticker Freeman*

SYNOPSIS:

Suffering from homesickness after being sent to live with his grandmother, following his parents' separation, Johnny turns to kindly Uncle Remus for comfort and guidance in his stories of Brer Rabbit, Brer Fox and Brer Bear.

SOUNDTRACK: Disneyland 1205

* * * * * * * * * *

SO THIS IS LOVE
Warner Bros., 1953

Producer: Henry Blanke
Director: Gordon Douglas
Screenplay: John Monks, Jr.; based on Grace Moore's autobiography

Choreography: LeRoy Prinz
Music and Lyrics: see below with song titles
Running time: 101 minutes, color

CAST:

Kathryn Grayson (*Grace Moore*); Merv Griffin (*Buddy Nash*); Joan Weldon (*Ruth Obre*); Walter Abel (*Colonel James Moore*); Rosemary De Camp (*Aunt Laura Stokley*); Jeff Donnell (*Henrietta Van Dyke*); Douglas Dick (*Bryan Curtis*); Ann Doran (*Mrs. Moore*); Margaret Field (*Edna Wallace*); Mabel Albertson (*Mary Garden*); Fortunio Bonanova (*Dr. Marafioti*); Marie Windsor (*Marilyn Montgomery*); Noreen Corcoran (*Grace at age 8*) and Lillian Bronson (*Mrs. Wilson Green*).

SONGS:

The Waltz Song (*Roméo et Juliette*) - *Charles Gounod*
Ciribiribin - *Alberto Pestalozza and Rudolf Thaler*
I'm Just Wild About Harry - *Eubie Blake and Noble Sissle*
The Kiss Waltz - *Vincent Youmans, Harold Adamson and Mack Gordon*
I Kiss Your Hand, Madame - *Ralph Erwin, Sam M. Lewis and Joe Young*
I Wish I Could Shimmy Like My Sister Kate - *Armand J. Piron*
Oh Me, Oh My, Oh You - *Vincent Youmans and Arthur Francis*
Time On My Hands - *Vincent Youmans, Harold Adamson and Mack Gordon*
Remember - *Irving Berlin*

SYNOPSIS:

The biography of opera star Grace Moore from her childhood in Jellicoe, Tennesse up through her début, in the rôle of "Mimi" in *La Bohème*, at the Metropolitan Opera in New York City.

SOUNDTRACK: No soundtrack available

* * * * * * * * *

THE SOUND OF MUSIC
20th Century Fox, 1965

Producer: Robert Wise
Director: Robert Wise
Screenplay: Ernest Lehman; based on the stage musical book by Howard Lindsay and Russel Crouse
Choreography: Marc Breaux and Dee Dee Wood

Music and Lyrics: Richard Rodgers and Oscar Hammerstein II
Running time: 172 minutes, color

CAST:

Julie Andrews (*Maria*); Christopher Plummer* (*Captain Georg Von Trapp*); Eleanor Parker (*Baroness Elsa Schröeder*); Richard Haydn (*Max Detweiler*); Peggy Wood (*Mother Abbess*); Charmian Carr (*Liesl*); Nicholas Hammond (*Friedrich*); Heather Menzies (*Louisa*); Duane Chase (*Kurt*); Angela Cartwright (*Brigitta*); Debbie Turner (*Marta*); Kym Karath (*Gretl*); Daniel Truhitte (*Rolf*); Norma Varden (*Frau Schmidt*); Gil Stuart (*Franz*) and Ben Wright (*Herr Zeller*).

vocals dubbed by Bill Lee

SONGS:

The Sound of Music; Maria; I Have Confidence*; Sixteen Going On Seventeen; My Favorite Things; Do-Re-Mi; Edelweiss; The Lonely Goatherd; So Long, Farewell; Climb Ev'ry Mountain; Something Good*.

music and lyrics by Richard Rodgers

SYNOPSIS:

When widowed Capt. Von Trapp hires Maria, a young postulant from the nearby Salzburg Abbey, to care for his seven children he never expected to fall in love with her--or that they would have to flee to Switzerland to escape the Nazi invasion of their native Austria.

SOUNDTRACK: RCA LSOD-2005

* * * * * * * * *

SOUTH PACIFIC
20th Century Fox, 1958

Producer: Buddy Adler
Director: Joshua Logan
Screenplay: Paul Osborn; based on the stage musical book by Oscar Hammerstein
          II and Joshua Logan
Choreography: LeRoy Prinz
Music and Lyrics: Richard Rodgers and Oscar Hammerstein II
Running time: 171 minutes, color

CAST:

Rossano Brazzi* (*Emile de Becque*); Mitzi Gaynor (*Ensign Nellie Forbush*); John Kerr** (*Lt. Joseph Cable*); Ray Walston (*Luther Billis*); Russ Brown (*Captain Brackett*); Juanita Hall*** (*Bloody Mary*); France Nuyen (*Liat*); Floyd Simmons (*Commander Bill Harbison*); Candace Lee (*Ngana*); Warren Hsieh (*Jerome*); Ken Clark**** (*Stewpot*); Jack Mullaney (*The Professor*) and Tom Laughlin (*Lt. Buzz Adams*).

   *vocals dubbed by Giorgio Tozzi
  **vocals dubbed by Bill Lee
 ***vocals dubbed by Muriel Smith
****vocals dubbed by Thurl Ravenscroft

SONGS:

Bloody Mary; There is Nothing like a Dame; Bali Ha'i; A Cockeyed Optimist; Twin Soliloquies; Some Enchanted Evening; Dites-moi; Younger than Springtime; I'm Gonna Wash That Man Right Outa My Hair; I'm in Love With a Wonderful Guy; Happy Talk; Honey Bun; My Girl Back Home; (You've Got To Be) Carefully Taught; This Nearly Was Mine.

SYNOPSIS:

On a Pacific island during WWII, two love stories are played out against a backdrop of racial prejudice--the French planter Emile de Becque and Navy nurse Nellie Forbush and Marine lieutenant Joe Cable and the young native girl Liat.

SOUNDTRACK: RCA AYL1-3681

* * * * * * * * * *

SPEEDWAY
Metro-Goldwyn-Mayer, 1968

Producer: Douglas Laurence
Director: Norman Taurog
Screenplay: Phillip Shuken
Music and Lyrics: Mel Glazer and Stephen Schlaks
Running time: 94 minutes, color

CAST:

Elvis Presley (*Steve Grayson*); Nancy Sinatra (*Susan Jacks*); Bill Bixby (*Kenny*

Donford); Gale Gordon (*R.W. Hepworth*); William Schallert (*Abel Esterlake*); Victoria Meyerink (*Ellie Esterlake*); Ross Hagen (*Paul Dado*) and Carl Ballantine (*Birdie Kebner*).

SONGS:

Speedway; Let Yourself Go; Your Groovy Self*; Your Time Hasn't Come Yet, Baby; He's Your Uncle, Not Your Dad; Who Are You? (Who Am I?); There Ain't Nothin' Like a Song.

*music and lyrics by Lee Hazelwood

SYNOPSIS:

Thanks to his manager's imbezzling, race car driver Steve Grayson finds he owes the I.R.S. $145,000 in back taxes that is going to be garnered from his winnings.

SOUNDTRACK: RCA LSP-3989

* * * * * * * * *

SPINOUT
Metro-Goldwyn-Mayer, 1966

Producer: Joe Pasternak
Director: Norman Taurog
Screenplay: Theodore J. Flicker and George Kirgo
Choreography: Jack Baker
Music and Lyrics: see below with song titles
Running time: 90 minutes, color

CAST:

Elvis Presley (*Mike McCoy*); Shelley Fabares (*Cynthia Foxhugh*); Diane McBain (*Diana St. Clair*); Deborah Walley (*Les*); Dodie Marshall (*Susan*); Jack Mullaney (*Curly*); Will Hutchins (*Lt. Tracy Richards*); Warren Berlinger (*Philip Short*); Jimmy Hawkins (*Larry*); Carl Betz (*Howard Foxhugh*); Cecil Kellaway (*Bernard Ranley*); Una Merkel (*Violet Ranley*); Frederic Worlock (*Blodgett*) and Dave Barry (*Harry*).

SONGS:

Stop, Look, Listen - *Joy Byers*
Adam and Evil - *Fred Wise and Randy Starr*
All That I Am - *Sid Tepper and Roy C. Bennett*

322

Never Say Yes - *Doc Pomus and Mort Shuman*
Am I Ready? - *Sid Tepper and Roy C. Bennett*
Beach Shack - *Bill Giant, Bernie Baum and Florence Kaye*
Spinout - *Sid Wayne, Ben Weisman and Dee Fuller*
Smorgasbord - *Sid Tepper and Roy C. Bennett*
I'll Be Back - *Sid Wayne and Ben Weisman*

SYNOPSIS:

Mike McCoy is the leader of a rock band who finds his professional and social life being disrupted by pretty--but spoiled--Cynthia Foxhugh.

SOUNDTRACK: RCA APL1-2560

* * * * * * * * *

SPRINGTIME IN THE ROCKIES
20th Century Fox, 1942

Producer: William LeBaron
Director: Irving Cummings
Screenplay: Walter Bullock and Ken Englund, adaptation by Jacques Thery; based
                on a story by Philip Wylie
Choreography: Hermes Pan
Music and Lyrics: Harry Warren and Mack Gordon
Running time: 91 minutes, color

CAST:

Betty Grable (*Vicky Lane*); John Payne (*Dan Christy*); Cesar Romero (*Victor Prince*); Carmen Miranda (*Rosita Murphy*); Charlotte Greenwood (*Phoebe Gray*); Edward Everett Horton (*McTavish*); Frank Orth (*Bickle*); Harry Hayden (*Brown*); Jackie Gleason (*Agent*) and Harry James (*Himself*).

SONGS:

Run Little Raindrop, Run; I Had the Craziest Dream; Chattanooga Choo Choo; A Poem Set to Music; Pan Americana Jubilee.

SYNOPSIS:

After breaking his promise to her to be faithful, entertainer Vicky Lane leaves her boyfriend and partner Dan Christy to team up with Victor Prince in a new act to open at the resort hotel at Lake Louise, in the Canadian Rockies.

SOUNDTRACK: Titania 507 (with *Sweet Rosie O'Grady*)

* * * * * * * * *

STAR!
20th Century Fox, 1968

Producer: Saul Chaplin
Director: Robert Wise
Screenplay: William Fairchild
Choreography: Michael Kidd
Music and Lyrics: see below with song titles
Running time: 175 minutes, color

CAST:

Julie Andrews (*Gertrude Lawrence*); Richard Crenna (*Richard Aldrich*); Daniel Massey (*Noël Coward*); Michael Craig (*Sir Anthony Spencer*); Robert Reed (*Charles Fraser*); Bruce Forsyth (*Arthur Lawrence*); Beryl Reid (*Rose*); Jenny Agutter (*Pamela*); John Collin (*Jack Roper*); Alan Oppenheimer (*André Charlot*); Garrett Lewis (*Jack Buchanan*); Richard Karlan (*David Holtzman*) and Lynley Lawrence (*Billie Carleton*).

SONGS:

Star! - *James Van Heusen and Sammy Cahn*
Down at the Old Bull and Bush - *Harry Von Tilzer, P. Krone, Andrew B. Sterling and Russell Hunting*
Piccadilly - *Paul Morande, Walter Williams and Bruce Seiver*
Oh, It's a Lovely War - *Maurice Scott and J.P. Long*
My Garden of Joy - *Saul Chaplin*
Forbidden Fruit - *Noël Coward*
'N Everything - *B.G. DeSylva, Gus Kahn and Al Jolson*
Burlington Bertie From Bow - *William Hargreaves*
Parisian Pierrot - *Noël Coward*
Limehouse Blues - *Douglas Furber and Philip Brahm*
Someone to Watch Over Me - *George Gerhswin and Ira Gershwin*
Dear Little Girl - *George Gershwin and Ira Gershwin*
Some Day I'll Find You - *Noël Coward*
The Physician - *Cole Porter*
Do, Do, Do - *George Gershwin and Ira Gershwin*
Has Anybody Seen Our Ship? - *Noël Coward*
My Ship - *Kurt Weill and Ira Gershwin*
Jenny - *Kurt Weill and Ira Gershwin*

SYNOPSIS:

The life of British musical stage star Gertrude Lawrence from her childhood through to her starring role in *Lady in the Dark*.

SOUNDTRACK: 20th Century Fox 5102

* * * * * * * * *

A STAR IS BORN
Warner Bros., 1954

Producer: Sidney Luft
Director: George Cukor
Screenplay: Moss Hart; based on the screenplay by Dorothy Parker, Alan Campbell
       and Robert Carson
Choreography: Richard Barstow
Music and Lyrics: Harold Arlen and Ira Gershwin
Running time: 176 minutes, color

CAST:

Judy Garland (*Esther Blodgett*); James Mason (*Norman Maine*); Jack Carson (*Matt Libby*); Charles Bickford (*Oliver Niles*); Tommy Noonan (*Danny McGuire*); Lucy Marlow (*Lola Lavery*) and Amanda Blake (*Susan*).

SONGS:

Gotta Have Me Go With You; The Man That Got Away; Born in a Trunk*; Here's What I'm Here For; It's a New World; Someone At Last; Lose That Long Face.

**music and lyrics by Leonard Gershe*

SYNOPSIS:

When young aspiring actress Esther Blodgett marries movie star Norman Maine she finds that as a career blossoms his gradually fades away.

SOUNDTRACK: Columbia BL-1201

* * * * * * * * *

A STAR IS BORN
Warner Bros., 1976

Producer: Jon Peters
Director: Frank Pierson
Screenplay: John Gregory Dunne, Joan Didion and Frank Pierson; based on a story
            by William Wellman and Robert Carson
Choreography: David Winters
Music and Lyrics: see below with song titles
Running time: 140 minutes, color

CAST:

Barbra Streisand (*Esther Hoffman*); Kris Kristofferson (*John Norman Howard*); Gary
Busey (*Bobby Ritchie*); Oliver Clark (*Gary Danziger*); Paul Mazursky (*Brian*); Joanne
Linville (*Freddie*); M.G. Kelly (*Bebe Jesus*) and Marta Heflin (*Quentin*).

SONGS:

Watch Closely Now - *Paul Williams and Kenny Ascher*
Spanish Lies - *Paul Williams and Kenny Ascher*
Hellacious Acres - *Paul Williams and Kenny Ascher*
Queen Bee - *Rupert Holmes*
Everything - *Rupert Holmes and Paul Williams*
Lost Inside Of You - *Barbra Streisand and Leon Russell*
Evergreen - *Barbra Streisand, Leon Russell and Paul Williams*
The Woman in the Moon - *Paul Williams and Kenny Ascher*
I Believe in Love - *Kenny Loggins, Marilyn Bergman and Alan Bergman*
Crippled Cow - *Donna Weiss*
With One More Look At You - *Paul Williams and Kenny Ascher*

SYNOPSIS:

Second musical remake of the 1937 film has John Norman Howard, an alcoholic,
drug-addicted rock star on his way down when he meets and falls in love with Esther
Hoffman, an aspiring singer who is unable to save him from himself.

SOUNDTRACK: Columbia JS-34403

* * * * * * * * *

STARS OVER BROADWAY
Warner Bros., 1935

Producer: Sam Bischoff
Director: William Keighley

326

Screenplay: Jerry Wald, Julius J. Epstein and Patsy Flick; based on a story by Mildred Cram
Choreography: Busby Berkeley and Bobby Connolly
Music and Lyrics: see below with song titles
Running time: 90 minutes, B/W

CAST:

Pat O'Brien (*Al McGillevray*); Jane Froman (*Joan Garrett*); James Melton (*Jan King*); Jean Muir (*Nora Wyman*); Frank McHugh (*Bugs Cramer*); Eddie Conrad (*Freddy*); William Ricciardi (*Signor Minotti*) and Marie Wilson (*Molly*).

SONGS:

Carry Me Back to the Lone Prairie - *Carson J. Robison*
Celeste Aide (*Aida*) - *Giuseppe Verdi*
You Let Me Down - *Harry Warren and Al Dubin*
Where Am I? - *Harry Warren and Al Dubin*
At Your Service, Madame - *Harry Warren and Al Dubin*
Avé Maria - *Franz Schubert*

SYNOPSIS:

After Al McGillevray discovers hotel porter Jan King he begins to groom him for stardom as an opera singer, but in his rush Jan begins to neglect his voice.

SOUNDTRACK: No soundtrack available

* * * * * * * * *

STATE FAIR
20th Century Fox, 1945

Producer: William Perlberg
Director: Walter Lang
Screenplay: Oscar Hammerstein II, Sonya Levien and Paul Green; based on the novel by Philip Strong
Music and Lyrics: Richard Rodgers and Oscar Hammerstein II
Running time: 100 minutes, color

CAST:

Jeanne Crain* (*Margie Frake*); Dana Andrews (*Pat Gilbert*); Dick Haymes (*Wayne Frake*); Vivian Blaine (*Emily Joyce*); Charles Winninger (*Abel Frake*); Fay Bainter

(*Melissa Frake*); Donald Meek (*Mr. Hippenstahl*); Frank McHugh (*McGee*) and Percy Kilbride (*Miller*).

vocals dubbed by Louanne Hogan

SONGS:

Our State Fair; It Might As Well Be Spring; That's For Me; Isn't It Kind of Fun?; It's a Grand Night For Singing.

SYNOPSIS:

The Frake family goes to the Iowa State Fair where father Abel hopes for a blue ribbon for his prize hog, mother Melissa first place for her mincemeat and children Margie and Wayne are looking for new romances.

SOUNDTRACK: Classic International Filmusicals 3009 (with *Centennial Summer*)

* * * * * * * * * *

STATE FAIR
20th Century Fox, 1962

Producer: Charles Brackett
Director: José Ferrer
Screenplay: Richard Breen, adaptation by Oscar Hammerstein II, Sonya Levien and
                    Paul Green; based on the novel by Philip Strong
Choreography: Nick Castle
Music and Lyrics: Richard Rodgers and Oscar Hammerstein II
Running time: 118 minutes, color

CAST:

Pat Boone (*Wayne Frake*); Bobby Darin (*Jerry Dundee*); Pamela Tiffin* (*Margie Frake*); Ann-Margret (*Emily Porter*); Tom Ewell (*Able Frake*); Alice Faye (*Melissa Frake*); Wally Cox (*Mr. Hipplewaite*); David Brandon (*Harry*); Clem Harvey (*Doc Cramer*); Linda Henrich (*Betty Jean*) and Edward "Tap" Canutt (*Red Hoerter*).

vocals dubbed by Anita Gordon

SONGS:

Our State Fair; It Might As Well Be Spring; That's For Me; More Than Just a Friend; Isn't It Kind of Fun?; Never Say No to a Man; Willing and Eager; It's a

Grand Night For Singing; This Isn't Heaven; It's the Little Things in Texas.

SYNOPSIS:

Remake of the 1945 musical film about the Frake family and their experiences at the 1961 Texas State Fair in Dallas. The emphasis is on daughter Margie's romance with broadcaster Jerry Dundee and son Wayne's involvement with entertainer Emily Porter.

SOUNDTRACK: Dot 29011

* * * * * * * * *

STEP LIVELY
RKO, 1944

Producer: Robert Fellows
Director: Tim Whelan
Screenplay: Warren Duff and Peter Milne; based on the play *Room Service* by John Murray and Allen Boretz
Choreography: Ernst Matray
Music and Lyrics: Jule Styne and Sammy Cahn
Running time: 88 minutes, B/W

CAST:

Frank Sinatra (*Glenn Russell*); George Murphy (*Gordon Miller*); Adolphe Menjou (*Mr. Wagner*); Gloria De Haven (*Christine Marlowe*); Walter Slezak (*Joe Gribble*); Eugene Pallette (*Mr. Jenkins*); Wally Brown (*Binion*); Alan Carney (*Harry*); Grant Mitchell (*Dr. Gladstone*) and Anne Jeffreys (*Miss Abbott*).

SONGS:

Where Does Love Begin?; Come Out, Come Out, Wherever You Are; As Long As There's Music; Some Other Time; Why Must There Be an Opening Song?; Ask the Madame.

SYNOPSIS:

Fast-talking producer Gordon Miller has conned his hotel manager brother-in-law out of his tab, backer Mr. Jenkins out of a big check and playwright Glenn Russell out of his life's savings--all to stage his big new show.

SOUNDTRACK: Hollywood Soundstage 412

329

* * * * * * * * * *

THE STORK CLUB
Paramount, 1945

Producer: B.G. DeSylva
Director: Hal Walker
Screenplay: B.G. DeSylva and John McGowan
Choreography: Billy Daniel
Music and Lyrics: see below with song titles
Running time: 98 minutes, B/W

CAST:

Betty Hutton (*Judy Peabody*); Barry Fitzgerald (*J.B. "Pop" Bates*); Don DeFore (*Danny Wilton*); Robert Benchley (*Tom Curtis*); Bill Goodwin (*Sherman Billingsley*); Iris Adrian (*Gwen*); Mikhail Rasumny (*Coretti*); Andy Russell (*Johnny Nolan*) and Mary Young (*Mrs. J.B. Bates*).

SONGS:

Doctor, Lawyer, Indian Chief - *Hoagy Carmichael and Paul Francis Webster*
I'm a Square in the Social Circle - *Ray Evans and Jay Livingston*
In the Shade of the Old Apple Tree - *Harry H. Williams and Egbert Van Alstyne*
If I Had a Dozen Hearts - *Harry Revel and Paul Francis Webster*
Love Me - *Jule Styne and Sammy Cahn*

SYNOPSIS:

Stork Club hat-check girl Judy Peabody saves millionaire J.B. Bates from drowning so he decides to be her anonymous benefactor.

SOUNDTRACK: Caliban 6020

* * * * * * * * * *

THE STORY OF VERNON AND IRENE CASTLE
RKO, 1939

Producer: George Haight
Director: H.C. Potter
Screenplay: Richard Sherman, adaptation by Oscar Hammerstein II and Dorothy Yost; based on stories by Irene Castle
Choreography: Hermes Pan

330

Music and Lyrics: see below with song titles
Running time: 90 minutes, B/W

CAST:

Fred Astaire (*Vernon Castle*); Ginger Rogers (*Irene Foote Castle*); Walter Brennan (*Walter*); Edna May Oliver (*Maggie Sutton*); Lew Fields (*Himself*); Etienne Girardot (*Papa Aubel*); Janet Beecher (*Mrs. Foote*); Rolfe Sedan (*Emile Aubel*); Robert Strange (*Dr. Foote*); Clarence Derwent (*Papa Louis*); Sonny Lamont (*Charlie*); Leonid Kinskey (*Artist*) and Donald MacBride (*Hotel Manager*).

SONGS:

By the Beautiful Sea - *Harry Carroll and Harold Atteridge*
Row, Row, Row - *William Jerome and James V. Monaco*
The Yama Yama Man - *Karl Hoschna and Collin Davis*
Come, Josephine in My Flying Machine - *Fred Fisher and Alfred Bryan*
By the Light of the Silvery Moon (instrumental) - *Gus Edwards and Edward Madden*
Oh, You Beautiful Doll! - *Fred Fisher and Alfred Bryan*
Only When You're in My Arms - *Con Conrad, Harry Ruby and Bert Kalmar*
Waitin' For the Robert E. Lee (instrumental) - *Abel Baer and L. Wolfe Gilbert*
Darktown Strutters' Ball - *Shelton Brooks*
Too Much Mustard - *Cecil Macklin*
It's a Long, Long Way to Tipperary - *Harry H. Williams and Jack Judge*
Hello, Hello, Who's Your Lady Friend? - *Bert Lee, Harry Fragson and Worten David*

SYNOPSIS:

Husband and wife Vernon and Irene Castle are the dance team sensation throughout the world as the film chronicles their successes in the years 1913-1918.

SOUNDTRACK: Caliban 6000 (with *Daddy Long Legs*)

* * * * * * * * * *

STOWAWAY
20th Century Fox, 1936

Producer: Darryl F. Zanuck
Director: William A. Seiter
Screenplay: William Conselman, Arthur Sheekman and Nat Perrin; based on a story
           by Samuel G. Engel
Music and Lyrics: Harry Revel and Mack Gordon
Running time: 86 minutes, B/W

CAST:

Shirley Temple (*Barbara "Ching-Ching" Stewart*); Robert Young (*Tommy Randall*); Alice Faye (*Susan Parker*); Eugene Pallette (*The Colonel*); Helen Westley (*Mrs. Hope*); Arthur Treacher (*Atkins*); J. Edward Bromberg (*Judge Booth*); Astrid Allwyn (*Kay Swift*); Allan Lane (*Richard Hope*); Robert Grieg (*Captain*); Jayne Regan (*Dora Day*); Philip Ahn (*Sun Lo*); Willie Fung (*Chang*); Julius Tannen (*First Mate*); Paul McVey (*Second Mate*); William Stack (*Alfred Kruikshank*); Helen Jerome Eddy (*Mrs. Kruikshank*) and Honorable Wu (*Li Zi*).

SONGS:

Good Night, My Love; You Gotta S-M-I-L-E to be H-A-double P-Y; One Never Knows, Does One?; That's What I Want For Christmas*.

music and lyrics by Irving Caesar and Gerald Marks

SYNOPSIS:

Ching-Ching, the orphan of missionaries, accidentally stows away in Tommy Randall's car as it's being loaded on board a ship in Shanghai. When she's discovered, Tommy offers to adopt her but the authorities won't let him because he is not married.

SOUNDTRACK: No soundtrack available

* * * * * * * * *

STRIKE ME PINK
United Artists, 1936

Producer: Samuel Goldwyn
Director: Norman Taurog
Screenplay: Frank Butler, Francis Martin and Philip Rapp
Choreography: Robert Alton
Music and Lyrics: Harold Arlen and Lew Brown
Running time: 100 minutes, B/W

CAST:

Eddie Cantor (*Eddie Pink*); Ethel Merman (*Joyce Lenox*); Sally Eilers (*Claribel Hayes*); Parkyakarkus (*Harry Park*); William Frawley (*Copple*); Helen Lowell (*Ma Carson*); Gordon Jones (*Butch Carson*); Brian Donlevy (*Vance*); Jack LaRue (*Thrust*) and Sunnie O'Dea (*Sunnie*).

First You Leave Me High, Then You Leave Me Low; The Lady Dances; Calabash Pipe; Shake It Off With Rhythm.

SYNOPSIS:

Eddie Pink is a mild-mannered tailor who becomes something of a hero when he's appointed the manager of a local amusement park that's the target of a gangster.

SOUNDTRACK: No soundtrack available

* * * * * * * * *

STRIKE UP THE BAND
Metro-Goldwyn-Mayer, 1940

Producer: Arthur Freed
Director: Busby Berkeley
Screenplay: John Monks, Jr. and Fred F. Finklehoffe
Choreography: Busby Berkeley
Music and Lyrics: see below with song titles
Running time: 120 minutes, B/W

CAST:

Mickey Rooney (*Jimmy Connors*); Judy Garland (*Mary Holden*); June Preisser (*Barbara Frances Morgan*); William Tracy (*Philip Turner*); Larry Nunn (*Willie Brewster*); Margaret Early (*Annie*); Ann Shoemaker (*Mrs. Connors*); Francis Pierlot (*Mr. Judd*); Virginia Brissac (*Mrs. May Holden*); George Lessey (*Mr. Morgan*); Enid Bennett (*Mrs. Morgan*); Milton Kibbee (*Mr. Holden*); Howard Hickman (*Doctor*); Sarah Edwards (*Miss Hodges*); Helen Jerome Eddy (*Mrs. Brewster*) and Paul Whiteman (*Himself*).

SONGS:

Our Love Affair - *Roger Edens and Arthur Freed*
Do the La Conga - *Roger Edens*
Nell of New Rochelle - *Roger Edens*
Heaven Protect the Working Girl - *A. Baldwin Sloane and Edgar Smith*
Drummer Boy - *Roger Edens*
Strike Up the Band - *George Gershwin and Ira Gershwin*

Riverwood High School senior Jimmy Connors has formed a dance orchestra but needs to raise $200 in order to get them to Chicago to compete in a radio contest for Paul Whiteman.

SOUNDTRACK: Curtain Calls 100/9-10 (with *Girl Crazy*)

* * * * * * * * * *

THE STUDENT PRINCE
Metro-Goldwyn-Mayer, 1954

Producer: Joe Pasternak
Director: Richard Thorpe
Screenplay: William Ludwig and Sonya Levien; based on the stage musical book by
                  Dorothy Donnelly
Choreography: Hermes Pan
Music and Lyrics: Sigmund Romberg and Dorothy Donnelly
Running time: 107 minutes, color

CAST:

Ann Blyth (*Kathie*); Edmund Purdom* (*Prince Karl Franz*); John Ericson (*Count Von Asterburg*); Louis Calhern (*King Ferdinand*); Edmund Gwenn (*Professor Juttner*); S.Z. Sakall (*Joseph Ruder*); Betta St. John (*Princess Johanna*); John Williams (*Lutz*); Evelyn Varden (*Queen Matilda*); John Hoyt (*Prime Minister*); Richard Anderson (*Lucas*) and Charles Davis (*Hubert*).

vocals dubbed by Mario Lanza

SONGS:

To the Inn We're Marching; Come Boys, Let's All Be Gay, Boys (Students' March Song); Summertime in Heidelberg*; Drink, Drink, Drink; Serenade; Deep in My Heart, Dear; Beloved*; I'll Walk With God*; Golden Days.

music and lyrics by Nicholas Brodsky and Paul Francis Webster

SYNOPSIS:

To better prepare him for the future throne, and his upcoming marriage, King Ferdinand of Karlsburg sends his grandson Karl Franz to the university in Heidelberg where he falls in love with an innkeeper's niece.

334

SOUNDTRACK: No soundtrack available

* * * * * * * * *

SUMMER HOLIDAY
Metro-Goldwyn-Mayer, 1948

Producer: Arthur Freed
Director: Rouben Mamoulian
Screenplay: Irving Brecher and Jean Holloway; based on a screenplay by Albert
        Hackett and Frances Goodrich
Choreography: Charles Walters
Music and Lyrics: Harry Warren and Ralph Blane
Running time: 92 minutes, color

CAST:

Mickey Rooney (*Richard Miller*); Gloria De Haven (*Muriel McComber*); Walter
Huston (*Mr. Nat Miller*); Frank Morgan (*Uncle Sid*); Butch Jenkins (*Tommy Miller*);
Marilyn Maxwell (*Belle*); Agnes Moorehead (*Aunt Lily*); Selena Royle (*Mrs. Essie
Miller*); Michael Kirby (*Arthur Miller*); Shirley Johns (*Mildred Miller*) and John
Alexander (*Mr. McComber*).

SONGS:

Our Home Town; Afraid to Fall in Love; Dan-Dan-Dannville High; The Stanley
Steamer; Independence Day; While the Men Are All Drinking; You're Next; Weary
Blues; The Sweetest Kid I Ever Met.

SYNOPSIS:

Musical version of Thornton Wilder's *Ah, Wilderness!* follows the life of the Miller
family of Dannville, Connecticut in the summer of 1906, especially middle son
Richard and his girlfriend Muriel McComber.

SOUNDTRACK: Four Jays HW-602

* * * * * * * * *

SUMMER MAGIC
Buena Vista, 1963

Producer: Walt Disney
Director: James Neilson

Screenplay: Sally Benson; based on the novel *Mother Carey's Chickens* by Kate
            Douglas Wiggin
Music and Lyrics: Richard M. Sherman and Robert B. Sherman
Running time: 100 minutes, color

CAST:

Hayley Mills (*Nancy Carey*); Burl Ives (*Osh Popham*); Dorothy McGuire* (*Margaret Carey*); Deborah Walley (*Cousin Julia Carey*); Eddie Hodges (*Gilly Carey*); Jimmy Mathers (*Peter Carey*); Michael J. Pollard (*Digby Popham*); Wendy Turner (*Lallie Joy Popham*); Una Merkel (*Maria Popham*); James Stacy (*Charles Bryant*) and Peter Brown (*Tom Hamilton*).

**vocals dubbed by Marilyn Hooven*

SONGS:

Flitterin'; Beautiful Beulah; Summer Magic; The Ugly Bug Ball; The Pink of Perfection; On the Front Porch; Femininity.

SYNOPSIS:

Upon learning that she has no money, widow Margaret Carey moves her family to a run-down house in Maine where the landlord doesn't charge them any rent because the wealthy owner isn't expected back for a long time.

SOUNDTRACK: Buena Vista 4025

* * * * * * * * *

SUMMER STOCK
Metro-Goldwyn-Mayer, 1950

Producer: Joe Pasternak
Director: Charles Walters
Screenplay: George Wells and Sy Gomberg; based on a story by Sy Gomberg
Choreography: Nick Castle
Music and Lyrics: Harry Warren and Mack Gordon
Running time: 109 minutes, color

CAST:

Judy Garland (*Jane Falbury*); Gene Kelly (*Joe D. Ross*); Eddie Bracken (*Orville Wingait*); Gloria De Haven (*Abigail Falbury*); Marjorie Main (*Esmé*); Phil Silvers

(*Herb Blake*); Ray Collins (*Jasper G. Wingait*); Nita Bieber (*Sarah Higgins*); Carleton Carpenter (*Artie*) and Hans Conried* (*Harrison I. Keath*).

**vocals dubbed by Pete Roberts*

SONGS:

If You Feel Like Singing, Sing; Happy Harvest; Dig-Dig-Dig For Your Dinner; Mem'ry Island; Portland Fancy (instrumental); You Wonderful You*; Friendly Star**; Heavenly Music**; Get Happy***.

   **music and lyrics by Harry Warren, Saul Chaplin and Jack Brooks*
  ***music and lyrics by Saul Chaplin*
***music and lyrics by Harold Arlen and Ted Koehler*

SYNOPSIS:

Joe Ross' acting troupe descends on his girlfriend Abigail's farm causing havoc with her sister Jane's efforts to bring in the harvest.

SOUNDTRACK: MGM 2-SES-52ST (with *Everything I Have is Yours* and *I Love Melvin*)

* * * * * * * * * *

SUNDAY IN THE PARK WITH GEORGE
Karl-Lorimar Video, 1985

Producer: Iris Merlis
Director: James Lapine and Terry Hughes
Book: James Lapine
Choreography: Randolyn Zinn
Music and Lyrics: Stephen Sondheim
Running time: 147 minutes, color

CAST:

Mandy Patinkin (*Georges Seurat/George*); Bernadette Peters (*Dot/Marie*); Dana Ivey (*Yvonne/Naomi Eisen*); Charles Kimborough (*Jules/Bob Greenburg*); Cris Groenendaal (*Louis/Billy Webster*); Brent Spiner (*Franz/Dennis*); Mary D'Arcy (*Celeste #2/Elaine*); Judith Moore (*Nurse/Mrs./Harriet Pawling*); Barbara Bryne (*Old Lady/Blair Daniels*); William Parry (*Boatman/Charles Redmond*); Nancy Opel (*Frieda/Betty*) and Robert Westenberg (*Soldier/Alex*).

SONGS:

Sunday in the Park With George; No Life; Colors and Light; Gossip; The Day Off; Everybody Loves Louis; Finishing the Hat; We Do Not Belong Together; Beautiful; Sunday; It's Hot Up Here; Putting It Together; Children and Art; Lesson #8; Move On.

SYNOPSIS:

Nineteenth century French neo-impressionistic painter Georges Seurat's famous painting *A Sunday Afternoon on the Island of La Grande Jatte* is the basis for this musical about his life and the effect of his work on his friends and family.

SOUNDTRACK: RCA HBC1-5042

* * * * * * * * *

SUN VALLEY SERENADE
20th Century Fox, 1941

Producer: Milton Sperling
Director: Bruce Humberstone
Screenplay: Robert Ellis and Helen Logan; based on a story by Art Arthur and Robert Harari
Choreography: Hermes Pan
Music and Lyrics: Harry Warren and Mack Gordon
Running time: 85 minutes, B/W

CAST:

Sonja Henie (*Karen Benson*); John Payne (*Ted Scott*); Glenn Miller (*Phil Corey*); Milton Berle (*Nifty Allen*); Lynn Bari* (*Vivian Dawn*); Joan Davis (*Miss Carstairs*); The Nicholas Brothers (*Dancers*); William Davidson (*Murray*) and Dorothy Dandridge (*Singer*).

**vocals dubbed by Pat Friday*

SONGS:

I Know Why and So Do You; At Last; It Happened in Sun Valley; Chattanooga Choo Choo; The World is Waiting to Waltz Again; I'm Lena the Ballerina; The Kiss Polka.

338

SYNOPSIS:

Ted Scott is the pianist for Phil Corey's band playing an engagement at the resort in Sun Valley, Idaho when he finds he must look after Karen Benson, the Norwegian refugee he's sponsering. When it turns out that Karen is a champion skater, Ted arranges for her to perform when singer Vivian Dawn walks out in a huff.

SOUNDTRACK: No soundtrack available

* * * * * * * * * *

SWEENEY TODD-THE DEMON BARBER OF FLEET STREET
RKO/Nederlander, 1982

Producer: Bonnie Burns
Director: Harold Prince and Terry Hughes
Book: Hugh Wheeler; based on the play *Sweeney Todd-The Demon Barber of Fleet Street* by Christopher Bond
Choreography: Larry Fuller
Music and Lyrics: Stephen Sondheim
Running time: 138 minutes, color

CAST:

Angela Lansbury (*Mrs. Nellie Lovett*); George Hearn (*Sweeney Todd*); Cris Groenendaal (*Anthony Hope*); Edmund Lyndeck (*Judge Turpin*); Betsy Joslyn (*Johanna Barker*); Ken Jennings (*Tobias Ragg*); Sara Woods (*Beggar Woman*); Calvin Remsberg (*Beadle Bamford*) and Sal Mistretta (*Pirelli*).

SONGS:

Prologue/The Ballad of Sweeney Todd; No Place Like London; The Barber and His Wife; The Worst Pies in London; Poor Thing; My Friends; Green Finch and Linnet Bird; Ah, Miss; Johanna; Pirelli's Miracle Elixir; The Contest; Wait; Kiss Me; Ladies and Their Sensitivities; Pretty Women; Epiphany; A Little Priest; God, That's Good!; By the Sea; The Letter; Not While I'm Around; Parlor Songs; Epilogue.

SYNOPSIS:

In 19th century London Benjamin Barker returns to seek revenge on those who falsely accused him and had him sentenced to prison abroad--in the guise of a barber named Sweeney Todd.

SOUNDTRACK: RCA CBL2-3379

* * * * * * * * *

SWEET CHARITY
Universal, 1969

Producer: Robert Arthur
Director: Bob Fosse
Screenplay: Peter Stone; based on the stage musical book by Neil Simon
Choreography: Bob Fosse
Music and Lyrics: Cy Coleman and Dorothy Fields
Running time: 148 minutes, color

CAST:

Shirley MacLaine (*Charity Hope Valentine*); John McMartin (*Oscar Lindquist*); Chita Rivera (*Nickie*); Paula Kelly (*Helene*); Stubby Kaye (*Herman*); Ricardo Montalban (*Vittorio Vitale*); Barbara Bouchet (*Ursula*); Suzanne Charny (*Dancer in Pompeii Club*); Alan Hewitt (*Mr. Nicholsby*); Dante D'Paulo (*Charlie*); Ben Vereen (*Dancer in Pompeii Club*); Lee Roy Reams (*Dancer in Pompeii Club*); Al Lanti (*"Big Spender"*); John Wheeler (*"Rhythm of Life" dancer*) and Sammy Davis, Jr. (*Big Daddy*).

SONGS:

My Personal Property; Big Spender; Rich Man's Frug (instrumental); If My Friends Could See Me Now; There's Gotta Be Something Better Than This; It's a Nice Face; Rhythm of Life; Sweet Charity; I'm a Brass Band; I Love to Cry at Weddings; Where Am I Going?

SYNOPSIS:

Eternal optimist Charity Hope Valentine, a taxi dancer, constantly searches for "Mr. Right"--in all the wrong places.

SOUNDTRACK: Decca 71502

* * * * * * * * *

SWEET DREAMS
Tri-Star, 1985

Producer: Bernard Schwartz
Director: Karel Reisz
Screenplay: Robert Getchell

340

Choreography: Susan Scanlan
Music and Lyrics: see below with song titles
Running time: 115 minutes, color

CAST:

Jessica Lange* (*Patsy Cline*); Ed Harris (*Charlie Dick*); Ann Wedgeworth (*Hilda Hensley*); David Clennon (*Randy Hughes*); James Staley (*Gerald Cline*); Gary Gasabara (*Woodhouse*); P.J. Soles (*Wanda*); Caitlin Kelch (*Sylvia Hensley*); Bruce Kirby (*Arthur Godfrey*); Robert L. Dasch (*John Hensley*) and Jerry Haynes (*Owen Bradley*).

vocals dubbed by Patsy Cline

SONGS:

San Antonio Rose - *Bob Hill*
Blue Moon of Kentucky - *Bill Monroe*
Lovesick Blues - *Irving Mills and Cliff Friend*
Seven Lonely Days - *Earl Shuman, Alden Shuman and Marshall Brown*
Your Cheatin' Heart - *Hank Williams*
Walking After Midnight - *Don Hecht and Alan Block*
Foolin' Around - *Harlan Howard and Buck Owens*
Bill Bailey, Won't You Please Come Home? - *Hughie Cannon*
I Fall to Pieces - *Hank Cochran and Harlan Howard*
Crazy - *Willie Nelson*
She's Got You - *Hank Cochran*
Sweet Dreams - *Don Gibson*

SYNOPSIS:

Biography of country singer Patsy Cline from her start in a Winchester, Virginia club through her turbulent second marriage to Charlie Dick and tragic early death in a private plane crash.

SOUNDTRACK: MCA 39301

* * * * * * * * *

SWEETHEARTS
Metro-Goldwyn-Mayer, 1938

Producer: Hunt Stromberg
Director: W.S. Van Dyke II

Screenplay: Dorothy Parker and Alan Campbell; based on the stage musical book by Harry B. Smith and Fred DeGresac
Choreography: Albertina Rasch
Music and Lyrics: Victor Herbert, Robert Wright and George Forrest
Running time: 120 minutes, color

CAST:

Jeanette MacDonald (*Gwen Marlowe*); Nelson Eddy (*Ernest Lane*); Frank Morgan (*Felix Lehman*); Ray Bolger (*Hans*); Florence Rice (*Kay Jordan*); Mischa Auer (*Leo Kronk*); Herman Bing (*Oscar Engel*); George Barbier (*Benjamin Silver*); Reginald Gardiner (*Norman Trumpett*); Fay Holden (*Hannah*); Allyn Joslyn (*Dink*); Lucille Watson (*Mrs. Marlowe*); Gene Lockhart (*Cousin Augustus*); Kathleen Lockhart (*Aunt Amelia*); Berton Churchill (*Uncle Sheridan*); Terry Kilburn (*Brother*); Raymond Walburn (*Orlando*); Douglas McPhail (*Harvey Horton*); Betty Jaynes (*Una Wilson*) and Olin Howland (*Appleby*).

SONGS:

Wooden Shoes; Every Lover Must Meet His Fate; Sweethearts; Auld Lang Syne*; Pretty as a Picture; Game of Love; Keep It Dark (*The Prince of Pilsen*)**; Badinage; On Parade; Little Gray Home in the West***.

traditional
**music and lyrics by Gustav Landers and Frank Pixley*
***music and lyrics by Hermann Löhr and Wilmot D. Eardley*

SYNOPSIS:

Gwen Marlowe and Ernest Lane are the married stars of Felix Lehman's show *Sweethearts* and look forward to celebrating their sixth wedding anniversary--which is also the show's--when Hollywood agent Norman Trumpett tries to lure them away.

SOUNDTRACK: No soundtrack available

* * * * * * * * *

SWEET ROSIE O'GRADY
20th Century Fox, 1943

Producer: William Perlberg
Director: Irving Cummings
Screenplay: Ken Englund
Choreography: Hermes Pan

Music and Lyrics: Harry Warren and Mack Gordon
Running time: 76 minutes, color

CAST:

Betty Grable (*Madeleine Marlowe*); Robert Young (*Sam Mackeever*); Adolphe Menjou (*Morgan*); Reginald Gardiner (*Duke Charles*); Virginia Grey (*Edna Van Dyke*); Phil Regan (*Composer*); Sig Rumann (*Joe Flugelman*); Alan Dinehart (*Arthur Skinner*) and Hobart Cavanaugh (*Clark*).

SONGS:

My Heart Tells Me; The Wishing Waltz; Get Your Police Gazette; My Sam; Going to the Country Fair; Waiting at the Church.

SYNOPSIS:

Singer Madeleine Marlowe goes to London with the hopes of getting Duke Charles to marry her but *Police Gazette* reporter Sam Mackeever has other ideas about her marital future.

SOUNDTRACK: Titania 507 (with *Springtime in the Rockies*)

* * * * * * * * *

SWING TIME
RKO, 1936

Producer: Pandro S. Berman
Director: George Stevens
Screenplay: Howard Lindsay and Allan Scott; based on a story by Erwin Gelsey
Choreography: Hermes Pan
Music and Lyrics: Jerome Kern and Dorothy Fields
Running time: 103 minutes, B/W

CAST:

Fred Astaire (*John "Lucky" Garnett*); Ginger Rogers (*Penelope "Penny" Carroll*); Victor Moore (*Ed-"Pop"*); Helen Broderick (*Mabel Anderson*); Eric Blore (*Mr. Gordon*); Betty Furness (*Margaret Watson*); Georges Metaxa (*Ricardo Romero*) and Landers Stevens (*Judge Watson*).

Pick Yourself Up; The Way You Look Tonight; The Waltz in Swing Time (instrumental); A Fine Romance; Bojangles of Harlem; Never Gonna Dance.

SYNOPSIS:

Dancer/gambler John Garnett goes to New York to try and raise $20,000 in order to prove to his fiancée's father that he is respectable. But while doing so he meets and falls in love with dance instructress Penny Carroll.

SOUNDTRACK: Sountrak 106 (with *Shall We Dance?*)

* * * * * * * * * *

THE SWORD IN THE STONE
Buena Vista, 1963

Producer: Walt Disney
Director: Wolfgang Reitherman
Screenplay: Bill Peet; based on the book by T.H. White
Music and Lyrics: Richard M. Sherman and Robert B. Sherman
Running time: 75 minutes, color

VOCAL TALENTS:

Ricky Sorenson (*Wart*); Sebastian Cabot (*Sir Ector*); Karl Swenson (*Merlin*); Junius Matthews (*Archimedes*); Alan Napier (*Sir Pellinore*); Norman Alden (*Kay*) and Martha Wentworth (*Madame Mim/Granny Squirrel*).

SONGS:

The Legend of the Sword in the Stone; Higitus Figitus; That's What Makes the World Go Round; A Most Befuddling Thing; Mad Madame Mim.

SYNOPSIS:

Animated tale of the story of how the boy named Wart grew up to become King Arthur (with a little help from Merlin!)

SOUNDTRACK: Disneyland 1236

T

TAKE ME OUT TO THE BALL GAME
Metro-Goldwyn-Mayer, 1949

Producer: Arthur Freed
Director: Busby Berkeley
Screenplay: Harry Tugend and George Wells; based on a story by Gene Kelly and
          Stanley Donen
Choreography: Gene Kelly and Stanley Donen
Music and Lyrics: Betty Comden, Adolph Green and Roger Edens
Running time: 90 minutes, color

CAST:

Gene Kelly (*Eddie O'Brien*); Frank Sinatra (*Dennis Ryan*); Esther Williams (*K.C. Higgins*); Betty Garrett (*Shirley Delwyn*); Jules Munshin (*Nat Goldberg*); Edward Arnold (*Joe Lorgan*); Tom Dugan (*Slappy Burke*) and Richard Lane (*Michael Gilhuley*).

SONGS:

Take Me Out to the Ball Game*; Yes Indeedy; O'Brien to Ryan to Goldberg; She's the Right Girl For Me; It's Fate, Baby, It's Fate; It's Strictly U.S.A.; The Hat My Dear Old Father Wore Upon St. Patrick's Day**.

  **music and lyrics by Jack Norworth and Albert Von Tilzer*
***music and lyrics by William Jerome and Jean Schwartz*

SYNOPSIS:

When new owner K.C. Higgins comes to Florida to take over ownership of the Wolves' baseball club she finds that she has more than she can handle with ladies' man Eddie O'Brien and shy Dennis Ryan.

SOUNDTRACK: Curtain Calls 100/18

* * * * * * * * *

TEA FOR TWO
Warner Bros., 1950

Producer: William Jacobs
Director: David Butler

Screenplay: Harry Clork; based on the stage musical book *No, No, Nanette* by Otto
           Harbach and Frank Mandel
Choreography: LeRoy Prinz
Music and Lyrics: see below with song titles
Running time: 97 minutes, color

CAST:

Doris Day (*Nanette Carter*); Gordon MacRae (*Jimmy Smith*); Gene Nelson (*Tommy Trainor*); Patrice Wymore (*Beatrice Darcy*); Eve Arden (*Pauline Hastings*); Billy DeWolfe (*Larry Blair*); S.Z. Sakall (*J. Maxwell Bloomhaus*); Bill Goodwin (*William Early*); Virginia Gibson (*Mabel Wiley*); Crauford Kent (*Stevens*); Mary Eleanor Donahue (*Lynne*) and Johnny McGovern (*Richard*).

SONGS:

Crazy Rhythm - *Irving Caesar, Joseph Meyer and Roger Wolfe Kahn*
I Only Have Eyes For You - *Harry Warren and Al Dubin*
Tea For Two - *Vincent Youmans and Irving Caesar*
Charleston (instrumental) - *Cecil Mack and Jimmy Johnson*
I Want To Be Happy - *Vincent Youmans and Irving Caesar*
Do, Do, Do - *George Gershwin and Ira Gershwin*
Oh Me! Oh My! - *Vincent Youmans and Ira Gershwin*
No, No, Nanette - *Vincent Youmans and Otto Harbach*

SYNOPSIS:

Heiress Nanette Carter loses all of her money in the 1929 Wall Street crash--a fact that her Uncle Max keeps from her even though she has promised to back Larry Blair's new show. Her uncle promises her, however, that she can have the money if she can only say "No" for 24 hours.

SOUNDTRACK: No soundtrack available

* * * * * * * * *

TEXAS CARNIVAL
Metro-Goldwyn-Mayer, 1951

Producer: Jack Cummings
Director: Charles Walters
Screenplay: Dorothy Kingsley; based on a story by George Wells and Dorothy
            Kingsley
Choreography: Hermes Pan

Music and Lyrics: Harry Warren and Dorothy Fields
Running time: 77 minutes, color

CAST:

Esther Williams (*Debbie Telford*); Red Skelton (*Cornie Quinell*); Howard Keel (*Slim Shelby*); Ann Miller (*Sunshine Jackson*); Paula Raymond (*Marilla Sabinas*); Keenan Wynn (*Dan Sabinas*); Tom Tully (*Sheriff Jackson*); Glenn Strange (*Tex Hodgkins*); Dick Wessel (*Concessionaire*); Donald MacBride (*Concessionaire*); Marjorie Wood (*Mrs. Gaytes*); Hans Conried (*Hotel Clerk*) and Thurston Hall (*Mr. Gaytes*).

SONGS:

Carnie's Pitch; Whoa! Emma; It's Dynamite; Deep in the Heart of Texas*; Clap Your Hands*; Young Folks Should Get Married.

music and lyrics by June Hershey and Don Swander

SYNOPSIS:

Carnival performers Cornie Quinell and Debbie Telford are mistaken for Texas millionaire Dan Sabinas and his sister Marilla and the more they try to get out of their predicament, the deeper they get.

SOUNDTRACK: No soundtrack available

* * * * * * * * *

THAT LADY IN ERMINE
20th Century Fox, 1948

Producer: Ernst Lubitsch
Director: Ernst Lubitsch
Screenplay: Samson Raphaelson
Choreography: Hermes Pan
Music and Lyrics: Leo Robin and Frederick Hollander
Running time: 93 minutes, color

CAST:

Betty Grable (*Francesca/Angelina*); Douglas Fairbanks, Jr. (*Colonel/Duke*); Cesar Romero (*Mario*); Walter Abel (*Major Horvath/Benvenuto*); Reginald Gardiner (*Alberto*); Harry Davenport (*Luigi*); Virginia Campbell (*Theresa*) and Whit Bissell (*Guilio*).

SONGS:

Ooh! What'll I Do? (To That Wild Hungarian); This Melody Has to Be Right; This is the Moment; There's Something About Midnight; The Jester's Song; What a Crisis; What Do You See?

SYNOPSIS:

Countess Francesca must find a way to defend her castle against an invading army led by a handsome colonel. Unable to come up with a solution she falls asleep and dreams of her ancestor who found herself in a similar situation and advises her accordingly.

SOUNDTRACK: No soundtrack available

* * * * * * * * *

THAT MIDNIGHT KISS
Metro-Goldwyn-Mayer, 1949

Producer: Joe Pasternak
Director: Norman Taurog
Screenplay: Bruce Manning and Tamara Hovey
Music and Lyrics: see below with song titles
Running time: 96 minutes, color

CAST:

Kathryn Grayson (*Prudence Budell*); José Iturbi (*Himself*); Ethel Barrymore (*Abigail Trent Budell*); Mario Lanza (*Johnny Donnetti*); Keenan Wynn (*Artie Geoffrey Glenson*); J. Carrol Naish (*Papa Donnetti*); Jules Munshin (*Michael Pemberton*); Thomas Gomez (*Guido Russino Betelli*); Marjorie Reynolds (*Mary*); Mimi Aguglia (*Mama Donnetti*); Arthur Treacher (*Hutchins*) and Ann Codee (*Mme. Bouget*).

SONGS:

Down Among the Sheltering Palms - *Abe Olman and James Brockman*
Celeste Aida (*Aida*) - *Giuseppe Verdi*
They Didn't Believe Me - *Jerome Kern and Herbert Reynolds*
Three O'Clock in the Morning - *Julian Robledo and Dorothy Terriss*
I Know, I Know, I Know - *Bronislau Kaper and Bob Russell*

348

SYNOPSIS:

Wealthy Philadelphia patroness Abigail Trent Budell creates a new civic opera, directed by José Iturbi, to give her granddaughter Prudence a chance at a career. But when tempermental tenor Guido Betelli quits a local truck driver named Johnny Donnetti is called upon to fill the role.

SOUNDTRACK: No soundtrack available

* * * * * * * * *

THAT NIGHT IN RIO
20th Century Fox, 1941

Producer: Fred Kohlmar
Director: Irving Cummings
Screenplay: George Seaton, Bess Meredyth, Hal Long and Samuel Hoffenstein;
        based on a play by Rudolph Lothar and Hans Adler
Choreography: Hermes Pan
Music and Lyrics: Harry Warren and Mack Gordon
Running time: 90 minutes, color

CAST:

Alice Faye (*Baroness*); Don Ameche (*Larry Martin/Baron Duarte*); Carmen Miranda (*Carmen*); S.Z. Sakall (*Renna*); J. Carrol Naish (*MacLado*); Curt Bois (*Salles*) and Leonid Kinskey (*Pierre*).

SONGS:

I Yi, Yi, Yi, Yi (I Like You Very Much); Chica, Chica, Boom, Chic; The Baron is in Conference; Boa Noite (Good Night); They Met in Rio.

SYNOPSIS:

Entertainer Larry Martin agrees to impersonate Baron Duarte for the Baroness in order to fool his business associates who are unaware that he is out-of-town--trying to secure finacial support for his failing company.

SOUNDTRACK: Curtain Calls 100/14 (with *Weekend in Havana*)

* * * * * * * * *

349

THERE'S NO BUSINESS LIKE SHOW BUSINESS
20th Century Fox, 1954

Producer: Sol C. Siegel
Director: Walter Lang
Screenplay: Phoebe Ephron and Henry Ephron; based on a story by Lamar Trotti
Choreography: Robert Alton
Music and Lyrics: Irving Berlin
Running time: 117 minutes, color

CAST:

Ethel Merman (*Molly Donahue*); Donald O'Connor (*Tim Donahue*); Marilyn Monroe (*Victoria Hoffman/Vicky Parker*); Dan Dailey (*Terry Donahue*); Johnnie Ray (*Steve Donahue*); Mitzi Gaynor (*Katie Donahue*); Hugh O'Brien (*Charlie Gibbs*); Frank McHugh (*Eddie Duggan*); Rhys Williams (*Father Dineen*); Lee Patrick (*Marge*) and Richard Eastham (*Lew Harris*).

SONGS:

When That Midnight Choo Choo Leaves For Alabam'; Play a Simple Melody; A Pretty Girl is Like a Melody; You'd Be Surprised; Let's Have Another Cup of Coffee; Alexander's Ragtime Band; After You Get What You Want; Remember; If You Believe; Heat Wave; A Man Chases a Girl; Lazy; A Sailor's Not a Sailor Till a Sailor's Been Tattooed; There's No Business Like Show Business.

SYNOPSIS:

Molly and Terry Donahue find their vaudeville act breaking up as their three children--Steve, Tim and Katie--each begin to branch out in their own lives and careers.

SOUNDTRACK: Decca 8091

* * * * * * * * *

THIN ICE
20th Century Fox, 1937

Producer: Raymond Griffith
Director: Sidney Lanfield
Screenplay: Boris Ingster and Milton Sperling; based on the play *Der Komet* by
          Attila Orbok
Choreography: Harry Losee

Music and Lyrics: Sidney D. Mitchell and Lew Pollack
Running time: 78 minutes, B/W

CAST:

Sonja Henie (*Lili Heiser*); Tyrone Power (*Prince Rudolph*); Arthur Treacher (*Nottingham*); Raymond Walburn (*Uncle Dornik*); Joan Davis (*Orchestra Leader*); Sig Rumann (*Prime Minister*); Alan Hale (*Baron*); Maurice Cass (*Count*); George Givot (*Alex*) and Leah Ray (*Singer*).

SONGS:

My Swiss Hill Billy; My Secret Love Affair; I'm Olga From the Volga*; Over Night.

music and lyrics by Mack Gordon and Harry Revel

SYNOPSIS:

Prince Rudolph decides to take a break from the pressures of royal duty and at a small Swiss village he meets skating instructress Lili Heiser. Soon she is beseiged by people who want her to use her influence with the prince to their advantage.

SOUNDTRACK: No soundtrack available

* * * * * * * * *

THIS TIME FOR KEEPS
Metro-Goldwyn-Mayer, 1947

Producer: Joe Pasternak
Director: Richard Thorpe
Screenplay: Gladys Lehman; based on a story by Erwin Gelsey and Lorraine
              Fielding
Choreography: Stanley Donen
Music and Lyrics: see below with song titles
Running time: 105 minutes, color

CAST:

Esther Williams (*Leonora Cambaretti*); Jimmy Durante (*Ferdi Farro*); Lauritz Melchior (*Richard Herald*); Johnnie Johnston (*Dick Johnson*); Xavier Cugat (*Himself*); Dame May Whitty (*Grandma Cambaretti*); Sharon McManus (*Deborah Cambaretti*); Dick Simmons (*Gordon Coome*); Mary Stuart (*Frances Allenbury*);

Ludwig Stossel (*Peter*); Dorothy Parker (*Merle*) and Nella Walker (*Mrs. Harriet Allenbury*).

SONGS:

A Little Bit of This, a Little Bit of That - *Jimmy Durante*
Easy to Love - *Cole Porter*
I Love to Dance - *Burton Lane and Ralph Freed*
Why Don't They Let Me Sing a Love Song? - *Benny Davis and Harry Akst*
M'Appari (*Martha*) - *Friedrich Von Flotow*
Ten Percent Off - *Sammy Fain and Ralph Freed*
Inka Dinka Doo - *Jimmy Durante and Ben Ryan*
I'll Be With You in Apple Blossom Time - *Albert Von Tilzer and Neville Fleeson*
Jingle Bells - *J.S. Pierpont*
No Wonder They Fell in Love - *Sammy Fain and Ralph Freed*
The Guy Who Found the Lost Chord - *Jimmy Durante*
When It's Lilac Time on Mackinac Island - *Leslie Kirk*
Chiquita Banana - *Leonard MacKenzie, Garth Montgomery and William Wirges*
La donna è mobile (*Rigoletto*) - *Giuseppe Verdi*

SYNOPSIS:

Dick Johnson, son of opera singer Richard Herald, decides to try and find the girl who kissed him while he was in a hospital during WWII.

SOUNDTRACK: No soundtrack available

* * * * * * * * *

THOROUGHLY MODERN MILLIE
Universal, 1967

Producer: Ross Hunter
Director: George Roy Hill
Screenplay: Richard Morris
Choreography: Joe Layton
Music and Lyrics: see below with song titles
Running time: 138 minutes, color

CAST:

Julie Andrews (*Millie Dilmount*); James Fox (*Jimmy Smith*); Mary Tyler Moore (*Miss Dorothy Brown*); Carol Channing (*Muzzy Van Hossmere*); John Gavin (*Trevor Graydon*); Philip Ahn (*Tea*); Cavada Humphrey (*Miss Flannery*); Jack Soo (*Oriental*

#1); Pat Morita (*Oriental #2*); Ann Dee (*Torch Singer*) and Beatrice Lillie (*Mrs. Meers*).

SONGS:

Thoroughly Modern Millie - *James Van Heusen and Sammy Cahn*
The Tapioca - *James Van Heusen and Sammy Cahn*
Baby Face - *Benny Davis and Harry Akst*
Drink La Chaim - *Sylvia Neufeld*
Jazz Baby - *William Jerome and Blanche Merrill*
Jimmy - *Jay Thompson*
Do It Again - *George Gershwin and B.G. DeSylva*
Poor Butterfly - *John Golden and Raymond Hubbell*
Rose of Washington Square - *James Hanley and Ballard MacDonald*

SYNOPSIS:

Millie Dilmount, a "modern", is out to get herself a career and then marry her boss but true love and a white slavery ring get in the way of her plans.

SOUNDTRACK: Decca 71500

* * * * * * * * *

THREE FOR THE SHOW
Columbia, 1955

Producer: Jonie Taps
Director: H.C. Potter
Screenplay: Edward Hope and Leonard Stern; based on the play *Too Many Husbands* by Somerset Maugham
Choreography: Jack Cole
Music and Lyrics: see below with song titles
Running time: 93 minutes, color

CAST:

Betty Grable (*Julie*); Jack Lemmon (*Marty Stewart*); Marge Champion (*Gwen Howard*); Gower Champion (*Vernon Loundes*); Myron McCormick (*Mike Hudson*) and Paul Harvey (*Colonel Wharton*).

SONGS:

Which One? - *Lester Lee and Ned Washington*

I've Got a Crush On You - *George Gershwin and Ira Gershwin*
I've Been Kissed Before - *Bob Russell*
How Come You Like Me Like You Do? - *Gene Austin and Roy Bergere*
Down Boy! - *Hoagy Carmichael and Harold Adamson*

SYNOPSIS:

After the Air Force informs Julie that her husband Marty Stewart has been shot down and is presumed dead she marries his partner Vernon Loundes. Problems arise when Marty returns very much alive and Julie can't decide which one she wants.

SOUNDTRACK: No soundtrack available

* * * * * * * * * *

THREE LITTLE GIRLS IN BLUE
20th Century Fox, 1946

Producer: Mack Gordon
Director: Bruce Humberstone
Screenplay: Valentine Davies, adaptation by Brown Holmes, Lynn Starling, Robert
        Ellis and Helen Logan; based on a play by Stephen Powys
Choreography: Seymour Felix and Babe Pearce
Music and Lyrics: Josef Myrow and Mack Gordon
Running time: 91 minutes, color

CAST:

June Haver (*Pamela Charters*); George Montgomery* (*Van Dam Smith*); Vivian Blaine (*Elizabeth Charters*); Celeste Holm (*Miriam*); Vera-Ellen** (*Myra Charters*); Frank Latimore (*Steve Harrington*); Charles Smith*** (*Mike*); Charles Halton (*Hoskins*); Ruby Dandridge (*Mammy*); Thurston Hall (*Colonel*) and Clinton Rosemond (*Ben*).

  vocals dubbed by Ben Gage
 **vocals dubbed by Carol Stewart*
***vocals dubbed by Del Porter*

SONGS:

I Like Mike; On the Board Walk (In Atlantic City); A Farmer's Life is a Very Merry Life; Three Little Girls in Blue; Somewhere in the Night; You Make Me Feel So Young; Always a Lady; This is Always*.

354

*music and lyrics by Harry Warren and Mack Gordon

<u>SYNOPSIS</u>:

Pamela, Elizabeth and Myra go to Atlantic City, New Jersey in search of husbands in 1905 and find Van, Mike and Steve just what they're looking for.

SOUNDTRACK: Hollywood Soundstage 410

* * * * * * * * *

THREE LITTLE WORDS
Metro-Goldwyn-Mayer, 1950

Producer: Jack Cummings
Director: Richard Thorpe
Screenplay: George Wells
Choreography: Hermes Pan
Music and Lyrics: see below with song title
Running time: 102 minutes, color

<u>CAST</u>:

Fred Astaire (*Bert Kalmar*); Red Skelton (*Harry Ruby*); Vera-Ellen* (*Jessie Brown Kalmar*); Arlene Dahl (*Eileen Percy Kalmar*); Keenan Wynn (*Charlie Kope*); Gale Robbins (*Terry Lordel*); Gloria De Haven (*Mrs. Carter De Haven*); Phil Regan (*Himself*); Harry Shannon (*Clanahan*); Debbie Reynolds** (*Helen Kane*); Paul Harvey (*Al Masters*); Carleton Carpenter (*Dan Healy*) and George Metkovich (*Al Schacht*).

 vocals dubbed by Anita Ellis
**vocals dubbed by Helen Kane*

<u>SONGS</u>:

Where Did You Get That Girl? - *Harry Puck and Bert Kalmar*
She's Mine, All Mine - *Harry Ruby and Bert Kalmar*
My Sunny Tennessee - *Harry Ruby, Herman Ruby and Bert Kalmar*
So Long, Oo-Long, How Long You Gonna Be? - *Harry Ruby and Bert Kalmar*
Who's Sorry Now? - *Harry Ruby, Bert Kalmar and Ted Snyder*
Come On Papa - *Harry Ruby and Edgar Leslie*
Nevertheless (I'm in Love With You) - *Harry Ruby and Bert Kalmar*
All Alone Monday - *Harry Ruby and Bert Kalmar*
I Wanna Be Loved By You - *Herbert Stothart, Harry Ruby and Bert Kalmar*

Up in the Clouds - *Harry Ruby and Bert Kalmar*
Thinking Of You - *Harry Ruby and Bert Kalmar*
Hooray For Captain Spaulding - *Harry Ruby and Bert Kalmar*
I Love You So Much - *Harry Ruby and Bert Kalmar*
You Are My Lucky Star - *Nacio Herb Brown and Arthur Freed*
Three Little Words - *Harry Ruby and Bert Kalmar*

SYNOPSIS:

The biography of songwriters Bert Kalmar and Harry Ruby with the emphasis on the ups-and-downs of their personal relationship.

SOUNDTRACK: MGM 2-SES-45ST (with *Till the Clouds Roll By*)

* * * * * * * * *

THREE SAILORS AND A GIRL
Warner Bros., 1953

Producer: Sammy Cahn
Director: Roy Del Ruth
Screenplay: Roland Kibbee and Devery Freeman; based on a play by George S.
         Kaufman
Choreography: LeRoy Prinz
Music and Lyrics: Sammy Fain and Sammy Cahn
Running time: 95 minutes, color

CAST:

Jane Powell (*Penny Weston*); Gordon MacRae (*"Choir Boy" Jones*); Gene Nelson (*Twitch*); Sam Levene (*Joe Woods*); Jack E. Leonard (*Porky*); George Givot (*Emilio Rossi*); Veda Ann Borg (*Fay Foss*); Archer MacDonald (*Melvin Webster*); Raymond Greenleaf (*B.P. Morrow*); Henry Slate (*Hank*); Grandon Rhodes (*George Abbott*); David Bond (*Moss Hart*); Alex Gerry (*Ira Gershwin*) and Burt Lancaster (*Marine*).

SONGS:

You're But Oh So Right; Kiss Me or I'll Scream; Face to Face; The Lately Song (I Got Butterflies); There Must Be a Reason; When It's Love; My Heart is a Singing Heart; Show Me a Happy Woman and I'll Show You a Miserable Man; Embraceable You*; Home is Where the Heart Is.

music and lyrics by George Gershwin and Ira Gershwin

356

SYNOPSIS:

Fast-talking producer Joe Woods convinces sailors Choir Boy, Twitch and Porky to invest $50,000 in a new show he's putting on--without telling them it's already in big trouble.

SOUNDTRACK: No soundtrack available

* * * * * * * * *

TICKLE ME
Allied Artists, 1965

Producer: Ben Schwalb
Director: Norman Taurog
Screenplay: Elwood Ullmann and Edward Bernds
Choreography: David Winters
Music and Lyrics: see below with song titles
Running time: 90 minutes, color

CAST:

Elvis Presley (*Lonnie Beale*); Jocelyn Lane (*Pam Merritt*); Julie Adams (*Vera Radford*); Jack Mullaney (*Stanley Potter*); Merry Anders (*Estelle Penfield*); Bill Williams (*Deputy Sturdivant*); Edward Faulkner (*Brad Bentley*) and Connie Gilchrist (*Hilda*).

SONGS:

It's a Long, Lonely Highway - *Doc Pomus and Mort Shuman*
It Feels So Right - *Ben Weisman and Fred Wise*
(Such an) Easy Question - *Otis Blackwell and Winfield Scott*
Dirty, Dirty Feeling - *Jerry Leiber and Mike Stoller*
Put the Blame On Me - *Norman Blagman, Fred Wise and Kathleen G. Twomey*
I'm Yours - *Don Robertson and Hal Blair*
Night Rider - *Doc Pomus and Mort Shuman*
I Feel That I've Known You Forever - *Doc Pomus and Alan Jeffreys*
Slowly But Surely - *Sid Wayne and Ben Weisman*

SYNOPSIS:

Rodeo rider Lonnie Beale, looking for work between seasons, finds employment on Vera Radford's dude ranch--for women only!

SOUNDTRACK: RCA EPA-4383

* * * * * * * * *

TIME OUT FOR RHYTHM
Columbia, 1941

Producer: Irving Starr
Director: Sidney Salkow
Screenplay: Edmund L. Hartmann, Bert Lawrence and Bert Granet; based on a play
        by Alex Ruben
Choreography: LeRoy Prinz
Music and Lyrics: Saul Chaplin and Sammy Cahn
Running time: 75 minutes, B/W

CAST:

Ann Miller (*Kitty Brown*); Rudy Vallee (*Daniel J. Collins*); Rosemary Lane (*Frances Lewis*); Allen Jenkins (*Off-Beat Davis*); Joan Merrill (*Herself*); Richard Lane (*Mike Armstrong*); Stanley Andrews (*James Anderson*) and the Three Stooges (*Themselves*).

SONGS:

Did Anyone Ever Tell You?; Boogie Woogie Man; Time Out For Rhythm; Twiddlin' My Thumbs; As If You Didn't Know; Obviously the Gentleman Prefers to Dance; The Rio de Janeiro.

SYNOPSIS:

Daniel Collins and Mike Armstrong decide to go into business as theatrical agents but soon find their partnership in jeopardy over dancer Kitty Brown.

SOUNDTRACK: No soundtrack available

* * * * * * * * *

THE TIME, THE PLACE AND THE GIRL
Warner Bros., 1946

Producer: Alex Gottlieb
Director: David Butler
Screenplay: Francis Swann, Agnes Christine Johnston and Lynn Starling; based on
        the story by Leonard Lee
Choreography: LeRoy Prinz

Music and Lyrics: Arthur Schwartz and Leo Robin
Running time: 105 minutes, color

CAST:

Dennis Morgan (*Steven Ross*); Jack Carson (*Jeff Howard*); Janis Paige (*Sue Jackson*); Martha Vickers (*Victoria Cassel*); S.Z. Sakall (*Ladislaus Cassel*); Alan Hale (*John Braden*); Angela Greene (*Elaine Winters*); Donald Woods (*Martin Drew*); Florence Bates (*Mme. Lucia Cassel*) and Carmen Cavallaro (*Himself*).

SONGS:

I Happened to Walk Down First Street; A Solid Citizen of the Solid South; Oh, But I Do; Through a Thousand Dreams; A Gal in Calico; A Rainy Night in Rio.

SYNOPSIS:

After Steve Ross and Jeff Howard have their nightclub closed down by symphony conductor Ladislaus Cassel's business manager, Cassel agrees to finance their new Broadway show if his granddaughter Vicky can have a part in it.

SOUNDTRACK: Titania 511 (with *The Paleface* and *Son of Paleface*)

* * * * * * * * *

TIN PAN ALLEY
20th Century Fox, 1940

Producer: Kenneth McGowan
Director: Walter Lang
Screenplay: Robert Ellis and Helen Logan; based on a story by Pamela Harris
Choreography: Seymour Felix
Music and Lyrics: see below with song titles
Running time: 92 minutes, B/W

CAST:

Alice Faye (*Katie Blane*); Betty Grable (*Lily Blane*); Jack Oakie (*Harry Calhoun*); John Payne (*Francis "Skeets" Harrigan*); Allen Jenkins (*Casey*); Esther Ralston (*Nora Bayes*); John Leder (*Reggie Carstair*); Elisha Cook, Jr. (*Joe Codd*); Billy Gilbert (*"The Sheik"*); Fred Keating (*Harvey Raymond*) and Tyler Brooke (*Bert Melville*).

SONGS:

You Say the Sweetest Things (Baby) - *Harry Warren and Mack Gordon*
On Moonlight Bay - *Edward Madden and Percy Wenrich*
Honeysuckle Rose - *Andy Razaf and Thomas "Fats" Waller*
Moonlight and Roses - *Ben Black, Neil Moret and Edwin H. Lemare*
America, I Love You - *Edgar Leslie and Archie Gottler*
Goodbye Broadway, Hello France - *C. Francis Reisner, Benny Davis and Billy Baskette*
The Sheik of Araby - *Harry B. Smith, Francis Wheeler and Ted Snyder*
K-K-K-Katy - *Geoffrey O'Hara*

SYNOPSIS:

Skeets Harrigan and Harry Calhoun are struggling Tin Pan Alley song publishers who find sisters Katie and Lily Blane the perfect team to pitch their new songs.

SOUNDTRACK: Sountrak 110

* * * * * * * * *

THE TOAST OF NEW ORLEANS
Metro-Goldwyn-Mayer, 1950

Producer: Joe Pasternak
Director: Norman Taurog
Screenplay: Sy Gomberg and George Wells
Choreography: Eugene Loring
Music and Lyrics: Nicholas Brodsky and Sammy Cahn
Running time: 97 minutes, color

CAST:

Kathryn Grayson (*Suzette Micheline*); Mario Lanza (*Pepe Abellard Duvalle*); David Niven (*Jacques Riboudeaux*); Rita Moreno (*Tina*); James Mitchell (*Pierre*); J. Carrol Naish (*Nicky Duvalle*); Clinton Sundberg (*Oscar*); Richard Hageman (*Maestro Pietro Trellini*); Sig Arno (*Mayor*); Romo Vincent (*Manuelo*) and Wallis Clark (*Mr. O'Neill*).

SONGS:

The Toast of New Orleans; Be My Love; Tina Lina; Je suis titania (*Mignon*)*; Boom Biddy Boom Boom; I'll Never Love You; Song of the Bayou; Love Duet (*Madama Butterfly*)**.

360

*music and lyrics by Ambroise Thomas
**music and lyrics by Giacomo Puccini

SYNOPSIS:

In turn-of-the-century Louisiana, New Orleans Opera director Jacques Riboudeaux hears shrimp fisherman Pepe Duvalle sing at his village festival and soon the young man finds that his tenor is a perfect complement to resident diva Suzette Micheline.

SOUNDTRACK: Azel 104

* * * * * * * * * *

TOMMY
Columbia, 1975

Producer: Robert Stigwood and Ken Russell
Director: Ken Russell
Screenplay: Ken Russell; based on the musical drama by Peter Townshend, Keith Moon and John Entwhistle
Choreography: Gillian Gregory
Music and Lyrics: Peter Townshend
Running time: 111 minutes, color

CAST:

Ann-Margret (*Nora Walker Hobbs*); Oliver Reed (*Frank Hobbs*); Roger Daltrey (*Tommy Walker*); Elton John (*The Pinball Wizard*); Eric Clapton (*Preacher*); Keith Moon (*Uncle Ernie*); Jack Nicholson (*The Specialist*); Robert Powell (*Captain Walker*); Paul Nicholas (*Cousin Kevin*); Tina Turner (*The Acid Queen*); Barry Winch (*Young Tommy*); Victoria Russell (*Sally Simpson*); Arthur Brown (*Priest*); Ben Aris (*Rev. Simpson*) and Mary Holland (*Mrs. Simpson*).

SONGS:

Tommy; It's a Boy; You Didn't Hear It (1921); Amazing Journey; Christmas; Cousin Kevin; The Acid Queen; Do You Think It's Alright?; Fiddle About*; Pinball Wizard; There's a Doctor (I've Found); Go to the Mirror Boy; Tommy Can You Hear Me?; Smash the Mirror; Sensation; Miracle Cure; Sally Simpson; I'm Free; Welcome; Tommy's Holiday Camp**; We're Not Gonna Take It; See Me, Feel Me.

*music and lyrics by John Entwhistle
**music and lyrics by Keith Moon

SYNOPSIS:

Film version of the rock opera by The Who is the story of a "deaf, dumb and blind kid" who finds a release from his own insulated world in the game of pinball.

SOUNDTRACK: MCA 10005

* * * * * * * * *

TOM SAWYER
United Artists, 1973

Producer: Arthur P. Jacobs
Director: Don Taylor
Screenplay: Richard M. Sherman and Robert B. Sherman; based on the book by
        Mark Twain
Choreography: Danny Daniels
Music and Lyrics: Richard M. Sherman and Robert B. Sherman
Running time: 104 minutes, color

CAST:

Johnny Whitaker (*Tom Sawyer*); Celeste Holm (*Aunt Polly*); Jeff East (*Huckleberry Finn*); Warren Oates (*Muff Potter*); Jodie Foster (*Becky Thatcher*); Noah Keen (*Judge Thatcher*); Lucille Benson (*Widder Douglas*); Susan Joyce (*Cousin Mary*); Joshua Hill Lewis (*Cousin Sidney*) and Kunu Hank (*Injun Joe*).

SONGS:

River Song*; Tom Sawyer; Gratifaction; A Man's Gotta Be (What He's Born to Be); How Come?; If'n I Was God; Freebootin'; Aunt Polly's Soliloquy; Hannibal Mo-(Zouree)!

*vocal by Charlie Pride

SYNOPSIS:

Life on the Mississippi River in the mid-19th century is full of adventures for a trio of young friends: Tom Sawyer, Becky Thatcher and Huckleberry Finn.

SOUNDTRACK: United Artists LA057-F

* * * * * * * * *

362

tom thumb
Metro-Goldwyn-Mayer, 1958

Producer: George Pal
Director: George Pal
Screenplay: Ladislas Foder; based on a story by the Brothers Grimm
Choreography: Alex Romero
Music and Lyrics: Fred Spielman, Janice Torre, Kermit Goell and Peggy Lee
Running time: 92 minutes, color

CAST:

Russ Tamblyn (*tom thumb*); Alan Young (*Woody*); Terry-Thomas (*Ivan*); June Thorburn (*Queenie*); Jessie Matthews* (*Anna*); Bernard Miles (*Jonathan*); Peter Sellers (*Tony*); Ian Wallace (*The Cobbler*); Peter Bull (*The Town Crier*); Peter Butterworth (*Kapellmeister*); Stan Freberg (*voice of "Yawning Man"*) and Dal McKennon (*voice of "Con-fu-shon"*).

vocals dubbed by Norma Zimmer

SONGS:

After All These Years; Are You a Dream?; tom thumb's song; Talented Shoes; The Yawning Song.

SYNOPSIS:

The classic fairy tale about a woodcutter named Jonathan and his wife Anna who are granted a son by the Forest Queen--a tiny son only as high as a thumb.

SOUNDTRACK: MGM CH-104

* * * * * * * * *

TONIGHT AND EVERY NIGHT
Columbia, 1945

Producer: Victor Saville
Director: Victor Saville
Screenplay: Lesser Samuels and Abem Finkel; based on the play *Heart of a City* by Lesley Storm
Choreography: Jack Cole and Val Raset
Music and Lyrics: Jule Styne and Sammy Cahn
Running time: 92 minutes, color

CAST:

Rita Hayworth* (*Rosalind Bruce*); Lee Bowman (*Squadron Leader Paul Lundy*); Janet Blair (*Judy Kane*); Marc Platt (*Tommy Lawson*); Leslie Brooks (*Angela*); Professor Lamberti (*"The Great Waldo"*); Dusty Anderson (*Toni*); Stephen Crane (*Leslie Wiggins*); Jim Bannon (*LIFE Photographer*); Florence Bates (*Mrs. May Tolliver*); Ernest Cossart (*Sam Royce*); Philip Merivale (*Rev. Gerald Lundy*); Patrick O'Moore (*David Long*) and Ann Codee (*Annette*).

vocals dubbed by Martha Meers

SONGS:

What Does an English Girl Think Of a Yank?; You Excite Me; The Boy I Left Behind; Tonight and Every Night; Cry and You Cry Alone; Anywhere.

SYNOPSIS:

Rosalind Bruce, Judy Kane and Tommy Lawson are performers in the Music Box Revue at the Windmill Music Hall in London during the Blitz of WWII. Even during the bombing raids the show never missed a performance.

SOUNDTRACK: No soundtrack available

* * * * * * * * * *

TOO MANY GIRLS
RKO, 1940

Producer: George Abbott and Harry Edington
Director: George Abbott
Screenplay: John Twist; based on the stage musical book by George Marion, Jr.
Choreography: LeRoy Prinz
Music and Lyrics: Richard Rodgers and Lorenz Hart
Running time: 85 minutes, B/W

CAST:

Lucille Ball (*Consuelo "Connie" Casey*); Richard Carlson (*Clint Kelly*); Ann Miller (*Pepe*); Eddie Bracken (*Jojo Jordan*); Frances Langford (*Eileen Eilers*); Desi Arnaz (*Manuelito Lynch*); Hal LeRoy (*Al Terwilliger*); Libby Bennett (*Tallulah Lou*); Harry Shannon (*Harvey Casey*); Douglas Walton (*Beverly Waverly*); Chester Clute (*Harold L. Lister*); Tiny Person (*Midge Martin*); Ivy Scott (*Mrs. Tewksbury*) and Byron Shores (*Sheriff Andaluz*).

SONGS:

Heroes in the Fall; You're Nearer; Pottawatomie; Cause We All Got Cake; Spic and Spanish; Love Never Went to College; Look Out; I Didn't Know What Time It Was; The Conga.

SYNOPSIS:

To keep his daughter Connie out of trouble at Pottawatomie College (in Stop Gap, New Mexico), Harvey Casey hires four Ivy League football players--Clint, Jojo, Al and Manuelito--as her bodyguards (without her knowledge).

SOUNDTRACK: No soundtrack available

* * * * * * * * *

TOP HAT
RKO, 1935

Producer: Pandro S. Berman
Director: Mark Sandrich
Screenplay: Dwight Taylor and Allan Scott; based on the stage musical book *The Gay Divorcée* by Dwight Taylor
Choreography: Hermes Pan and Fred Astaire
Music and Lyrics: Irving Berlin
Running time: 101 minutes, B/W

CAST:

Fred Astaire (*Jerry Travers*); Ginger Rogers (*Dale Tremont*); Edward Everett Horton (*Horace Hardwick*); Helen Broderick (*Madge Hardwick*); Erik Rhodes (*Alberto Beddini*) and Eric Blore (*Bates*).

SONGS:

No Strings; Isn't This a Lovely Day?; Top Hat, White Tie and Tails; Cheek to Cheek; The Piccolino.

SYNOPSIS:

When dancer Jerry Travers falls in love with Dale Tremont she mistakenly thinks he is the husband of her friend Helen.

SOUNDTRACK: Sountrak 105 (with *The Gay Divorcée*)

* * * * * * * * *

TWO GUYS FROM TEXAS
Warner Bros., 1948

Producer: Alex Gottlieb
Director: David Butler
Screenplay: I.A.L. Diamond and Allen Boretz; based on a play by Louis Pelletier,
        Jr. and Robert Sloane
Choreography: LeRoy Prinz
Music and Lyrics: Jule Styne and Sammy Cahn
Running time: 86 minutes, B/W

CAST:

Dennis Morgan (*Steve Carroll*); Jack Carson (*Danny Foster*); Dorothy Malone (*Joan Winston*); Penny Edwards (*Maggie Reed*); Forrest Tucker (*Sheriff Tex Bennett*); Fred Clark (*Dr. Straeger*); Gerald Mohr (*Link Jessup*); John Alvin (*Jim Crocker*); Andrew Tombes (*"The Texan"*); Monte Blue (*Pete Nash*) and Mel Blanc (*voice of "Bugs Bunny"*).

SONGS:

There's Music in the Land; I Don't Care If It Rains All Night; A Texan Who Loves Texas; Every Day I Love You Just a Little Bit More; I Wanna Be a Cowboy in the Movies; Hankerin'; At the Rodeo.

SYNOPSIS:

Out-of-work entertainers Steve Carroll and Danny Foster find themselves stranded at a Texas dude ranch on their way to a job offer in California. Complicating matters is Danny's intense fear of any animal and a case of mistaken identity in a local robbery.

SOUNDTRACK: No soundtrack available

* * * * * * * * *

TWO TICKETS TO BROADWAY
RKO, 1951

Producer: Howard Hughes
Director: James V. Kern
Screenplay: Sid Silvers and Hal Kantner; based on a story by Sammy Cahn

Choreography: Busby Berkeley
Music and Lyrics: see below with song titles
Running time: 106 minutes, color

CAST:

Tony Martin (*Dan Carter*); Janet Leigh (*Nancy Peterson*); Gloria De Haven (*Hannah Holbrook*); Eddie Bracken (*Lew Conway*); Ann Miller (*Joyce Campbell*); Barbara Lawrence (*S.F. "Foxy" Rogers*); Bob Crosby (*Himself*); Joe Smith (*Harry*); Charles Dale (*Leo*); Taylor Holmes (*Willard Glendon*) and Buddy Baer (*Sailor*).

SONGS:

Pelican Falls High - *Jule Styne and Leo Robin*
There's No Tomorrow - *Al Hoffman, Leo Corday and Leon Carr*
Manhattan - *Richard Rodgers and Lorenz Hart*
Baby, You'll Never Be Sorry - *Jule Styne and Leo Robin*
The Closer You Are - *Jule Styne and Leo Robin*
The Worry Bird - *Jule Styne and Leo Robin*
Let's Make Comparisons - *Bob Crosby and Sammy Cahn*
Prologue (*Pagliacci*) - *Ruggiero Leoncavallo*
It Began in Yucatan - *Jule Styne and Leo Robin*
Big Chief Hole-in-the-Ground - *Jule Styne and Leo Robin*
Are You a Beautiful Dream? - *Jule Styne and Leo Robin*

SYNOPSIS:

Fast-talking agent Lew Conway convinces his client, singer Dan Carter, that if he can get together a production number with some pretty girls then he can get a spot on Bob Crosby's television show.

SOUNDTRACK: No soundtrack available

* * * * * * * * *

TWO WEEKS WITH LOVE
Metro-Goldwyn-Mayer, 1950

Producer: Jack Cummings
Director: Roy Rowland
Screenplay: John Larkin and Dorothy Kingsley; based on a story by John Larkin
Choreography: Busby Berkeley
Music and Lyrics: see below with song titles
Running time: 92 minutes, color

CAST:

Jane Powell (*Patti Robinson*); Ricardo Montalban (*Demi Armendez*); Louis Calhern (*Horatio Robinson*); Ann Harding (*Katherine Robinson*); Phyllis Kirk (*Valerie Streseman*); Carleton Carpenter (*Billy Finlay*); Debbie Reynolds (*Melba Robinson*); Clinton Sundberg (*Mr. Finlay*); Gary Gray (*McCormick Robinson*); Tommy Rettig (*Ricky Robinson*) and Charles Smith (*Eddie Gavin*).

SONGS:

A Heart That's Free - *Thomas T. Railey and Alfred G. Robyn*
That's How I Need You - *Joseph McCarthy and Joe Goodwin*
The Oceana Roll - *Roger Lewis and Lucien Denni*
Aba Daba Honeymoon - *Arthur Fields and Walter Donovan*
By the Light of the Silvery Moon - *Gus Edwards and Edward Madden*
Beautiful Lady - *Ivan Caryll and C.H.S. McClellan*
My Hero - *Stanislau Stange and Oscar Straus*
Row, Row, Row - *William Jerome and James V. Monaco*

SYNOPSIS:

On their annual two-week vacation with their parents, Patti and Melba Robinson find romance and adventure at Kissamee-in-the-Catskills.

SOUNDTRACK: MGM 2-SES-49ST (with *Good News* and *In the Good Old Summertime*)

U

THE UNSINKABLE MOLLY BROWN
Metro-Goldwyn-Mayer, 1964

Producer: Lawrence Weingarten
Director: Charles Walters
Screenplay: Helen Deutsch; based on the stage musical book by Richard Morris
Choreography: Peter Gennero
Music and Lyrics: Meredith Willson
Running time: 128 minutes, color

CAST:

Debbie Reynolds (*Molly Brown*); Harve Presnell (*Johnny Brown*); Ed Begley (*Shamus Tobin*); Hermione Baddeley (*Buttercup Grogan*); Audrey Christie (*Gladys McGraw*); Jack Kruschen (*Christmas Morgan*); Vassili Lambrinos (*Prince Louis de Laniere*); Martita Hunt (*Grand Duchess Elise Lupovinova*); Harvey Lembeck (*Polak*); George Mitchell (*Monsignor Ryan*) and Grover Dale (*Jam*).

SONGS:

I Ain't Down Yet; Colorado, My Home; Belly Up to the Bar, Boys; I'll Never Say No; He's My Friend; Leadville Johnny Brown (Soliloquy).

SYNOPSIS:

Based on the true-life story of Molly Tobin who set off from her dirt farm to make her fortune. She found love and wealth with a rich miner named Johnny Brown and went on to become a hero in the sinking of the *S.S. Titanic*.

SOUNDTRACK: MGM SE-4232

* * * * * * * * *

UP IN ARMS
RKO, 1944

Producer: Samuel Goldwyn
Director: Elliott Nugent
Screenplay: Don Hartman, Allen Boretz and Robert Pirosh; suggested by the
            character *The Nervous Wreck* by Owen Davis
Choreography: Danny Dare

Music and Lyrics: Harold Arlen and Ted Koehler
Running time: 106 minutes, color

CAST:

Danny Kaye (*Danny Weems*); Dinah Shore (*Virginia Merrill*); Dana Andrews (*Joe Nelson*); Constance Dowling (*Mary Morgan*); Louis Calhern (*Colonel Ashley*); George Matthews (*Blackie*); Benny Baker (*Butterball*); Elisha Cook, Jr. (*Info Jones*); Lyle Talbot (*Sergeant Gelsey*); Walter Catlett (*Major Breck*) and Knox Manning (*Narrator*).

SONGS:

Theatre Lobby Number (Manic-Depressive Presents)*; Now I Know; Tess' Torch Song; Melody in 4-F*; Jive Number; All Out For Freedom.

music and lyrics by Sylvia Fine and Max Leibman

SYNOPSIS:

Hypochondriac Danny Weems is drafted into the Army during WWII and ends up capturing an entire Japanese regiment--single-handedly! Remake of *Whoopee*.

SOUNDTRACK: Sountrak 113

V

THE VAGABOND KING
Paramount, 1956

Producer: Pat Duggan
Director: Michael Curtiz
Screenplay: Ken Englund and Noel Langley; based on the stage musical book by
              Brian Hooker and William H. Post
Choreography: Hanya Holm
Music and Lyrics: Rudolf Friml, Brian Hooker and William H. Post
Running time: 88 minutes, color

CAST:

Kathryn Grayson (*Catherine de Vaucelles*); Oreste (*François Villon*); Rita Moreno (*Huguette*); Walter Hampden (*King Louis XI*); Sir Cedric Hardwicke (*Tristan*); Leslie Nielsen (*Thibault*); William Prince (*Rene*); Jack Lord (*Ferrebone*); Billy Vine (*Jacques*); Harry McNaughton (*Colin*); Florence Sundstrom (*Laughing Margot*); Lucie Lancaster (*Margaret*); Raymond Bramley (*"The Scar"*); Gregory Morton (*Gen. Antoine de Chabannes*); Richard Tone (*Quicksilver*); Ralph Sumpter (*Bishop of Paris and Turin*); G. Thomas Duggan (*Charles, Duke of Burgundy*); Gavin Gordon (*Majordomo*); Joel Ashley (*Duke of Normandy*); Ralph Clinton (*Duke of Anjou*); Gordon Mills (*Duke of Bourbon*) and Vincent Price (*Narrator*).

SONGS:

Bon Jour*; Lord, I'm Glad I Know Thee*; Vive La You; Some Day; Comparisons*; Only a Rose; This Same Heart*; Watch Out For the Devil; Huguette's Waltz; Song of the Vagabonds.

**music and lyrics by Rudolf Friml and Johnny Burke*

SYNOPSIS:

François Villon is the "King of the Vagabonds" who agrees to help King Louis XI save his throne from attack by the Duke of Burgundy--before the King has him executed for treason.

SOUNDTRACK: No soundtrack available

* * * * * * * *

371

VICTOR/VICTORIA
Metro-Goldwyn-Mayer, 1982

Producer: Blake Edwards and Tony Adams
Director: Blake Edwards
Screenplay: Blake Edwards; based on the film *Viktor and Viktoria* by Rheinhold
         Schuenzel and Hans Hoemburg
Choreography: Paddy Stone
Music and Lyrics: Henry Mancini and Leslie Bricusse
Running time: 133 minutes, color

CAST:

Julie Andrews (*Victoria Grant*); James Garner (*King Marchand*); Robert Preston
(*Carol "Toddy" Todd*); Lesley Ann Warren (*Norma Cassidy*); Alex Karras (*Squash
Bernstein*); John Rhys-Davies (*André Cassel*); Graham Stark (*Waiter*); Malcolm
Jamieson (*Richard*) and Peter Arne (*Labisse*).

SONGS:

Gay Paree; King's Can-Can (instrumental); Le Jazz Hot; You and Me; Crazy World;
Chicago, Illinois; The Shady Dame From Seville.

SYNOPSIS:

Paris during the Depression: Out-of-work opera singer Victoria Grant forms a
partnership with out-of-work gay cabaret singer Carol Todd for her to pretend to be
a gay, male, *female* impersonator.

SOUNDTRACK: PolyGram MG-1-5407

* * * * * * * * *

VIVA LAS VEGAS
Metro-Goldwyn-Mayer, 1964

Producer: Jack Cummings and George Sidney
Director: George Sidney
Screenplay: Sally Benson
Choreography: David Winters
Music and Lyrics: see below with song titles
Running time: 86 minutes, color

<u>CAST</u>:

Elvis Presley (*Lucky Jackson*); Ann-Margret (*Rusty Martin*); Cesare Danova (*Count Elmo Mancini*); William Demarest (*Mr. Martin*); Nicky Blair (*Shorty Farnsworth*) and Jack Carter (*Himself*).

<u>SONGS</u>:

The Yellow Rose of Texas - *Don George*
The Lady Loves Me - *Sid Tepper and Roy C. Bennett*
Come On, Everybody - *Stanley Chianese*
Today, Tomorrow and Forever - *Bill Giant, Bernie Baum and Florence Kaye*
The Climb - *Don George*
What'd I Say - *Ray Charles*
If You Think I Don't Need You - *Bob West*
Appreciation - *Marvin More and Bernie Wayne*
Viva Las Vegas - *Doc Pomus*
I Need Somebody to Lean On - *Doc Pomus*
My Rival - *Marvin More and Bernie Wayne*

<u>SYNOPSIS</u>:

Race car driver Lucky Jackson needs some big money to get his car's engine out of hock but finds that task easier than competing with an Italian count for the attentions of swim instructor Rusty Martin.

SOUNDTRACK: Lucky Records 711

W

WABASH AVENUE
20th Century Fox, 1950

Producer: William Perlberg
Director: Henry Koster
Screenplay: Harry Tugend and Charles Lederer
Choreography: Billy Daniel
Music and Lyrics: Josef Myrow and Mack Gordon
Running time: 92 minutes, color

CAST:

Betty Grable (*Ruby Summers*); Victor Mature (*Andy Clark*); Phil Harris (*Uncle Mike*); Reginald Gardiner (*English Eddie*); James Barton (*Hogan*); Barry Kelley (*Bouncer*); Margaret Hamilton (*Tillie Hutch*) and Jacqueline Dalya (*Cleo*).

SONGS:

Clean Up Chicago; Wilhelmina; Baby, Won't You Say You Love Me?; May I Tempt You With a Big Rosy Apple?; Down on Wabash Avenue; I Remember You*; Honeymoon**; I Wish I Could Shimmy Like My Sister Kate***.

  *music and lyrics by Johnny Mercer and Victor Schertzinger
 **music and lyrics by Joseph E. Howard, Will Hough and Frank Adams
***music and lyrics by Armand J. Piron

SYNOPSIS:

Andy and Mike are partners in a Wabash Avenue club who don't quite trust each other but both have their eye on Ruby Summers, the girl who sings and dances in the club.

SOUNDTRACK: No soundtrack available

* * * * * * * * *

WAIKIKI WEDDING
Paramount, 1937

Producer: Arthur Hornblow, Jr.
Director: Frank Tuttle

Screenplay: Frank Butler, Don Hartman, Walter DeLeon and Francis Martin; based on a story by Frank Butler and Don Hartman
Choreography: LeRoy Prinz
Music and Lyrics: Leo Robin and Ralph Rainger
Running time: 90 minutes, B/W

CAST:

Bing Crosby (*Tony Marvin*); Bob Burns (*Shad Buggle*); Martha Raye (*Myrtle Finch*); Shirley Ross (*Georgia Smith*); George Barbier (*J.P. Todhunter*); Leif Erickson (*Victor*); Grady Sutton (*Everett Todhunter*); Granville Bates (*Uncle Herman*); Anthony Quinn (*Kimo*); Mitchell Lewis (*Koalani*) and George Regas (*Mua Mua*).

SONGS:

Sweet Leilani*; Okolehao; In a Little Hula Heaven; Blue Hawaii; Sweet is the Word For You.

music and lyrics by Harry Owens and Jimmy Lovell

SYNOPSIS:

Assigned to act as tour guide to Georgia Smith who won a Hawaiian vacation in a contest, public relations Tony Marvin finds his hands full when she insists on bringing her friend Myrtle Finch along.

SOUNDTRACK: No soundtrack available

* * * * * * * * *

WEEKEND IN HAVANA
20th Century Fox, 1941

Producer: William LeBaron
Director: Walter Lang
Screenplay: Karl Tunberg and Darrell Ware
Choreography: Hermes Pan
Music and Lyrics: Harry Warren and Mack Gordon
Running time: 83 minutes, color

CAST:

Alice Faye (*Nan Spencer*); Carmen Miranda (*Rosita Rivas*); John Payne (*Jay Williams*); Cesar Romero (*Monte Blanca*); Cobina Wright, Jr. (*Terry McCracken*);

George Barbier (*Walter McCracken*); Sheldon Leonard (*Boris*); Leonid Kinskey (*Rafael*); Chris-Pin Martin (*Driver*); Billy Gilbert (*Arbolado*) and Hal K. Dawson (*Mr. Marks*).

SONGS:

The Man With the Lollypop Song; A Weekend in Havana; Tropical Magic; The Nango; Romance and Rhumba*; When I Love I Love.

*music and lyrics by Mack Gordon and James V. Monaco

SYNOPSIS:

When the cruise ship Nan Spencer is taking accidentally runs aground the company send Jay Williams to make sure she gets to Havana. Although he has a fiancée in New York, Jay finds that the attentions paid to Nan by Monte Blanca more than a little disquieting.

SOUNDTRACK: Curtain Calls 100/14 (with *That Night in Rio*)

* * * * * * * * *

THE WEST POINT STORY
Warner Bros., 1950

Producer: Louis F. Edelman
Director: Roy Del Ruth
Screenplay: John Monks, Jr., Charles Hoffman and Irving Wallace; based on a story
        by Irving Wallace
Choreography: LeRoy Prinz and Johnny Boyle, Jr.
Music and Lyrics: Jule Styne and Sammy Cahn
Running time: 107 minutes, B/W

CAST:

James Cagney (*Elwin Bixby*); Virginia Mayo (*Eve Dillon*); Doris Day (*Jan Wilson*); Gordon MacRae (*Tom Fletcher*); Gene Nelson (*Hal Courtland*); Alan Hale, Jr. (*Bull Gilbert*); Roland Winters (*Harry Eberhart*); Wilton Graff (*Lt. Colonel Martin*); Jerome Cowan (*Mr. Jocelyn*) and Frank Ferguson (*Commandant*).

SONGS:

One Hundred Days 'Til June; The Kissing Rock; Ten Thousand Sheep; The Military Polka; You Love Me; The Corps; B'klyn; It Could Only Happen in Brooklyn.

376

SYNOPSIS:

Elwin Bixby is hired by producer Harry Eberhart to direct the West Point cadets' annual "100th Day Show"--and to lure Eberhart's nephew Tom Fletcher away from the Army and onto the stage.

SOUNDTRACK: Titania 501 (with *My Dream is Yours*)

* * * * * * * * * *

WEST SIDE STORY
United Artists, 1961

Producer: Robert Wise
Director: Robert Wise and Jerome Robbins
Screenplay: Ernest Lehman; based on the stage musical book by Arthur Laurents
Choreography: Jerome Robbins
Music and Lyrics: Leonard Bernstein and Stephen Sondheim
Running time: 152 minutes, color

CAST:

Natalie Wood* (*Maria*); Richard Beymer** (*Tony*); Russ Tamblyn (*Riff*); George Chakiris (*Bernardo*); Rita Moreno (*Anita*); Simon Oakland (*Lt. Schrank*); William Bramley (*Officer Krupke*); Ned Glass (*Doc*); John Astin (*"Glad Hand"*); Tucker Smith (*Ice*); Jose de Vega (*Chino*); Eliot Feld (*Baby John*); Tony Mordente (*Action*); David Winters (*Arab*); Bert Michaels (*Snowboy*); David Bean (*Tiger*); Robert Banas (*Joyboy*); Scooter Teague (*Big Deal*); Harvey Hohnecker (*Mouthpiece*); Tommy Abbott (*Gee Tar*); Susan Oakes (*Anybodys*); Gina Trikonis (*Graciella*); Carole D'Andrea (*Velma*); Jay Norman (*Pepe*); Gus Trikonis (*Indio*); Eddie Verso (*Juano*); Jaime Rogers (*Loco*); Larry Roquemore (*Rocco*); Robert Thompson (*Luis*); Nick Covacevich (*Toro*); Roy Del Campo (*Del Campo*); Andre Tayir (*Chile*); Yvonne Othon (*Consuela*); Suzie Kaye (*Rosalia*) and Joanne Meya (*Francisca*).

 *vocals dubbed by Marni Nixon
**vocals dubbed by Jim Bryant

SONGS:

Prologue (instrumental); Jet Song; Something's Coming; Dance at the Gym (instrumental); Maria; America; Tonight; Gee, Officer Krupke; I Feel Pretty; One Hand, One Heart; Quintet; Somewhere; Cool; A Boy Like That; I Have a Love.

SYNOPSIS:

The Lower West Side of New York City is the "turf" that two rival gangs--the Anglo Jets and the Puerto Rican Sharks--are willing to do anything to control and young lovers Tony and Maria find themselves caught between them.

SOUNDTRACK: Columbia 2070

* * * * * * * * *

WHEN YOU'RE IN LOVE
Columbia, 1937

Producer: Everett Riskin
Director: Robert Riskin
Screenplay: Robert Riskin; based on an idea by Ethel Hill and Cedric Worth
Choreography: Leon Leonidoff
Music and Lyrics: see below with song titles
Running time: 110 minutes, B/W

CAST:

Grace Moore (*Louise Fuller*); Cary Grant (*Jimmy Hudson*); Aline MacMahon (*Marianne Woods*); Henry Stephenson (*Walter Mitchell*); Thomas Mitchell (*Hank Miller*); Catherine Doucet (*Jane Summers*); Luis Alberni (*Luis Perugini*); Gerald Oliver Smith (*Gerald Meeker*); Emma Dunn (*Mrs. Hamilton*); George Pearce (*Mr. Hamilton*) and Frank Puglia (*Carlos*).

SONGS:

Siboney - *Ernest Lecuona and Dolly Morse*
The Whistling Boy - *Jerome Kern and Dorothy Fields*
Our Song - *Jerome Kern and Dorothy Fields*
In the Gloaming - *Meta Orred and Annie F. Harrison*
Minnie the Moocher - *Cab Calloway, Irving Mills and Clarence Gaskill*
Serenade (*Roméo et Juliette*) - *Charles Gounod*

SYNOPSIS:

Opera singer Louise Fuller agrees to a marriage of convenience with artist Jimmy Hudson in order to re-enter the United States to sing at a concert for her patron, Walter Mitchell.

SOUNDTRACK: Caliban 6044

378

* * * * * * * * *

WHITE CHRISTMAS
Paramount, 1954

Producer: Robert Emmett Dolan
Director: Michael Curtiz
Screenplay: Norman Krasna, Norman Panama and Melvin Frank
Choreography: Robert Alton
Music and Lyrics: Irving Berlin
Running time: 120 minutes, color

CAST:

Bing Crosby (*Bob Wallace*); Danny Kaye (*Phil Davis*); Rosemary Clooney (*Betty Haines*); Vera-Ellen* (*Judy Haines*); Dean Jagger (*General Waverly*); Mary Wickes (*Emma Allen*); John Brascia (*Joe*) and Anne Whitfield (*Susan Waverly*).

vocals dubbed by Trudy Stevens

SONGS:

White Christmas; The Old Man; Heat Wave; Let Me Sing and I'm Happy; Blue Skies; Sisters; The Best Things Happen While You're Dancing; Snow; Mandy; Count Your Blessings Instead of Sheep; Choreography; Love, You Didn't Do Right By Me; What Can You Do With a General?; Gee, I Wish I Was Back in the Army.

SYNOPSIS:

Entertainers Bob Wallace and Phil Davis follow sisters Betty and Judy Haines from Florida to the Columbia Inn in Vermont where they have an engagement--only to discover that it belongs to their former commanding officer, General Waverly. With the hotel in financial difficulty the foursome decide to put on a show to help raise money to pay off the debt.

SOUNDTRACK: Decca DL-8083

* * * * * * * * *

WHOOPEE
United Artists, 1930

Producer: Florenz Ziegfeld and Samuel Goldwyn
Director: Thornton Freeland

Screenplay: William M. Conselman and William Anthony McGuire; based on the play *The Nervous Wreck* by Owen Davis
Choreography: Busby Berkeley
Music and Lyrics: Walter Donaldson and Gus Kahn
Running time: 94 minutes, color

CAST:

Eddie Cantor (*Henry Williams*); Ethel Shutta (*Mary Custer*); Paul Gregory (*Wanenis*); Eleanor Hunt (*Sally Morgan*); John Rutherford (*Sheriff Bob Wells*); Walter Law (*Judd Morgan*); Spencer Charters (*Jerome Underwood*); Albert Hackett (*Chester Underwood*) and Chief Caupolican (*Black Eagle*).

SONGS:

Mission Number; I'll Still Belong to You*; Making Whoopee; A Girlfriend of a Boyfriend of Mine; My Baby Just Cares For Me; High Stetson Hat; The Song of the Setting Sun.

music and lyrics by Edward Eliscu and Nacio Herb Brown

SYNOPSIS:

Henry Williams is a hypochondriac who is in Arizona for his health. While there he tries to help Sally Morgan marry her true love and that gets him involved with the local Indian tribe and a crooked sheriff.

SOUNDTRACK: Meet-Patti Discs PRW-1930 (with *Puttin' On the Ritz*)

* * * * * * * * * *

WILLY WONKA AND THE CHOCOLATE FACTORY
Paramount, 1971

Producer: David L. Wolper and Stan Margulies
Director: Mel Stuart
Screenplay: Roald Dahl, based on his book *Charlie and the Chocolate Factory*
Choreography: Howard Jeffrey
Music and Lyrics: Anthony Newley and Leslie Bricusse
Running time: 98 minutes, color

CAST:

Gene Wilder (*Willy Wonka*); Jack Albertson (*Grandpa Joe*); Peter Ostrum (*Charlie*

Bucket); Michael Bollner (*Augustus Gloop*); Ursula Reit (*Mrs. Gloop*); Denise Nickerson (*Violet Beauregarde*); Leonard Stone (*Mr. Beauregarde*); Julie Dawn Cole (*Veruca Salt*); Roy Kinnear (*Mr. Salt*); Paris Themmen (*Mike TeeVee*); Dodo Denny (*Mrs. TeeVee*); Diana Sowle (*Mrs. Bucket*); Franziska Liebling (*Grandma Josephine*); Ernest Ziegler (*Grandpa George*); Dora Altmann (*Grandma Georgina*); Aubrey Wood (*Mr. Bill*) and Gunter Meisner (*Mr. Slugworth*).

SONGS:

The Candy Man; Cheer Up, Charlie; (I've Got a) Golden Ticket; Pure Imagination; Oompa Loompa; I Want It Now.

SYNOPSIS:

Musical fantasy about a young boy named Charlie Bucket who wins a ticket for a special tour of the candy factory of eccentric inventor Willy Wonka.

SOUNDTRACK: Paramount 6012

* * * * * * * * *

WINTERTIME
20th Century Fox, 1943

Producer: William LeBaron
Director: John Brahm
Screenplay: E. Edwin Moran, Jack Jevne and Lynn Starling; based on a story by Arthur Kober
Choreography: Kenny Williams
Music and Lyrics: Nacio Herb Brown and Leo Robin
Running time: 90 minutes, B/W

CAST:

Sonja Henie (*Nora*); Jack Oakie (*Skip*); Cesar Romero (*Brad*); Carole Landis (*Flossie*); S.Z. Sakall (*Ostegaard*); Cornell Wilde (*Freddie*) and Woody Herman (*Himself*).

SONGS:

Later Tonight; Dancing in the Dawn; Wintertime; I Like It Here; I'm All A-Twitter Over You; Drums and Dreams; We Always Get Our Girl.

SYNOPSIS:

After Skip convinces Mr. Ostegaard to invest in his hotel in Quebec, it's up to Ostegaard's niece Nora to star in an ice show to help raise money for the hotel-- and also fall in love with Freddie.

SOUNDTRACK: No soundtrack available

* * * * * * * * * *

WITH A SONG IN MY HEART
20th Century Fox, 1952

Producer: Lamar Trotti
Director: Walter Lang
Screenplay: Lamar Trotti
Choreography: Billy Daniel
Music and Lyrics: see below with song titles
Running time: 116 minutes, color

CAST:

Susan Hayward* (*Jane Froman*); Rory Calhoun (*John Burns*); David Wayne (*Don Ross*); Thelma Ritter (*Clancy*); Robert Wagner (*G.I. Paratrooper*); Helen Wescott (*Jennifer March*); Una Merkel (*Sister Marie*); Max Showalter (*Harry Guild*); Lyle Talbot (*Radio Director*); Leif Erickson (*General*) and George Offerman (*Muleface*).

vocals dubbed by Jane Froman

SONGS:

Hoe That Corn - *Jack Woodford and Max Showalter*
That Old Feeling - *Sammy Fain and Lew Brown*
I'm Through With Love - *Gus Kahn, Matty Malneck and Fud Livingston*
Get Happy - *Harold Arlen and Ted Koehler*
Blue Moon - *Richard Rodgers and Lorenz Hart*
On the Gay White Way - *Ralph Rainger and Leo Robin*
The Right Kind of Love - *Charles Henderson and Don George*
With a Song in My Heart - *Richard Rodgers and Lorenz Hart*
Embraceable You - *George Gershwin and Ira Gershwin*
Tea For Two - *Vincent Youmans and Irving Caesar*
It's a Good Day - *Dave Barbour and Peggy Lee*
They're Either Too Young or Too Old - *Arthur Schwartz and Frank Loesser*
I'll Walk Alone - *Jule Styne and Sammy Cahn*

382

America the Beautiful - *Samuel Ward and Katherine Lee Bates*
Give My Regards to Broadway - *George M. Cohan*
Chicago - *Fred Fisher*
Carry Me Back to Old Virginny - *James Bland*
Maine Stein Song - *Lincoln Colcord and E.A. Fensted*
Back Home Again in Indiana - *James F. Hanley and Ballard MacDonald*
Alabamy Bound - *B.G. DeSylva, Ray Henderson and Bud Green*
Deep in the Heart of Texas - *June Hershey and Don Swander*
Dixie - *Daniel D. Emmett*

SYNOPSIS:

The film chronicles the life of singer Jane Froman, who survived a shattered leg as a result of a plane crash during a WWII U.S.O. tour and still kept on performing despite countless operations and almost constant pain.

SOUNDTRACK: No soundtrack available

* * * * * * * * *

THE WIZ
Universal, 1978

Producer: Rob Cohen
Director: Sidney Lumet
Screenplay: Joel Schumacher; based on the stage musical book by William F. Brown
Choreography: Louis Johnson
Music and Lyrics: Charlie Smalls
Running time: 133 minutes, color

CAST:

Diana Ross (*Dorothy*); Michael Jackson (*The Scarecrow*); Nipsey Russell (*The Tinman*); Ted Ross (*The Lion*); Mabel King (*Evillene*); Theresa Merritt (*Aunt Em*); Thelma Carpenter (*Miss One*); Lena Horne (*Glinda the Good*) and Richard Pryor (*The Wiz*).

SONGS:

The Feeling That We Have; Can I Go On?; He's the Wizard; Soon As I Get Home; You Can't Win; Ease On Down the Road; What Would I Do If I Could Feel?; Slide Some Oil to Me; (I'm a) Mean Ole Lion; Be a Lion; Is This What Feeling Gets? (Dorothy's Theme)*; Don't Nobody Bring Me No Bad News; A Brand New Day; Believe in Yourself (Dorothy); Home.

music and lyrics by Quincy Jones, Nick Ashford and Valerie Simpson

SYNOPSIS:

The L. Frank Baum story is updated to present-day New York City with Dorothy as a disillusioned schoolteacher who embarks on an odyssey through the "jungles" of Manhattan.

SOUNDTRACK: MCA 2-14000

* * * * * * * * * *

THE WIZARD OF OZ
Metro-Goldwyn-Mayer, 1939

Producer: Mervyn LeRoy
Director: Victor Fleming
Screenplay: Noel Langley, Florence Ryerson and Edgar Allan Woolf; based on the
                    book by L. Frank Baum
Choreography: Bobby Connolly
Music and Lyrics: Harold Arlen and E.Y. Harburg
Running time: 119 minutes, sepia-tone and color

CAST:

Judy Garland (*Dorothy Gale*); Ray Bolger (*Hunk/"The Scarecrow"*); Jack Haley (*Hickory/"The Tin Woodsman"*); Bert Lahr (*Zeke/"The Cowardly Lion"*); Frank Morgan (*Professor Marvel/"The Wizard"*); Margaret Hamilton (*Miss Gulch/"The Wicked Witch of the West"*); Billie Burke (*Glinda, the Good Witch*); Charles Grapewin (*Uncle Henry*); Clara Blandick (*Auntie Em*) and the Singer Midgets (*The Munchkins*).

SONGS:

Over the Rainbow; Ding-Dong! The Witch is Dead; Munchkinland; Follow the Yellow Brick Road; We're Off to See the Wizard; If I Only Had a Brain; If I Only Had a Heart; If I Only Had the Nerve; The Merry Old Land of Oz; If I Were the King of the Forest.

SYNOPSIS:

The classic childrens' tale about a little Kansas farm girl who (thanks to a tornado) suddenly finds herself over the rainbow in search of the mystical Wizard of Oz.

384

SOUNDTRACK: MGM 3996

* * * * * * * * *

THE WONDERFUL WORLD OF THE BROTHERS GRIMM
Metro-Goldwyn-Mayer, 1962

Producer: George Pal
Director: Henry Levin and George Pal
Screenplay: David P. Harmon, Charles Beaumont and William Roberts; based on the
    book *Die Brüder Grimm* by Dr. Herrmann Gerstner
Choreography: Alex Romero
Music and Lyrics: Bob Merrill
Running time: 135 minutes, color

CAST:

Laurence Harvey (*Wilhelm Grimm/The Cobbler*); Karl Boehm (*Jacob Grimm*); Claire
Bloom (*Dorothea Grimm*); Walter Slezak (*Stossel*); Barbara Eden (*Greta Heinrich*);
Oscar Homolka (*The Duke*); Arnold Stang (*Rumplestiltskin*); Martita Hunt (*The
Storyteller*); Ian Wolfe (*Gruber*); Bryan Russell (*Friedrich Grimm*); Tammy Marihugh
(*Pauline Grimm*); Russ Tamblyn (*The Woodsman/tom thumb*); Yvette Mimieux (*The
Princess*); Jim Backus (*The King*); Beulah Bondi (*The Gypsy*); Clinton Sundberg (*The
Prime Minister*); Walter Brooke (*The Mayor*); Sandra Gale Bettin (*The Ballerina*);
Terry-Thomas (*Ludwig*) and Buddy Hackett (*Hans*).

SONGS:

The Wonderful World of the Brothers Grimm (instrumental); Gypsy Fire
(instrumental); The Dancing Princess; Ah-Oom; Above the Stars (instrumental);
Christmas Land; The Singing Bone*; Dee-Are-A-Gee-O-En.

music and lyrics by Bob Merrill and Charles Beaumont

SYNOPSIS:

The life of the Grimm brothers, Jacob and Wilhelm, and how they came to write
their famous fairy tales.

SOUNDTRACK: MGM 1E3

X

XANADU
Universal, 1980

Producer: Lawrence Gordon
Director: Robert Greenwalk
Screenplay: Richard Christian Danus and Marc Reid Rubel
Choreography: Kenny Ortega and Jerry Trent
Music and Lyrics: John Farrar and Jeff Lynne
Running time: 88 minutes, color

CAST:

Olivia Newton-John (*Kira*); Gene Kelly (*Danny McGuire*); Michael Beck (*Sonny Malone*); James Sloyan (*Simpson*); Fred McCarren (*Richie*); Dimitra Arliss (*Helen*); Katie Hanley (*Sandra*); Ren Woods (*Jo*) and the Tubes (*Rock Group at Nightclub*).

SONGS:

I'm Alive*; Magic; Whenever You're Away From Me; Suddenly**; Dancin'; Don't Walk Away*; All Over the World*; The Fall*; Suspended in Time; Xanadu.

 *vocal by The Electric Light Orchestra
**vocal duet with Cliff Richard

SYNOPSIS:

A muse named Kira helps bring together retired musician Danny McGuire and frustrated artist Sonny Malone in order to realize Danny's dream of opening a new nightclub--Xanadu.

SOUNDTRACK: MCA 6100

386

Y

YANKEE DOODLE DANDY
Warner Bros., 1942

Producer: Hal B. Wallis
Director: Michael Curtiz
Screenplay: Robert Buckner and Edmund Joseph; based on a story by Robert
        Buckner
Choreography: LeRoy Prinz and Seymour Felix
Music and Lyrics: George M. Cohan
Running time: 126 minutes, B/W (has been colorized)

CAST:

James Cagney (*George M. Cohan*); Joan Leslie (*Mary*); Walter Huston (*Jerry Cohan*); Richard Whorf (*Sam Harris*); George Tobias (*Dietz*); Irene Manning (*Fay Templeton*); Rosemary De Camp (*Nellie Cohan*); Jeanne Cagney (*Josie Cohan*); S.Z. Sakall (*Schwab*); George Barbier (*Erlanger*); Eddie Foy, Jr. (*Eddie Foy, Sr.*); Frances Langford (*Singer at Rally*) and Capt. Jack Young (*The President*).

SONGS:

I Was Born in Virginia; The Warmest Baby in the Bunch; Harrigan; Yankee Doodle Dandy; All Aboard For Old Broadway*; Give My Regards to Broadway; Oh, You Wonderful Girl; Blue Skies, Grey Skies; The Barbers' Ball; Mary is a Grand Old Name; Forty-Five Minutes From Broadway; So Long, Mary; You're a Grand Old Flag; Over There; Nellie Kelly, I Love You; The Man Who Owns Broadway; Molly Malone; Billie; Off the Record.

music and lyrics by Jack Scholl and M.K. Jerome

SYNOPSIS:

The life of the famous composer-performer George M. Cohan is told through a series of flashbacks as on older George recalls his career to President Franklin D. Roosevelt.

SOUNDTRACK: Curtain Calls 100/13

* * * * * * * * *

YENTL
United Artists, 1983

Producer: Barbra Streisand
Director: Barbra Streisand
Screenplay: Jack Rosenthal and Barbra Streisand; based on *Yentl, the Yeshiva Boy*
                    by Issac Bashevis Singer
Choreography: Gillian Lynne
Music and Lyrics: Michel Legrand, Alan Bergman and Marilyn Bergman
Running time: 134 minutes, color

CAST:

Barbra Streisand (*Yentl/Anshull*); Mandy Patinkin (*Avigdor*); Amy Irving (*Hadass*);
Nehemiah Persoff (*Papa*); Steven Hill (*Reb Alter Vishkower*); Ruth Goring (*Esther rachel*) and Allan Corduner (*Shimmele*).

SONGS:

Where is it Written?; Papa, Can You Hear Me?; This is One of Those Moments; No
Wonder; The Way He Makes Me Feel; Tomorrow Night; Will Someone Ever Look
at Me That Way?; No Matter What Happens; A Piece of Sky.

SYNOPSIS:

Forbidden by law from an education, a young Jewish woman named Yentl disguises
herself as a boy named Anshull in order to become a scholar in turn-of-the-century
Poland.

SOUNDTRACK: Columbia JS-39152

* * * * * * * * *

YOLANDA AND THE THIEF
Metro-Goldwyn-Mayer, 1945

Producer: Arthur Freed
Director: Vincente Minelli
Screenplay: Irving Brecher; based on a story by Jacques Thery and Ludwig
                    Bemelmans
Choreography: Eugene Loring
Music and Lyrics: Harry Warren and Arthur Freed
Running time: 108 minutes, color

CAST:

Fred Astaire (*Johnny Parkson Riggs*); Lucille Bremer* (*Yolanda Aquaviva*); Frank

388

Morgan (*Victor Budlow Trout*); Mildred Natwick (*Aunt Amarilla*); Mary Nash (*Duenna*); Leon Ames (*Mr. Candle*); Ludwig Stossel (*School Teacher*); Jane Green (*Mother Superior*); Remo Bufano (*Puppeteer*); Francis Pierlot (*Padre*); Leon Belasco (*Taxi Driver*); Ghislaine Perreau (*Gigi*); Charles La Torre (*Police Lieutenant*) and Michael Visaroff (*Major Domo*).

vocals dubbed by Trudy Erwin

SONGS:

This is a Day For Love; Angel; Will You Marry Me?; Yolanda; Coffee Time.

SYNOPSIS:

Convent-reared Yolanda Aquaviva prays to her guardian angel for guidance in handling her vast financial estate--and con-man Johnny Riggs overhears her prayer and pretends to be the angel, "Mr. Brown", in order to swindle her out of her money.

SOUNDTRACK: Hollywood Soundstage 5001 (with *You'll Never Get Rich*)

* * * * * * * * *

YOU CAN'T HAVE EVERYTHING
20th Century Fox, 1937

Producer: Lawrence Schwab
Director: Norman Taurog
Screenplay: Harry Tugend, Jack Yellen and Karl Tunberg; based on a story by
         Gregory Ratoff
Choreography: Harry Losee
Music and Lyrics: Harry Revel and Mack Gordon
Running time: 100 minutes, B/W

CAST:

Alice Faye (*Judith Poe Wells*); Don Ameche (*George Macrea*); Charles Winninger (*Sam Gordon*); The Ritz Brothers (*Themselves*); Louise Hovick (*Lulu Riley*); Tony Martin (*Bobby Walker*); Arthur Treacher (*Bevins*); Phyllis Brooks (*Evelyn Moore*) and David Rubinoff (*Himself*).

SONGS:

You Can't Have Everything; Danger, Love at Work; Please Pardon Us, We're in

Love; The Loveliness of You; Afraid to Dream.

SYNOPSIS:

Judith Wells is an aspiring playwright who falls for producer George Macrea but when his girlfriend Lulu threatens to make trouble she decides to return to her hometown--and her former job as a song plugger.

SOUNDTRACK: Titania 508 (with *The Duchess of Idaho*)

* * * * * * * * *

YOU CAN'T RUN AWAY FROM IT
Columbia, 1956

Producer: Dick Powell
Director: Dick Powell
Screenplay: Claude Binyon and Robert Riskin; based on the short story by Samuel Hopkins Adams
Choreography: Robert Sidney
Music and Lyrics: Gene DePaul and Johnny Mercer
Running time: 95 minutes, color

CAST:

June Allyson (*Ellie Andrews*); Jack Lemmon (*Peter Warren*); Charles Bickford (*A.A. Andrews*); Allyn Joslyn (*Joe Gordon*); Paul Gilbert (*George Shapely*); Stubby Kaye (*Fred Tootin*); Henny Youngman (*Bus Driver*); Jack Albertson (*Motel Manager*) and Jim Backus (*Danker*).

SONGS:

You Can't Run Away From It*; Howdy, Friends and Neighbors; Temporarily Yours; Scarecrow Ballet (instrumental); Thumbin' a Ride.

vocal by The Four Aces

SYNOPSIS:

Musical remake of *It Happened One Night* has heiress Ellie Andrews trying to get back to her groom after being "kidnapped" from her wedding by men who work for her father. She's aided in her quest by reporter Peter Warren who's hoping for a big story.

390

SOUNDTRACK: Decca 8396

* * * * * * * * *

YOU'LL NEVER GET RICH
Columbia, 1941

Producer: Samuel Bischoff
Director: Sidney Lanfield
Screenplay: Michael Fessier and Ernest Pagano
Choreography: Robert Alton
Music and Lyrics: Cole Porter
Running time: 88 minutes, B/W

CAST:

Fred Astaire (*Robert Curtis*); Rita Hayworth (*Sheila Winthrop*); Robert Benchley (*Martin Cortland*); John Hubbard (*Captain Tom Barton*); Osa Massen (*Sonya*); Frieda Inescort (*Mrs. Julia Cortland*); Guinn Williams (*Kewpie*); Donald MacBride (*Top Sergeant*); Cliff Nazarro (*Swivel Tongue*); Marjorie Gateson (*Aunt Louise*); Ann Shoemaker (*Mrs. Barton*); Sunnie O'Dea (*Marjorie*); Emmett Vogan (*Jenkins*); Paul Philips (*Captain Nolan*); Harold Goodwin (*Captain Williams*); Frank Ferguson (*Justice of the Peace*) and Boyd Davis (*Colonel Shiller*).

SONGS:

The Boogie Barcarolle (instrumental); Shootin' the Works for Uncle Sam; Since I Kissed My Baby Goodbye; The A-stairable Rag (instrumental); So Near and Yet So Far; The Wedding Cake March.

SYNOPSIS:

Choreographer Robert Curtis gets drafted into the Army and is soon spending most of his time either in the guardhouse or trying to romance pretty Sheila Winthrop, one of his former dance partners and the girlfriend of his captain.

SOUNDTRACK: Hollywood Soundstage 5001 (with *Yolanda and the Thief*)

* * * * * * * * *

YOUNG AT HEART
Warner Bros., 1955

Producer: Henry Blanke
Director: Gordon Douglas
Screenplay: Julius J. Epstein and Lenore Coffe, adaptation by Liam O'Brien; based
            on a story by Fannie Hurst
Music and Lyrics: see below with song titles
Running time: 117 minutes, color

CAST:

Doris Day (*Laurie Tuttle*); Frank Sinatra (*Barney Sloan*); Gig Young (*Alex Burke*);
Ethel Barrymore (*Aunt Jessie*); Dorothy Malone (*Fran Tuttle*); Robert Keith
(*Professor Gregory Tuttle*); Elisabeth Fraser (*Amy Tuttle*); Alan Hale, Jr. (*Bob
Neary*) and Lonny Chapman (*Ernie Nichols*).

SONGS:

Young at Heart - *Johnny Richards and Carolyn Leigh*
Till My Love Comes Back to Me - *Felix Mendelssohn and Paul Francis Webster*
Ready, Willing and Able - *Floyd Huddleston and Al Rinker*
Hold Me in Your Arms - *Ray Heindorf, Charles Henderson and Don Pippin*
Someone to Watch Over Me - *George Gershwin and Ira Gershwin*
Just One of Those Things - *Cole Porter*
One For My Baby - *Harold Arlen and Johnny Mercer*
There's a Rising Moon For Every Falling Star - *Sammy Fain and Paul Francis*
                                              Webster
You, My Love - *James Van Heusen and Mack Gordon*

SYNOPSIS:

Composer Alex Burke falls in love with Laurie Tuttle but her two sisters, Fran and
Amy, are entranced by him too. Further complicating the situation is Alex's arranger,
Barney Sloan, a down-on-his-luck drifter who falls hard for Laurie.

SOUNDTRACK: Titania 500 (with *April in Paris*)

* * * * * * * * * *

YOU'RE MY EVERYTHING
20th Century Fox, 1949

Producer: Lamar Trotti
Director: Walter Lang
Screenplay: Lamar Trotti and Will H. Hays, Jr.; based on a story by George Jessel
Choreography: Nick Castle

Music and Lyrics: see below with song titles
Running time: 94 minutes, color

CAST:

Dan Dailey (*Timothy O'Connor*); Anne Baxter (*Hannah Adams O'Connor*); Anne Revere (*Jane Adams*); Stanley Ridges (*Henry Mercer*); Shari Robinson (*Jane O'Connor*); Henry O'Neil (*Professor Adams*); Selena Royle (*Mrs. Adams*); Alan Mowbray (*Joe Blanton*); George Nokes (*Mark Adams*); Phyllis Kennedy (*Elizabeth*); Charles Lane (*Eddie Plummer*) and Mack Gordon (*Songwriter*).

SONGS:

I Want To Be Teacher's Pet - *Josef Myrow and Mack Gordon*
The Varsity Drag - *B.G. DeSylva, Lew Brown and Ray Henderson*
You're My Everything - *Harry Warren, Mort Dixon and Joe Young*
I Think You're Wonderful - *Carl Sigman and Bob Hilliard*
Chattanooga Choo Choo - *Harry Warren and Mack Gordon*
I Can't Begin to Tell You - *Mack Gordon and James V. Monaco*
Would You Like to Take a Walk? - *Harry Warren, Mort Dixon and Billy Rose*
On the Good Ship Lollipop - *Richard Whiting and Sidney Clare*

SYNOPSIS:

Star-struck Hannah Adams marries vaudeville star Tim O'Connor but when they go to Hollywood for Tim's screen test it's Hannah who is suddenly offered a contract.

SOUNDTRACK: No soundtrack available

* * * * * * * * * *

YOU WERE NEVER LOVELIER
Columbia, 1942

Producer: Louis F. Edelman
Director: William A. Seiter
Screenplay: Michael Fessier, Ernest Pagano; based on the screenplay *The Gay Señorita* by Carlos Olivari and Sixto Pondal Rios
Choreography: Val Raset
Music and Lyrics: Jerome Kern and Johnny Mercer
Running time: 97 minutes, B/W

CAST:

Fred Astaire (*Robert Davis*); Rita Hayworth* (*Maria Acuña*); Adolphe Menjou (*Eduardo Acuña*); Leslie Brooks (*Cecy Acuña*); Adele Mara (*Lita Acuña*); Isobel Elsom (*Mrs. Maria Castro*); Gus Schilling (*Fernando*); Barbara Brown (*Mrs. Delfina Acuña*); Douglas Leavitt (*Juan Castro*); Catherine Craig (*Julia Acuña*); Kathleen Howard (*Grandmother Acuña*); Mary Field (*Louise*); Larry Parks (*Tony*); Stanley Brown (*Roddy*); Lina Romay (*Singer*); Kirk Alyn (*Groom*) and Xavier Cugat (*Himself*).

*vocals dubbed by Nan Wynn

SONGS:

Chiu Chiu*; Dearly Beloved; Ding-Dong Bell; Audition Dance (instrumental); I'm Old-Fashioned; The Shorty George; Wedding in the Spring; You Were Never Lovelier; These Orchids.

*music and lyrics by Nicanor Molinare

SYNOPSIS:

Buenas Aires hotel magnate Eduardo Acuña hires unemployed dancer Bob Davis to impersonate the mysterious sender of orchids to his daughter Maria--but the sender is really Acuña trying to dispell her notions of a knight in shining armour.

SOUNDTRACK: Curtain Calls 100/24 (with *Cover Girl*)

Z

ZIEGFELD GIRL
Metro-Goldwyn-Mayer, 1941

Producer: Pandro S. Berman
Director: Robert Z. Leonard
Screenplay: Marguerite Roberts and Sonya Levien; based on a story by William
  Anthony McGuire
Choreography: Busby Berkeley
Music and Lyrics: see below with song titles
Running time: 131 minutes, B/W

CAST:

James Stewart (*Gilbert Young*); Judy Garland (*Susan Gallagher*); Hedy LaMarr
(*Sandra Kolter*); Lana Turner (*Sheila Regan/Sheila Hale*); Tony Martin (*Frank
Merton*); Jackie Cooper (*Jerry Regan*); Ian Hunter (*Geoffrey Collis*); Charles
Winninger (*Ed "Pop" Gallagher*); Edward Everett Horton (*Noble Sage*); Philip Dorn
(*Franz Kolter*); Paul Kelly (*John Slayton*); Eve Arden (*Patsy Dixon*); Dan Dailey
(*Jimmy Walters*); Al Shean (*Himself*); Fay Holden (*Mrs. Regan*); Felix Bressart
(*Mischa*); Rose Hobart (*Mrs. Frank Merton*); Bernard Nedell (*Nick Capalini*); Ed
McNamara (*Mr. Regan*); Mae Busch (*Jenny*); Renie Riano (*Annie*) and Josephine
Whittell (*Perkins*).

SONGS:

You Stepped Out of a Dream - *Nacio Herb Brown and Gus Kahn*
Whispering - *John Schonberger, Richard Coburn and Vincent Rose*
I'm Always Chasing Rainbows - *Frederick Chopin, Harry Carroll and Joseph
  McCarthy*
Caribbean Love Song - *Roger Edens and Ralph Freed*
Minnie From Trinidad - *Roger Edens*
Mr. Gallagher and Mr. Shean - *Edward Gallagher and Al Shean*
You Gotta Pull Strings - *Walter Donaldson and Harold Adamson*
You Never Looked So Beautiful - *Walter Donaldson and Harold Adamson*

SYNOPSIS:

Susan Gallagher, Sandra Kolter and Sheila Regan are all chosen to be Ziegfeld girls
but when their big break comes their methods of handling fame prove to be very
different.

SOUNDTRACK: Classic International Filmusicals 3006

INDEXES

Shows & Performers

INDEX: SHOWS & PERFORMERS

413

INDEX: SHOWS & PERFORMERS

INDEX: SHOWS & PERFORMERS

420

Producers

Directors

Writers

426

Choreographers

Songs & Songwriters

432

435

INDEX: SONGS & SONGWRITERS

INDEX: SONGS & SONGWRITERS

INDEX: SONGS & SONGWRITERS

447

INDEX: SONGS & SONGWRITERS

454

INDEX: SONGS & SONGWRITERS

INDEX: SONGS & SONGWRITERS

INDEX: SONGS & SONGWRITERS

462

Bibliography

Eames, John Douglas. *The M.G.M. Story*. New York: Crown Publishers, 1975

Fordin, Hugh. *The World of Entertainment*. New York: Avon Books, 1975

Green, Stanley. *Broadway Musicals: Show By Show*. Milwaukee, Wisconsin: Hal Leonard Books, 1987

Harewood, The Earl of. *The Definitive Kobbé's Opera Book*. New York: G.P. Putnam's Sons, 1987

Harris, Steve. *Film, Television and Stage Music on Phonograph Records*. Jefferson, NC and London: McFarland & Company, Inc., 1988

Kobal, John. *Gotta Sing, Gotta Dance*. New York: Hamlyn, 1971

Lax, Roger and Smith, Frederick. *The Great Song Thesaurus*. New York: Oxford University Press, 1984

Maltin, Leonard. *The Disney Films*. New York: Bonanza Books, 1973

Maltin, Leonard. *T.V. Movies and Video Guide*. New York: Signet, 1988

Marill, Alvin H. *Samuel Goldwyn Presents*. South Brunswick and New York: A.S. Barnes and Company, 1976

Michael, Paul. *The American Movies*. New York: Garland Books, 1969

Nash, Jay Robert and Ross, Stanley Ralph. *The Motion Picture Guide: 1927-1983*. Chicago, Illinois: Cinebooks, Inc., 1986

Raymond, Jack. *Show Music on Record*. New York: Frederick Ungar Publishing, 1982

Thomas, Lawrence B. *The M.G.M. Years*. New York: Columbia House, 1972

Thomas, Tony and Solomon, Aubrey. *The Films of 20th Century Fox*. Secaucus, New Jersey: Citadel Press, 1985

Willis, John. *Screen World, Volume 37 (1986)*. New York: Crown Publishers

*This book was designed by Sheryl Aumack
and printed by Sea-Maid Press.*

*The Sea-Maid logo was designed by
Allan Corwin.*

*The text type - 6, 10, 12 and 14 point Times Roman
and Times Roman Italic - was set on an
I.B.M. PC/2 30-286.*

*The headline type was set by hand and composed
of various sizes of Balmoral, Murray Hill Bold,
Pointille and Times Roman.*

The text paper is long-grain, 20 pound white paper.

The printing was done by high-speed Xerography.